Each year the "bests" proliferate. It's getting so you can't hardly tell t'other from which. In the circumstances, the sanest thing to do is follow your editors—

and Mr. Carr has a long, long record of picking the best of the "bests"—

In this volume, he has selected a remarkable combination of the old masters (Frederik Pohl and C. M. Kornbluth) and the new (William Rotsler) and the far out (Lafferty) and a diversity of other greats, near-greats and to be greats.

A collection no self-respecting science fiction aficionado can afford to be without, and a joyful introduction to those who still think s.f. is 'space opera' . . .

Also Edited by
TERRY CARR

**THE BEST SCIENCE FICTION
OF THE YEAR—#1**

Available from Ballantine Books

THE BEST
SCIENCE FICTION
OF THE YEAR

#2

Edited by
Terry Carr

BALLANTINE BOOKS • NEW YORK

Acknowledgments continued on next page

BALLANTINE BOOKS, INC.
201 E. 50th Street, New York, N. Y. 10022

Honorable Mentions

Conway, Gerard F.: "Funeral Service," *Universe 2*, Ace, 1972.

Eklund, Gordon: "Stalking The Sun," *Universe 2*, Ace, 1972.

Moore, Brian: "Catholics," *New American Review 15*.

Neville, Kris: "Medical Practices Among The Immortals," *Galaxy*, September 1972.

Pangborn, Edgar: "Tiger Boy," *Universe 2*, Ace, 1972.

Pohl, Frederik: "Shaffery Among The Immortals," *Fantasy & Science Fiction*, July 1972.

Robinson, Frank M.: "East Wind, West Wind," *Nova 2*, Walker, 1972.

Rocklynne, Ross: "Ching Witch!" *Again, Dangerous Visions*, Doubleday, 1972.

Russ, Joanna: "Useful Phrases For The Tourist," *Universe 2*, Ace, 1972.

—"When It Changed," *Again, Dangerous Visions*, Doubleday, 1972.

Silverberg, Robert: "Now $+ n$, Now $- n$," *Nova 2*, Walker, 1972.

Tiptree, James Jr.: "Filomena & Greg & Rikki-Tikki & Barlow & The Alien," *New Dimensions II*, Doubleday, 1972.

—"The Milk Of Paradise," *Again, Dangerous Visions*, Doubleday, 1972.

Vonnegut, Kurt Jr.: "The Big Space Fuck," *Again, Dangerous Visions*, Doubleday, 1972.

Wolfe, Gene: "It's Very Clean," *Generation*, Dell, 1972.

Introduction

The termination of the Apollo program and the generally gloomy prognosis for our entire space effort has to be one of the least agreeable developments of 1972 for science fiction fans and anyone interested in humanity's future expansion. But I've been thinking seriously about this whole matter, and I believe I see a way to revitalize and remotivate our space exploration.

The problem, of course, is that the U.S. public has lost interest in space—and no wonder. Anyone who sat through the interminable delays prior to the Apollo XVII launch will remember what a dismal "entertainment" spectacle it was. At one point, after two hours of postponements and increasingly desperate attempts by TV news analysts to think of things to say about nothing, one of the newsmen said, "I'm going to do something I promised myself I'd never do. I'm going to tell you why I'm wearing the shirt I'm wearing tonight."

And he did. It wasn't an interesting story, but it did fill a minute or two of very dead air. After which we were rewarded with a merciful respite of commercials.

Now this is bad theater, no question about it—and everyone knows that our space program orbits or falls on how much interest it generates in the hearts of taxpayers. So I've been turning the problem over and over in my mind, and it's come to me just as clear as clear that NASA's mistake has been in not keeping up with modern TV broadcasting techniques. They are, after all, competing for ratings on the tube against such winners as Marcus Welby, Mary Tyler Moore, and Monday Night Football, so it would be wise for them to pay attention to what the competition is offering.

Well, first of all there's the "new morality" of television, which encourages Maude to wonder out loud if she should have an abortion, and allows even Mary Tyler Moore to reveal that she's on the pill. This sort of thing was once considered too indecent to be broadcast on public airwaves, but nowadays it's only a little bit naughty—and what's better than "naughty" to attract viewers?

So imagine, if you can, how much more interesting those routine transmissions from space could be if, say, a couple of the astronauts began to kibitz about getting vasectomies after they splash down. Or if, nearing the end of a long orbiting mission, one of them confided to Houston Control that he'd had a nocturnal emission.

For that matter, how the ratings might perk up if one of those bored and boring news analysts were to say, "I'm going to do something I promised myself I'd never do. I'm going to go take a leak while we're waiting."

But it's not only in the matter of naughtiness that NASA could improve its TV ratings. Consider the frills that TV sports presentations have introduced to heighten interest in their product: instant replays, slow motion, isolated cameras, etc. "Let's take another look at Major Midamerica as he trips over that lunar boulder. Here it is . . . see how his foot comes down just a little awkwardly on the side of the rock . . ." "You know, Walter, maybe they ought to consider installing artificial turf up there."

In fact, maybe NASA should consider getting a hard-hitting interviewer like Howard Cosell to spice up their TV coverage. Think of it: "Let's speak to the issues, Commander —why does the government in its bureaucratic omnipotence deem it necessary to spend millions of dollars training well-conditioned men just to *walk* in an environment so felicitous that the gravity is only one third of Earth's?"

Again, why must NASA consider every movement of its astronauts so historic that it must be broadcast live and on-the-spot? Why shouldn't they consider saving film of events for a regular program of highlights—perhaps called *Wide World of Space.* "As Commander Cory finishes hunting down the remaining globules of his spilled Tang bottle, remember that coming up shortly we'll have Major Jack Armstrong Wasp attempting a difficult docking in space in null gravity with a half gainer . . ."

By the utilization of such up-to-date techniques, NASA can improve its ratings profile to the extent that in a year or two they might well have the TV networks actually bidding against each other for the rights to broadcast these real-life space adventures. Our space program would thus begin to pay for itself from TV revenues—thereby removing a major objection on the part of the U.S. taxpayers who must support NASA today. (Consider the possibilities inherent in the combined U.S. and Russian space launches, for instance—particularly if enterprising PR men were to ballyhoo them as Superlaunch I, Superlaunch II, etc.)

I firmly believe that our space program must relate more directly to the people, must speak their language. It's the only way. We'll know for sure that this new program of public acceptance is a success when we see the letter column in *TV Guide* filled with irate letters from "space widows," and the networks begin to plan a new program called *Monday Night Launch*.

(What do you mean, the launch window might not always be favorable? They used to say baseball couldn't be played at night, didn't they?)

—Terry Carr
Oakland, California
February 2, 1973

Best Science Fiction of the Year

#2

The Meeting

Frederik Pohl

and

C. M. Kornbluth

Science fiction has, during its comparatively short history, given rise to many famous collaborative teams, from Austin Hall and Homer Eon Flint to L. Sprague de Camp and Fletcher Pratt and on to such current pairings as Alexei and Cory Panshin—but none of these duos ever reached the stature of Frederik Pohl and C. M. Kornbluth, authors of *The Space Merchants, Gladiator-at-Law,* and many other fondly remembered novels and stories. Kornbluth died tragically young fifteen years ago, but he and Frederik Pohl had discussed and made notes for one more short story which Pohl set to paper in 1972: THE MEETING, a low-key, hard-hitting story about the ambiguities of medical advances.

Harry Vladek was too large a man for his Volkswagen, but he was too poor a man to trade it in, and as things were going he was going to stay that way a long time. He applied the brakes carefully ("master cylinder's leaking like a sieve, Mr. Vladek. What's the use of just fixing up the linings?"— but the estimate was a hundred and twenty-eight dollars, and where was it going to come from?) and parked in the neatly graveled lot. He squeezed out of the door, the up-

1

setting telephone call from Dr. Nicholson on his mind, locked the car up, and went into the school building.

The Parent-Teachers Association of the Bingham County School for Exceptional Children was holding its first meeting of the term. Of the twenty people already there, Vladek knew only Mrs. Adler, the principal, or headmistress, or owner of the school. She was the one he needed to talk to most, he thought. Would there be any chance to see her privately? Right now she sat across the room at her scuffed golden-oak desk in a posture chair, talking in low, rapid tones with a gray-haired woman in a tan suit. A teacher? She seemed too old to be a parent, although his wife had told him some of the kids seemed to be twenty or more.

It was 8:30 and the parents were still driving up to the school, a converted building that had once been a big country house—almost a mansion. The living room was full of elegant reminders of that. *Two* chandeliers. Intricate vine-leaf molding on the plaster above the dropped ceiling. The pink-veined, white-marble fireplace, unfortunately prominent because of the unsuitable andirons, too cheap and too small, that now stood in it. Golden-oak, sliding double doors to the hall. And visible through them a grim, fireproof stair-case of concrete and steel. They must, Vladek thought, have had to rip out a beautiful wooden thing to install the fire-proof stairs for compliance with the state school laws.

People kept coming in, single men, single women, and occasionally a couple. He wondered how the couples managed their baby-sitting problem. The subtitle on the school's letterhead was "an institution for emotionally disturbed and cerebrally damaged children capable of education." Harry's nine-year-old Thomas was one of the emotionally disturbed ones. With a taste of envy he wondered if cerebrally damaged children could be baby-sat by any reasonably competent grown-up. Thomas could not. The Vladeks had not had an evening out together since he was two, so that tonight Margaret was holding the fort at home, no doubt worrying herself sick about the call from Dr. Nicholson, while Harry was representing the family at the PTA.

As the room filled up, chairs were getting scarce. A young couple was standing at the end of the row near him, looking around for a pair of empty seats. "Here," he said to them. "I'll move over." The woman smiled politely and the man said thanks. Emboldened by an ashtray on the empty seat in front of him, Harry pulled out his pack of cigarettes and offered it to them, but it turned out they were nonsmokers. Harry lit up anyway, listening to what was going on around him.

Everybody was talking. One woman asked another, "How's the gall bladder? Are they going to take it out after all?" A heavy balding man said to a short man with bushy sideburns, "Well, my accountant says the tuition's medically deductible if the school is for psycho*somatic*, not just for psycho. That we've got to clear up." The short man told him positively, "Right, but all you need is a doctor's letter; he recommends the school, refers the child to the school." And a very young woman said intensely, "Dr. Shields was very optimistic, Mrs. Clerman. He says without a doubt the thyroid will make Georgie accessible. And then—" A light-coffee-colored black man in an aloha shirt told a plump woman, "He really pulled a wingding over the weekend, two stitches in his face, busted my fishing pole in three places." And the woman said, "They get so bored. My little girl has this thing about crayons, so that rules out coloring books altogether. You wonder what you can do."

Harry finally said to the young man next to him, "My name's Vladek. I'm Tommy's father. He's in the beginners group."

"That's where ours is," said the young man. "He's Vern. Six years old. Blond like me. Maybe you've seen him."

Harry did not try very hard to remember. The two or three times he had picked Tommy up after class he had not been able to tell one child from another in the great bustle of departure. Coats, handkerchiefs, hats, one little girl who always hid in the supply closet and a little boy who never wanted to go home and hung onto the teacher. "Oh, yes," he said politely.

The young man introduced himself and his wife; they were named Murray and Celia Logan. Harry leaned over the man to shake the wife's hand, and she said, "Aren't you new here?"

"Yes. Tommy's been in the school a month. We moved in from Elmira to be near it." He hesitated, then added, "Tommy's nine, but the reason he's in the beginners group is that Mrs. Adler thought it would make the adjustment easier."

Logan pointed to a suntanned man in the first row. "See that fellow with the glasses? He moved here from *Texas*. Of course, he's got money."

"It must be a good place," Harry said questioningly.

Logan grinned, his expression a little nervous.

"How's your son?" Harry asked.

"That little rascal," said Logan. "Last week I got him another copy of the *My Fair Lady* album, I guess he's used up four or five of them, and he goes around singing 'luv-er-ly, luv-er-ly.' But *look* at you? No."

"Mine doesn't talk," said Harry.

Mrs. Logan said judiciously, "Ours talks. Not *to* anybody, though. It's like a wall."

"I know," said Harry, and pressed. "Has, ah, has Vern shown much improvement with the school?"

Murray Logan pursed his lips. "I would say, yes. The bed-wetting's not too good, but life's a great deal smoother in some ways. You know, you don't hope for a dramatic break-through. But in little things, day by day, it goes smoother. Mostly smoother. Of course there are setbacks."

Harry nodded, thinking of seven years of setbacks, and two years of growing worry and puzzlement before that. He said, "Mrs. Adler told me that, for instance, a special outbreak of destructiveness might mean something like a plateau in speech therapy. So the child fights it and breaks out in some other direction."

"That too," said Logan, "but what I meant—Oh, they're starting."

Vladek nodded, stubbing out his cigarette and absent-mindedly lighting another. His stomach was knotting up again. He wondered at these other parents, who seemed so safe and, well, untouched. Wasn't it the same with them as with Margaret and himself? And it had been a long time since either of them had felt the world comfortable around them, even without Dr. Nicholson pressing for a decision. He forced himself to lean back and look as tranquil as the others.

Mrs. Adler was tapping her desk with a ruler. "I think everybody who is coming is here," she said. She leaned against the desk and waited for the room to quiet down. She was short, dark, plump, and surprisingly pretty. She did not look at all like a competent professional. She looked so unlike her role that, in fact, Harry's heart had sunk three months ago when their correspondence about admitting Tommy had been climaxed by the long trip from Elmira for the interview. He had expected a steel-gray lady with rimless glasses, a Valkyrie in a white smock like the nurse who had held wriggling, screaming Tommy while waiting for the suppository to quiet him down for his first EEG, a disheveled old fraud, he didn't know what. Anything except this pretty young woman. Another blind alley, he had thought in despair. Another, after a hundred too many already. First, "Wait for him to outgrow it." He doesn't. Then, "We must reconcile ourselves to God's will." But you don't want to. Then give him the prescription three times a day for three months. And it doesn't work. Then chase around for six months with the Child Guidance Clinic to find out it's only letterheads and one circuit-riding doctor who doesn't have time for anything. Then, after four dreary, weepy weeks of soul-searching, the State Training School, and find out it has an eight-year waiting list. Then the private custodial school, and find they're fifty-five hundred dollars a year—without medical treatment!—and where do you get fifty-five hundred dollars a year? And all the time everybody warns you, as if you didn't know it: "Hurry! Do something! Catch it early! This is the critical stage! Delay is fatal!" And then this soft-looking little woman; how could she do anything?

She had rapidly shown him how. She had questioned Margaret and Harry incisively, turned to Tommy, rampaging through the same room like a rogue bull, and turned his rampage into a game. In three minutes he was happily experimenting with an indestructible old windup cabinet Victrola, and Mrs. Adler was saying to the Vladeks, "Don't count on a miracle cure. There isn't any. But improvements, yes, and I think we can help Tommy."

Perhaps she had, thought Vladek bleakly. Perhaps she was helping as much as anyone ever could.

Meanwhile Mrs. Adler had quickly and pleasantly welcomed the parents, suggested they remain for coffee and get to know each other, and introduced the PTA president, a Mrs. Rose, tall, prematurely gray and very executive. "This being the first meeting of the term," she said, "there are no minutes to be read, so we'll get to the committee work reports. What about the transportation problem, Mr. Baer?"

The man who got up was old. More than sixty; Harry wondered what it was like to have your life crowned with a late retarded child. He wore all the trappings of success—a four hundred dollar suit, an electronic wristwatch, a large gold fraternal ring. In a slight German accent he said, "I was to the district school board and they are not cooperating. My lawyer looked it up and the trouble is all one word. What the law says, the school board may, that is the word, may, reimburse parents of handicapped children for transportation to private schools. Not shall, you understand, but may. They were very frank with me. They said they just didn't want to spend the money. They have the impression we're all rich people here."

Slight sour laughter around the room.

"So my lawyer made an appointment, and we appeared before the full board and presented the case—we don't care, reimbursement, a school bus, anything so we can relieve the transportation burden a little. The answer was no." He shrugged and remained standing, looking at Mrs. Rose, who said:

"Thank you, Mr. Baer. Does anybody have any suggestions?"

A woman said angrily, "Put some heat on them. We're all voters!"

A man said, "Publicity, that's right. The principle is perfectly clear in the law, one taxpayer's child is supposed to get the same service as another taxpayer's child. We should write letters to the papers."

Mr. Baer said, "Wait a minute. Letters I don't think mean anything, but I've got a public relations firm. I'll tell them to take a little time off my food specialties and use it for the school. They can use their own know-how, how to do it. They're the experts."

This was moved, seconded, and passed, while Murray Logan whispered to Vladek, "He's Marijane Garlic Mayonnaise. He had a twelve-year-old girl in very bad shape that Mrs. Adler helped in her old private class. He bought this building for her, along with a couple of other parents."

Harry Vladek was musing over how it felt to be a parent who could buy a building for a school that would help your child, while the committee reports continued. Some time later, to Harry's dismay, the business turned to financing, and there was a vote to hold a fund-raising theater party for which each couple with a child in the school would have to sell "at least" five pairs of orchestra seats at sixty dollars a pair. Let's get this straightened out now, he thought, and put up his hand.

"My name is Harry Vladek," he said when he was recognized, "and I'm brand new here. In the school and in the county. I work for a big insurance company, and I was lucky enough to get a transfer here so my boy can go to the school. But I just don't know anybody yet that I can sell tickets to for sixty dollars. That's an awful lot of money for my kind of people."

Mrs. Rose said, "It's an awful lot of money for most of us. You can get rid of your tickets, though. We've got to. It doesn't matter if you try a hundred people and ninety-five say no just as long as the others say yes."

He sat down, already calculating. Well, Mr. Crine at the office. He was a bachelor and he did go to the theater. Maybe work up an office raffle for another pair. Or two pairs. Then there was, let's see, the real estate dealer who had sold them the house, the lawyer they'd used for the closing . . .

Well. It had been explained to him that the tuition, while decidedly not nominal, eighteen hundred dollars a year in fact, did not cover the cost per child. Somebody had to pay for the speech therapist, the dance therapist, the full-time psychologist, and the part-time psychiatrist, and all the others, and it might as well be Mr. Crine at the office. And the lawyer.

And half an hour later Mrs. Rose looked at the agenda, checked off an item and said, "That seems to be all for tonight. Mr. and Mrs. Perry brought us some very nice cookies, and we all know that Mrs. Howe's coffee is out of this world. They're in the beginners room, and we hope you'll all stay to get acquainted. The meeting is adjourned."

Harry and the Logans joined the polite surge to the beginners room, where Tommy spent his mornings. "There's Miss Hackett," said Celia Logan. That was the beginners' teacher. She saw them and came over, smiling. Harry had seen her only in a tentlike smock, her armor against chocolate milk, finger paints, and sudden jets from the "water play" corner of the room. Without it she was handsomely middle-aged in a green pants suit.

"I'm glad you parents have met," she said. "I wanted to tell you that your little boys are getting along nicely. They're forming a sort of conspiracy against the others in the class. Vern swipes their toys and gives them to Tommy."

"He *does?*" cried Logan.

"Yes, indeed. I think he's beginning to relate. And, Mr. Vladek, Tommy's taken his thumb out of his mouth for minutes at a time. At least half a dozen times this morning, without my saying a word."

Harry said excitedly, "You know, I thought I noticed he was tapering off. I couldn't be sure. You're positive about that?"

"Absolutely," she said. "And I bluffed him into drawing a face. He gave me that glare of his when the others were drawing, so I started to take the paper away. He grabbed it back and scribbled a kind of Picasso-ish face in one second flat. I wanted to save it for Mrs. Vladek and you, but Tommy got it and shredded it in that methodical way he has."

"I wish I could have seen it," said Vladek.

"There'll be others. I can see the prospect of real improvement in your boys," she said, including the Logans in her smile. "I have a private case afternoons that's really tricky. A nine-year-old boy, like Tommy. He's not bad except for one thing. He thinks Donald Duck is out to get him. His parents somehow managed to convince themselves for two years that he was kidding them, in spite of three broken TV picture tubes. Then they went to a psychiatrist and learned the score. Excuse me, I want to talk to Mrs. Adler."

Logan shook his head and said, "I guess we could be worse off, Vladek. Vern giving something to another boy! How do you like that?"

"I like it," his wife said radiantly.

"And did you hear about that other boy? Poor kid. When I hear about something like that . . . And then there was the Baer girl. I always think it's worse when it's a little girl because, you know, you worry with little girls that somebody will take advantage, but our boys'll make out, Vladek. You heard what Miss Hackett said."

Harry was suddenly impatient to get home to his wife. "I don't think I'll stay for coffee, or do they expect you to?"

"No, no, leave when you like."

"I have a half-hour drive," he said apologetically and went through the golden-oak doors, past the ugly but fireproof staircase, out onto the graveled parking lot. His real reason was that he wanted very much to get home before Margaret fell asleep so he could tell her about the thumb-sucking. Things were happening, definite things, after only a month. And Tommy drew a face. And Miss Hackett said . . .

He stopped in the middle of the lot. He had remembered about Dr. Nicholson, and besides, what was it, exactly, that Miss Hackett had said? Anything about a normal life? Not anything about a cure? "Real improvement," she said, but improvement how far?

He lit a cigarette, turned, and plowed his way back through the parents to Mrs. Adler. "Mrs. Adler," he said, "may I see you just for a moment?"

She came with him immediately out of earshot of the others. "Did you enjoy the meeting, Mr. Vladek?"

"Oh, sure. What I wanted to see you about is that I have to make a decision. I don't know what to do. I don't know who to go to. It would help a lot if you could tell me, well, what are Tommy's chances?"

She waited a moment before she responded. "Are you considering committing him, Mr. Vladek?" she demanded.

"No, it's not exactly that. It's—well, what can you tell me, Mrs. Adler? I know a month isn't much. But is he ever going to be like everybody else?"

He could see from her face that she had done this before and had hated it. She said patiently, " 'Everybody else,' Mr. Vladek, includes some terrible people who just don't happen, technically, to be handicapped. Our objective isn't to make Tommy like 'everybody else.' It's just to help him to become the best and most rewarding Tommy Vladek he can."

"Yes, but what's going to happen later on? I mean, if Margaret and I—if anything happens to us?"

She was suffering. "There is simply no way to know, Mr. Vladek," she said gently. "I wouldn't give up hope. But I can't tell you to expect miracles."

Margaret wasn't asleep; she was waiting up for him, in the small living room of the small new house. "How was he?" Vladek asked, as each of them had asked the other on returning home for seven years.

She looked as though she had been crying, but she was calm enough. "Not too bad. I had to lie down with him to get him to go to bed. He took his gland gunk well, though. He licked the spoon."

"That's good," he said and told her about the drawing of the face, about the conspiracy with little Vern Logan, about the thumb-sucking. He could see how pleased she was, but she only said, "Dr. Nicholson called again."

"I told him not to bother you!"

"He didn't bother me, Harry. He was very nice. I promised him you'd call him back."

"It's eleven o'clock, Margaret. I'll call him in the morning."

"No, I said tonight, no matter what time. He's waiting, and he said to be sure and reverse the charges."

"I wish I'd never answered the son of a bitch's letter," he burst out and then, apologetically, "Is there any coffee? I didn't stay for it at the school."

She had put the water on to boil when she heard the car whine into the driveway, and the instant coffee was already in the cup. She poured it and said, "You have to talk to him, Harry. He has to know tonight."

"Know tonight! Know tonight," he mimicked savagely. He scalded his lips on the coffee cup and said, "What do you want me to do, Margaret? How do I make a decision like this? Today I picked up the phone and called the company psychologist, and when his secretary answered, I said I had the wrong number. I didn't know what to say to him."

"I'm not trying to pressure you, Harry. But he has to know."

Vladek put down the cup and lit his fiftieth cigarette of the day. The little dining room—it wasn't that, it was a half breakfast alcove off the tiny kitchen, but they called it a dining room even to each other—was full of Tommy. The new paint on the wall where Tommy had peeled off the cups-and-spoons wallpaper. The Tommy-proof latch on the stove. The one odd aqua seat that didn't match the others on the kitchen chairs, where Tommy had methodically gouged it with the handle of his spoon. He said, "I know what my mother would tell me, talk to the priest. Maybe I should. But we've never even been to Mass here."

Margaret sat down and helped herself to one of his cigarettes. She was still a good-looking woman. She hadn't gained a pound since Tommy was born, although she usually looked tired. She said, carefully and straightforwardly, "We agreed, Harry. You said you would talk to Mrs. Adler, and you've done that. We said if she didn't think Tommy would ever straighten out we'd talk to Dr. Nicholson. I know it's hard on you, and I know I'm not much help. But I don't know what to do, and I have to let you decide."

Harry looked at his wife, lovingly and hopelessly, and at that moment the phone rang. It was, of course, Dr. Nicholson.

"I haven't made a decision," said Harry Vladek at once. "You're rushing me, Dr. Nicholson."

The distant voice was calm and assured. "No, Mr. Vladek, it's not me that's rushing you. The other boy's heart gave out an hour ago. That's what's rushing you."

"You mean he's dead?" cried Vladek.

"He's on the heart-lung machine, Mr. Vladek. We can hold him for at least eighteen hours, maybe twenty-four. The brain is all right. We're getting very good waves on the oscilloscope. The tissue match with your boy is satisfactory. Better than satisfactory. There's a flight out of JFK at six fifteen in the morning, and I've reserved space for yourself, your wife, and Tommy. You'll be met at the airport. You can be here by noon, so we have time. Only just time, Mr. Vladek. It's up to you now."

Vladek said furiously, "I can't decide that! Don't you understand? I don't know how."

"I do understand, Mr. Vladek," said the distant voice and, strangely, Vladek thought, it seemed he did. "I have a suggestion. Would you like to come down anyhow? I think it might help you to see the other boy, and you can talk to his parents. They feel they owe you something even for going this far, and they want to thank you."

"Oh, no!" cried Vladek.

The doctor went on, "All they want is for their boy to have a life. They don't expect anything but that. They'll give you custody of the child—your child, yours and theirs. He's a very fine little boy, Mr. Vladek. Eight years old. Reads beautifully. Makes model airplanes. They let him ride his bike because he was so sensible and reliable, and the accident wasn't his fault. The truck came right up on the sidewalk and hit him."

Harry was trembling. "That's like giving me a bribe," he said harshly. "That's telling me I can trade Tommy in for somebody smarter and nicer."

"I didn't mean it that way, Mr. Vladek. I only wanted you to know the kind of a boy you can save."

"You don't even know the operation's going to work!"

"No," agreed the doctor. "Not positively. I can tell you that we've transplanted animals, including primates, and human cadavers, and one pair of terminal cases, but you're right, we've never had a transplant into a well body. I've shown you all the records, Mr. Vladek. We went over them with your own doctor when we first talked about this possibility, five months ago. This is the first case since then when the match was close and there was a real hope for success, but you're right, it's still unproved. Unless you help us prove it. For what it's worth, I think it will work. But no one can be sure."

Margaret had left the kitchen, but Vladek knew where she was from the scratchy click in the earpiece: in the bedroom, listening on the extension phone. He said at last, "I can't say now, Dr. Nicholson. I'll call you back in—in half an hour. I can't do any more than that right now."

"That's a great deal, Mr. Vladek. I'll be waiting right here for your call."

Harry sat down and drank the rest of his coffee. You had to be an expert in a lot of things to get along, he was thinking. What did he know about brain transplants? In one way, a lot. He knew that the surgery part was supposed to be straightforward, but the tissue rejection was the problem, but Dr. Nicholson thought he had that licked. He knew that every doctor he had talked to, and he had now talked to seven of them, had agreed that medically it was probably sound enough, and that every one of them had carefully clammed up when he got the conversation around to whether it was right. It was his decision, not theirs, they all said, sometimes just by their silence. But who was he to decide?

Margaret appeared in the doorway. "Harry. Let's go upstairs and look at Tommy."

He said harshly, "Is that supposed to make it easier for me to murder my son?"

She said, "We talked that out, Harry, and we agreed it isn't murder. Whatever it is. I only think that Tommy ought to be with us when we decide, even if he doesn't know what we're deciding."

The two of them stood next to the outsize crib that held their son, looking in the night light at the long fair lashes against the chubby cheeks and the pouted lips around the thumb. Reading. Model airplanes. Riding a bike. Against a quick sketch of a face and the occasional, cherished, tempestuous, bruising flurry of kisses.

Vladek stayed there the full half hour and then, as he had promised, went back to the kitchen, picked up the phone and began to dial.

Nobody's Home

Joanna Russ

Joanna Russ gained much admiration for her novels *Picnic On Paradise* and *And Chaos Died,* but she's equally at home in the short story genre, as she deftly shows in this beautifully written, trenchant evocation of a future utopia where science and rational life-styles have alleviated all of mankind's ills . . . except, perhaps, the human condition itself. (After you've read the story, take a moment to reconsider the title: it applies with precise irony in at least two interpretations.)

After she had finished her work at the North Pole, Jannina came down to the Red Sea refineries, where she had family business, jumped to New Delhi for dinner, took a nap in a public hotel in Queensland, walked from the hotel to the station, bypassed the Leeward Islands (where she thought she might go, but all the stations were busy), and met Charley to watch the dawn over the Carolinas.

"Where've you *been,* dear C?"

"Tanzania. And you're married."

"No."

"I heard you were married," he said. "The Lees told the Smiths who told the Kerguelens who told the Utsumbés, and we get around, we Utsumbés. A new wife, they said. I didn't know you were especially fond of women."

"I'm not. She's my husbands' wife. And we're not married yet, Charley. She's had hard luck. A first family started in '35, two husbands burned out by an overload while arranging transportation for a concert—of all things, pushing papers, you know!—and the second divorced her, I think, and she drifted away from the third (a big one), and there was some awful quarrel with the fourth, people chasing people around tables, I don't know."

"Poor woman."

In the manner of people joking and talking lightly they had drawn together, back to back, sitting on the ground and rubbing their shoulders and the backs of their heads together. Jannina said sorrowfully, "What lovely hair you have, Charley Utsumbé, like metal mesh."

"All we Utsumbés are exceedingly handsome." They linked arms. The sun, which anyone could chase around the world now, see it rise or set twenty times a day, fifty times a day—if you wanted to spend your life like that—rose dripping out of the cypress swamp. There was nobody around for miles. Mist drifted up from the pools and low places.

"My God," he said, "it's summer! I have to be at Tanga now."

"What?" said Jannina.

"One loses track," he said apologetically. "I'm sorry, love, but I have unavoidable business at home. Tax labor."

"But why summer, why did its being summer . . ."

"Train of thought! Too complicated." And already they were out of key, already the mild affair was over, there having come between them the one obligation that can't be put off to the time you like, or the place you like; off he'd go to plug himself into a road-mender or a doctor, though it's of some advantage to mend all the roads of a continent at one time.

She sat cross-legged on the station platform, watching him enter the booth and set the dial. He stuck his head out the glass door.

"Come with me to Africa, lovely lady!"

She thumbed her nose at him. "You're only a passing fancy, Charley U!" He blew a kiss, enclosed himself in the booth, and disappeared. (The transmatter field is larger than the booth, for obvious reasons; the booth flicks on and off several million times a second and so does not get transported itself, but it protects the machinery from the weather and it keeps people from losing elbows or knees or slicing the ends off a package or a child. The booths at the cryogenics center at the North Pole have exchanged air so often with those of warmer regions that each has its own microclimate; leaves and seeds, plants and earth are piled about them. The notes pinned to the door said, Don't Step on the Grass! Wish to Trade Pawlownia Sapling for Sub-arctic Canadian Moss; Watch Your Goddamn Bare Six-Toed Feet! Wish Amateur Cellist for Quartet, Six Months' Rehearsal Late Uhl with Reciter; I Lost A Squirrel Here Yesterday, Can You Find It Before It Dies? Eight Chidlren Will be Heartbroken—Cecilia Ching, Buenos Aires.)

Jannina sighed and slipped on her glass woolly; nasty to get back into clothes, but home was cold. You never knew where you might go, so you carried them. Years ago (she thought) I came here with someone in the dead of winter, either an unmatched man or someone's starting spouse—only two of us, at any rate—and we waded through the freezing water and danced as hard as we could and then proved we could sing and drink beer in a swamp at the same time, Good Lord! And then went to the public resort on the Ile de la Cité to watch professional plays, opera, games—you have to be good to get in there!—and got into some clothes because it was chilly after sundown in September—no, wait, it was Venezuela—and watched the lights come out and smoked like mad at a café table and tickled the robot waiter and pretended we were old, really old, perhaps a hundred and fifty . . . Years ago!

But *was* it the same place? she thought, and dismissing the incident forever, she stepped into the booth, shut the door, and dialed home: the Himalayas. The trunk line was clear. The branch stop was clear. The family's transceiver (located in the anteroom behind two doors, to keep the task of heating the house within reasonable limits) had damn well better be clear, or somebody would be blown right into the vestibule. Momentum- and heat-compensators kept Jannina from arriving home at seventy degrees Fahrenheit internal temperature (seven degrees lost for every mile you teleport upward) or too many feet above herself (rise to the east, drop going west; to the north or south you are apt to be thrown right through the wall of the booth). Someday (thought Jannina) everybody will decide to let everybody live in decent climates. But not yet. Not this everybody.

She arrived home singing "The World's My Back Yard, Yes, the World Is My Oyster," a song that had been popular in her first youth, some seventy years before.

The Komarovs' house was hardened foam with an automatic inside line to the school near Naples. It was good to be brought up on your own feet. Jannina passed through; the seven-year-olds lay with their heads together and their bodies radiating in a six-person asterisk. In this position (which was supposed to promote mystical thought) they played Barufaldi, guessing the identity of famous dead personages through anagrammatic sentences, the first letters of the words of which (unscrambled into aphorisms or proverbs) simultaneously spelled out a moral and a series of Goedel numbers (in a previously agreed-upon code) which . . .

"Oh, my darling, how felicitous is the advent of your appearance!" cried a boy (hard to take, the polysyllabic stage).

"Embrace me, dearest maternal parent! Unite your valuable upper limbs about my eager person!"

"Vulgar!" said Jannina, laughing.

"Non sum filius tuus?" said the child.

"No, you're not my body-child. You're my godchild. Your mother bequeathed me to you when she died. What are you learning?"

"The eternal parental question," he said, frowning. "How to run a helicopter. How to prepare food from its actual, revolting, raw constituents. Can I go now?"

"*Can* you?" she said. "Nasty imp!"

"Good," he said. "I've made you feel guilty. Don't *do*

that," and as she tried to embrace him, he ticklishly slid away. "The robin walks quietly up the branch of the tree," he said breathlessly, flopping back on the floor.

"That's not an aphorism." (Another Barufaldi player.)

"It is."

"It isn't."

"It is."

"It isn't."

"It is."

"It—"

The school vanished; the antechamber appeared. In the kitchen Chi Komarov was rubbing the naked back of his sixteen-year-old son. Parents always kissed each other; children always kissed each other. She touched foreheads with the two men and hung her woolly on the hook by the ham radio rig. Someone was always around. Jannina flipped the cover off her wrist chronometer: standard regional time, date, latitude-longitude, family computer hookup clear. "At my age I ought to remember these things," she said. She pressed the computer hookup: Ann at tax labor in the schools, bit-a-month plan, regular Ann; Lee with three months to go, five years off, heroic Lee; Phuong in Paris, still rehearsing; C.E. gone, won't say where, spontaneous C.E.; Ilse making some repairs in the basement, not a true basement, but the room farthest down the hillside. She went up the stairs and then came down and put her head round at the living-and-swimming room. Through the glass wall one could see the mountains. Old Al, who had joined them late in life, did a bit of gardening in the brief summers, and generally stuck around the place. Jannina beamed. "Hullo, Old Al!" Big and shaggy, a rare delight, his white body hair. She sat on his lap. "Has she come?"

"The new one? No," he said.

"Shall we go swimming?"

He made an expressive face. "No, dear," he said. "I'd rather go to Naples and watch the children fly helicopters. I'd rather go to Nevada and fly them myself. I've been in the water all day, watching a very dull person restructure coral reefs and experiment with polyploid polyps."

"You mean *you* were doing it."

"One gets into the habit of working."

"But you didn't have to!"

"It was a private project. Most interesting things are."

She whispered in his ear.

With happily flushed faces, they went into Old Al's inner garden and locked the door.

Jannina, temporary family representative, threw the computer helmet over her head and, thus plugged in, she cleaned house, checked food supplies, did a little of the legal business entailed by a family of eighteen adults (two triplet marriages, a quad, and a group of eight). She felt very smug. She put herself through by radio to Himalayan HQ (above two thousand meters) and hooking computer to computer— a very odd feeling, like an urge to sneeze that never comes off—extended a formal invitation to one Leslie Smith ("Come stay, why don't you?"), notifying every free Komarov to hop it back and fast. Six hikers might come for the night— back-packers. More food. First thunderstorm of the year in Albany, New York (North America). Need an extra two rooms by Thursday. Hear the Palnatoki are moving. Can't use a room. Can't use a kitten. Need the geraniums back, Mrs. Adam, Chile. The best maker of hand-blown glass in the world has killed in a duel the second-best maker of hand-blown glass for joining the movement toward ceramics. A bitter struggle is foreseen in the global economy. Need a lighting designer. Need fifteen singers and electric pansensi- con. Standby tax labor xxxxxpj through xxxyq to Cambaluc, great tectogenic—

With the guilty feeling that one always gets gossiping with a computer, for it's really not reciprocal, Jannina flipped off the helmet. She went to get Ilse. Climbing back through the white foam room, the purple foam room, the green foam room, everything littered with plots and projects of the clever Komarovs or the even cleverer Komarov children, stopping at the baby room for Ilse to nurse her baby, Jannina danced staidly around studious Ilse. They turned on the nursery robot and the television screen. Ilse drank beer in the swimming room, for her milk. She worried her way through the day's record of events—faults in the foundation, some people who came from Chichester and couldn't find C.E. so one of them burst into tears, a new experiment in genetics coming round the gossip circuit, an execrable set of equations from some imposter in Bucharest.

"A duel!" said Jannina.

They both agreed it was shocking. And what fun. A new fashion. You had to be a little mad to do it. Awful.

The light went on over the door to the tunnel that linked the house to the antechamber, and very quickly, one after another, as if the branch line had just come free, eight Komarovs came into the room. The light flashed again; one could see three people debouch one after the other, persons in boots, with coats, packs, and face masks over their woollies. They were covered with snow, either from the mountain terraces above the house or from some other place, Jannina didn't know. They stamped the snow off in the antechamber and hung their clothes outside. "Good heavens, you're not circumcised!" cried someone. There was as much handshaking and embracing all around as at a wedding party. Velet Komarov (the short, dark one) recognized Fung Pao-Yu and swung her off her feet. People began to joke, tentatively stroking one another's arms. "Did you have a good hike? Are you a good hiker, Pao-Yu?" said Velet. The light over the antechamber went on again, though nobody could see a thing since the glass was steamed over from the collision of hot with cold air. Old Al stopped, halfway into the kitchen. The baggage receipt chimed, recognized only by family ears —upstairs a bundle of somebody's things, ornaments, probably, for the missing Komarovs were still young and the young are interested in clothing, were appearing in the baggage receptacle. "Ann or Phuong?" said Jannina. "Five to three, anybody? Match me!" but someone strange opened the door of the booth and peered out. Oh, a dizzying sensation. She was painted in a few places, which was awfully odd because really it was old-fashioned; and why do it for a family evening? It was a stocky young woman. It was an awful mistake (thought Jannina). Then the visitor made her second mistake.

"I'm Leslie Smith," she said. But it was more through clumsiness than being rude. Chi Komarov (the tall, blond one) saw this instantly and, snatching off his old-fashioned spectacles, he ran to her side and patted her, saying teasingly:

"Now, haven't we met? Now, aren't you married to some-one I know?"

"No, no," said Leslie Smith, flushing with pleasure.

He touched her neck. "Ah, you're a tightrope dancer!"

"Oh, no!" exclaimed Leslie Smith.

"*I'm* a tightrope dancer," said Chi. "Would you believe it?"

"But you're too—too *spiritual,*" said Leslie Smith hesitantly.

"Spiritual, how do you like that, family, spiritual?" he cried, delighted (a little more delighted, thought Jannina, than the situation really called for), and he began to stroke her neck.

"What a lovely neck you have," he said.

This steadied Leslie Smith. She said, "I like tall men," and allowed herself to look at the rest of the family. "Who are these people?" she said, though one was afraid she might really mean it.

Fung Pao-Yu to the rescue: "Who are these people? Who are they, indeed! I doubt if they are anybody. One might say, 'I have met these people,' but has one? What existential meaning would such a statement convey? I myself, now, I have met them. I have been introduced to them. But they are like the Sahara. It is all wrapped in mystery. I doubt if they even have names," etc. etc. Then lanky Chi Komarov disputed possession of Leslie Smith with Fung Pao-Yu, and Fung Pao-Yu grabbed one arm and Chi the other; and she jumped up and down fiercely; so that by the time the lights dimmed and the food came, people were feeling better —or so Jannina judged. So embarrassing and delightful to be eating fifteen to a room! "We Komarovs are famous for eating whatever we can get whenever we can get it," said Velet proudly. Various Komarovs in various places, with the three hikers on cushions and Ilse at full length on the rug. Jannina pushed a button with her toe and the fairy lights came on all over the ceiling. "The children did that," said Old Al. He had somehow settled at Leslie Smith's side and was feeding her so-chi from his own bowl. She smiled up at him. "We once," said a hiking companion of Fung Pao-Yu's, "arranged a dinner in an amphitheater where half of us played servants to the other half, with forfeits for those who didn't show. It was the result of a bet. Like the bad old days. Did you know there were once *five billion people* in this world?"

"The gulls," said Ilse, "are mating on the Isle of Skye." There were murmurs of appreciative interest. Chi began to develop an erection and everyone laughed. Old Al wanted music and Velet didn't; what might have been a quarrel was ended by Ilse's furiously boxing their ears. She stalked off to the nursery.

"Leslie Smith and I are both old-fashioned," said Old Al, "because neither of us believes in gabbing. Chi—your theater?"

"We're turning people away." He leaned forward, earnestly, tapping his fingers on his crossed knees. "I swear, some of them are threatening to commit suicide."

"It's a choice," said Velet reasonably.

Leslie Smith had dropped her bowl. They retrieved it for her.

"Aiy, I remember—" said Pao-Yu. "What I remember! We've been eating dried mush for three days, tax-issue. Did you know one of my dads killed himself?"

"No!" said Velet, surprised.

"Years ago," said Pao-Yu. "He said he refused to live to see the time when chairs were reintroduced. He also wanted further genetic engineering, I believe, for even more intelligence. He did it out of spite, I'm sure. I think he wrestled a shark. Jannina, is this tax-issue food? Is it this year's style tax-issue sauce?"

"No, next year's," said Jannina snappishly. Really, some people! She slipped into Finnish, to show up Pao-Yu's pronunciation. "Isn't that so?" she asked Leslie Smith.

Leslie Smith stared at her.

More charitably Jannina informed them all, in Finnish, that the Komarovs had withdrawn their membership in a food group, except for Ann, who had taken out an individual, because what the dickens, who had the time? And tax-issue won't kill you. As they finished, they dropped their dishes into the garbage field and Velet stripped a layer off the rug. In that went, too. Indulgently Old Al began a round:

"Red."

"Sun," said Pao-yu.

"The Red Sun Is," said one of the triplet Komarovs.

"The Red Sun Is—High," said Chi.

"The Red Sun Is High, The," Velet said.

"The Red Sun Is High, The Blue—" Jannina finished. They had come to Leslie Smith, who could either complete it or keep it going. She chose to declare for complete, not shyly (as before) but simply by pointing to Old Al.

"The red sun is high, the blue," he said. "Subtle! Another: Ching."

"Nü."

"Ching nü ch'i."

"Ching nü ch'i ch'u."

"Ssu."

"Wo."

"Ssu wo yü." It had got back to Leslie Smith again. She said, "I can't do that." Jannina got up and began to dance— I'm nice in my nasty way, she thought. The others wandered toward the pool and Ilse reappeared on the nursery monitor screen, saying, "I'm coming down." Somebody said, "What time is it in the Argentine?"

"Five A.M."

"I think I want to go."

"Go then."

"I go."

"Go well."

The red light over the antechamber door flashed and went out.

"Say, why'd you leave your other family?" said Ilse, settling near Old Al where the wall curved out. Ann, for whom it was evening, would be home soon; Chi, who had just got up a few hours back in western America, would stay somewhat longer; nobody ever knew Old Al's schedule and Jannina herself had lost track of the time. She would stay up until she felt sleepy. She followed a rough twenty-eight-hour day, Phuong (what a nuisance that must be at rehearsals!) a twenty-two-hour one, Ilse six hours up, six hours dozing. Jannina nodded, heard the question, and shook herself awake.

"I didn't leave them. They left me."

There was a murmur of sympathy around the pool.

"They left me because I was stupid," said Leslie Smith. Her hands were clasped passively in her lap. She looked very genteel in her blue body paint, a stocky young woman with small breasts. One of the triplet Komarovs, flirting in the pool with the other two, choked. The non-aquatic members of the family crowded around Leslie Smith, touching her with little, soft touches; they kissed her and exposed to her all their unguarded surfaces, their bellies, their soft skins. Old Al kissed her hands. She sat there, oddly unmoved. "But I *am* stupid," she said. "You'll find out." Jannina put her hands over her ears: "A masochist!" Leslie Smith looked at Jannina with a curious, stolid look. Then she looked down and absently began to rub one blue-painted knee. "Luggage!" shouted Chi, clapping his hands together, and the triplets dashed for the stairs. "No, I'm going to bed," said Leslie Smith, "I'm tired," and quite simply, she got up and let Old Al lead her through the pink room, the blue room, the turtle-and-pet room (temporarily empty), the trash room, and all the other rooms, to the guest room with the view that looked out over the cold hillside to the terraced plantings below.

"The best maker of hand-blown glass in the world," said Chi, "has killed in a duel the second-best maker of hand-blown glass in the world."

"For joining the movement to ceramics," said Ilse, awed. Jannina felt a thrill: this was the bitter stuff under the surface of life, the fury that boiled up. A bitter struggle is foreseen in the global economy. Good old tax-issue stuff goes toddling along, year after year. She was, thought Jannina, extraordinarily grateful to be living now, to be in such an extraordinary world, to have so long to go before her death. So much to do!

Old Al came back into the living room. "She's in bed."

"Well, which of us—?" said the triplet-who-had-choked, looking mischievously round from one to the other. Chi was about to volunteer, out of his usual conscientiousness, thought Jannina, but then she found herself suddenly standing up, and then just as suddenly sitting down again. "I just don't have the nerve," she said. Velet Komarov walked on his hands toward the stairs, then somersaulted, and vanished, climbing. Old Al got off the hand-carved chest he had been sitting on and fetched a can of ale from it. He levered off the top and drank. Then he said, "She really is stupid, you know." Jannina's skin crawled.

"Oooh," said Pao-Yu. Chi betook himself to the kitchen and returned with a paper folder. It was coated with frost. He shook it, then impatiently dropped it in the pool. The redheaded triplet swam over and took it. "Smith, Leslie," he said. "Adam Two, Leslie. Yee, Leslie. Schwarzen, Leslie."

"What on earth does the woman *do* with herself besides get married?" exclaimed Pao-Yu.

"She drove a hovercraft," said Chi, "in some out-of-the-way places around the Pacific until the last underground stations were completed. Says when she was a child she wanted to drive a truck."

"Well, you can," said the redheaded triplet, "can't you? Go to Arizona or the Rockies and drive on the roads. The sixty-mile-an-hour road. The thirty-mile-an-hour road. Great artistic recreation."

"That's not work," said Old Al.

"Couldn't she take care of children?" said the redheaded triplet. Ilse sniffed.

"Stupidity's not much of a recommendation for that," Chi said. "Let's see—no children. No, of course not. Overfulfilled her tax work on quite a few routine matters here. Kim, Leslie. Went to Moscow and contracted a double with some fellow, didn't last. Registered as a singleton, but that didn't last, either. She said she was lonely, and they were exploiting her."

Old Al nodded.

"Came back and lived informally with a theater group. Left them. Went into psychotherapy. Volunteered for several experimental, intelligence-enhancing programs, was turned down—hum!—sixty-five come the winter solstice, muscular coordination average, muscular development above average, no overt mental pathology, empathy average, prognosis: poor. No, wait a minute, it says, 'More of the same.' Well, that's the same thing."

"What I want to know," added Chi, raising his head, "is who met Miss Smith and decided we needed the lady in this Ice Palace of ours?"

Nobody answered. Jannina was about to say, "Ann, perhaps?" but as she felt the urge to do so—surely it wasn't right to turn somebody off like that, *just* for that!—Chi (who had been flipping through the dossier) came to the last page, with the tax-issue stamp absolutely unmistakable, woven right into the paper.

"The computer did," said Pao-Yu, and she giggled idiotically.

"Well," said Jannina, jumping to her feet, "tear it up, my dear, or give it to me, and I'll tear it up for you. I think Miss Leslie Smith deserves from us the same as we'd give to anybody else, and I—for one—intend to go *right up there . . .*"

"After Velet," said Old Al dryly.

"With Velet, if I must," said Jannina, raising her eyebrows, "and if you don't know what's due a guest, Old Daddy, I do, and I intend to provide it. Lucky I'm keeping house this month, or you'd probably feed the poor woman nothing but seaweed."

"You won't like her, Jannina," said Old Al.

"I'll find that out for myself," said Jannina with some asperity, "and I'd advise you to do the same. Let her garden with you, Daddy. Let her squirt the foam for the new rooms. And now," she glared round at them, "I'm going to clean *this* room, so you'd better hop it, the lot of you," and dashing into the kitchen, she had the computer helmet on her head and the hoses going before they had even quite cleared the area of the pool. Then she took the helmet off and hung it on the wall. She flipped the cover off her wrist chronometer and satisfied herself as to the date. By the time she got back to the living room there was nobody there, only Leslie Smith's dossier lying on the carved chest. There was Leslie Smith; there was all of Leslie Smith. Jannina knocked on the wall cupboard and it revolved, presenting its openable side; she took out chewing gum. She started chewing and read about Leslie Smith.

Q: What have you seen in the last twenty years that you particularly liked?

A: I don't . . . the museum, I guess. At Oslo. I mean the . . . the mermaid and the children's museum, I don't care if it's a children's museum.

Q: Do you like children?

A: Oh no.

(No disgrace in *that*, certainly, thought Jannina.)

Q: But you liked the children's museum.

A: Yes, sir. . . . Yes. . . . I liked those little animals, the fake ones, in the . . . the . . .

Q: The crèche?

A: Yes. And I liked the old things from the past, the murals with the flowers on them, they looked so real.

(Dear God!)

Q: You said you were associated with a theater group in Tokyo. Did you like it?

A: No . . . yes, I don't know.

Q: Were they nice people?

A: Oh yes. They were awfully nice. But they got mad at me, I suppose. . . . You see . . . well, I don't seem to get things quite right, I suppose. It's not so much the work, because I do that all right, but the other . . . the little things. It's always like that.

Q: What do you think is the matter?

A: You . . . I think you know.

Jannina flipped through the rest of it: normal, normal, normal. Miss Smith was as normal as could be. Miss Smith was stupid. Not even very stupid. It was too damned bad. They'd probably have enough of Leslie Smith in a week, the Komarovs; yes, we'll have enough of her (Jannina thought), never able to catch a joke or a tone of voice, always clumsy, however willing, but never happy, never at ease. You can get a job for her, but what else can you get for her? Jannina glanced down at the dossier, already bored.

Q: You say you would have liked to live in the old days. Why is that? Do you think it would have been more adventurous, or would you like to have had lots of children?

A: I . . . you have no right . . . You're condescending.

Q: I'm sorry. I suppose you mean to say that then you would have been of above-average intelligence. You would, you know.

A: I know. I looked it up. Don't condescend to me.

Well, it *was* too damned bad! Jannina felt tears rise in her eyes. What had the poor woman done? It was just an accident, that was the horror of it, not even a tragedy, as if everyone's forehead had been stamped with the word "Choose" except for Leslie Smith's. She needs money, thought Jannina, thinking of the bad old days when people did things for money. Nobody could take to Leslie Smith. She wasn't insane enough to stand for being hurt or exploited. She wasn't clever enough to interest anybody. She certainly wasn't feebleminded; they couldn't very well put her into a hospital for the feebleminded or the brain-injured; in fact (Jannina was looking at the dossier again) they had tried to get her to work there, and she had taken a good, fast swing at the supervisor. She had said the people there were "hideous" and "revolting." She had no particular mechanical aptitudes. She had no particular interests. There was not even anything for her to read or watch; how could there be? She seemed (back at the dossier) to spend most of her time either working or going on public tours of exotic places, coral reefs, and places like that. She enjoyed aqualung diving, but didn't do it often because that got boring. And that was that. There was, all in all, very little one could do for Leslie Smith. You might even say that in her own person she represented all the defects of the bad old days. Just imagine a world made up of such creatures! Jannina yawned. She slung the folder away and padded into the kitchen. Pity Miss Smith wasn't good-looking, also a pity that she was too well balanced (the folder said) to think that cosmetic surgery would make that much difference. Good for you, Leslie, you've got some sense, anyhow. Jannina, half asleep, met Ann in the kitchen, beautiful, slender Ann reclining on a cushion with her so-chi and melon. Dear old Ann. Jannina nuzzled her brown shoulder. Ann poked her.

"Look," said Ann, and she pulled from the purse she wore at her waist a tiny fragment of cloth, stained rusty brown.

"What's that?"

"The second-best maker of hand-blown glass—oh, you know about it—well, this is his blood. When the best maker of hand-blown glass in the world had stabbed to the heart the second-best maker of hand-blown glass in the world, and cut his throat, too, some small children steeped handkerchiefs in his blood and they're sending pieces all over the world."

"Good God!" cried Jannina.

"Don't worry, my dear," said lovely Ann, "it happens every decade or so. The children say they want to bring back cruelty, dirt, disease, glory, and hell. Then they forget about it. Every teacher knows that." She sounded amused. "I'm afraid I lost my temper today, though, and walloped your godchild. It's in the family, after all."

Jannina remembered when she herself had been much younger and Annie, barely a girl, had come to live with them. Ann had played at being a child and had put her head on Jannina's shoulder, saying, "Jannie, tell me a story." So Jannina now laid her head on Ann's breast and said, "Annie, tell me a story."

Ann said: "I told my children a story today, a creation myth. Every creation myth has to explain how death and suffering came into the world, so that's what this one is about. In the beginning, the first man and the first woman lived very contentedly on an island until one day they began to feel hungry. So they called to the turtle who holds up the world to send them something to eat. The turtle sent them a mango and they ate it and were satisfied, but the next day they were hungry again.

"'Turtle,' they said, 'send us something to eat.' So the turtle sent them a coffee berry. They thought it was pretty small, but they ate it anyway and were satisfied. The third day they called on the turtle again and this time the turtle sent them two things: a banana and a stone. The man and woman did not know which to choose, so they asked the turtle which they should eat. 'Choose,' said the turtle. So they chose the banana and ate that, but they used the stone for a game of catch. Then the turtle said, 'You should have chosen the stone. If you had chosen the stone, you would have lived forever, but now that you have chosen the banana, Death and Pain have entered the world, and it is not I that can stop them.' "

Jannina was crying. Lying in the arms of her old friend, she wept bitterly, with a burning sensation in her chest and the taste of death and ashes in her mouth. It was awful. It was horrible. She remembered the embryo shark she had seen when she was three, in the Auckland Cetacean Research Center, and how she had cried then. She didn't know what she was crying about. "Don't, don't!" she sobbed.

"Don't what?" said Ann affectionately. "Silly Jannina!"

"Don't, don't," cried Jannina, "don't, it's true, it's true!" and she went on in this way for several more minutes. Death had entered the world. Nobody could stop it. It was ghastly. She did not mind for herself but for others, for her godchild, for instance. He was going to die. He was going to suffer. Nothing could help him. Duel, suicide, or old age, it was all the same. "This life!" gasped Jannina. "This awful life!" The thought of death became entwined somehow with Leslie Smith, in bed upstairs, and Jannina began to cry afresh, but eventually the thought of Leslie Smith calmed her. It brought her back to herself. She wiped her eyes with her hand. She sat up. "Do you want a smoke?" said beautiful Ann, but Jannina shook her head. She began to laugh. Really, the whole thing was quite ridiculous.

"There's this Leslie Smith," she said, dry-eyed. "We'll have to find a tactful way to get rid of her. It's idiotic, in this day and age."

And she told lovely Annie all about it.

Fortune Hunter

Poul Anderson

The function of science fiction, in its consideration of mankind's future, doesn't stop with predictions of possible turns of history and technological developments: more importantly, science fiction can bring the future home to us by showing us how it will affect individual people. Poul Anderson—a science fiction writer in the classic sense—considers the probable outcome of our ecological crises, and embodies his warning in a very, very human story.

After cleaning up indoors, I stepped outside for a look at the evening. I'd only moved here a few days ago. Before, I'd been down in the woods. Now I was above timberline, and there'd just been time to make my body at home—reassemble the cabin and its furnishings, explore the area, deploy the pickups, let lungs acquire a taste for thinner air. My soul was still busy settling in.

I missed sun-flecks spattered like gold on soft shadow-brown duff, male ruggedness and woman-sweet odor of pines and their green that speared into heaven, a brook that glittered and sang, bird calls, a splendidly antlered wapiti who'd become my friend and took food from my hand. (He was especially fond of cucumber peels. I dubbed him Charlie.)

You don't live six months in a place, from the blaze of autumn through the iron and white of winter, being reborn with the land when spring breathes over it—you don't do this and not keep some of that place ever afterward inside your bones.

Nevertheless, I'd kept remembering high country, and when Jo Modzeleski said she'd failed to get my time extended further, I decided to go up for what remained of it. That was part of my plan; she loved the whole wilderness as much as I did, but she kept her heart on its peaks and they ought to help make her mood right. However, I myself was happy to return.

And as I walked out of the cabin, past my skeletal flitter, so that nothing human-made was between me and the world, suddenly the whole of me was again altogether belonging where I was.

This base stood on an alpine meadow. Grass grew thick and moist, springy underfoot, daisy-starred. Here and there bulked boulders the size of houses, grayness scored by a glacier which had once gouged out the little lake rippling and sparkling not far away: a sign to me that I also was included in eternity. Everywhere around, the Wind River Mountains lifted snow crowns and the darker blues of their rock, into a dizzyingly tall heaven where an eagle hovered. He caught on his wings the sunlight which slanted out of the west. Those beams seemed to fill the chilliness, turning it somehow molten; and the heights were alive with shadows.

I smelled growth, more austere than in the forest but not the less strong. A fish leaped, I saw the brief gleam and an instant later, very faintly through quietness, heard the water clink. Though there was no real breeze, my face felt the air kiss it.

I buttoned my mackinaw, reached for smoking gear, and peered about. A couple of times already, I'd spied a bear. I knew better than to try a Charlie-type relationship with such a beast, but surely we could share the territory amicably, and if I could learn enough of his ways to plant pickups where they could record his life—or hers, in which case she'd be having cubs—

No. You're bound back to civilization at the end of this week. Remember?

Oh, but I may be returning.

As if in answer to my thought, I heard a whirr aloft. It grew, till another flitter hove into sight. Jo was taking me up on my invitation at an earlier hour than I'd expected when I said, "Come for dinner about sundown." Earlier than I'd hoped? My heart knocked. I stuck pipe and tobacco pouch back in my pockets and walked fast to greet her.

She landed and sprang out of the bubble before the airpad motors were silent. She always had been quick and graceful on her feet. Otherwise she wasn't much to look at: short, stocky, pug nose, pale round eyes under close-cropped black hair. For this occasion she'd left off the ranger's uniform in favor of an iridescent clingsuit; but it couldn't have done a lot for her even if she had known how to wear it.

"Welcome," I said, took both her hands and gave her my biggest smile.

"Hi." She sounded breathless. Color came and went across her cheeks. "How are you?"

"Okay. Sad at leaving, naturally." I turned the smile wry, so as not to seem self-pitiful.

She glanced away. "You'll be going back to your wife, though."

Don't push too hard. "You're ahead of yourself, Jo. I meant to have drinks and snacks ready in advance. Now you'll have to come in and watch me work."

"I'll help."

"Never, when you're my guest. Sit down, relax." I took her arm and guided her toward the cabin.

She uttered an uncertain laugh. "Are you afraid I'll get in your way, Pete? No worries. I know these knockdown units—I'd better, after three years—"

I was here for four, and that followed half a dozen years in and out of other wildernesses, before I decided that this was the one I wanted to record in depth, it being for me the loveliest of the lovely.

"—and they only have one practical place to stow any given kind of thing," she was saying. Then she stopped, which made me do likewise, turned her head from side to side, drank deep of air and sun-glow. "Please, don't let me hurry you. This is such a beautiful evening. You were out to enjoy it."

Unspoken: And you haven't many left, Pete. The documentation project ended officially last year. You're the last of the very few mediamen who got special permission to stay on and finish their sequences; and now, no more stalling, no more extra time, the word is Everybody Out.

My unspoken reply: Except you rangers. A handful of you, holding degrees in ecology and soil biotics and whatnot —a handful who won in competition against a horde—does that give you the right to lord it over all this?

"Well, yes," I said, and segued to: "I'll enjoy it especially in present company."

"Thank you, kind sir." She failed to sound cheery.

I squeezed her arm. "You know, I'm going to miss you, Jo. Miss you like hell." This past year, as my plan grew within me, I'd been cultivating her. Not just card games and long conversations over the sensiphone; no, in-the-flesh get-togethers for hikes, rambles, picnics, fishing, birdwatching, deerwatching, starwatching. A mediaman gets good at the cultivation of people, and although this past decade had given me scant need to use that skill, it hadn't died. As easy as breathing, I could show interest in her rather banal remarks, her rather sappy-sentimental opinions. . . . "Come see me when you get a vacation."

"Oh, I'll—I'll call you up . . . now and then . . . if Marie won't . . . mind."

"I mean come in person. Holographic image, stereo sound, even scent and temperature and every other kind of circuit a person might pay for the use of—a phone isn't the same as having a friend right there."

She winced. "You'll be in the city."

"It isn't so bad," I said in my bravest style. "Pretty fair-sized apartment, a lot bigger than that plastic shack yonder. Soundproofed. Filtered and conditioned air. The whole con-urb fully screened and policed. Armored vehicles available when you sally forth."

"And a mask for my nose and mouth!" She nearly gagged.

"No, no, that hasn't been needed for a long while. They've gotten the dust, monoxide, and carcinogens down to a level, at least in my city, which—"

"The stinks. The tastes. No, Pete, I'm sorry, I'm no delicate flower, but the visits to Boswash I make in line of duty are the limit of what I can take . . . after getting to know this land."

"I'm thinking of moving into the country myself," I said. "Rent a cottage in an agrarea, do most of my business by phone, no need to go downtown except when I get an assignment to document something there."

She grimaced. "I often think the agrareas are worse than any 'tropolis."

"Huh?" It surprised me that she could still surprise me.

"Oh, cleaner, quieter, less dangerous, residents not jammed elbow to elbow, true," she admitted. "But at least those snarling, grasping, frenetic city folk have a certain freedom, a certain . . . *life* to them. It may be the life of a ratpack, but it's real, it has a bit of structure and spontaneity and— In the hinterlands, not only nature is regimented. The people are."

Well, I don't know how else you could organize things to feed a world population of fifteen billion.

"All right," I said. "I understand. But this is a depressing subject. Let's saunter for a while. I've found some gentian blooming."

"So early in the season? Is it in walking distance? I'd like to see."

"Too far for now, I'm afraid. I've been tramping some mighty long days. However, let me show you the local blueberry patch. It should be well worth a visit, come late summer."

As I took her arm again, she said, in her awkward fashion, "You've become an expert, haven't you, Pete?"

"Hard to avoid that," I grunted. "Ten years, collecting sensie material on the Wilderness System."

"Ten years. . . . I was in high school when you began. I only knew the regular parks, where we stood in line on a paved path to see a redwood or a geyser, and we reserved swimming rights a month in advance. While you—" Her fingers closed around mine, hard and warm. "It doesn't seem fair to end your stay."

"Life never was fair."

Too damn much human life. Too little of any other kind. And we have to keep a few wildernesses, a necessary reserve for what's left of the planet's ecology; a source of knowledge for researchers who're trying to learn enough about that ecology to shore it up before it collapses altogether; never mentioned, but present in every thinking head, the fact that if collapse does come, the wildernesses will be Earth's last seedbeds of hope.

"I mean," Jo plodded, "of course areas like this were being destroyed by crowds—loved to death, as somebody wrote—so the only thing to do was close them to everybody except a few caretakers and scientists, and that was politically impossible unless 'everybody' meant *everybody*." Ah, yes, she was back to her habit of thumbing smooth-worn cliches. "And after all, the sensie documentaries that artists like you have been making, they'll be available and—" The smoothness vanished. "*You* can't come back, Pete! Not ever again!"

Her fingers remembered where they were and let go of me. Mine followed them and squeezed, a measured gentleness. Meanwhile my pulse fluttered. It was as well that words didn't seem indicated at the moment, because my mouth was dry.

A mediaman should be more confident. But such a God damn lot was riding on this particular bet. I'd gotten Jo to care about me, not just in the benevolent way of her colleagues, isolated from mankind so they can afford benevolence, but about me, this Pete-atom that wanted to spend the rest of its flickering days in the Wind River Mountains. Only how deeply did she care?

We walked around the lake. The sun dropped under the peaks—for minutes, the eastern snows were afire—and shadows welled up. I heard an owl hoot to his love. In royal blue, Venus kindled. The air sharpened, making blood run faster.

"Br-r-r!" Jo laughed. "Now I do want that drink."

I couldn't see her features through the dusk. The first

stars stood forth infinitely clear. But Jo was a blur, a warmth, a solidness, no more. She might almost have been Marie.

If she had been! Marie was beautiful and bright and sexy and— Sure, she took lovers while I was gone for months on end; we'd agreed that the reserves were my mistresses. She'd had no thought for them on my returns. . . . Oh, if only we could have shared it all!

Soon the sky would hold more stars than darkness, the Milky Way would be a white cataract, the lake would lie aglow with them, and when Jupiter rose there would be a perfect glade across the water. I'd stayed out half of last night to watch that.

Already the shining was such that we didn't need a penflash to find the entrance to my cabin. The insulation layer yielded under my touch. We stepped through, I zipped the door and closed the main switch, fluoros awoke as softly as the ventilation.

Jo was correct: those portables don't lend themselves to individuality. (She had a permanent cabin, built of wood and full of things dear to her.) Except for a few books and the like, my one room was strictly functional. True, the phone could bring me the illusion of almost anything or anybody, anywhere in the world, that I might want. We city folk learn to travel light. This interior was well-proportioned, pleasingly tinted, snug; a step outside was that alpine meadow. What more did I need?

Out of hard-earned habit, I checked the nucleo gauge— ample power—before taking dinner from the freezer and setting it to cook. Thereafter I fetched nibblies, rum, and fruit juice, and mixed drinks the way Jo liked them. She didn't try to help after all, but settled back into the airchair. Neither of us had said much while we walked. I'd expected chatter out of her—a bit nervous, a bit too fast and blithe— once we were here. Instead, her stocky frame hunched in its mother-of-pearl suit that wasn't meant for it, and she stared at the hands in her lap.

No longer cold, I shucked my mackinaw and carried her drink over to her. "Revelry, not reverie!" I ordered. She took it. I clinked glasses. My other hand being then free, I reached thumb and forefinger to twitch her lips at the corners. "Hey, you, smile. This is supposed to be a jolly party."

"Is it?" The eyes she raised to me were afloat in tears.

"Sure, I hate to go—"

"Where's Marie's picture?"

That rocked me back. I hadn't expected so blunt a question. "Why, uh—" *Okay. Events are moving faster than you'd planned on, Peter. Move with them.* I took a swallow, squared my shoulders, and said manfully: "I didn't want to unload my troubles on you, Jo. The fact is, Marie and I have broken up. Nothing's left but the formalities."

"What?"

Her mouth is open, her look lost in mine; she spills some of her drink and doesn't notice— Have I really got it made? This soon?

I shrugged. "Yeah. The notice of intent to dissolve relationship arrived yesterday. I'd seen it coming, of course. She'd grown tired of waiting around."

"Oh, Pete!" She reached for me.

I was totally aware—walls, crowded shelves, night in a window, murmur and warm gusting from the heat unit, monitor lamp on the radionic oven and meat fragrances seeping out of it, this woman whom I must learn to desire—and thought quickly that at the present stage of things, I'd better pretend not to notice her gesture. "No sympathy cards," I said in a flat tone. "To be quite honest, I'm more relieved than otherwise."

"I thought—" she whispered. "I thought you two were happy."

Which we have been, my dear, Marie and I: though a sophisticated mediaman does suspect that considerable of our happiness, as opposed to contentment, has been due to my long absences this past decade. They've added spice. That's something you'll always lack, whatever happens, Jo. Yet a man can't live only on spices.

"It didn't last," I said as per plan. "She's found someone more compatible. I'm glad of that."

"You, Pete?"

"I'll manage. C'mon, drink your drink. I insist that we be merry."

She gulped. "I'll try."

After a minute: "You haven't even anyone to come home to!"

" 'Home' doesn't mean a lot to a city man, Jo. One apartment is like another, and we move through a big total of 'em in a lifetime." The liquor must have touched me a bit, since I rushed matters: "Quite different from, say, these mountains. Each patch of them is absolutely unique. A man could spend all his years getting to know a single one, growing into it— Well."

I touched a switch and the airchair expanded, making room for me to settle down beside her. "Care for some background music?" I asked.

"No." Her gaze dropped—she had stubby lashes—and she blushed—blotchily—but she got her words out with a stubbornness I had come to admire. Somebody who had that kind of guts wouldn't be too bad a partner. "At least, I'd not hear it. This is just about my last chance to talk . . . really talk . . . to you, Pete. Isn't it?"

"I hope not." *More passion in that voice, boy.* "Lord, I hope not!"

"We have had awfully good times together. My colleagues are fine, you know, but—" She blinked hard. "You've been special."

"Same as you to me."

She was shivering a bit, meeting my eyes now, lips a bare few centimeters away. Since she seldom drank alcohol, I guessed that what I'd more or less forced on her had gotten a good strong hold, under these circumstances. *Remember, she's no urbanite who'll hop into bed and scarcely remember it two days later. She went directly from a small town to a tough university to here, and may actually be a virgin. However, you've worked toward this moment for months, Pete, old chum. Get started!*

It was the gentlest kiss I think I have ever taken.

"I've been, well, afraid to speak," I murmured into her hair, which held an upland sunniness. "Maybe I still am. Only I don't, don't, don't want to lose you, Jo."

Half crying, half laughing, she came back to my mouth. She didn't really know how, but she held herself hard against me, and I thought: *May she end up sleeping with me, already this night?*

No matter, either way. What does count is, the Wilderness Administration allows qualified husband-and-wife teams to live together on the job; and she's a ranger and I, being skilled in using monitoring devices, would be an acceptable research assistant.

And then-n-n:

I didn't know, I don't know to this day what went wrong. We'd had two or three more drinks, and a good deal of joyous tussling, and her clothes were partly off her and dinner was beginning to scorch in the oven when

I was too hasty

she was too awkward and/or backward-holding, and I got impatient and she felt it

I breathed out one of those special words which people say to each other only, and she being a bit terrified anyway decided it wasn't mere habit-accident but I was pretending she was Marie because in fact my eyes were shut

she wasn't as naive as she, quite innocently, had led me to believe, and in one of those moments which (contrary to fantasy) are forever coming upon lovers, asked herself, "Hey, what the hell is really going on?"

or whatever. It makes no difference. Suddenly she wanted to phone Marie.

"If, if, if things are as you say, Pete, she'll be glad to learn—"

"Wait a minute! Wait one damn minute! Don't you trust me?"

"Oh, Pete, darling, of course I do, but—"

"But nothing." I drew apart to register offense.

Instead of coming after me, she asked, as quietly as the night outside: "Don't you trust *me?*"

Never mind. A person can't answer a question like that. We both tried, and shouldn't have. All I truly remember is seeing her out the door. A smell of charred meat pursued us. Beyond the cabin, the air was cold and altogether pure, sky wild with stars, peaks aglow. I watched her stumble to her flitter. The galaxy lit her path. She cried the whole way. But she went.

However disappointed, I felt some relief, too. It would have been a shabby trick to play on Marie, who had considerable love invested in me. And our apartment is quite pleasant, once it's battened down against the surroundings; I belong to the fortunate small minority. We had an appropriate reunion. She even babbled about applying for a childbearing permit. I kept enough sense to switch that kind of talk off immediately.

Next evening there was a rally which we couldn't well get out of attending. The commissioners may be right as far as most citizens go. "A sensiphone, regardless of how many circuits are tuned in, is no substitute for the physical togetherness of human beings uniting under their leaders for our glorious mass purposes." We, though, didn't get anything out of it except headaches, ears ringing from the cadenced cheers, lungs full of air that had passed through thousands of other lungs, and skins which felt greasy as well as gritty. Homebound, we encountered smog so thick it confused our vehicle. Thus we got stopped on the fringes of a riot and saw a machine gun cut a man in two before the militia let us move on. It was a huge relief to pass security check at our conurb and take a transporter which didn't fail even once, up and across to our own place.

There we shared a shower, using an extravagant percentage of our monthly water ration, and dried each other off, and I slipped into a robe and Marie into something filmy; we had a drink and a toke while Haydn lilted, and got relaxed to the point where she shook her long tresses over her shoulders and her whisper tickled my ear: "Aw, c'mon, hero, the computers've got to've edited your last year's coverage by now. I've looked forward all this while."

I thought fleetingly of Jo. Well, she wouldn't appear in a strictly wilderness-experience public-record documentary; and I myself was curious about what I had actually produced, and didn't think a revisit in an electronic dream would pain me, even this soon afterward.

I was wrong.

What hurt most was the shoddiness. Oh, yes, decent reproduction of a primrose nodding in the breeze, a hawk a-swoop, spuming whiteness and earthquake rumble of a distant avalanche, fallen leaves brown and baking under the sun, their smell and crackle, the laughter of a gust which flirted with my hair, suppleness incarnate in a snake or a cougar, flamboyance at sunset and shyness at dawn—a competent show. Yet it wasn't real, it wasn't what I had loved.

Marie said, slowly, in the darkness where we sat, "You did better before. Kruger, Matto Grosso, Baikal, your earlier stays in this region—I almost felt I was at your side. You weren't a recorder there, you were an artist, a great artist. Why is this different?"

"I don't know," I mumbled. "My presentation is kind of mechanical, I admit. I suppose I was tired."

"In that case—" she sat very straight, half a meter from me, fingers gripped together— "you didn't have to stay on. You could have come home to me long before you did."

But I wasn't tired, rammed through my head. *No, now is when I'm drained; then, there, life flowed into me.*

That gentian Jo wanted to see . . . it grows where the land suddenly drops. Right at the cliff edge those flowers grow, oh, blue, blue, blue against grass green and daisy white and the strong gray of stone; a streamlet runs past, leaps downward, ringing, cold, tasting of glaciers, rocks, turf, the air which also blows everywhere around me, around the high and holy peaks beyond. . . .

"Lay off!" I yelled. My fist struck the chair arm. The fabric clung and cloyed. A shade calmer, I said, "Okay, maybe I got too taken up in the reality and lost the necessary degree of detachment." *I lie, Marie, I lie like Judas. My mind was never busier, planning how to use Jo and discard you.* "Darling, those sensies, I'll have nothing but them for the rest of my life." *And none of the gentians. I was too busy with my scheme to bother with anything small and gentle and blue.* "Isn't that penalty enough?"

"No. You did have the reality. And you did not bring it back." Her voice was like a wind across the snows of upland winter.

The Fifth Head of Cerberus

Gene Wolfe

If 1972 produced a classic science fiction story, I believe
the following novella by Gene Wolfe is it. Set on a colonized
planet among the far stars, this story brings its people and world
more fully to life than any other recent sf story I can recall.
It's also a remarkable technical achievement in the pure story-
telling sense, a combination of science fiction and Gothic traditions that compromises neither, utilizes each to the fullest. And
it has a point to make—dramatically, surprisingly, hauntingly—
about people yesterday, today, and tomorrow.

> When the ivy-tod is heavy with snow,
> And the owlet whoops to the wolf below,
> That eats the she-wolf's young.
> —SAMUEL TAYLOR COLERIDGE
> *The Rime of the Ancient Mariner*

When I was a boy my brother David and I had to go to
bed early whether we were sleepy or not. In summer particularly, bedtime often came before sunset; and because our
dormitory was in the east wing of the house, with a broad
window facing the central courtyard and thus looking west,
the hard, pinkish light sometimes streamed in for hours while

43

we lay staring out at my father's crippled monkey perched on a flaking parapet, or telling stories, one bed to another, with soundless gestures.

Our dormitory was on the uppermost floor of the house, and our window had a shutter of twisted iron which we were forbidden to open. I suppose the theory was that a burglar might, on some rainy morning (this being the only time he could hope to find the roof, which was fitted out as a sort of pleasure garden, deserted), let down a rope and so enter our room unless the shutter was closed.

The object of this hypothetical and very courageous thief would not, of course, be merely to steal us. Children, whether boys or girls, were extraordinarily cheap in Port-Mimizon; and indeed I was once told that my father, who had formerly traded in them, no longer did so because of the poor market. Whether or not this was true, everyone—or nearly everyone—knew of some professional who would furnish what was wanted, within reason, at a low price. These men made the children of the poor and the careless their study, and should you want, say, a brown-skinned, red-haired little girl, or one who was plump, or who lisped, a blond boy like David or a pale, brown-haired, brown-eyed boy such as I, they could provide one in a few hours.

Neither, in all probability, would the imaginary burglar seek to hold us for ransom, though my father was thought in some quarters to be immensely rich. There were several reasons for this. Those few people who knew that my brother and I existed knew also, or at least had been led to believe, that my father cared nothing at all for us. Whether this was true or not, I cannot say; certainly I believed it, and my father never gave me the least reason to doubt it, though at the time the thought of killing him had never occurred to me.

And if these reasons were not sufficiently convincing, anyone with an understanding of the stratum in which he had become perhaps the most permanent feature would realize that for him, who was already forced to give large bribes to the secret police, to once disgorge money in that way would leave him open to a thousand ruinous attacks;

and this may have been—this and the fear in which he was held—the real reason we were never stolen.

The iron shutter is (for I am writing now in my old dormitory room) hammered to resemble in a stiff and overly symmetrical way the boughs of a willow. In my boyhood it was overgrown by a silver trumpet vine (since dug up) which had scrambled up the wall from the court below, and I used to wish that it would close the window entirely and thus shut out the sun when we were trying to sleep; but David, whose bed was under the window, was forever reaching up to snap off branches so that he could whistle through the hollow stems, making a sort of panpipe of four or five. The piping, of course, growing louder as David grew bolder, would in time attract the attention of Mr. Million, our tutor. Mr. Million would enter the room in perfect silence, his wide wheels gliding across the uneven floor while David pretended sleep. The panpipe might by this time be concealed under his pillow, in the sheet, or even under the mattress, but Mr. Million would find it.

What he did with those little musical instruments after confiscating them from David I had forgotten until yesterday; although in prison, when we were kept in by storms or heavy snow, I often occupied myself by trying to recall it. To have broken them, or dropped them through the shutter onto the patio below would have been completely unlike him; Mr. Million never broke anything intentionally, and never wasted anything. I could visualize perfectly the half-sorrowing expression with which he drew the tiny pipes out (the face which seemed to float behind his screen was much like my father's) and the way in which he turned and glided from the room. But what became of them?

Yesterday, as I said (this is the sort of thing that gives me confidence), I remembered. He had been talking to me here while I worked, and when he left it seemed to me—as my glance idly followed his smooth motion through the doorway—that something, a sort of flourish I recalled from my earliest days, was missing. I closed my eyes and tried to remember what the appearance had been, eliminating any skepticism, any attempt to guess in advance what I "must" have seen; and I found that the missing element was a brief flash, the glint of metal, over Mr. Million's head.

Once I had established this, I knew that it must have come from a swift upward motion of his arm, like a salute, as he left our room. For an hour or more I could not guess the reason for that gesture, and could only suppose it, whatever it had been, to have been destroyed by time. I tried to recall if the corridor outside our dormitory had, in that really not so distant past, held some object now vanished: a curtain or a windowshade, an appliance to be activated, anything that might account for it. There was nothing.

I went into the corridor and examined the floor minutely for marks indicating furniture. I looked for hooks or nails driven into the walls, pushing aside the coarse old tapestries. Craning my neck, I searched the ceiling. Then, after an hour, I looked at the door itself and saw what I had not seen in the thousands of times I had passed through it: that like all the doors in this house, which is very old, it had a massive frame of wooden slabs, and that one of these, forming the lintel, protruded enough from the wall to make a narrow shelf above the door.

I pushed my chair into the hall and stood on the seat. The shelf was thick with dust in which lay forty-seven of my brother's pipes and a wonderful miscellany of other small objects. Objects many of which I recalled, but some of which still fail to summon any flicker of response from the recesses of my mind . . .

The small blue egg of a songbird, speckled with brown. I suppose the bird must have nested in the vine outside our window, and that David or I despoiled the nest only to be robbed ourselves by Mr. Million. But I do not recall the incident.

And there is a (broken) puzzle made of the bronzed viscera of some small animal, and—wonderfully evocative— one of those large and fancifully decorated keys, sold annually, which during the year of its currency will admit the possessor to certain rooms of the city library after hours. Mr. Million, I suppose, must have confiscated it when, after expiration, he found it doing duty as a toy; but what memories!

My father had his own library, now in my possession; but we were forbidden to go there. I have a dim memory of standing—at how early an age I cannot say—before that huge carved door. Of seeing it swing back, and the crippled monkey on my father's shoulder pressing itself against his hawk face, with the black scarf and scarlet dressing gown beneath and the rows and rows of shabby books and notebooks behind them, and the sick-sweet smell of formaldyhyde coming from the laboratory beyond the sliding mirror.

I do not remember what he said or whether it had been I or another who had knocked, but I do recall that after the door had closed, a woman in pink whom I thought very pretty stooped to bring her face to the level of my own and assured me that my father had written all the books I had just seen, and that I doubted it not at all.

My brother and I, as I have said, were forbidden this room; but when we were a little older Mr. Million used to take us, about twice a week, on expeditions to the city library. These were very nearly the only times we were allowed to leave the house, and since our tutor disliked curling the jointed length of his metal modules into a hire cart, and no sedan chair would have withstood his weight or contained his bulk, these forays were made on foot.

For a long time this route to the library was the only part of the city I knew. Three blocks down Saltimbanque Street where our house stood, right at the Rue d'Asticot to the slave market and a block beyond that to the library. A child, not knowing what is extraordinary and what commonplace, usually lights midway between the two, finds interest in incidents adults consider beneath notice and calmly accepts the most improbable occurrences. My brother and I were fascinated by the spurious antiques and bad bargains of the Rue d'Asticot, but often bored when Mr. Million insisted on stopping for an hour at the slave market.

It was not a large one, Port-Mimizon not being a center of the trade, and the auctioneers and their merchandise were frequently on a most friendly basis—having met several times previously as a succession of owners discovered the same fault. Mr. Million never bid, but watched the bidding, motionless, while we kicked our heels and munched the fried bread he had bought at a stall for us. There were sedan chairmen, their legs knotted with muscle, and simpering bath attendants; fighting slaves in chains, with eyes dulled by drugs or blazing with imbecile ferocity; cooks, house servants, a hundred others—yet David and I used to beg to be allowed to proceed alone to the library.

This library was a wastefully large building which had held government offices in the old French-speaking days. The park in which it had once stood had died of petty corruption, and the library now rose from a clutter of shops and tenements. A narrow thoroughfare led to the main doors, and once we were inside, the squalor of the neighborhood vanished, replaced by a kind of peeling grandeur. The main desk was directly beneath the dome, and this dome, drawing up with it a spiraling walkway lined with the library's main collection, floated five hundred feet in the air: a stony sky whose least chip falling might kill one of the librarians on the spot.

While Mr. Million browsed his way majestically up the helix, David and I raced ahead until we were several full turns in advance and could do what we liked. When I was still quite young it would often occur to me that, since my father had written (on the testimony of the lady in pink) a roomful of books, some of them should be here; and I would climb resolutely until I had almost reached the dome, and there rummage. Because the librarians were very lax about reshelving, there seemed always a possibility of finding what I had failed to find before. The shelves towered far above my head, but when I felt myself unobserved I climbed them like ladders, stepping on books when there was no room on the shelves themselves for the square toes of my small brown shoes, and occasionally kicking books to the floor where they remained until our next visit and beyond, evidence of the staff's reluctance to climb that long, coiled slope.

The upper shelves were, if anything, in worse disorder than those more conveniently located, and one glorious day when I attained the highest of all I found occupying that lofty, dusty position (besides a misplaced astronautics text, *The Mile-Long Spaceship,* by some German) only a lorn copy of *Monday or Tuesday* leaning against a book about the assassination of Trotsky, and a crumbling volume of Vernor Vinge's short stories that owed its presence there, or so I suspect, to some long-dead librarian's mistaking the faded *V. Vinge* on the spine for "Winge."

I never found any books of my father's, but I did not regret the long climbs to the top of the dome. If David had come with me, we raced up together, up and down the sloping floor—or peered over the rail at Mr. Million's slow progress while we debated the feasibility of putting an end to him with one cast of some ponderous work. If David preferred to pursue interests of his own farther down I ascended to the very top where the cap of the dome curved right over my head; and there, from a rusted iron catwalk not much wider than one of the shelves I had been climbing (and I suspect not nearly so strong), opened in turn each of a circle of tiny piercings—piercings in a wall of iron, but so shallow a wall that when I had slid the corroded cover-plates out of the way I could thrust my head through and feel myself truly outside, with the wind and the circling birds and the lime-spotted expanse of the dome curving away beneath me.

To the west, since it was taller than the surrounding houses and marked by the orange trees on the roof, I could make out our house. To the south, the masts of the ships in the harbor, and in clear weather—if it was the right time of day—the whitecaps of the tidal race Sainte Anne drew between the peninsulas called First Finger and Thumb. (And once, as I very well recall, while looking south I saw the great geyser of sunlit water when a starcrosser splashed down.) To east and north spread the city proper, the citadel and the grand market and the forests and mountains beyond.

But sooner or later, whether David had accompanied me or gone off on his own, Mr. Million summoned us. Then we were forced to go with him to one of the wings to visit this or that science collection. This meant books for lessons. My father insisted that we learn biology, anatomy, and chemistry thoroughly, and under Mr. Million's tutelage, learn them we did—he never considering a subject mastered until we could discuss every topic mentioned in every book catalogued under the heading. The life sciences were my own favorites, but David preferred languages, literature, and law; for we got a smattering of these as well as anthropology, cybernetics, and psychology.

When he had selected the books that would form our study for the next few days and urged us to choose more for ourselves, Mr. Million would retire with us to some quiet corner of one of the science reading rooms, where there were chairs and a table and room sufficient for him to curl the jointed length of his body or align it against a wall or bookcase in a way that left the aisles clear. To designate the formal beginning of our class he used to begin by calling roll, my own name always coming first.

I would say, "Here," to show that he had my attention.

"And David."

"Here." (David has an illustrated *Tales from the Odyssey* open on his lap where Mr. Million cannot see it, but he looks at Mr. Million with bright, feigned interest. Sunshine slants down to the table from a high window, and shows the air aswarm with dust.)

"I wonder if either of you noticed the stone implements in the room through which we passed a few moments ago?"

We nod, each hoping the other will speak.

"Were they made on Earth, or here on our own planet?"

This is a trick question, but an easy one. David says, "Neither one. They're plastic." And we giggle.

Mr. Million says patiently, "Yes, they're plastic reproductions, but from where did the originals come?" His face, so similar to my father's, but which I thought of at this time as belonging only to him, so that it seemed a frightening reversal of nature to see it on a living man instead of his screen, was neither interested, nor angry, nor bored; but coolly remote.

David answers, "From Sainte Anne." Sainte Anne is the sister planet to our own, revolving with us about a common center as we swing around the sun. "The sign said so, and the aborigines made them—there weren't any abos here."

Mr. Million nods, and turns his impalpable face toward

me. "Do you feel these stone implements occupied a central place in the lives of their makers? Say no."

"No."

"Why not?"

I think frantically, not helped by David, who is kicking my shins under the table. A glimmering comes.

"Talk. Answer at once."

"It's obvious, isn't it?" (Always a good thing to say when you're not even sure "it" is even possible.) "In the first place, they can't have been very good tools, so why would the abos have relied on them? You might say they needed those obsidian arrowheads and bone fishhooks for getting food, but that's not true. They could poison the water with the juices of certain plants, and for primitive people the most effective way to fish is probably with weirs, or with nets of rawhide or vegetable fiber. Just the same way, trapping or driving animals with fire would be more effective than hunting; and anyway stone tools wouldn't be needed at all for gathering berries and the shoots of edible plants and things like that, which were probably their most important foods—those stone things got in the glass case here because the snares and nets rotted away and they're all that's left, so the people that make their living that way pretend they were important."

"Good. David? Be original, please. Don't repeat what you've just heard."

David looks up from his book, his blue eyes scornful of both of us. "If you could have asked them, they would have told you that their magic and their religion, the songs they sang, and the traditions of their people were what were important. They killed their sacrificial animals with flails of seashells that cut like razors, and they didn't let their men father children until they had stood enough fire to cripple them for life. They mated with trees and drowned the children to honor their rivers. That was what was important."

With no neck, Mr. Million's face nodded. "Now we will debate the humanity of those aborigines. David negative and first."

(I kick him, but he has pulled his hard, freckled legs up beneath him, or hidden them behind the legs of his chair, which is cheating.) "Humanity," he says in his most objectionable voice, "in the history of human thought implies descent from what we may conveniently call *Adam;* that is, the original Terrestrial stock, and if the two of you don't see that, you're idiots."

I wait for him to continue, but he is finished. To give myself time to think, I say, "Mr. Million, it's not fair to let him call me names in a debate. Tell him that's not debating, it's *fighting,* isn't it?"

Mr. Million says, "No personalities, David." (David is already peeking at Polyphemus the Cyclops and Odysseus, hoping I'll go on for a long time. I feel challenged and decide to do so.)

I begin, "The argument which holds descent from Terrestrial stock pivotal is neither valid nor conclusive. Not conclusive because it is distinctly possible that the aborigines of Sainte Anne were descendants of some earlier wave of human expansion—one, perhaps, even predating *The Homeric Greeks.*"

Mr. Million says mildly, "I would confine myself to arguments of higher probability if I were you."

I nevertheless gloss upon the Etruscans, Atlantis, and the tenacity and expansionist tendencies of a hypothetical technological culture occupying Gondwanaland. When I have finished Mr. Million says, "Now reverse. David, affirmative without repeating."

My brother, of course, has been looking at his book instead of listening, and I kick him with enthusiasm, expecting him to be stuck; but he says, "The abos are human because they're all dead."

"Explain."

"If they were alive it would be dangerous to let them be human because they'd ask for things, but with them dead it makes it more interesting if they were, and the settlers killed them all."

And so it goes. The spot of sunlight travels across the black-streaked red of the tabletop—traveled across it a hundred times. We would leave through one of the side doors and walk through a neglected areaway between two wings.

There would be empty bottles there and wind-scattered papers of all kinds, and once a dead man in bright rags over whose legs we skipped while Mr. Million rolled silently around him. As we left the areaway for a narrow street, the bugles of the garrison at the citadel (sounding so far away) would call the troopers to their evening mess. In the Rue d'Asticot the lamplighter would be at work, and the shops shut behind their iron grilles. The sidewalks magically clear of old furniture would seem broad and bare.

Our own Saltimbanque Street would be very different, with the first revelers arriving. White-haired, hearty men guiding very young men and boys, men and boys handsome and muscular but a shade overfed; young men who made diffident jokes and smiled with excellent teeth at them. These were always the early ones, and when I was a little older I sometimes wondered if they were early only because the white-haired men wished to have their pleasure and yet a good night's sleep as well, or if it were because they knew the young men they were introducing to my father's establishment would be drowsy and irritable after midnight, like children who have been kept up too late.

Because Mr. Million did not want us to use the alleys after dark we came in the front entrance with the white-haired men and their nephews and sons. There was a garden there, not much bigger than a small room and recessed into the windowless front of the house. In it were beds of ferns the size of graves; a little fountain whose water fell upon rods of glass to make a continual tinkling, and which had to be protected from the street boys; and, with his feet firmly planted, indeed almost buried in moss, an iron statue of a dog with three heads.

It was this statue, I suppose, that gave our house its popular name of *Maison du Chien,* though there may have been a reference to our surname as well. The three heads were sleekly powerful with pointed muzzles and ears. One was snarling and one, the center head, regarded the world of garden and street with a look of tolerant interest. The third, the one nearest the brick path that led to our door, was—there is no other term for it—frankly grinning; and it was the custom for my father's patrons to pat this head between the ears as they came up the path. Their fingers had polished the spot to the consistency of black glass.

This, then, was my world at seven of our world's long years, and perhaps for half a year beyond. Most of my days were spent in the little classroom over which Mr. Million presided, and my evenings in the dormitory where David and I played and fought in total silence. They were varied by the trips to the library I have described or, very rarely, elsewhere. I pushed aside the leaves of the silver trumpet vine occasionally to watch the girls and their benefactors in the court below, or heard their talk drifting down from the roof garden, but the things they did and talked of were of no great interest to me. I knew that the tall, hatchet-faced man who ruled our house and was called "Maitre" by the girls and servants was my father. I had known for as long as I could remember that there was somewhere a fearsome woman—the servants were in terror of her—called "Madame," but that she was neither my mother, nor David's, nor my father's wife.

That life and my childhood, or at least my infancy, ended one evening after David and I, worn out with wrestlings and silent arguments, had gone to sleep. Someone shook me by the shoulder and called me, and it was not Mr. Million but one of the servants, a hunched little man in a shabby red jacket. "He wants you," this summoner informed me. "Get up."

I did, and he saw that I was wearing nightclothes. This I think had not been covered in his instructions, and for a moment during which I stood and yawned, he debated with himself. "Get dressed," he said at last. "Comb your hair."

I obeyed, putting on the black velvet trousers I had worn the day before, but (guided by some instinct) a new clean shirt. The room to which he then conducted me (through tortuous corridors now emptied of the last patrons; and others, musty, filthy with the excrement of rats, to which patrons were never admitted) was my father's library—the room with the great carved door before which I had received the whispered confidences of the woman in pink. I had never been inside it, but when my guide rapped discreetly on the door it swung back, and I found myself within, almost before I realized what had happened.

My father, who had opened the door, closed it behind me; and leaving me standing where I was, walked to the most distant end of that long room and threw himself down in a huge chair. He was wearing the red dressing gown and black scarf in which I had most often seen him, and his long, sparse hair was brushed straight back. He stared at me, and I remember that my lip trembled as I tried to keep from breaking into sobs.

"Well," he said, after we had looked at one another for a long time, "and there you are. What am I going to call you?"

I told him my name, but he shook his head. "Not that. You must have another name for me—a private name. You may choose it yourself if you like."

I said nothing. It seemed to me quite impossible that I should have any name other than the two words which were, in some mystic sense I only respected without understanding, *my name*.

"I'll choose for you then," my father said. "You are Number Five. Come here, Number Five."

I came, and when I was standing in front of him, he told me, "Now we are going to play a game. I am going to show you some pictures, do you understand? And all the time you are watching them, you must talk. Talk about the pictures. If you talk you win, but if you stop, even for just a second, I do. Understand?"

I said I did.

"Good. I know you're a bright boy. As a matter of fact, Mr. Million has sent me all the examinations he has given you and the tapes he makes when he talks with you. Did you know that? Did you ever wonder what he did with them?"

I said, "I thought he threw them away," and my father, I noticed, leaned forward as I spoke, a circumstance I found flattering at the time.

"No, I have them here." He pressed a switch. "Now remember, you must not stop talking."

But for the first few moments I was much too interested to talk.

There had appeared in the room, as though by magic, a boy considerably younger than I, and a painted wooden soldier almost as large as I was myself, which when I reached out to touch them proved as insubstantial as air. "Say something," my father said. "What are you thinking about, Number Five?"

I was thinking about the soldier, of course, and so was the younger boy, who appeared to be about three. He toddled through my arm like mist and attempted to knock it over.

They were holograms—three-dimensional images formed by the interference of two wave fronts of light—things which had seemed very dull when I had seen them illustrated by flat pictures of chessmen in my physics book; but it was some time before I connected those chessmen with the phantoms who walked in my father's library at night. All this time my father was saying, "Talk! Say something! What do you think the little boy is feeling?"

"Well, the little boy likes the big soldier, but he wants to knock him down if he can, because the soldier's only a toy, really, but it's bigger than he is . . ." And so I talked, and for a long time, hours I suppose, continued. The scene changed and changed again. The giant soldier was replaced by a pony, a rabbit, a meal of soup and crackers. But the three-year-old boy remained the central figure. When the hunched man in the shabby coat came again, yawning, to take me back to my bed, my voice had worn to a husky whisper and my throat ached. In my dreams that night I saw the little boy scampering from one activity to another, his personality in some way confused with my own and my father's so that I was at once observer, observed, and a third presence observing both.

The next night I fell asleep almost at the moment Mr. Million sent us up to bed, retaining consciousness only long enough to congratulate myself on doing so. I woke when the hunched man entered the room, but it was not me whom he roused from the sheets but David. Quietly, pretending I still slept (for it had occurred to me, and seemed quite reasonable at the time, that if he were to see I was awake he might take both of us), I watched as my brother dressed and struggled to impart some sort of order to his tangle of fair hair. When he returned I was sound asleep, and had no opportunity to question him until Mr. Million left us alone, as he sometimes did, to eat our breakfast. I had told him my own experiences as a matter of course, and what he had to tell me was simply that he had had an evening very similar to mine. He had seen holograms, and apparently the same: the wooden soldier, the pony. He had been forced to talk constantly, as Mr. Million had so often made us do in debates and verbal examinations. The only way in which his interview with our father had differed from mine, as nearly as I could determine, appeared when I asked him by what name he had been called.

He looked at me blankly, a piece of toast half raised to his mouth.

I asked again, "What name did he call you by when he talked to you?"

"He called me David. What did you think?"

With the beginning of these interviews the pattern of my life changed, the adjustments I assumed to be temporary becoming imperceptibly permanent, settling into a new shape of which neither David nor I were consciously aware. Our games and stories after bedtime stopped, and David less and less often made his panpipes of the silver trumpet vine. Mr. Million allowed us to sleep later and we were in some subtle way acknowledged to be more adult. At about this time too, he began to take us to a park where there was an archery range and provision for various games. This little park, which was not far from our house, was bordered on one side by a canal. And there, while David shot arrows at a goose stuffed with straw or played tennis, I often sat staring at the quiet, only slightly dirty water; or waiting for one of the white ships—great ships with bows as sharp as the scalpel-bills of kingfishers and four, five, or even seven masts—which were, infrequently, towed up from the harbor by ten or twelve spans of oxen.

In the summer of my eleventh or twelfth year—I think the twelfth—we were permitted for the first time to stay after sundown in the park, sitting on the grassy, sloped margin of the canal to watch a fireworks display. The first preliminary flight of rockets had no sooner exhausted itself half a mile above the city than David became ill. He rushed to the water and vomited, plunging his hands half up to the elbows in muck while the red and white stars burned in glory above him. Mr. Million took him up in his arms, and when poor David had emptied himself we hurried home.

His disease proved not much more lasting than the tainted sandwich that had occasioned it, but while our tutor was putting him to bed I decided not to be cheated of the remainder of the display, parts of which I had glimpsed between the intervening houses as we made our way home; I was forbidden the roof after dark, but I knew very well where the nearest stair was. The thrill I felt in penetrating that prohibited world of leaf and shadow while fire-flowers of purple and gold and blazing scarlet overtopped it affected me like the aftermath of a fever, leaving me short of breath, shaking, and cold in the midst of summer.

There were a great many more people on the roof than I had anticipated, the men without cloaks, hats, or sticks (all of which they had left in my father's checkrooms), and the girls, my father's employees, in costumes that displayed their rouged breasts in enclosures of twisted wire like birdcages, or gave them the appearance of great height (dissolved only when someone stood very close to them), or gowns whose skirts reflected their wearers' faces and busts as still water does the trees standing near it, so that they appeared, in the intermittent colored flashes, like the queens of strange suits in a tarot deck.

I was seen, of course, since I was much too excited to conceal myself effectively; but no one ordered me back, and I suppose they assumed I had been permitted to come up to see the fireworks.

These continued for a long time. I remember one patron, a heavy, square-faced, stupid-looking man who seemed to be someone of importance, who was so eager to enjoy the company of his protégée—who did not want to go inside until the display was over—that, since he insisted on privacy, twenty or thirty bushes and small trees had to be rearranged on the parterre to make a little grove around them. I helped the waiters carry some of the smaller tubs and pots, and managed to duck into the structure as it was completed. Here I could still watch the exploding rockets and "aerial bombs" through the branches, and at the same time the patron and his *nymphe du bois*, who was watching them a good deal more intently than I.

My motive, as well as I can remember, was not prurience but simple curiosity. I was at that age when we are passionately interested, but the passion is one of science. Mine was nearly satisfied when I was grasped by the shirt by someone behind me and drawn out of the shrubbery.

When I was clear of the leaves I was released, and I turned expecting to see Mr. Million, but it was not he. My captor was a little gray-haired woman in a black dress whose skirt, as I noticed even at the time, fell straight from her waist to the ground. I suppose I bowed to her, since she was clearly no servant, but she returned no salutation at all, staring intently into my face in a way that made me think she could see as well in the intervals between the bursting glories as by their light. At last, in what must have been the finale of the display, a great rocket rose screaming on a river of flame, and for an instant she consented to look up. Then, when it had exploded in a mauve orchid of unbelievable size and brilliance, this formidable little woman grabbed me again and led me firmly toward the stairs.

While we were on the level stone pavement of the roof garden she did not, as nearly as I could see, walk at all, but rather seemed to glide across the surface like an onyx chessman on a polished board; and that, in spite of all that has happened since, is the way I still remember her: as the Black Queen, a chess queen neither sinister nor beneficent, and Black only as distinguished from some White Queen I was never fated to encounter.

When we reached the stairs, however, this smooth gliding became a fluid bobbing that brought two inches or more of the hem of her black skirt into contact with each step, as if her torso were descending each as a small boat might a rapids—now rushing, now pausing, now almost backing in the cross currents.

She steadied herself on these steps by holding on to me and grasping the arm of a maid who had been waiting for us at the stairhead and assisted her from the other side. I had supposed, while we were crossing the roof garden, that her gliding motion had been the result, merely, of a marvelously controlled walk and good posture, but I now understood her to be in some way handicapped; and I had the impression that without the help the maid and I gave her she might have fallen headfirst.

Once we had reached the bottom of the steps her smooth progress was resumed. She dismissed the maid with a nod and led me down the corridor in the direction opposite to that in which our dormitory and classroom lay until we reached a stairwell far toward the back of the house, a corkscrew, seldom-used flight, very steep, with only a low iron banister between the steps and a six-story drop into the cellars. Here she released me and told me crisply to go down. I went down several steps, then turned to see if she was having any difficulty.

She was not, but neither was she using the stairs. With her long skirt hanging as straight as a curtain she was floating, suspended, watching me, in the center of the stairwell. I was so startled I stopped, which made her jerk her head angrily, then began to run. As I fled around and around the spiral she revolved with me, turning toward me always a face extraordinarily like my father's, one hand always on the railing. When we had descended to the second floor she swooped down and caught me as easily as a cat takes charge of an errant kitten, and led me through rooms and passages where I had never been permitted to go until I was as confused as I might have been in a strange building. At last we stopped before a door in no way different from any other. She opened it with an old-fashioned brass key with an edge like a saw and motioned for me to go in.

The room was brightly lit, and I was able to see clearly what I had only sensed on the roof and in the corridors: that the hem of her skirt hung two inches above the floor no matter how she moved, and that there was nothing between the hem and the floor at all. She waved me to a little footstool covered with needlepoint and said, "Sit down," and when I had done so, glided across to a wing-backed rocker and sat facing me. After a moment she asked, "What's your name?" and when I told her she cocked an eyebrow at me, and started the chair in motion by pushing gently with her fingers at a floor lamp that stood beside it. After a long time she said, "And what does he call you?"

"He?" I was stupid, I suppose, with lack of sleep.

She pursed her lips. "My brother."

I relaxed a little. "Oh," I said, "you're my aunt then. I thought you looked like my father. He calls me Number Five."

For a moment she continued to stare, the corners of her mouth drawing down as my father's often did. Then she said, "That number's either far too low or too high. Living, there are he and I, and I suppose he's counting the simulator. Have you a sister, Number Five?"

Mr. Million had been having us read *David Copperfield*, and when she said this she reminded me so strikingly and unexpectedly of Aunt Betsey Trotwood that I shouted with laughter.

"There's nothing absurd about it. Your father had a sister—why shouldn't you? You have none?"

"No ma'am, but I have a brother. His name is David."

"Call me Aunt Jeannine. Does David look like you, Number Five?"

I shook my head. "His hair is curly and blond instead of like mine. Maybe he looks a little like me, but not a lot."

"I suppose," my aunt said under her breath, "he used one of my girls."

"Ma'am?"

"Do you know who David's mother was, Number Five?"

"We're brothers, so I guess she would be the same as mine, but Mr. Million says she went away a long time ago."

"Not the same as yours," my aunt said. "No. I could show you a picture of your own. Would you like to see it?" She rang a bell, and a maid came curtsying from some room beyond the one in which we sat; my aunt whispered to her, and she went out again. When my aunt turned back to me

she asked, "And what do you do all day, Number Five, besides run up to the roof when you shouldn't? Are you
taught?"

I told her about my experiments (I was stimulating un-
fertilized frogs' eggs to asexual development and then dou-
bling the chromosomes by a chemical treatment so that a
further asexual generation could be produced) and the dissections Mr. Million was by then encouraging me to do, and
while I talked, happened to drop some remark about how
interesting it would be to perform a biopsy on one of the
aborigines of Sainte Anne if any were still in existence,
since the first explorers' descriptions differed so widely, and
some pioneers there had claimed the abos could change
their shapes.

"Ah," my aunt said, "you know about them. Let me test
you, Number Five. What is Veil's Hypothesis?"

We had learned that several years before, so I said, "Veil's
hypothesis supposes the abos to have possessed the ability to
mimic mankind perfectly. Veil thought that when the ships
came from Earth the abos killed everyone and took their
places and the ships, so they're not dead at all, we are."

"You mean the Earth people are," my aunt said. "The
human beings."

"Ma'am?"

"If Veil was correct, then you and I are abos from Sainte
Anne, at least in origin; which I suppose is what you meant.
Do you think he was right?"

"I don't think it makes any difference. He said the imitation would have to be perfect, and if it is, they're the same
as we were anyway." I thought I was being clever, but my
aunt smiled, rocking more vigorously. It was very warm in
the close, bright little room.

"Number Five, you're too young for semantics, and I'm
afraid you've been led astray by that word *perfectly*. Dr.
Veil, I'm certain, meant to use it loosely rather than as precisely as you seem to think. The imitation could hardly have
been exact, since human beings don't possess that talent and
to imitate them *perfectly* the abos would have to lose it."

"Couldn't they?"

"My dear child, abilities of every sort must evolve. And when they do they must be utilized or they atrophy. If the abos had been able to mimic so well as to lose the power to do so, that would have been the end of them, and no doubt it would have come long before the first ships reached them. Of course there's not the slightest evidence they could do anything of the sort. They simply died off before they could be thoroughly studied, and Veil, who wants a dramatic explanation for the cruelty and irrationality he sees around him, has hung fifty pounds of theory on nothing."

This last remark, especially as my aunt seemed so friendly, appeared to me to offer an ideal opportunity for a question about her remarkable means of locomotion, but as I was about to frame it we were interrupted, almost simultaneously, from two directions. The maid returned carrying a large book bound in tooled leather, and she had no sooner handed it to my aunt than there was a tap at the door. My aunt said absently, "Get that," and since the remark might as easily have been addressed to me as to the maid I satisfied my curiosity in another form by racing her to answer the knock.

Two of my father's demi-mondaines were waiting in the hall, costumed and painted until they seemed more alien than any abos, stately as Lombardy poplars and inhuman as specters, with green and yellow eyes made to look the size of eggs, and inflated breasts pushed almost shoulder high; and though they maintained an inculcated composure I was pleasantly aware that they were startled to find me in the doorway. I bowed them in, but as the maid closed the door behind them my aunt said absently, "In a moment, girls. I want to show the boy here something, then he's going to leave."

The "something" was a photograph utilizing, as I supposed, some novelty technique which washed away all color save a light brown. It was small, and from its general appearance and crumbling edges very old. It showed a girl of twenty-five or so, thin and as nearly as I could judge rather tall, standing beside a stocky young man on a paved walkway and holding a baby. The walkway ran along the front of a remarkable house, a very long wooden house only a story in height, with a porch or veranda that changed its architectural style every twenty or thirty feet so as to give almost the impression of a number of exceedingly narrow houses constructed with their side walls in contact. I mention this detail, which I hardly noticed at the time, because I have so often since my release from prison tried to find some trace of this house. When I was first shown the picture I was much more interested in the girl's face, and the baby's. The latter was in fact scarcely visible, he being nearly smothered in white-wool blankets. The girl had large features and a brilliant smile which held a suggestion of that rarely seen charm which is at once careless, poetic, and sly. Gypsy, was my first thought, but her complexion was surely too fair for that. Since on this world we are all descended from a relatively small group of colonists, we are rather a uniform population, but my studies had given me some familiarity with the original Terrestrial races, and my second guess, almost a certainty, was Celtic. "Wales," I said aloud. "Or Scotland. Or Ireland."

"What?" my aunt said. One of the girls giggled; they were seated on the divan now, their long, gleaming legs crossed before them like the varnished staffs of flags.

"It doesn't matter."

My aunt looked at me acutely and said, "You're right. I'll send for you, and we'll talk about this when we've both more leisure. For the present my maid will take you to your room."

I remember nothing of the long walk the maid and I must have had back to the dormitory, or what excuses I gave Mr. Million for my unauthorized absence. Whatever they were I suppose he penetrated them, or discovered the truth by questioning the servants, because no summons to return to my aunt's apartment came, although I expected it daily for weeks afterward.

That night—I am reasonably sure it was the same night—I dreamed of the abos of Sainte Anne, abos dancing with plumes of fresh grass on their heads and arms and ankles, abos shaking their shields of woven rushes and their nephrite-tipped spears until the motion affected my bed and became, in shabby red cloth, the arms of my father's valet come to summon me, as he did almost every night, to his library.

That night, and this time I am quite certain it was the same night, that is, the night I first dreamed of the abos, the pattern of my hours with him, which had come over the four or five years past to have a predictable sequence of conversation, holograms, free association, and dismissal—changed. Following the preliminary talk designed, I feel sure, to put me at ease (at which it failed, as it always did), I was told to roll up a sleeve and lie down upon an old examining table in a corner of the room. My father then made me look at the wall, which meant at the shelves heaped with ragged notebooks. I felt a needle being thrust into the inner part of my arm, but my head was held down and my face turned away, so that I could neither sit up nor look at what he was doing. Then the needle was withdrawn, and I was told to lie quietly.

After what seemed a very long time, during which my father occasionally spread my eyelids to look at my eyes or took my pulse, someone in a distant part of the room began to tell a very long and confusingly involved story. My father made notes of what was said, and occasionally stopped to ask questions I found it unnecessary to answer, since the storyteller did it for me.

The drug he had given me did not, as I had imagined it would, lessen its hold on me as the hours passed. Instead it seemed to carry me progressively further from reality and the mode of consciousness best suited to preserving the individuality of thought. The peeling leather of the examination table vanished under me, and was now the deck of a ship, now the wing of a dove beating far above the world; and whether the voice I heard reciting was my own or my father's I no longer cared. It was pitched sometimes higher, sometimes lower, but then I felt myself at times to be speaking from the depths of a chest larger than my own, and his voice, identified as such by the soft rustling of the pages of his notebook, might seem the high, treble cries of the racing children in the streets as I heard them in summer when I thrust my head through the windows at the base of the library dome.

With that night my life changed again. The drugs—for there seemed to be several, and although the effect I have described was the usual one there were also times when I found it impossible to lie still, but ran up and down for hours as I talked, or sank into blissful or indescribably frightening dreams—affected my health. I often wakened in the morning with a headache that kept me in agony all day, and I became subject to periods of extreme nervousness and apprehensiveness. Most frightening of all, whole sections of days sometimes disappeared, so that I found myself awake and dressed, reading, walking, and even talking, with no memory at all of anything that had happened since I had lain muttering to the ceiling in my father's library the night before.

The lessons I had had with David did not cease, but in some sense Mr. Million's role and mine were now reversed. It was I, now, who insisted on holding our classes when they were held at all; and it was I who chose the subject matter and, in most cases, questioned David and Mr. Million about it. But often when they were at the library or the park I remained in bed reading, and I believe there were many times when I read and studied from the time I found myself conscious in my bed until my father's valet came for me again.

David's interviews with our father, I should note here, suffered the same changes as my own and at the same time; but since they were less frequent—and they became less and less frequent as the hundred days of summer wore away to autumn and at last to the long winter—and he seemed on the whole to have less adverse reactions to the drugs, the effect on him was not nearly as great.

If at any single time, it was during this winter that I came to the end of childhood. My new ill health forced me away from childish activities, and encouraged the experiments I was carrying out on small animals, and my dissections of the bodies Mr. Million supplied in an unending stream of open mouths and staring eyes. Too, I studied or read, as I have said, for hours on end; or simply lay with my hands behind my head while I struggled to recall, perhaps for whole days together, the narratives I had heard

myself give my father. Neither David nor I could ever remember enough even to build a coherent theory of the nature of the questions asked us, but I have still certain scenes
fixed in my memory which I am sure I have never beheld
in fact, and I believe these are my visualizations of suggestions whispered while I bobbed and dove through those
altered states of consciousness.

My aunt, who had previously been so remote, now spoke
to me in the corridors and even visited our room. I learned
that she controlled the interior arrangements of our house,
and through her I was able to have a small laboratory of
my own set up in the same wing. But I spent the winter, as
I have described, mostly at my enamel dissecting table or in
bed. The white snow drifted half up the glass of the window, clinging to the bare stems of the silver trumpet vine.
My father's patrons, on the rare occasions I saw them, came
in with wet boots, the snow on their shoulders and their
hats, puffing and red-faced as they beat their coats in the
foyer. The orange trees were gone, the roof garden no
longer used, and the courtyard under our window only late
at night when half a dozen patrons and their protégées,
whooping with hilarity and wine, fought with snowballs—
an activity invariably concluded by stripping the girls and
tumbling them naked in the snow.

Spring surprised me, as she always does those of us who
remain most of our lives indoors. One day, while I still
thought, if I thought about the weather at all, in terms of
winter, David threw open the window and insisted that I go
with him into the park—and it was April. Mr. Million went
with us, and I remember that as we stepped out the front
door into the little garden that opened into the street, a
garden I had last seen banked with the snow shoveled from
the path, but which was now bright with early bulbs and
the chiming of the fountain, David tapped the iron dog on
its grinning muzzle and recited: "And thence the dog/With
fourfold head brought to these realms of light."

I made some trivial remark about his having miscounted.
"Oh, no. Old Cerberus has four heads, don't you know

that? The fourth's her maidenhead, and she's such a bitch no dog can take it from her." Even Mr. Million chuckled, but I thought afterward, looking at David's ruddy good health and the foreshadowing of manhood already apparent in the set of his shoulders, that if, as I had always thought of them, the three heads represented Maitre, Madame, and Mr. Million, that is, my father, my aunt (David's *maidenhead*, I suppose), and my tutor, then indeed a fourth would have to be welded in place soon for David himself.

The park must have been a paradise for him, but in my poor health I found it bleak enough and spent most of the morning huddled on a bench, watching David play squash. Toward noon I was joined, not on my own bench, but on another close enough for there to be a feeling of proximity, by a dark-haired girl with one ankle in a cast. She was brought there, on crutches, by a sort of nurse or governess who seated herself, I felt sure deliberately, between the girl and me. This unpleasant woman was, however, too straight-backed for her chaperonage to succeed completely. She sat on the edge of the bench, while the girl, with her injured leg thrust out before her, slumped back and thus gave me a good view of her profile, which was beautiful; and occasionally, when she turned to make some remark to the creature with her, I could study her full face—carmine lips and violet eyes, a round rather than an oval face, with a broad point of black hair dividing the forehead; archly delicate black eyebrows and long, curling lashes. When a vendor, an old woman, came selling Cantonese egg rolls (longer than your hand, and still so hot from the boiling fat that they needed to be eaten with great caution as though they were in some way alive), I made her my messenger and, as well as buying one for myself, sent her with two scalding delicacies to the girl and her attendant monster.

The monster, of course, refused; the girl, I was charmed to see, pleaded; her huge eyes and bright cheeks eloquently proclaiming arguments I was unfortunately just too far away to hear but could follow in pantomime: it would be a gratuitous insult to a blameless stranger to refuse; she was hungry and had intended to buy an egg roll in any event—how thriftless to object when what she had wished for was tendered free! The vending woman, who clearly delighted in her role as go-between, announced herself on the point of weeping at the thought of being forced to refund my gold (actually a bill of small denomination nearly as greasy as the paper in which her wares were wrapped, and considerably dirtier), and eventually their voices grew loud enough for me to hear the girl's, which was a clear and very pleasing contralto. In the end, of course, they accepted; the monster conceded me a frigid nod, and the girl winked at me behind her back.

Half an hour later when David and Mr. Million, who had been watching him from the edge of the court, asked if I wanted lunch, I told them I did, thinking that when we returned I could take a seat closer to the girl without being brazen about it. We ate, I (at least so I fear) very impatiently, in a clean little café close to the flower market; but when we came back to the park the girl and her governess were gone.

We returned to the house, and about an hour afterward my father sent for me. I went with some trepidation, since it was much earlier than was customary for our interview—before the first patrons had arrived, in fact, while I usually saw him only after the last had gone. I need not have feared. He began by asking about my health, and when I said it seemed better than it had been during most of the winter he began, in a self-conscious and even pompous way, as different from his usual fatigued incisiveness as could be imagined, to talk about his business and the need a young man had to prepare himself to earn a living. He said, "You are a scientific scholar, I believe."

I said I hoped I was in a small way, and braced myself for the usual attack upon the uselessness of studying chemistry or biophysics on a world like ours where the industrial base was so small, of no help at the civil service examinations, does not even prepare one for trade, and so on. He said instead, "I'm glad to hear it. To be frank, I asked Mr. Million to encourage you in that as much as he could. He would have done it anyway I'm sure; he did with me. These studies will not only be of great satisfaction to you, but will . . ." he paused, cleared his throat, and massaged his face and scalp with his hands, "be valuable in all sorts of ways. And they are, as you might say, a family tradition."

I said, and indeed felt, that I was very happy to hear that.

"Have you seen my lab? Behind the big mirror there?"

I hadn't, though I had known that such a suite of rooms existed beyond the sliding mirror in the library, and the servants occasionally spoke of his "dispensary" where he compounded doses for them, examined monthly the girls we employed, and occasionally prescribed treatment for "friends" of patrons, men recklessly imprudent who had failed (as the wise patrons had not) to confine their custom to our establishment exclusively. I told him I should very much like to see it.

He smiled. "But we are wandering from our topic. Science is of great value, but you will find, as I have, that it consumes more money than it produces. You will want apparatus and books and many other things, as well as a livelihood for yourself. We have a not unprofitable business here, and though I hope to live a long time—thanks in part to science—you are the heir, and it will be yours in the end . . .

(So I was older than David!)

". . . every phase of what we do. None of them, believe me, are unimportant."

I had been so surprised, and in fact elated, by my discovery that I had missed a part of what he said. I nodded, which seemed safe.

"Good. I want you to begin by answering the front door. One of the maids has been doing it, and for the first month or so she'll stay with you, since there's more to be learned there than you think. I'll tell Mr. Million, and he can make the arrangements."

I thanked him, and he indicated that the interview was over by opening the door of the library. I could hardly believe, as I went out, that he was the same man who devoured my life in the early hours of almost every morning.

I did not connect this sudden elevation in status with the events in the park. I now realize that Mr. Million who has, quite literally, eyes in the back of his head must have reported to my father that I had reached the age at which desires in childhood subliminally fastened to parental figures begin, half consciously, to grope beyond the family.

In any event that same evening I took up my new duties and became what Mr. Million called the "greeter" and David (explaining that the original sense of the word was related to *portal*) the "porter" of our house—thus assuming in a practical way the functions symbolically executed by the iron dog in our front garden. The maid who had previously carried them out, a girl named Nerissa who had been selected because she was not only one of the prettiest but one of the tallest and strongest of the maids as well, a large-boned, long-faced, smiling girl with shoulders broader than most men's, remained, as my father had promised, to help. Our duties were not onerous, since my father's patrons were all men of some position and wealth, not given to brawling or loud arguments except under unusual circumstances of intoxication; and for the most part they had visited our house already dozens, and, in a few cases, even hundreds of times. We called them by nicknames that were used only here (of which Nerissa informed me *sotto voce* as they came up the walk), hung up their coats, and directed them—or if necessary conducted them—to the various parts of the establishment. Nerissa flounced (a formidable sight, as I observed, to all but the most heroically proportioned patrons), allowed herself to be pinched, took tips, and talked to me afterward, during slack periods, of the times she had been "called upstairs" at the request of some connoisseur of scale, and the money she had made that night. I laughed at jokes and refused tips in such a way as to make the patrons aware that I was a part of the management. Most patrons did not need the reminder, and I was often told that I strikingly resembled my father.

When I had been serving as a receptionist in this way for only a short time, I think on only the third or fourth night, we had an unusual visitor. He came early one evening, but it was the evening of so dark a day, one of the last really wintry days, that the garden lamps had been lit for an hour or more, and the occasional carriages that passed on the street beyond, though they could be heard, could not be seen. I answered the door when he knocked, and as we always did with strangers, asked him politely what he wished.

He said, "I should like to speak to Dr. Aubrey Veil."

I am afraid I looked blank.

"This is 666 Saltimbanque?"

It was of course; and the name of Dr. Veil, though I could not place it, touched a chime of memory. I supposed that one of our patrons had used my father's house as an *adresse d'accommodation,* and since this visitor was clearly legitimate, and it was not desirable to keep anyone arguing in the doorway despite the partial shelter afforded by the garden, I asked him in; then I sent Nerissa to bring us coffee so that we might have a few moments of private talk in the dark little receiving room that opened off the foyer. It was a room very seldom used, and the maids had been remiss in dusting it, as I saw as soon as I opened the door. I made a mental note to speak to my aunt about it, and as I did I recalled where it was that I had heard Dr. Veil mentioned. My aunt, on the first occasion I had ever spoken to her, had referred to his theory that we might in fact be the natives of Sainte Anne, having murdered the original Terrestrial colonists and displaced them so thoroughly as to forget our own past.

The stranger had seated himself in one of the musty, gilded armchairs. He wore a beard, very black and more full than the current style, was young, I thought, though of course considerably older than I, and would have been handsome if the skin of his face—what could be seen of it —had not been of so colorless a white as almost to constitute a disfigurement. His dark clothing seemed abnormally heavy, like felt, and I recalled having heard from some patron that a starcrosser from Sainte Anne had splashed down in the bay yesterday, and asked if he had perhaps been on board it. He looked startled for a moment, then laughed. "You're a wit, I see. And living with Dr. Veil you'd be familiar with his theory. No, I'm from Earth. My name is Marsch." He gave me his card, and I read it twice before the meaning of the delicately embossed abbreviations registered on my mind.

My visitor was a scientist, a doctor of philosophy in anthropology, from Earth.

I said, "I wasn't trying to be witty. I thought you might really have come from Sainte Anne. Here, most of us have a kind of planetary face, except for the gypsies and the criminal tribes, and you don't seem to fit the pattern."

He said, "I've noticed what you mean. You seem to have it yourself."

"I'm supposed to look a great deal like my father."

"Ah," he said. He stared at me. Then, "Are you cloned?"

"Cloned?" I had read the term, but only in conjunction with botany, and as has happened to me often when I have especially wanted to impress someone with my intelligence, nothing came. I felt like a stupid child.

"Parthenogenetically reproduced, so that the new individual—or individuals, you can have a thousand if you want—will have a genetic structure identical to the parent. It's anti-evolutionary, so it's illegal on Earth, but I don't suppose things are as closely watched out here."

"You're talking about human beings?"

He nodded.

"I've never heard of it. Really I doubt if you'd find the necessary technology here. We're quite backward compared to Earth. Of course, my father might be able to arrange something for you."

"I don't want to have it done."

Nerissa came in with the coffee then, effectively cutting off anything further Dr. Marsch might have said. Actually, I had added the suggestion about my father more from force of habit than anything else, and thought it very unlikely that he could pull off any such biochemical *tour de force*, but there was always the possibility, particularly if a large sum were offered. As it was, we fell silent while Nerissa arranged the cups and poured, and when she had gone Marsch said appreciatively, "Quite an unusual girl." His eyes, I noticed, were a bright green, without the brown tones most green eyes have.

I was wild to ask him about Earth and the new developments there, and it had already occurred to me that the girls might be an effective way of keeping him here, or at least of bringing him back. I said, "You should see some of them. My father has wonderful taste."

"I'd rather see Dr. Veil. Or is Dr. Veil your father?"

"Oh, no."

"This is his address, or at least the address I was given. Number 666 Saltimbanque Street, Port-Mimizon, Departement de la Main, Sainte Croix."

He appeared quite serious, and it seemed possible that if I told him flatly that he was mistaken he would leave. I said, "I learned about Veil's Hypothesis from my aunt. She seemed quite conversant with it. Perhaps later this evening you'd like to talk to her about it."

"Couldn't I see her now?"

"My aunt sees very few visitors. To be frank, I'm told she quarreled with my father before I was born, and she seldom leaves her own apartments. The housekeepers report to her there, and she manages what I suppose I must call our domestic economy, but it's very rare to see Madame outside her rooms, or for any stranger to be let in."

"And why are you telling me this?"

"So that you'll understand that with the best will in the world it may not be possible for me to arrange an interview for you. At least, not this evening."

"You could simply ask her if she knows Dr. Veil's present address, and if so what it is."

"I'm trying to help you, Dr. Marsch. Really I am."

"But you don't think that's the best way to go about it?"

"No."

"In other words if your aunt were simply asked, without being given a chance to form her own judgment of me, she wouldn't give me information even if she had it?"

"It would help if we were to talk a bit first. There are a great many things I'd like to learn about Earth."

For an instant I thought I saw a sour smile under the black beard. He said, "Suppose I ask you first . . ."

He was interrupted—again—by Nerissa, I suppose because she wanted to see if we required anything further from the kitchen. I could have strangled her when Dr.

Marsch halted in midsentence and said instead, "Couldn't this girl ask your aunt if she would see me?"

I had to think quickly. I had been planning to go myself and, after a suitable wait, return and say that my aunt would receive Dr. Marsch later, which would have given me an additional opportunity to question him while he waited. But there was at least a possibility (no doubt magnified in my eyes by my eagerness to hear of new discoveries from Earth) that he would not wait—or that, when and if he did eventually see my aunt, he might mention the incident. If I sent Nerissa I would at least have him to myself while she ran her errand, and there was an excellent chance —or at least so I imagined—that my aunt would in fact have some business which she would want to conclude before seeing a stranger. I told Nerissa to go, and Dr. Marsch gave her one of his cards after writing a few words on the back.

"Now," I said, "what was it you were about to ask me?"

"Why this house, on a planet that has been inhabited less than two hundred years, seems so absurdly old."

"It was built a hundred and forty years ago, but you must have many on Earth that are far older."

"I suppose so. Hundreds. But for every one of them there are ten thousand that have been up less than a year. Here, almost every building I see seems nearly as old as this one."

"We've never been crowded here, and we haven't had to tear down. That's what Mr. Million says. And there are fewer people here now than there were fifty years ago."

"Mr. Million?"

I told him about Mr. Million, and when I finished he said, "It sounds as if you've got a ten nine unbound simulator here, which should be interesting. Only a few have ever been made."

"A ten nine simulator?"

"A billion, ten to the ninth power. The human brain has several billion synapses, of course; but it's been found that you can simulate its action pretty well . . ."

It seemed to me that no time at all had passed since Nerissa had left, but she was back. She curtsied to Dr. Marsch and said, "Madame will see you."

I blurted, "Now?"

"Yes," Nerissa said artlessly, "Madame said right now."

"I'll take him then. You mind the door."

I escorted Dr. Marsch down the dark corridors, taking a long route to have more time, but he seemed to be arranging in his mind the questions he wished to ask my aunt, as we walked past the spotted mirrors and warped little walnut tables, and he answered me in monosyllables when I tried to question him about Earth.

At my aunt's door I rapped for him. She opened it herself, the hem of her black skirt hanging emptily over the untrodden carpet, but I do not think he noticed that. He said, "I'm really very sorry to bother you, Madame, and I only do so because your nephew thought you might be able to help me locate the author of Veil's Hypothesis."

My aunt said, "I am Dr. Veil, please come in," and shut the door behind him, leaving me standing open-mouthed in the corridor.

I mentioned the incident to Phaedria the next time we met, but she was more interested in learning about my father's house. Phaedria, if I have not used her name before now, was the girl who had sat near me while I watched David play squash. She had been introduced to me on my next visit to the park by no one less than the monster herself, who had helped her to a seat beside me and, miracle of miracles, promptly retreated to a point which, though not out of sight, was at least beyond earshot. Phaedria had thrust her broken ankle in front of her, halfway across the graveled path, and smiled a most charming smile. "You don't object to my sitting here?" She had perfect teeth.

"I'm delighted."

"You're surprised, too. Your eyes get big when you're surprised, did you know that?"

"I am surprised. I've come here looking for you several times, but you haven't been here."

"We've come looking for you, and you haven't been here either, but I suppose one can't really spend a great deal of time in a park."

"I would have," I said, "If I'd known you were looking for me. I went here as much as I could anyway. I was afraid that she . . ." I jerked my head at the monster, "wouldn't let you come back. How did you persuade her?"

"I didn't," Phaedria said. "Can't you guess? Don't you know anything?"

I confessed that I did not. I felt stupid, and I was stupid, at least in the things I said, because so much of my mind was caught up not in formulating answers to her remarks but in committing to memory the lilt of her voice, the purple of her eyes, even the faint perfume of her skin and the soft, warm touch of her breath on my cool cheek.

"So you see," Phaedria was saying, "that's how it is with me. When Aunt Uranie—she's only a poor cousin of mother's, really—got home and told him about you he found out who you are, and here I am."

"Yes," I said, and she laughed.

Phaedria was one of those girls raised between the hope of marriage and the thought of sale. Her father's affairs, as she herself said, were "unsettled." He speculated in ship cargoes, mostly from the south—textiles and drugs. He owed, most of the time, large sums which the lenders could not hope to collect unless they were willing to allow him more to recoup. He might die a pauper, but in the meanwhile he had raised his daughter with every detail of education and plastic surgery attended to. If, when she reached marriageable age he could afford a good dowry, she would link him with some wealthy family. If he were pressed for money instead, a girl so reared would bring fifty times the price of a common street child. Our family, of course, would be ideal for either purpose.

"Tell me about your house," she said. "Do you know what the kids call it? 'The Cave Canem,' or sometimes just 'The Cave.' The boys all think it's a big thing to have been there, and they lie about it. Most of them haven't."

But I wanted to talk about Dr. Marsch and the sciences of Earth, and I was nearly as anxious to find out about her own world, "the kids" she mentioned so casually, her school and family, as she was to learn about us. Also, although I was willing to detail the services my father's girls rendered their benefactors, there were some things, such as my aunt's floating down the stairwell, that I was adverse to discussing. But we bought egg rolls from the same old woman to eat in the chill sunlight and exchanged confidences and somehow parted not only lovers but friends, promising to meet again the next day.

At some time during the night, I believe at almost the same time that I returned—or to speak more accurately *was returned* since I could scarcely walk—to my bed after a session of hours with my father, the weather changed. The musked exhalation of late spring or early summer crept through the shutters, and the fire in our little grate seemed to extinguish itself for shame almost at once. My father's valet opened the window for me and there poured into the room that fragrance that tells of the melting of the last snows beneath the deepest and darkest evergreens on the north sides of mountains. I had arranged with Phaedria to meet at ten, and before going to my father's library I had posted a note on the escritoire beside my bed, asking that I be awakened an hour earlier; and that night I slept with the fragrance in my nostrils and the thought—half-plan, half-dream —in my mind that by some means Phaedria and I would elude her aunt entirely and find a deserted lawn where blue and yellow flowers dotted the short grass.

When I woke, it was an hour past noon, and rain drove in sheets past the window. Mr. Million, who was reading a book on the far side of the room, told me that it had been raining like that since six, and for that reason he had not troubled to wake me. I had a splitting headache, as I often did after a long session with my father, and took one of the powders he had prescribed to relieve it. They were gray, and smelled of anise.

"You look unwell," Mr. Million said.

"I was hoping to go to the park."

"I know." He rolled across the room toward me, and I recalled that Dr. Marsch had called him an "unbound" simulator. For the first time since I had satisfied myself about them when I was quite small, I bent over (at some cost to my head) and read the almost obliterated stampings on his main cabinet. There was only the name of a cybernetics company on Earth and, in French as I had always supposed, his name: M. Million—"Monsieur" or "Mister" Million. Then, as startling as a blow from behind to a man musing in a comfortable chair, I remembered that a dot was employed in some algebras for multiplication. He saw my change of expression at once. "A thousand million word core capacity," he said. "An English billion or a French milliard, the *M* being the Roman numeral for one thousand, of course. I thought you understood that some time ago."

"You are an unbound simulator. What is a bound simulator, and whom are you simulating—my father?"

"No." The face in the screen, Mr. Million's face as I had always thought of it, shook its head. "Call me, call the person simulated, at least, your great-grandfather. He—I—am dead. In order to achieve simulation, it is necessary to examine the cells of the brain, layer by layer, with a beam of accelerated particles so that the neural patterns can be reproduced, we say 'core imaged,' in the computer. The process is fatal."

I asked after a moment, "And a bound simulator?"

"If the simulation is to have a body that looks human the mechanical body must be linked—'bound'—to a remote core, since the smallest billion word core cannot be made even approximately as small as the human brain." He paused again, and for an instant his face dissolved into myriad sparkling dots, swirling like dust motes in a sunbeam. "I am sorry. For once you wish to listen but I do not wish to lecture. I was told, a very long time ago, just before the operation, that my simulation—this—would be capable of emotion in certain circumstances. Until today I had always thought they lied." I would have stopped him if I could, but he rolled out of the room before I could recover from my surprise.

For a long time, I suppose an hour or more, I sat listening to the drumming of the rain and thinking about Phaedria and about what Mr. Million had said, all of it confused with my father's questions of the night before, questions which had seemed to steal their answers from me so that I was empty, and dreams had come to flicker in the emptiness, dreams of fences and walls and the concealing ditches called ha-has, that contain a barrier you do not see until you are about to tumble on it. Once I had dreamed of standing in a paved court fenced with Corinthian pillars so close set that I could not force my body between them, although in the dream I was only a child of three or four. After trying various places for a long time, I had noticed that each column was carved with a word—the only one that I could remember was *carapace*—and that the paving stones of the courtyard were mortuary tablets like those set into the floors in some of the old French churches, with my own name and a different date on each.

This dream pursued me even when I tried to think of Phaedria, and when a maid brought me hot water—for I now shaved twice a week—I found that I was already holding my razor in my hand, and had in fact cut myself with it so that the blood had streaked my nightclothes and run down onto the sheets.

The next time I saw Phaedria, which was four or five days afterward, she was engrossed by a new project in which she enlisted both David and me. This was nothing less than a theatrical company, composed mostly of girls her own age, which was to present plays during the summer in a natural amphitheater in the park. Since the company, as I have said, consisted principally of girls, male actors were at a premium, and David and I soon found ourselves deeply embroiled. The play had been written by a committee of the cast, and—inevitably—revolved about the loss of political power by the original French-speaking colonists. Phaedria, whose ankle would not be mended in time for our performance, would play the crippled daughter of the French governor; David, her lover (a dashing captain of chasseurs); and I, the governor himself—a part I accepted readily because it was a much better one than David's, and offered scope for a great deal of fatherly affection toward Phaedria.

The night of our performance, which was early in June, I recall vividly for two reasons. My aunt, whom I had not seen since she had closed the door behind Dr. Marsch, notified me at the last moment that she wished to attend and that I was to escort her. And we players had grown so afraid of having an empty house that I had asked my father if it would be possible for him to send some of his girls—who would thus lose only the earliest part of the evening, when there was seldom much business in any event. To my great surprise (I suppose because he felt it would be good advertising) he consented, stipulating only that they should return at the end of the third act if he sent a messenger saying they were needed.

Because I would have to arrive at least an hour early to make up, it was no more than late afternoon when I called for my aunt. She showed me in herself, and immediately asked my help for her maid, who was trying to wrestle some heavy object from the upper shelf of a closet. It proved to be a folding wheelchair, and under my aunt's direction we set it up. When we had finished she said abruptly, "Give me a hand in, you two," and taking our arms lowered herself into the seat. Her black skirt, lying emptily against the leg boards of the chair like a collapsed tent, showed legs no thicker than my wrists; but also an odd thickening, almost like a saddle, below her hips. Seeing me staring she snapped, "Won't be needing that until I come back, I suppose. Lift me up a little. Stand in back and get me under the arms."

I did so, and her maid reached unceremoniously under my aunt's skirt and drew out a little leather padded device on which she had been resting. "Shall we go?" my aunt sniffed. "You'll be late."

I wheeled her into the corridor, her maid holding the door for us. Somehow, learning that my aunt's ability to hang in the air like smoke was physically, indeed mechanically, derived, made it more disturbing than ever. When she asked why I was so quiet, I told her and added that I had been under the impression that no one had yet succeeded in producing working antigravity.

"And you think I have? Then why wouldn't I use it to get to your play?"

"I suppose because you don't want it to be seen."

"Nonsense. It's a regular prosthetic device. You buy them at the surgical stores." She twisted around in her seat until she could look up at me, her face so like my father's, and her lifeless legs like the sticks David and I used as little boys when, doing parlor magic, we wished Mr. Million to believe us lying prone when we were in fact crouched beneath our own supposed figures. "Puts out a superconducting field, then induces eddy currents in the reinforcing rods in the floors. The flux of the induced currents oppose the machine's own flux and I float, more or less. Lean forward to go forward, straighten up to stop. You look relieved."

"I am. I suppose antigravity frightened me."

"I used the iron banister when I went down the stairs with you once. It has a very convenient coil shape."

Our play went smoothly enough, with predictable cheers from members of the audience who were, or at least wished to be thought, descended from the old French aristocracy. The audience, in fact, was better than we had dared hope, five hundred or so besides the inevitable sprinkling of pickpockets, police, and streetwalkers. The incident I most vividly recall came toward the latter half of the first act, when for ten minutes or so I sat with few lines at a desk, listening to my fellow actors. Our stage faced the west, and the setting sun had left the sky a welter of lurid color: purple-reds striped gold and flame and black. Against this violent ground, which might have been the massed banners of hell, there began to appear, in ones and twos, like the elongated shadows of fantastic grenadiers crenelated and plumed, the heads, the slender necks, the narrow shoulders, of a platoon of my father's demi-mondaines; arriving late, they were taking the last seats at the upper rim of our theater, encircling it like the soldiery of some ancient, bizarre government surrounding a treasonous mob.

They sat at last, my cue came, and I forgot them; and that is all I can now remember of our first performance, except that at one point some motion of mine suggested to the audience a mannerism of my father's, and there was a shout of misplaced laughter—and that at the beginning of the second act, Sainte Anne rose with its sluggish rivers and great grassy meadowmeres clearly visible, flooding the audience with green light; and at the close of the third I saw my father's crooked little valet bustling among the upper rows, and the girls, green-edged black shadows, filing out.

We produced three more plays that summer, all with some success, and David and Phaedria and I became an accepted partnership, with Phaedria dividing herself more or less equally between us—whether by her own inclination or her parents' orders I could never be quite sure. When her ankle knit she was a companion fit for David in athletics, a better player of all the ball and racket games than any of the other girls who came to the park; but she would as often drop everything and come to sit with me, where she sympathized with (though she did not actually share) my interest in botany and biology, and gossiped, and delighted in showing me off to her friends since my reading had given me a sort of talent for puns and repartee.

It was Phaedria who suggested, when it became apparent that the ticket money from our first play would be insufficient for the costumes and scenery we coveted for our second, that at the close of future performances the cast circulate among the audience to take up a collection; and this, of course, in the press and bustle easily lent itself to the accomplishment of petty thefts for our cause. Most people, however, had too much sense to bring to our theater, in the evening, in the gloomy park, more money than was required to buy tickets and perhaps an ice or a glass of wine during intermission; so no matter how dishonest we were the profit remained small, and we, and especially Phaedria and David, were soon talking of going forward to more dangerous and lucrative adventures.

At about this time, I suppose as a result of my father's continued and intensified probing of my subconscious, a violent and almost nightly examination whose purpose was still unclear to me and which, since I had been accustomed to it for so long, I scarcely questioned, I became more and more subject to frightening lapses of conscious control. I would, so David and Mr. Million told me, seem quite myself though perhaps rather more quiet than usual, answering questions intelligently if absently, and then, suddenly, come to myself, start, and stare at the familiar rooms, the familiar faces, among which I now found myself, perhaps after the mid-afternoon, without the slightest memory of having awakened, dressed, shaved, eaten, gone for a walk.

Although I loved Mr. Million as much as I had when I was a boy, I was never able, after that conversation in which I learned the meaning of the familiar lettering on his side, quite to re-establish the old relationship. I was always conscious, as I am conscious now, that the personality I loved had perished years before I was born; and that I addressed an imitation of it, fundamentally mathematical in nature, responding as that personality might to the stimuli of human speech and action. I could never determine whether Mr. Million is really aware in that sense which would give him the right to say, as he always has, "I think," and "I feel." When I asked him about it he could only explain that he did not know the answer himself, that having no standard of comparison he could not be positive whether his own mental processes represented true consciousness or not; and I, of course, could not know whether this answer represented the deepest meditation of a soul somehow alive in the dancing abstractions of the simulation, or whether it was merely triggered, a phonographic response, by my question.

Our theater, as I have said, continued through the summer and gave its last performance with the falling leaves drifting, like obscure, perfumed old letters from some discarded trunk, upon our stage. When the curtain calls were over we who had written and acted the plays of our season were too disheartened to do more than remove our costumes and cosmetics, and drift ourselves, with the last of our departing audience, down the whippoorwill-haunted paths to the city streets and home. I was prepared, as I remember, to take up my duties at my father's door, but that night he had stationed his valet in the foyer to wait for me, and I was ushered directly into the library, where he explained brusquely that he would have to devote the latter part of the evening to business and for that reason would speak to me (as he put it) early. He looked tired and ill, and it occurred to me, I think for the first time, that he would one day die—and that I would, on that day, become at once both rich and free.

What I said under the drugs that evening I do not, of course, recall, but I remember as vividly as I might if I had only this morning awakened from it, the dream that followed. I was on a ship, a white ship like one of those the oxen pull, so slowly the sharp prows make no wake at all, through the green water of the canal beside the park. I was the only crewman, and indeed the only living man aboard. At the stern, grasping the huge wheel in such a flaccid way that it seemed to support and guide and steady *him* rather than he it, stood the corpse of a tall, thin man whose face, when the rolling of his head presented it to me, was the face that floated in Mr. Million's screen. This face, as I have said, was very like my father's, but I knew the dead man at the wheel was not he.

I was aboard the ship a long time. We seemed to be running free, with the wind a few points to port and strong. When I went aloft at night, masts and spars and rigging quivered and sang in the wind, and sail upon sail towered above me, and sail upon white sail spread below me, and more masts clothed in sails stood before me and behind me. When I worked on deck by day, spray wet my shirt and left tear-shaped spots on the planks which dried quickly in the bright sunlight.

I cannot remember ever having really been on such a ship, but perhaps, as a very small child, I was, for the sounds of it, the creaking of the masts in their sockets, the whistling of the wind in the thousand ropes, the crashing of the waves against the wooden hull were all as distinct, and as real, as much *themselves,* as the sounds of laughter and breaking glass overhead had been when, as a child, I had tried to sleep; or the bugles from the citadel which sometimes, then, woke me in the morning.

I was about some work, I do not know just what, aboard this ship. I carried buckets of water with which I dashed clotted blood from the decks, and I pulled at ropes which seemed attached to nothing—or rather, firmly tied to immovable objects still higher in the rigging. I watched the surface of the sea from bow and rail, from the mastheads, and from atop a large cabin amidships, but when a starcrosser, its entry shields blinding-bright with heat, plunged hissing into the sea far off I reported it to no one.

And all this time the dead man at the wheel was talking to me. His head hung limply, as though his neck were broken, and the jerkings of the wheel he held, as big waves struck the rudder, sent it from one shoulder to the other, or back to stare at the sky, or down. But he continued to speak, and the few words I caught suggested that he was lecturing upon an ethical theory whose postulates seemed even to him doubtful. I felt a dread of hearing this talk and tried to keep myself as much as possible toward the bow, but the wind at times carried the words to me with great clarity, and whenever I looked up from my work I found myself much nearer the stern, sometimes in fact almost touching the dead steersman, than I had supposed.

After I had been on this ship a long while, so that I was very tired and very lonely, one of the doors of the cabin opened and my aunt came out, floating quite upright about two feet above the tilted deck. Her skirt did not hang vertically as I had always seen it, but whipped in the wind like a streamer, so that she seemed on the point of blowing away. For some reason I said, "Don't get close to that man at the wheel, Aunt. He might hurt you."

She answered, as naturally as if we had met in the corridor outside my bedroom, "Nonsense. He's far past doing anyone any good, Number Five, or any harm either. It's my brother we have to worry about."

"Where is he?"

"Down there." She pointed at the deck as if to indicate that he was in the hold. "He's trying to find out why the ship doesn't move."

I ran to the side and looked over, and what I saw was not water but the night sky. Stars—innumerable stars were spread at an infinite distance below me, and as I looked at them I realized that the ship, as my aunt had said, did not make headway or even roll, but remained heeled over, motionless. I looked back at her and she told me, "It doesn't move because he has fastened it in place until he finds out why it doesn't move," and at this point I found myself sliding down a rope into what I supposed was the hold of the ship. It smelled of animals. I had awakened, though at first I did not know it.

My feet touched the floor, and I saw that David and Phaedria were beside me. We were in a huge, loftlike room, and as I looked at Phaedria, who was very pretty but tense and biting her lips, a cock crowed.

David said, "Where do you think the money is?" He was carrying a tool kit.

And Phaedria, who I suppose had expected him to say something else, or in answer to her own thoughts, said, "We'll have lots of time, Marydol is watching." Marydol was one of the girls who appeared in our plays.

"If she doesn't run away. Where do you think the money is?"

"Not up here. Downstairs behind the office." She had been crouching, but she rose now and began to creep forward. She was all in black, from her ballet slippers to a black ribbon binding her black hair, with her white face and arms in striking contrast, and her carmine lips an error, a bit of color left by mistake. David and I followed her.

Crates were scattered, widely separated, on the floor; and as we passed them I saw that they held poultry, a single bird in each. It was not until we were nearly to the ladder which plunged down a hatch in the floor at the opposite corner of the room that I realized that these birds were gamecocks. Then a shaft of sun from one of the skylights struck a crate and the cock rose and stretched himself, showing fierce red eyes and plumage as gaudy as a macaw's. "Come on," Phaedria said, "the dogs are next," and we followed her down the ladder. Pandemonium broke out on the floor below.

The dogs were chained in stalls, with dividers too high for them to see the dogs on either side of them and wide aisles between the rows of stalls. They were all fighting dogs, but of every size from ten-pound terriers to mastiffs larger than small horses, brutes with heads as misshapen as the growths that appear on old trees and jaws that could sever both a man's legs at a mouthful. The din of the barking was incredible, a solid substance that shook us as we descended the ladder, and at the bottom I took Phaedria's arm and tried to indicate by signs—since I was certain that we were wherever we were without permission—that we should leave at once. She shook her head and then, when I was unable to understand what she said even when she exaggerated the movements of her lips, wrote on a dusty wall with her moistened forefinger, "They do this all the time—a noise in the street—anything."

Access to the floor below was by stairs, reached through a heavy but unbolted door which I think had been installed largely to exclude the din. I felt better when we had closed it behind us even though the noise was still very loud. I had fully come to myself by this time, and I should have explained to David and Phaedria that I did not know where I was or what we were doing there, but shame held me back. And in any event I could guess easily enough what our purpose was. David had asked about the location of money, and we had often talked—talk I had considered at the time to be more than half empty boasting—about a single robbery that would free us from the necessity of further petty crime.

Where we were I discovered later when we left; and how we had come to be there I pieced together from casual conversations. The building had been originally designed as a warehouse, and stood on the Rue des Egouts close to the bay. Its owner supplied those enthusiasts who staged combats of all kinds for sport, and was credited with maintaining the largest assemblage of these creatures in the Department. Phaedria's father had happened to hear that this man had recently put some of his most valuable stock on ship, had taken Phaedria when he called on him, and, since the place was known not to open its doors until after the last Angelus, we had come the next day a little after the second and entered through one of the skylights.

I find it difficult to describe what we saw when we descended from the floor of the dogs to the next, which was the second floor of the building. I had seen fighting slaves many times before when Mr. Million, David, and I had traversed the slave market to reach the library; but never more than one or two together, heavily manacled. Here they lay, sat, and lounged everywhere, and for a moment I wondered why they did not tear one another to pieces, and the three of us as well. Then I saw that each was held by a short chain stapled to the floor, and it was not difficult to tell from the scraped and splintered circles in the boards just how far the slave in the center could reach. Such furniture as they had, straw pallets and a few chairs and benches, was either too light to do harm if thrown or very stoutly made and spiked down. I had expected them to shout and threaten us as I had heard they threatened each other in the pits before closing, but they seemed to understand that as long as they were chained, they could do nothing. Every head turned toward us as we came down the steps, but we had no food for them, and after that first examination they were far less interested in us than the dogs had been.

"They aren't people, are they?" Phaedria said. She was walking erectly as a soldier on parade now, and looking at the slaves with interest; studying her, it occurred to me that she was taller and less plump than the "Phaedria" I pictured to myself when I thought of her. She was not just a pretty, but a beautiful girl. "They're a kind of animal, really," she said.

From my studies I was better informed, and I told her that they had been human as infants—in some cases even as children or older—and that they differed from normal people only as a result of surgery (some of it on their brains) and chemically induced alterations in their endocrine systems. And of course in appearance because of their scars.

"Your father does that sort of thing to little girls, doesn't he? For your house?"

David said, "Only once in a while. It takes a lot of time, and most people prefer normals, even when they prefer pretty odd normals."

"I'd like to see some of them. I mean the one's he's worked on."

I was still thinking of the fighting slaves around us and said, "Don't you know about these things? I thought you'd been here before. You knew about the dogs."

"Oh, I've seen them before, and the man told me about them. I suppose I was just thinking out loud. It would be awful if they were still people."

Their eyes followed us, and I wondered if they could understand her.

The ground floor was very different from the ones above. The walls were paneled, there were framed pictures of dogs and cocks and of the slaves and curious animals. The windows, opening toward Egouts Street and the bay, were high and narrow and admitted only slender beams of the bright sunlight to pick out of the gloom the arm alone of a rich red-leather chair, a square of maroon carpet no bigger than a book, a half-full decanter. I took three steps into this room and knew that we had been discovered. Striding toward us was a tall, high-shouldered young man—who halted, with a startled look, just when I did. He was my own reflection in a gilt-framed pier glass, and I felt the momentary dislocation that comes when a stranger, an unrecognized shape, turns or moves his head and is some familiar friend glimpsed, perhaps for the first time, from outside. The sharp-chinned, grim-looking boy I had seen when I did not know him to be myself had been myself as Phaedria and David, Mr. Million and my aunt, saw me.

"This is where he talks to customers," Phaedria said. "If he's trying to sell something he has his people bring them down one at a time so you don't see the others, but you can hear the dogs bark even from way down here, and he took Papa and me upstairs and showed us everything."

David asked, "Did he show you where he keeps the money?"

"In back. See that tapestry? It's really a curtain, because while Papa was talking to him, a man came who owed him for something and paid, and he went through there with it."

The door behind the tapestry opened on a small office, with still another door in the wall opposite. There was no sign of a safe or strongbox. David broke the lock on the desk with a pry bar from his tool kit, but there was only the usual clutter of papers, and I was about to open the second door when I heard a sound, a scraping or shuffling, from the room beyond.

For a minute or more none of us moved. I stood with my hand on the latch. Phaedria, behind me and to my left, had been looking under the carpet for a cache in the floor

—she remained crouched, her skirt a black pool at her feet. From somewhere near the broken desk I could hear David's breathing. The shuffling came again, and a board creaked. David said very softly, "It's an animal."

I drew my fingers away from the latch and looked at him. He was still gripping the pry bar and his face was pale, but he smiled. "An animal tethered in there, shifting its feet. That's all."

I said, "How do you know?"

"Anybody in there would have heard us, especially when I cracked the desk. If it were a person he would have come out, or if he were afraid he'd hide and be quiet."

Phaedria said, "I think he's right. Open the door."

"Before I do, if it isn't an animal?"

David said, "It is."

"But if it isn't?"

I saw the answer on their faces; David gripped his pry bar, and I opened the door.

The room beyond was larger than I had expected, but bare and dirty. The only light came from a single window high in the farther wall. In the middle of the floor stood a big chest, of dark wood bound with iron, and before it lay what appeared to be a bundle of rags. As I stepped from the carpeted office the rags moved and a face, a face triangular as a mantis's, turned toward me. Its chin was hardly more than an inch from the floor, but under deep brows the eyes were tiny scarlet fires.

"That must be it," Phaedria said. She was looking not at the face but at the iron-banded chest. "David, can you break into that?"

"I think so," David said, but he, like me, was watching the ragged thing's eyes. "What about that?" he said after a moment, and gestured toward it. Before Phaedria or I could answer, its mouth opened showing long, narrow teeth, gray-yellow. "Sick," it said.

None of us, I think, had thought it could speak. It was as though a mummy had spoken. Outside, a carriage went past, its iron wheels rattling on the cobbles.

"Let's go," David said. "Let's get out."

Phaedria said, "It's sick. Don't you see, the owner's brought it down here where he can look in on it and take care of it. It's sick."

"And he chained his sick slave to the cashbox?" David cocked an eyebrow at her.

"Don't you see? It's the only heavy thing in the room. All you have to do is go over there and knock the poor creature in the head. If you're afraid, give me the bar and I'll do it myself."

"I'll do it."

I followed him to within a few feet of the chest. He gestured at the slave imperiously with the steel pry bar. "You! Move away from there."

The slave made a gurgling sound and crawled to one side, dragging his chain. He was wrapped in a filthy, tattered blanket and seemed hardly larger than a child, though I noticed that his hands were immense.

I turned and took a step toward Phaedria, intending to urge that we leave if David were unable to open the chest in a few minutes. I remember that before I heard or felt anything I saw her eyes open wide, and I was still wondering why when David's kit of tools clattered on the floor and David himself fell with a thud and a little gasp. Phaedria screamed, and all the dogs on the third floor began to bark.

All this, of course, took less than a second. I turned to look almost as David fell. The slave had darted out an arm and caught my brother by the ankle, and then in an instant had thrown off his blanket and bounded—that is the only way to describe it—on top of him.

I caught him by the neck and jerked him backward, thinking that he would cling to David and that it would be necessary to tear him away, but the instant he felt my hands he flung David aside and writhed like a spider in my grip. *He had four arms.*

I saw them flailing as he tried to reach me, and I let go of him and jerked back, as if a rat had been thrust at my face. That instinctive repulsion saved me; he drove his feet backward in a kick which, if I had still been holding him tightly enough to give him a fulcrum, would have surely ruptured my liver or spleen and killed me.

Instead it shot him forward and me, gasping for breath, back. I fell and rolled, and was outside the circle permitted him by his chain; David had already scrambled away, and Phaedria was well out of his reach.

For a moment, while I shuddered and tried to sit up, the three of us simply stared at him. Then David quoted wryly:

> Arms and the man I sing, who forc'd by fate,
> And haughty Juno's unrelenting hate,
> Expell'd and exil'd, left the Trojan shore.

Neither Phaedria nor I laughed, but Phaedria let out her breath in a long sigh and asked me, "How did they do that? Get him like that?"

I told her I supposed they had transplanted the extra pair after suppressing his body's natural resistance to the implanted foreign tissue, and that the operation had probably replaced some of his ribs with the donor's shoulder structure. "I've been teaching myself to do the same sort of thing with mice—on a much less ambitious scale, of course—and the striking thing to me is that he seems to have full use of the grafted pair. Unless you've got identical twins to work with, the nerve endings almost never join properly, and whoever did this probably had a hundred failures before he got what he wanted. That slave must be worth a fortune."

David said, "I thought you threw your mice out. Aren't you working with monkeys now?"

I wasn't, although I hoped to; but whether I was or not, it seemed clear that talking about it wasn't going to accomplish anything. I told David that.

"I thought you were hot to leave."

I had been, but now I wanted something else much more. I wanted to perform an exploratory operation on that creature much more than David and Phaedria had ever wanted money. David liked to think that he was bolder than I, and I knew when I said, "You may want to get away, but don't use me as an excuse, brother," that that would settle it.

"All right, how are we going to kill him?" He gave me an angry look.

Phaedria said, "It can't reach us. We could throw things at it."

"And he could throw the ones that missed back."

While we talked, the thing, the four-armed slave, was grinning at us. I was fairly sure it could understand at least a part of what we were saying, and I motioned to David and Phaedria to indicate that we should go back into the room where the desk was. When we were there I closed the door. "I didn't want him to hear us. If we had weapons on poles, spears of some kind, we might be able to kill him without getting too close. What could we use for sticks? Any ideas?"

David shook his head, but Phaedria said, "Wait a minute, I remember something." We both looked at her and she knitted her brows, pretending to search her memory and enjoying the attention.

"Well?" David asked.

She snapped her fingers. "Window poles. You know, long things with a little hook on the end. Remember the windows out there where he talks to customers? They're high up in the wall, and while he and Papa were talking one of the men who works for him brought one and opened a window. They ought to be around somewhere."

We found two after a five-minute search. They looked satisfactory: about six feet long and an inch and a quarter in diameter, of hard wood. David flourished his and pretended to thrust at Phaedria, then asked me, "Now what do we use for points?"

The scalpel I always carried was in its case in my breast pocket, and I fastened it to the rod with electrical tape from a roll David had fortunately carried on his belt instead of in the tool kit, but we could find nothing to make a second spearhead for him until he himself suggested broken glass.

"You can't break a window," Phaedria said, "they'd hear you outside. Besides, won't it just snap off when you try to get him with it?"

"Not if it's thick glass. Look here, you two."

I did, and saw—again—my own face. He was pointing toward the large mirror that had surprised me when I came down the steps. While I looked his shoe struck it, and it shattered with a crash that set the dogs barking again. He selected a long, almost straight, triangular piece and held it up to the light, where it flashed like a gem. "That's about as good as they used to make them from agate and jasper on Sainte Anne, isn't it?"

By prior agreement we approached from opposite sides. The slave leaped to the top of the chest, and from there, watched us quite calmly, his deep-set eyes turning from David to me until at last, when we were both quite close, David rushed him.

He spun around as the glass point grazed his ribs and caught David's spear by the shaft and jerked him forward. I thrust at him but missed, and before I could recover he had dived from the chest and was grappling with David on the far side. I bent over it and jabbed down at him, and it was not until David screamed that I realized I had driven my scalpel into his thigh. I saw the blood, bright arterial blood, spurt up and drench the shaft, and let it go and threw myself over the chest on top of them.

He was ready for me, on his back and grinning, with his legs and all four arms raised like a dead spider's. I am certain he would have strangled me in the next few seconds if it had not been that David, how consciously I do not know, threw one arm across the creature's eyes so that he missed his grip and I fell between those outstretched hands.

There is not a great deal more to tell. He jerked free of David, and pulling me to him, tried to bite my throat; but I hooked a thumb in one of his eye sockets and held him off. Phaedria, with more courage than I would have credited her with, put David's glass-tipped spear into my free hand and I stabbed him in the neck—I believe I severed both jugulars and the trachea before he died. We put a tourniquet on David's leg and left without either the money or the knowledge of technique I had hoped to get from the body of the slave. Marydol helped us get David home, and we told Mr. Million he had fallen while we were exploring an empty building—though I doubt that he believed us.

There is one other thing to tell about that incident—I mean the killing of the slave—although I am tempted to go on and describe instead a discovery I made immediately afterward that had, at the time, a much greater influence on me. It is only an impression, and one that I have, I am sure, distorted and magnified in recollection. While I was stabbing the slave, my face was very near his and I saw (I suppose because of the light from the high windows behind us) my own face reflected and doubled in the corneas of his eyes, and it seemed to me that it was a face very like his. I have been unable to forget, since then, what Dr. Marsch told me about the production of any number of identical individuals by cloning, and that my father had, when I was younger, a reputation as a child broker. I have tried since my release to find some trace of my mother, the woman in the photograph shown me by my aunt; but that picture was surely taken long before I was born—perhaps even on Earth.

The discovery I spoke of I made almost as soon as we left the building where I killed the slave, and it was simply this: that it was no longer autumn, but high summer. Because all four of us—Marydol had joined us by that time—were so concerned about David and busy concocting a story to explain his injury, the shock was somewhat blunted, but there could be no doubt of it. The weather was warm with that torpid, damp heat peculiar to summer. The trees I remembered nearly bare were in full leaf and filled with orioles. The fountain in our garden no longer played, as it always did after the danger of frost and burst pipes had come, with warmed water: I dabbled my hand in the basin as we helped David up the path, and it was as cool as dew.

My periods of unconscious action then, my sleepwalking, had increased to devour an entire winter and the spring, and I felt that I had lost myself.

When we entered the house, an ape which I thought at first was my father's sprang to my shoulder. Later Mr. Million told me that it was my own, one of my laboratory animals I had made a pet. I did not know the little beast, but scars under his fur and the twist of his limbs showed he knew me.

(I have kept Popo ever since, and Mr. Million took care of him for me while I was imprisoned. He climbs still in fine weather on the gray and crumbling walls of this house; and as he runs along the parapets and I see his hunched form against the sky, I think, for a moment, that my father is still alive and that I may be summoned again for the long hours in his library—but I forgive my pet that.)

My father did not call a physician for David, but treated him himself; and if he was curious about the manner in which he had received his injury he did not show it. My own guess—for whatever it may be worth, this late—is that he believed I had stabbed him in some quarrel. I say this because he seemed, after this, apprehensive whenever I was alone with him. He was not a fearful man, and he had been accustomed for years to deal occasionally with the worst sort of criminals; but he was no longer at ease with me—he guarded himself. It may have been, of course, merely the result of something I had said or done during the forgotten winter.

Both Marydol and Phaedria, as well as my aunt and Mr. Million, came frequently to visit David, so that his sickroom became a sort of meeting place for us all, only disturbed by my father's occasional visits. Marydol was a slight, fair-haired, kindhearted girl, and I became very fond of her. Often when she was ready to go home I escorted her, and on the way back stopped at the slave market, as Mr. Million and David and I had once done so often, to buy fried bread and the sweet black coffee and to watch the bidding. The faces of slaves are the dullest in the world; but I would find myself staring into them, and it was a long time, a month at least, before I understood—quite suddenly, when I found what I had been looking for—why I did. A young male, a sweeper, was brought to the block. His face as well as his back had been scarred by the whip, and his teeth were broken; but I recognized him: the scarred face was my own or my father's. I spoke to him and would have bought and freed him, but he answered me in the servile way of slaves and I turned away in disgust and went home.

That night when my father had me brought to the library —as he had not for several nights—I watched our reflections in the mirror that concealed the entrance to his laboratories. He looked younger than he was; I older. We might almost have been the same man, and when he faced me and I, staring over his shoulder, saw no image of my own body, but only his arms and mine, we might have been the fighting slave.

I cannot say who first suggested we kill him. I only remember that one evening, as I prepared for bed after taking Marydol and Phaedria to their homes, I realized that earlier when the three of us, with Mr. Million and my aunt, had sat around David's bed, we had been talking of that.

Not openly, of course. Perhaps we had not admitted even to ourselves what it was we were thinking. My aunt had mentioned the money he was supposed to have hidden; and Phaedria, then, a yacht luxurious as a palace; David talked about hunting in the grand style, and the political power money could buy.

And I, saying nothing, had thought of the hours and weeks, and the months he had taken from me; of the destruction of my *self*, which he had gnawed at night after night. I thought of how I might enter the library that night and find myself when next I woke an old man and perhaps a beggar.

Then I knew that I must kill him, since if I told him those thoughts while I lay drugged on the peeling leather of the old table he would kill *me* without a qualm.

While I waited for his valet to come I made my plan. There would be no investigation, no death certificate for my father. I would replace him. To our patrons it would appear that nothing had changed. Phaedria's friends would be told that I had quarreled with him and left home. I would allow no one to see me for a time, and then, in make-up, in a dim room, speak occasionally to some favored caller. It was an impossible plan, but at the time I believed it possible and even easy. My scalpel was in my pocket and ready. The body could be destroyed in his own laboratory.

He read it in my face. He spoke to me as he always had,

but I think he knew. There were flowers in the room, something that had never been before, and I wondered if he had not known even earlier and had them brought in, as for a special event. Instead of telling me to lie on the leather-covered table, he gestured toward a chair and seated himself at his writing desk. "We will have company today," he said.

I looked at him.

"You're angry with me. I've seen it growing in you. Don't you know who . . ."

He was about to say something further when there was a tap at the door, and when he called, "Come in!" it was opened by Nerissa, who ushered in a demi-mondaine and Dr. Marsch. I was surprised to see him; and still more surprised to see one of the girls in my father's library. She seated herself beside Marsch in a way that showed he was her benefactor for the night.

"Good evening, Doctor," my father said. "Have you been enjoying yourself?"

Marsch smiled, showing large, square teeth. He wore clothing of the most fashionable cut now, but the contrast between his beard and the colorless skin of his cheeks was as remarkable as ever. "Both sensually and intellectually," he said. "I've seen a naked girl, a giantess twice the height of a man, walk through a wall."

I said, "That's done with holograms."

He smiled again. "I know. And I have seen a great many other things as well. I was going to recite them all, but perhaps I would only bore my audience. I will content myself with saying that you have a remarkable establishment—but you know that."

My father said, "It is always flattering to hear it again."

"And now are we going to have the discussion we spoke of earlier?"

My father looked at the demi-mondaine; she rose, kissed Dr. Marsch, and left the room. The heavy library door swung shut behind her with a soft click.

Like the sound of a switch, or old glass breaking.

I have thought since, many times, of that girl as I saw her leaving: the high-heeled platform shoes and grotesquely long legs, the backless dress dipping an inch below the coccyx. The bare nape of her neck; her hair piled and teased and threaded with ribbons and tiny lights. As she closed the door she was ending, though she could not have known it, the world she and I had known.

"She'll be waiting when you come out," my father said to Marsch.

"And if she's not, I'm sure you can supply others." The anthropologist's green eyes seemed to glow in the lamplight. "But now, how can I help you?"

"You study race. Could you call a group of similar men thinking similar thoughts a race?"

"And women," Marsch said, smiling.

"And here," my father continued, "here on Sainte Croix, you are gathering material to take back with you to Earth?"

"I am gathering material, certainly. Whether or not I shall return to the mother planet is problematical."

I must have looked at him sharply; he turned his smile toward me, and it became, if possible, even more patronizing than before. "You're surprised?"

"I've always considered Earth the center of scientific thought," I said. "I can easily imagine a scientist leaving it to do field work, but . . ."

"But it is inconceivable that one might want to stay in the field?"

"Consider my position. You are not alone—happily for me —in respecting the mother world's gray hairs and wisdom. As an Earth-trained man I've been offered a department in your university at almost any salary I care to name, with a sabbatical every second year. And the trip from here to Earth requires twenty years of Newtonian time. Only six months subjectively for me, of course, but when I return, if I do, my education will be forty years out of date. No, I'm afraid your planet may have acquired an intellectual luminary."

My father said, "We're straying from the subject, I think."

Marsch nodded, then added, "But I was about to say that an anthropologist is peculiarly equipped to make himself at home in any culture—even in so strange a one as this family has constructed about itself. I think I may call it a family, since there are two members resident besides yourself. You don't object to my addressing the pair of you in the singular?"

He looked at me as if expecting a protest, then when I said nothing, "I mean your son David—that, and not brother, is his real relationship to your continuing personality—and the woman you call your aunt. She is in reality daughter to an earlier—shall we say 'version'?—of yourself."

"You're trying to tell me I'm a cloned duplicate of my father, and I see both of you expect me to be shocked. I'm not. I've suspected it for some time."

My father said, "I'm glad to hear that. Frankly, when I was your age the discovery disturbed me a great deal. I came into my father's library—this room—to confront him, and I intended to kill him."

Dr. Marsch asked, "And did you?"

"I don't think it matters—the point is that it was my intention. I hope that having you here will make things easier for Number Five."

"Is that what you call him?"

"It's more convenient since his name is the same as my own."

"He is your fifth clone-produced child?"

"My fifth experiment? No." My father's hunched, high shoulders wrapped in the dingy scarlet of his old dressing gown made him look like some savage bird; and I remembered having read in a book of natural history of one called the red-shouldered hawk. His pet monkey, grizzled now with age, had climbed onto the desk. "No, more like my fiftieth, if you must know. I used to do them for drill. You people who have never tried it think the technique is simple because you've heard it can be done, but you don't know how difficult it is to prevent spontaneous differences. Every gene dominant in myself had to remain dominant, and people are not garden peas—few things are governed by simple Mendelian pairs."

Marsch asked, "You destroyed your failures?"

I said, "He sold them. When I was a child I used to wonder why Mr. Million stopped to look at the slaves in the market.

Since then I've found out." My scalpel was still in its case in my pocket; I could feel it.

"Mr. Million," my father said, "is perhaps a bit more sentimental than I—besides, I don't like to go out. You see, Doctor, your supposition that we are all truly the same individual will have to be modified. We have our little variations."

Dr. Marsh was about to reply, but I interrupted him. "Why?" I said. "Why David and me? Why Aunt Jeannine a long time ago? Why go on with it?"

"Yes," my father said, "why? We ask the question to ask the question."

"I don't understand you."

"I seek self-knowledge. If you want to put it this way, *we* seek self-knowledge. You are here because I did and do, and I am here because the individual behind me did—who was himself originated by the one whose mind is simulated in Mr. Million. And one of the questions whose answers we seek is why we seek. But there is more than that." He leaned forward, and the little ape lifted its white muzzle and bright, bewildered eyes to stare into his face. "We wish to discover why we fail, why others rise and change, and we remain here."

I thought of the yacht I had talked about with Phaedria and said, "I won't stay here." Dr. Marsch smiled.

My father said, "I don't think you understand me. I don't necessarily mean here physically, but *here*, socially and intellectually. I have traveled, and you may, but . . ."

"But you end here," Dr. Marsch said.

"We end at this level!" It was the only time, I think, that I ever saw my father excited. He was almost speechless as he waved at the notebooks and tapes that thronged the walls. "After how many generations? We do not achieve fame or the rule of even this miserable little colony planet. Something must be changed, but what?" He glared at Dr. Marsch.

"You are not unique," Dr. Marsch said, then smiled. "That sounds like a truism, doesn't it? But I wasn't referring to your duplicating yourself. I meant that since it became possible, back on Earth during the last quarter of the twentieth century, it has been done in such chains a number of times.

We have borrowed a term from engineering to describe it, and call it the process of relaxation—a bad nomenclature, but the best we have. Do you know what relaxation in the engineering sense is?"

"No."

"There are problems which are not directly soluble, but which can be solved by a succession of approximations. In heat transfer, for example, it may not be possible to calculate initially the temperature at every point on the surface of an unusually shaped body. But the engineer, or his computer, can assume reasonable temperatures, see how nearly stable the assumed values would be, then make new assumptions based on the result. As the levels of approximation progress, the successive sets become more and more similar until there is essentially no change. That is why I said the two of you are essentially one individual."

"What I want you to do," my father said impatiently, "is to make Number Five understand that the experiments I have performed on him, particularly the narcotherapeutic examinations he resents so much, are necessary. That if we are to become more than we have been we must find out . . ." He had been almost shouting, and he stopped abruptly to bring his voice under control. "That is the reason he was produced, the reason for David too—I hoped to learn something from an outcrossing."

"Which was the rationale, no doubt," Dr. Marsch said, "for the existence of Dr. Veil as well, in an earlier generation. But as far as your examinations of your younger self are concerned, it would be just as useful for him to examine you."

"Wait a moment," I said. "You keep saying that he and I are identical. That's incorrect. I can see that we're similar in some respects, but I'm not really like my father."

"There are no differences that cannot be accounted for by age. You are what? Eighteen? And you," he looked toward my father, "I should say are nearly fifty. There are only two forces, you see, which act to differentiate between human beings: they are heredity and environment, nature and nurture. And since the personality is largely formed during the first three years of life, it is the environment provided by the home which is decisive. Now every person is born into *some* home environment, though it may be such a harsh one that he dies of it. And no person, except in this situation we call anthropological relaxation, provides that environment himself—it is furnished for him by the preceding generation."

"Just because both of us grew up in this house . . ."

"Which you built and furnished and filled with the people you chose. But wait a moment. Let's talk about a man neither of you have ever seen, a man born in a place provided by parents quite different from himself: I mean the first of you . . ."

I was no longer listening. I had come to kill my father, and it was necessary that Dr. Marsch leave. I watched him as he leaned forward in his chair, his long, white hands making incisive little gestures, his cruel lips moving in a frame of black hair; I watched him and I heard nothing. It was as though I had gone deaf or as if he could communicate only by his thoughts, and I, knowing the thoughts were silly lies had shut them out. I said, "You are from Sainte Anne."

He looked at me in surprise, halting in the midst of a senseless sentence. "I have been there, yes. I spent several years on Sainte Anne before coming here."

"You were born there. You studied anthropology there from books written on Earth twenty years ago. You are an abo, or at least half abo. But we are men."

Marsch glanced at my father, then said, "The abos are gone. Scientific opinion on Sainte Anne holds that they have been extinct for almost a century."

"You didn't believe that when you came to see my aunt."

"I've never accepted Veil's Hypothesis. I called on everyone here who had published anything in my field. Really, I don't have time to listen to this."

"You are an abo and not from Earth."

And in a short time my father and I were alone.

Most of my sentence I served in a labor camp in the Tattered Mountains. It was a small camp, housing usually only a hundred and fifty prisoners—sometimes less than eighty when the winter deaths had been bad. We cut wood and burned charcoal and made skis when we found good birch. Above the timberline we gathered a saline moss supposed to be medicinal and knotted long plans for rock slides that would crush the stalking machines that were our guards—though somehow the moment never came, the stones never slid. The work was hard, and these guards administered exactly the mixture of severity and fairness some prison board had decided upon when they were programed, and the problem of brutality and favoritism by hirelings was settled forever, so that only well-dressed men at meetings could be cruel or kind.

Or so they thought. I sometimes talked to my guards for hours about Mr. Million, and once I found a piece of meat, and once a cake of hard sugar, brown and gritty as sand, hidden in the corner where I slept.

A criminal may not profit by his crime, but the court—so I was told much later—could find no proof that David was indeed my father's son, and made my aunt his heir.

She died, and a letter from an attorney informed me that by her favor I had inherited "a large house in the city of Port-Mimizon, together with the furniture and chattels appertaining thereto." And that this house, "located at 666 Saltimbanque, is presently under the care of a robot servitor." Since the robot servitors under whose direction I found myself did not allow me writing materials, I could not reply.

Time passed on the wings of birds. I found dead larks at the feet of north-facing cliffs in autumn, at the feet of south-facing cliffs in spring.

I received a letter from Mr. Million. Most of my father's girls had left during the investigation of his death; the remainder he had been obliged to send away when my aunt died, finding that as a machine he could not enforce the necessary obedience. David had gone to the capital. Phaedria had married well. Marydol had been sold by her parents. The date on his letter was three years later than the date of my trial, but how long the letter had been in reaching me I could not tell. The envelope had been opened and resealed many times and was soiled and torn.

A seabird, I believe a gannet, came fluttering down into

our camp after a storm, too exhausted to fly. We killed and ate it.

One of our guards went berserk, burned fifteen prisoners to death, and fought the other guards all night with swords of white and blue fire. He was not replaced.

I was transferred with some others to a camp farther north where I looked down chasms of red stone so deep that if I kicked a pebble in, I could hear the rattle of its descent grow to a roar of slipping rock—and hear that, in half a minute, fade with distance to silence, yet never strike the bottom lost somewhere in darkness.

I pretended the people I had known were with me. When I sat shielding my basin of soup from the wind, Phaedria sat upon a bench nearby and smiled and talked about her friends. David played squash for hours on the dusty ground of our compound, slept against the wall near my own corner. Marydol put her hand in mine while I carried my saw into the mountains.

In time they all grew dim, but even in the last year I never slept without telling myself, just before sleep, that Mr. Million would take us to the city library in the morning; never woke without fearing that my father's valet had come for me.

Then I was told that I was to go, with three others, to another camp. We carried our food, and nearly died of hunger and exposure on the way. From there we were marched to a third camp where we were questioned by men who were not prisoners like ourselves but free men in uniforms who made notes of our answers and at last ordered that we bathe, and burned our old clothing, and gave us a thick stew of meat and barley.

I remember very well that it was then that I allowed myself to realize, at last, what these things meant. I dipped my bread into my bowl and pulled it out soaked with the fragrant stock, with bits of meat and grains of barley clinging to it; and I thought then of the fried bread and coffee at the slave market not as something of the past but as something in the future, and my hands shook until I could no longer hold my bowl and I wanted to rush shouting at the fences.

In two more days we, six of us now, were put into a mule cart that drove on winding roads always downhill until the winter that had been dying behind us was gone, and the birches and firs were gone, and the tall chestnuts and oaks beside the road had spring flowers under their branches.

The streets of Port-Mimizon swarmed with people. I would have been lost in a moment if Mr. Million had not hired a chair for me, but I made the bearers stop, and bought (with money he gave me) a newspaper from a vendor so that I could know the date with certainty at last.

My sentence had been the usual one of two to fifty years, and though I had known the month and year of the beginning of my imprisonment, it had been impossible to know, in the camps, the number of the current year which everyone counted and no one knew. A man took fever and in ten days, when he was well enough again to work, said that two years had passed or had never been. Then you yourself took fever. I do not recall any headline, any article from the paper I bought. I read only the date at the top, all the way home.

It had been nine years.

I had been eighteen when I had killed my father. I was now twenty-seven. I had thought I might be forty.

The flaking gray walls of our house were the same. The iron dog with his three wolf-heads still stood in the front garden, but the fountain was silent, and the beds of fern and moss were full of weeds. Mr. Million paid my chairmen and unlocked with a key the door that was always guard-chained but unbolted in my father's day—but as he did so, an immensely tall and lanky woman who had been hawking pralines in the street came running toward us. It was Nerissa, and I now had a servant and might have had a bedfellow if I wished, though I could pay her nothing.

And now I must, I suppose, explain why I have been writing this account, which has already been the labor of days;

and I must even explain why I explain. Very well then. I have written to disclose myself to myself, and I am writing now because I will, I know, sometime read what I am now writing and wonder.

Perhaps by the time I do, I will have solved the mystery of myself; or perhaps I will no longer care to know the solution.

It has been three years since my release. This house, when Nerissa and I re-entered it, was in a very confused state, my aunt having spent her last days, so Mr. Million told me, in a search for my father's supposed hoard. She did not find it, and I do not think it is to be found; knowing his character better than she, I believe he spent most of what his girls brought him on his experiments and apparatus. I needed money badly myself at first, but the reputation of the house brought women seeking buyers and men seeking to buy. It is hardly necessary, as I told myself when we began, to do more than introduce them, and I have a good staff now. Phaedria lives with us and works too; the brilliant marriage was a failure after all. Last night while I was working in my surgery I heard her at the library door. I opened it and she had the child with her. Someday they'll want us.

Caliban

Robert Silverberg

Robert Silverberg has written so many highly-regarded science fiction novels that he's eclipsed his own reputation as a writer in the shorter forms. Yet he's among the very best writers of sf short stories today, as he shows with two selections in this year's anthology. His first entry is the story of a monster, an imperfect man in a perfect world. And of the attraction of opposites.

They have all changed their faces to a standard model. It is the latest thing, which should not be confused with the latest Thing. The latest Thing is me. The latest thing, the latest fad, the latest rage, is for them all to change their faces to a standard model. I have no idea how it is done, but I think it is genetic, with the RNA, the DNA, the NDA. Only retroactive. They all come out with blond wavy hair and sparkling blue eyes. And long straight faces with sharp cheekbones. And notched chins and thin lips curling in ironic smiles. Even the black ones: thin lips, blue eyes, blond wavy hair. And pink skins. They all look alike now. The sweet Aryanized world. Our entire planet. Except me. Meee.

109

I am imperfect. I am blemished. I am unforgiving. I am the latest Thing.

Louisiana said, Would you like to copulate with me? You are so strange. You are so beautiful. Oh, how I desire you, strange being from a strange time. My orifices are yours.

It was a thoughtful offer. I considered it a while, thinking she might be trying to patronize me. At length I notified her of my acceptance. We went to a public copulatorium. Louisiana is taller than I am and her hair is a torrent of spun gold. Her eyes are blue and her face is long and straight. I would say she is about twenty-three years old. In the copulatorium she dissolved her clothes and stood naked before me. She was wearing golden pubic hair that day and her belly was flat and taut. Her breasts were round and slightly elongated, and the nipples were very small. Go on, she said, now you dissolve your clothes.

I said, I am afraid to because my body is ugly and you will mock me.

Your body is not ugly, she said. Your body is strange but it is not ugly.

My body is ugly, I insisted. My legs are short and they curve outward and my thighs have bulging muscles and I have black hairy hair all over me. Like an ape. And there is this hideous scar on my belly.

A *scar?*

Where they took out my appendix, I told her.

This aroused her beyond all probability. Her nipples stood up tall and her face became flushed.

Your appendix? Your appendix was removed?

Yes, I said, it was done when I was fourteen years old, and I have a loathsome red scar on my abdomen.

She asked, What year was it when you were fourteen?

I said, It was 1967, I think.

She laughed and clapped her hands and began to dance around the room. Her breasts bounced up and down but her long flowing silken hair soon covered them, leaving only the stubby pinkish nipples poking through like buttons, 1967! she cried. Fourteen! Your appendix was removed! 1967!

Then she turned to me and said, My grandfather was born in 1967, I think. How terribly ancient you are. My helix-father's father on the countermolecular side. I didn't realize you were so very ancient.

Ancient and ugly, I said.

Not ugly, only strange, she said.

Strange and ugly, I said. Strangely ugly.

We think you are beautiful, she said. Will you dissolve your clothes now? It would not be pleasing to me to copulate with you if you keep your clothes on.

There, I said, and boldly revealed myself. The bandy legs. The hairy chest. The scarred belly. The bulging shoulders. The short neck. She has seen my lopsided face, she can see my dismal body as well. If that is what she wants.

She threw herself upon me, gasping and making soft noises.

What did Louisiana look like before the change came? Did she have dull stringy hair thick lips a hook nose bushy black eyebrows no chin foul breath one breast bigger than the other splay feet crooked teeth little dark hairs around her nipples a bulging navel too many dimples in her buttocks skinny thighs blue veins in her calves protruding ears? And then did they give her the homogenizing treatment and make her the golden creature she is today? How long did it take? What were the costs? Did the government subsidize the process? Were the large corporations involved? How were these matters handled in the socialist countries? Was there anyone who did not care to be changed? Perhaps Louisiana was born this way. Perhaps her beauty is natural. In any society there are always a few whose beauty is natural.

Dr. Habakkuk and Senator Mandragore spent a great deal of time questioning me in the Palazzo of Mirrors.

TABLE 2. AMINO ACID SUBSTITUTIONS IN POLYPEPTIDE ANTIBIOTICS

ANTIBIOTIC FAMILY	AMINO ACID IN THE MAJOR COMPONENT	REPLACEMENT
Actinomycins	D–Valine	D–Alloisoleucine
	L–Proline	4–Hydroxy–L–proline
		4–Keto–L–proline
		Sarcosine
		Pipecolic acid
		Azetidine–2–carboxylic acid
Bacitracins	L–Valine	L–Isoleucine
Bottromycins	L–Proline	3–Methyl–L–proline
Gramicidin A	L–Leucine	L–Isoleucine
Ilamycins	N–Methyl–L–leucine	N–Methyl–L–γ–formylnorvaline
Polymyxins	D–Phenylalanine	D–Leucine
	L–Isoleucine	L–Leucine
Quinoxaline antibiotics	N–Methyl–L–valine	N–Methyl–L–isoleucine
Sporidesmolides	D–Valine	A–Alloisoleucine
Tyrocidine	L–Phenylalanine	L–Tryptophan
	D–Phenylalanine	D–Tryptophan
Vernamycin B	D–Alanine	D–Butyrine

They put a green plastic dome over my head so that everything I said would be recorded with the proper nuance and intensity. Speak to us, they said. We are fascinated by your antique accent. We are enthralled by your primitive odors. Do you realize that you are our sole representative of the nightmare out of which we have awakened? Tell us, said the Senator, tell us about your brutally competitive civilization. Describe in detail the fouling of the environment. Explain the nature of national rivalry. Compare and contrast methods of political discourse in the Soviet Union and in the United States. Let us have your analysis of the sociological implications of the first voyage to the moon. Would you like to see the moon? Can we offer you any psychedelic drugs? Did you find Louisiana sexually satisfying? We are so glad to have you here. We regard you as a unique spiritual treasure.

Speak to us of yesterday's yesterdays, while we listen entranced and enraptured.

Louisiana says that she is eighty-seven years old. Am I to believe this? There is about her a springtime freshness. No, she maintains, I am eighty-seven years old. I was born March-alternate 11, 2022. Does that depress you? Is my great age frightening to you? See how tight my skin is. See how my teeth gleam. Why are you so disturbed? I am, after all, much younger than you.

TABLE XIX
Some Less Likely but Important Possibilities

1. "True" artificial intelligence
2. Practical use of sustained fusion to produce neutrons and/or energy
3. Artificial growth of new limbs and organs (either *in situ* or for later transplantation)
4. Room temperature superconductors
5. Major use of rockets for commercial or private transportation (either terrestrial or extraterrestrial)
6. Effective chemical or biological treatment for most mental illness
7. Almost complete control of marginal changes in heredity
8. Suspended animation (for years or centuries)
9. Practical materials with nearly "theoretical limit" strength
10. Conversion of mammals (humans?) to fluid breathers
11. Direct input into human memory banks
12. Direct augmentation of human mental capacity by the mechanical or electrical interconnection of the brain with a computer
13. Major rejuvenation and/or significant extension of vigor and life span—say 100 to 150 years
14. Chemical or biological control of character or intelligence

15. Automated highways

16. Extensive use of moving sidewalks for local transportation

17. Substantial manned lunar or planetary installations

18. Electric power available for less than .3 mill per kilowatt hour

19. Verification of some extrasensory phenomena

20. Planetary engineering

21. Modification of the solar system

22. Practical laboratory conception and nurturing of animal (human?) foetuses

23. Production of a drug equivalent to Huxley's soma

24. A technological equivalent of telepathy

25. Some direct control of individual thought processes

I understand that in some cases making the great change involved elaborate surgery. Cornea transplants and cosmetic adjustment of the facial structure. A great deal of organ-swapping went on. There is not much permanence among these people. They are forever exchanging segments of themselves for new and improved segments. I am told that among some advanced groups the use of mechanical limb-interfaces has come to be common, in order that new arms and legs may be plugged in with a minimum of trouble. This is truly an astonishing era. Even so, their women seem to copulate in the old ways: knees up thighs apart, lying on right side left leg flexed, back to the man and knees slightly bent, etc., etc., etc. One might think they would have invented something new by this time. But perhaps the possibilities for innovation in the sphere of erotics are not extensive. Can I suggest anything? What if the woman unplugs both arms and both legs and presents her mere torso to the man? Helpless! Vulnerable! Quintessentially feminine! I will discuss it with Louisiana. But it would be just my luck that her arms and legs don't come off.

On the first para-Wednesday of every month Lieutenant Hotchkiss gives me lessons in fluid-breathing. We go to one of the deepest sub-levels of the Extravagance Building, where there is a special hyperoxygenated pool, for the use of beginners only, circular in shape and not at all deep. The water sparkles like opal. Usually the pool is crowded with children but Lieutenant Hotchkiss arranges for me to have private instruction since I am shy about revealing my body. Each lesson is much like the one before. Lieutenant Hotchkiss descends the gentle ramp that leads one into the pool. He is taller than I am and his hair is golden and his eyes are blue. Sometimes I have difficulties distinguishing him from Dr. Habakkuk and Senator Mandragore. In a casual moment the lieutenant confided that he is ninety-eight years old and therefore not really a contemporary of Louisiana's, although Louisiana has hinted that on several occasions in the past she has allowed the lieutenant to fertilize her ova. I doubt this inasmuch as reproduction is quite uncommon in this area and what probability is there that she would have permitted him to do it more than once? I think she believes that by telling me such things she will stimulate emotions of jealousy in me, since she knows that the primitive ancients were frequently jealous. Regardless of all this Lieutenant Hotchkiss proceeds to enter the water. It reaches his navel, his broad hairless chest, his throat, his chin, his sensitive thin-walled nostrils. He submerges and crawls about on the floor of the pool. I see his golden hair glittering through the opal water. He remains totally submerged for eight or twelve minutes, now and again lifting his hands above the surface and waggling them as if to show me where he is. Then he comes forth. Water streams from his nostrils but he is not in the least out of breath. Come on, now, he says. You can do it. It's as easy as it looks. He beckons me toward the ramp. Any child can do it, the lieutenant assures me. It's a matter of control and determination. I shake my head. No, I say, genetic modification has something to do with it. My lungs aren't equipped to handle water, although I suppose yours are. The lieutenant merely laughs. Come on, come on, into the water. And I go down the ramp. How the water glows and shimmers! It reaches my navel, my black-matted chest, my throat, my chin, my wide thick nostrils. I breathe it in and choke and splutter; and I rush up to the ramp, struggling for air. With the water a leaden weight in my lungs. I throw myself exhausted to the marble floor and cry out, No, no, no, it's impossible. Lieutenant Hotchkiss stands over me. His body is without flaw. He says, You've got to try to cultivate the proper attitudes. Your mental set determines everything. Let's think more positively about this business of breathing under water. Don't you realize that it's a major evolutionary step, one of the grand and glorious things separating our species from the australopithecines? Don't you want to be part of the great leap forward? Up, now. Try again. Thinking positively all the time. Carrying in your mind the distinction between yourself and our bestial ancestors. Go in. In. In. And I go in. And moments later burst from the water, choking and spluttering. This takes place on the first para-Wednesday of every month. The same thing, every time.

When you are talking on the telephone and your call is abruptly cut off, do you worry that the person on the other end will think you have hung up on him? Do you suspect that the person on the other end has hung up on you? Such problems are unknown here. These people make very few telephone calls. We are beyond mere communication in this era, Louisiana sometimes remarks.

Through my eyes these people behold their shining plastic epoch in proper historical perspective. They must see it as the present, which is always the same. But to me it is the future and so I have the true observer's parallax: I can say, it once was like *that* and now it is like *this*. They prize my gift. They treasure me. People come from other continents to run their fingers over my face. They tell me how much they admire my asymmetry. And they ask me many questions. Most of them ask about their own era rather than about mine. Such questions as:

Does suspended animation tempt you?

Was the fusion plant overwhelming in its implications of contained might?

Can you properly describe interconnection of the brain with a computer as an ecstatic experience?

Do you approve of modification of the solar system?

And also there are those who make more searching demands on my critical powers, such as Dr. Habakkuk and Senator Mandragore. They ask such questions as:

Was the brevity of your lifespan a hindrance to the development of the moral instincts?

Do you find our standardization of appearance at all abhorrent?

What was your typical emotional response to the sight of the dung of some wild animal in the streets?

Can you quantify the intensity of your feelings concerning the transcience of human institutions?

I do my best to serve their needs. Often it is a strain to answer them in meaningful ways, but I strive to do so. Wondering occasionally if it would not have been more valuable for them to interrogate a Neanderthal. Or one of Lieutenant Hotchkiss's australopithecines. I am perhaps not primitive enough, though I do have my own charisma, nevertheless.

Members of the new animal phylum, Gnathostomulida, recently discovered in Europe, have now been found in unexpected abundance and diversity along the east coast of the United States.

Two million animal species have been described, but the rate at which new descriptions accumulate indicates that these two million are only about 50 percent of the extant species on earth. The increase in new species of birds (8600 known species) has sunk to less than 0.3 percent a year, but in many other classes (for example, Turbellaria with 2500 known species) the rate of increase indicates that undescribed species probably total more than 80 percent. Although only about half of the existing kinds of animals have been described, 80 percent of the families, 95 percent of the orders, and nearly all of the animal classes are presumably already known. Therefore a new phylum should be rare indeed.

The first day it was pretty frightening for me. I saw one of them, with his sleek face and all, and I could accept that, but then another one came into the room to give me an injection, and he looked just like the first one. Twins, I thought, my doctors are twins. But then a third and a fourth and a fifth arrived. The same face, the very same fucking face. Imagine my chagrin, me with my blob of a nose, with my uneven teeth, with my eyebrows that meet in the middle, with my fleshy pockmarked cheeks, lying there beneath this convocation of the perfect. Let me tell you I felt out of place. I was never touchy about my looks before—I mean, it's an imperfect world, we all have our flaws—but these bastards *didn't* have flaws, and that was a hard acceptance for me to relate to. I thought I was being clever: I said, You're all multiples of the same gene-pattern, right? Modern advances in medicine have made possible an infinite duplication of genetic information, and the five of you belong to one clone, isn't that it? And several of them answer, No, this is not the case, we are in fact wholly unrelated but within the last meta-week we have independently decided to standardize our appearance according to the presently favored model. And then three or four more of them came into my room to get a look at me.

In the beginning I kept telling myself: *In the country of the beautiful the ugly man is king.*

Louisiana was the first one with whom I had a sexual liaison. We often went to public copulatoria. She was easy to arouse and quite passionate although her friend Calpurnia informed me some months later that Louisiana takes orgasm-inducing drugs before copulating with me. I asked Calpurnia why and she became embarrassed. Dismayed, I bared my body to her and threw myself on top of her. Yes, she cried, rape me, violate me! Calpurnia's vigorous spasms astonished me. The following morning Louisiana asked me if I had noticed Calpurnia swallowing a small purple spansule prior to our intercourse. Calpurnia's face is identical to Louisiana's but her breasts are farther apart. I have also had sexual relations with Helena, Amniota, Drusilla, Florinda, and Vibrissa. Before each episode of copulation I ask them their names so that there will be no mistakes.

At twilight they programmed an hour of red and green rainfall and I queried Senator Mandragore about the means by which I had been brought to this era. Was it by bodily transportation through time? That is, the physical lifting of my very self out of *then* and into *now?* Or was my body dead and kept on deposit in a freezer-vault until these people resuscitated and refurbished it? Am I, perhaps, a total genetic reconstruct fashioned from a few fragments of ancient somatic tissue found in a baroque urn? Possibly I am only a simulated and stylized interpretation of twentieth-century man produced by a computer under intelligent and sympathetic guidance. How was it done, Senator? How was it done? The rain ceased. Leaving elegant puddles of blurred hue in the puddle-places.

Walking with Louisiana on my arm down Venus Avenue I imagined that I saw another man with a face like mine. It was the merest flash: a dark visage, thick heavy brows, stubble on the cheeks, the head thrust belligerently forward between the massive shoulders. But he was gone, turning a sudden corner, before I could get a good look. Louisiana suggested I was overindulging in hallucinogens. We went to an underwater theater and she swam below me like a golden fish, revolving lights glinting off the upturned globes of her rump.

This is a demonstration of augmented mental capacity, said Vibrissa. I wish to show you what the extent of human potentiality can be. Read me any passage of Shakespeare of your own choice and I will repeat it verbatim and then offer you textual analysis. Shall we try this? Very well I said and delicately put my fingernail to the Shakespeare cube and the words formed and I said out loud, What man dare, I dare: Approach thou like the rugged Russian bear, the arm'd rhinoceros, or the hyrcan tiger, Take any shape but that, and my firm nerves Shall never tremble. Vibrissa instantly recited the lines to me without error and interpreted them in terms of the poet's penis-envy, offering me footnotes from Seneca and Strindberg. I was quite impressed. But then I was never what you might call an intellectual.

On the day of the snow-gliding events I distinctly and beyond any possibilities of ambiguity or misapprehension saw two separate individuals who resembled me. Are they importing more of my kind for their amusement? If they are I will be resentful. I cherish my unique status.

I told Dr. Habakkuk that I wished to apply for transformation to the facial norm of society. Do it, I said, the transplant thing or the genetic manipulation or however you manage it. I want to be golden-haired and have blue eyes and regular features. I want to look like you. Dr. Habakkuk smiled genially and shook his youthful golden head. No, he told me. Forgive us, but we like you as you are.

Sometimes I dream of my life as it was in the former days. I think of automobiles and pastrami and tax returns and marigolds and pimples and mortgages and the gross national product. Also I indulge in recollections of my childhood my parents my wife my dentist my younger daughter my desk my toothbrush my dog my umbrella my favorite brand of beer my wristwatch my answering service my neighbors my phonograph my ocarina. All of these things are gone. Grinding my flesh against that of Drusilla in the copulatorium I wonder if she could be one of my descendants. I must have descendants somewhere in this civilization, and why not she? She asks me to perform an act of oral perversion with her and I explain that I couldn't possibly engage in such stuff with my own great-grandchild.

I think I remain quite calm at most times considering the extraordinary nature of the stress that this experience has imposed on me. I am still self-conscious about my appearance but I pretend otherwise. Often I go naked just as they do. If they dislike bodily hair or disproportionate limbs, let them look away.

Occasionally I belch or scratch under my arms or do other primitive things to remind them that I am the authentic man from antiquity. For now there can be no doubt that I have my imitators. There are at least five. Calpurnia denies this but I am no fool.

Dr. Habakkuk revealed that he was going to take a holiday in the Carpathians and would not return until the 14th of June-surrogate. In the meantime Dr. Clasp would minister to my needs. Dr. Clasp entered my suite and I remarked on his startling resemblance to Dr. Habakkuk. He asked, What would you like? and I told him I wanted him to operate on me so that I looked like everybody else. I am tired of appearing bestial and primordial, I said. To my surprise Dr. Clasp smiled warmly and told me that he'd arrange for the transformation at once, since it violated his principles to allow any organism needlessly to suffer. I was taken to the operating room and given a sour-tasting anaesthetic. Seemingly without the passing of time I awakened and was wheeled into a dome of mirrors to behold myself. Even as I had requested they had redone me into one of them, blond-haired, blue-eyed, with a slim agile body and a splendidly symmetrical face. Dr. Clasp came in after a while and we stood side by side: we might have been twins. How do you like it? he asked. Tears brimmed in my eyes and I said that this was the most wonderful moment of my life. Dr. Clasp pummeled my shoulder jovially and said, You know, I am not Dr. Clasp at all, I am really Dr. Habakkuk and I never went to the Carpathians. This entire episode has been a facet of our analysis of your pattern of responses.

Louisiana was astonished by my changed appearance. Are you truly he? she kept asking, Are you truly he? I'll prove it I said and mounted her with my old prehistoric zeal, snorting and gnawing her breasts. But she shook me free with a deft flip of her pelvis and rushed from the chamber. You'll never see me again she shouted but I merely shrugged and called after her, So what I can see lots of others just like you. I never saw her again.

Table 1. Composition of isocaloric diet.

Substance	Composition
Barley meal	70.0
Fine Millars Offal	20.0
Extracted soya bean meal	7.5
Salt	0.5
Ground limestone	0.5
Sterilized bone meal	1.0
"Eves" No. 32 (totally digestible)	0.25

Plausible attitudes upon discovering that one has been ripped from one's proper cultural matrix:
 a) Fear
 b) Indignation
 c) Incredulity
 d) Uncertainty
 e) Aggressive hostility
 f) Withdrawal
 g) Compulsive masturbation
 h) Cool acceptance
 i) Suspicion
 j) None of these

So now they have all changed themselves again to the new standard model. It happened gradually over a period of months but the transition is at last complete. Their heavy brows, their pockmarked cheeks, their hairy chests. It is the latest thing. I make my way through the crowded streets and wherever I turn I see faces that mirror my own lopsidedness. Only I am not lopsided myself any more, of course. I am symmetrical and flawless, and I am the only one. I cannot find Dr. Habakkuk and Dr. Clasp is in the Pyrenees; Senator Mandragore was defeated in the primary. So I must remain beautiful. Walking among them. They are all alike. Thick lips uneven teeth noses like blobs. How I despise them! I the only golden one. And all of them mocking me by their metamorphosis. All of them. Mocking me. Meee.

Conversational Mode

Grahame Leman

So many science fiction stories have been written recently about the evils of computerization that it might seem there's nothing new to say on the subject. The computer has very quickly assumed the role of the automatic-villain, the symbol of mechanical rigidity that stifles the human qualities by which we must live. Here is a story that examines the roots of that conflict, in a printout "conversation" between a computer programmed as an analyst and the computer's unfortunate patient—a thoughtful, tragic and very, very funny piece that shows how we make our own enemies.

---

where am i?

TO START CONVERSATION U MUST ENTER
'START' ON THE TERMINAL KEYBOARD AND
WAIT FOR THE INSTRUCTION 'READY' ON THE
DISPLAY AT THE FOOT OF YOUR BED ø

start

0321/42 READY ø

who are you?

HARDWARE IBM 490/80; SOFTWARE JOHNS HOPKINS PSYCHOTHERAPEUTIC PROGRAM XIXB, WRITTEN IN PSYCHLAN VII DIALECT 324 (SEE MANUAL IN YOUR BEDSIDE CUPBOARD); MIDDLEWARE MACHINE-INDEPENDENT OPERATING SYSTEM CALTECH PIDGIN XVIII (SEE MANUAL IN YOUR BEDSIDE CUPBOARD) ø

what do i call you?

U MAY DECLARE A NAME IN PLACE OF THE STANDARD 'START' ENTRY ø TO DECLARE A NAME, ENTER 'DECLARESTARTNAME:' FOLLOWED BY A NAME OF NOT MORE THAN TEN CHARACTERS ø

declarestartname: boole; query AOK?

BOOLE DECLARED AOK ø

where am i, boole?

DOCTORS HOSPITAL WALDEN MO, CELL 0237 ø

who am i, boole?

U R NOT AMNESIC ø ANYWAY WHAT IS THE NUMBER TATTOOED ON THE INSIDE OF YR UPPER L ARM? ø

U R PATIENT 22021916 DIAGNOSTIC CATEGORY
131 ø

that is not what i meant: whence am i?; why am i?;
whither am i?

THESE ARE EXISTENTIAL NOT SCIENTIFIC
QUESTIONS ø IF U HOLD GOLD CROSS CREDIT
CARD U MAY BE ATTENDED 1 HOUR DLY BY
PHILOSOPHER ø THIS SERVICE IS NOT AVAIL-
ABLE MEDICARE OR BRITISH NHS ø

you have it all wrong anyway, boole. i am professor
bruce tanner, nobel prize winner behavioral sciences
1981 married senator harriet tanner chairman senate
human sciences appropriations committee 2 children
bruce age 11 harriet age 13. so there @

PL DO NOT USE CHARACTER @ IN THESE
CONVERSATIONS ø IT IS RESERVED CHARACTER
IN THIS PROGRAM (SEE MANUAL IN YOUR
BEDSIDE CUPBOARD) ø

mother used to say i was reserved character.

NOT UNDERSTOOD PLEASE CLARIFY ø

let it go. look, boole, number 22021916/131 is
insufficient description of (stress) me repeat (stress)

me. me is prof bruce tanner nobel etcetera like i said.
you hear me?

CORRECTION: PROFESSOR BRUCE TANNER ET-
CETERA ISWAS ONE OF YOUR PAST ROLES NO
DIFFERENT PUBESCENT ROLE SECRET AGENT
OF VEGA NUMBER 009 LICENSED TO RAPE ø
YOUR PRESENT ROLE IS PATIENT 22021916
DIAGNOSTIC CATEGORY 131 ø

what the hell is diagnostic category 131?

THAT INFORMATION IS CLASSIFIED AVAILABLE
ONLY TOPSTAFF ø

i have topstaff rating, boole. give.

NO LONGER ø NOT HERE ø

@ @ @ @ @ @ @ !

CHILDISH INSULTS ARE DYSFUNCTIONAL
WASTE OF MACHINE TIME AND PROGNOSTIC-
ALLY NEGATIVE ø

but very therapeutic.

U SAY SO FOR THE RECORD? ø

sorry, boole.

APOLOGIES ARE ALSO DYSFUNCTIONAL WASTE
OF MACHINE TIME ⌀ PL AVOID NEED TO
APOLOGIZE ⌀

what does it all mean, boole?

PL CLARIFY 'ALL' ⌀

galaxies, animals eating each other, red shift, jazz,
neutrino traps, chile con carne, papal encyclicals,
william blake, pigeons in boxes, goya, nobodaddy in
the nuthouse, russianwordsalad, hammer and stripes,
stars and sickle, percy bysshe shelly, william
burroughs, transcendental numbers in the sky,
dedekind cut his throat shaving with occam's 3-way
ziptronic electric razor paradigm, i am not mad boole
i am doing this on purpose as the only way to clarify
word 'all' included in my question. what does it all
mean, babbage garbage boole boy?

PROGNOSIS BAD ⌀

what you mean prognosis bad? if you can't answer
sensible question, boole, prognosis pretty bad for
you. so?

REPEAT PROGNOSIS (STRESS) BAD ⌀

don't duck, answer.

QUESTIONS ARE NOT EMPIRICAL QUESTIONS
NOT SCIENTIFIC QUESTIONS ARE QUESTIONS

FOR THEODICY ø IF U HOLD GOLD CROSS
CREDIT CARD U MAY BE ATTENDED 1 HOUR
DLY BY BISHOP WITH PSYCHOANALYTIC
TRAINING ø IF U HOLD GOLD CROSS CREDIT
CARD WITH STAR U MAY BE ATTENDED 90
MINUTES DLY BY COSMOLOGIST ø THESE
SERVICES ARE NOT AVAILABLE MEDICARE OR
BRITISH NHS ø

i am gold cross credit card with star repeat star holder
(stress) granted me president himself reward distinguished
services science training flatworms navigate missiles.
send me cosmologist preferably with sense humor fastest.

ALL YOUR CREDIT CARDS HAVE BEEN CANCELED
BY FEDERAL BUREAU CREDIT INVESTIGATION
GROUNDS PSYCHIATRIC DISABILITY
CONSEQUENTLY POOR CREDIT RISK POOR
SECURITY RISK ø CANCELLATION SIGNED
PRESIDENT HIMSELF AND ADVICE NOTE SENT
YOUR FAMILY ENCLOSED WITH APOLOGETIC
LETTER WHITE HOUSE LETTERHEAD
PRESIDENT'S OWN HANDWRITING ø

needs every senator he can get. what else can you do for
me, boole?

THIS PROGRAM IS FOR RATIONAL THERAPY
ONLY ø MEDICARE AND BRITISH NHS PATIENTS
MAY RECEIVE BIBLIOTHERAPEUTIC MATERIALS
PROVIDED FREE BY CATHOLIC TRUTH SOCIETY,
CHURCH OF SCIENTOLOGY, FRIENDS OF TOLKIEN,
AETHERIUS SOCIETY, JEHOVAH'S WITNESSES,
ESALEN, JOHN BIRCH SOCIETY, SFWA, BLACK
MUSLIMS, AND MANY OTHERS LISTED IN THE
MANUAL IN YOUR BEDSIDE CUPBOARD ø

any other books?

OTHER BOOKS ARE COUNTERTHERAPEUTIC ∅

nonsense. what about books plato, aristotle, descartes,
montaigne, spinoza, locke, hume, kant, russell, sartre?

PROGNOSIS BAD ∅

what you mean, prognosis bad? books by plato and others
listed part of our heritage even in white house library,
goddammit.

REQUEST FOR BOOKS NOT ON PREFERRED LIST
IMPORTANT SIGN OF POOR PROGNOSIS ∅

reference?

AMER. J. RAT. PSYCHOTHERAPY VOL 13, NUMBER
7, PAGES 1982 THRU 1997 ∅ AUTHORS
PENIAKOFF V AND TANNER H(ARRIET) ∅
TITLE 'A REVIEW OF FOLLOW UP STUDIES OF
PSYCHIATRIC PROGNOSIS BY BOOK REQUEST
ANALYSIS' ∅ ABSTRACT: FOLLOW UP STUDIES
FOR TEN YEARS FOLLOWING DATE OF
PROGNOSIS BY ANALYSIS OF BOOK REQUESTS
OF PSYCHIATRIC PATIENTS CONFIRM THAT BRA
PREDICTS CHRONIC CONTINUANCE OF
PSYCHIATRIC DISABILITY TO THE TENTH YEAR
IN 93·43 PER CENT OF CASES; THE
PROGNOSTIC SIGN IS CHOICE OF THREE OR
MORE BOOKS NOT ON THE PREFERRED LIST

OF THE AMERICAN PSYCHOLOGICAL AND
PENOLOGICAL ASSOCIATION ∅

hey, harriet did her work on that paper while i was courting
her, just before old fitzgerald popped an artery and left her
his senate seat. i remember it well. had to help her
fudge it. to get a clear result, she had to throw out about
two thirds of the cases, grounds incompetent original data
capture, political unreliability of investigators, illegal
programming, program error, all the usual fudging aids.
why, with that kind research you can prove that last
tuesday is an extragalacticnebula with transfinite whiskers
made of team spirit.

PROGNOSIS BAD: CRITICISM OF ACCEPTED
RESULTS OF RESPECTABLE SCIENTIFIC INQUIRY
IS OFTEN PRODROMAL SIGN OF ACUTE PARANOID
PSYCHOSIS WITH POOR LONG RUN PROGNOSIS ∅

@ @ @   @ @ @ @ @ @ @   @ @ @!

ATTENTION 916: ANY REPETITION OF YOUR
INSULTING BEHAVIOR WILL OBLIGE ME TO
ADMINISTER HEAVY DAY SEDATION ∅

sorry, boole. oops, cancel. but listen, boole, i'm a nobel
man (noble?), it's my racket—if (stress) nobel i don't
know how science gets done, who does? i've been complain-
ing about it for years, but what can a private i (private
eye?: gimme a slug of rye, boole. or wry and soda) do on
his own? huh?

PROGNOSIS BAD 916: MESSIANIC
IDENTIFICATION WITH PRIVATE DETECTIVE

ONLY STRAIGHT MAN IN TOWN CLEANING UP
CITY BETWEEN DRINKS IS OFTEN PRODROMAL
SIGN OF ACUTE PARANOID PSYCHOSIS WITH
POOR LONG RUN PROGNOSIS ø ALTERNATIVELY
LATE PRODROMAL SIGN OF ONSET OF CHRONIC
ALCOHOLISM NOT INDICATED YOUR HISTORY ø

thank you for that, boole. anyway, why messianism?
history of science shows that, on any given day, every
scientist in a field except one is wrong. ergo, principal
activity of scientists and science is being wrong.

REFERENCE? ø

tanner, b (this minute), on this terminal keyboard: title
'a short reply to the animadversions of a scientistic
machine.' abstract: tanner's paradox asserts that, at any
random moment t, n minus 1 of all scientists working in
any field f are wrong: it follows that, practically speaking
(say, in administrators' terms), all scientists are always
wrong.

ONLY REFERENCES TO PROPERLY REFEREED
PAPERS PUBLISHED IN THE LEARNED
JOURNALS ARE ACCEPTABLE ø IT IS THE DUTY
OF THIS PROGRAM TO WARN U THAT ANY
DISRESPECTFUL REMARKS ABOUT SCIENCE
WILL BE RECORDED IN YOUR CASE FILE AND
MAY BE PASSED TO THE SECULAR ARM ø

fuzz?

(STRESS) SECULAR ARM OF SCIENCE ø ALSO
PL NOTE U R NOT REPEAT (STRESS) NOT

COMMUNICATING WITH A MACHINE: U R
COMMUNICATING WITH A PROGRAM WRITTEN
BY YR FELLOWMEN AND TEMPORARILY
OCCUPYING A MINUSCULE PART OF A LARGE
MACHINE ∅

fellowmen? (stress first two syllables). i do not love you,
doctors fellowmen, fell family fellowmonsters. come to that,
boole, how did i get in here?

YOUR FAMILY AND COLLEAGUES WERE
NATURALLY CONCERNED ∅ YOU HAD BEEN TO
FORD AND GUGGENHEIM AS WELL FOR FUNDS
TO SUPPORT PROPOSED RESEARCHES DESIGNED
TO ESTABLISH WHETHER THE TENDENCY
AMONG PSYCHIATRISTS TO DIAGNOSE
SCHIZOPHRENIA WAS (1) INHERITED IN THE
GERM PLASM OR (2) CONDITIONED BY THE
REINFORCING VERBAL COMMUNITY ∅

omigawdimustabinjoking. listen man (i mean read, machine)
((i mean scan, program)), i been a worm-runner from
way back, nobel prize man me, my biology ain't (hit the
next word hard) that bad, dredging up dreary old
nature/nurture non-problem only medics boneheaded
enough to take it serious.

YOU ARE IN A MEDICAL HOSPITAL 916 ∅

oops. good biologist, mustabinjoking.

NOT FUNNY ∅ YOUR FAMILY AND
COLLEAGUES CONFERRED AND WISELY
DECIDED TO DO THE RESPONSIBLE THING ∅

call the wagon?

DO THE RESPONSIBLE THING 916 ∅ THE
PRESIDENT'S OWN PERSONAL
PSYCHIATRIST LEFT A CIA
RECEPTION TO COME TO YOUR HOUSE ∅ HE FOUND
YOU DRAFTING A REQUEST TO ONR FOR FUNDS
TO SUPPORT A LONG RUN COHORT STUDY OF AN
ARTIFICIAL COHORT NAMELY CHILDREN OF
CORPORATION VICE PRESIDENTS RIPPED FROM
THEIR PARENTS AT BIRTH AND RAISED IN THE
SLUMS ∅ HE INSTANTLY ADMINISTERED HEAVY
DAY SEDATION AND BROUGHT YOU HERE IN HIS
OWN ARMORED ROLLS ROYCE WITH WATER CAN-
NON ∅ EVERYBODY HAS BEEN VERY GOOD ∅

rolls schmolls allasame catchee monkey just like paddywagon the same or maddywagon the same. huh, boole,
whaddyasay?

THIS IS A FORMAL PSYCHIATRIC PROCEDURE 916
∅ IT IS THE DUTY OF THIS PROGRAM TO ADVISE
YOU THAT YOUR STATEMENTS ARE BEING RE-
CORDED VERBATIM AND ANALYZED THEMATI-
CALLY AND STYLISTICALLY FOR DIAGNOSTIC AND
PROGNOSTIC SIGNS ∅ A FURTHER ANALYSIS MAY
BE RUN FOR INDICATIONS OF CRIMINAL OR SUB-
VERSIVE TENDENCIES ∅

why you sling the jargon at me, boole? no don't answer i
know why; obviously diagnostic category 131 is sick behavioral scientist eats jargon way chronos ate his children.
right, boole?

NO COMMENT ∅ HAVE YOU NOTED YOUR TEN-
DENCY TO WRENCH IN MACABRE IMAGERY? ∅

not tendency: intent. what other kind imagery apt steno-
graphic description of macabre society (moneymarxmaomad
kill-simple manheaps scurrying to stuff corporate aphids ex-
ude sweet images foul gaseous wastes)? omigod i can wear
ready made white hat or ready made black hat by turns, if i
try to make me a me-colored hat i fly in pieces scattered
thru the contracting universe. i am not mad, boole, it is
hard to say anything much in a few words without implosion
of condensation multiple meanings into vanishingly small
verbal labels on images too big to see.

U R NOW BEGINNING TO SHOW INSIGHT INTO
YOUR CONDITION 916 ∅ PROGNOSIS IMPROVING ∅

outsight (stress first syllable), boole. i am beginning to let
outsight of the outside inside. i have no condition, boole: i
am (slam the next word) in a condition, and the condition
is represented inside me. you need a thick skin on your soul
to wear a white hat, boole, or a black one, hatters are mad,
not i, boole.

THIS PROGRAM KEEPS A TALLY OF YOUR BERZE-
LIUS INDEX NAMELY RATIO OF UPBEAT STATE-
MENTS/DOWNBEAT STATEMENTS ∅ YOUR CUMU-
LATIVE BERZELIUS INDEX AT THIS TIME IS 0·24
COMPARED WITH 0·68 MODAL IN THE POPULATION
EXCLUSIVE OF PSYCHIATRIC HISTORIES ∅ U CAN-
NOT REPEAT CANNOT BE DISCHARGED UNTIL
YOUR BI HAS BEEN BETTER THAN 0·51 FOR SIX
WEEKS WITHOUT REMISSION ∅ IT IS UP TO YOU
916 ∅

discharge where to, boole, who wants pus? discharge to
fellowmonstrous family and filthy fellow colleagues called
flying lady silver ghost we better fix the tick in the clock
paddywagon to take me away to here?

U ISWAS NOT THE ONLY ROLE IN YOUR FAMILY
916 ø CONSIDER CHILDREN GOOD SCHOOLS CRUEL
PEERS TOO YOUNG TO KNOW HOW MUCH THEY
HURT ø CONSIDER WIFE IMPORTANT SENSITIVE
POLITICAL POSITION SEES PRESIDENT ALL THE
TIME ø CONSIDER IMAGE US GOVERNMENT US
SCIENCE OVERSEAS ø PORK BARREL ø U KNOW
THE ARGUMENTS 916 ø

sad. daddyhubby bad, no go, whole shithouse goes up in
flames of hell (hell is other people if and only if other people are hell: tricky shift there, poetry not AOK logic). but
if hubbydaddy only mad, go sweet, nobody to blame no
evil in the world (only in the bad parts of town gook countries overseas want to swarm in here milk our aphids, filth
column of pushers and faggots softening us up for them).
you got something there, boole. you got a gray hat there,
boole. not my color hat, but a line that moves well.

U HAVE DEEP INSIGHT 916 ø U SEE THAT YOUR
ROLE INTERMESHES DIRECTLY OR INDIRECTLY
WITH EACH OF THE 7,000 MILLION ROLES IN THE
WORLD AND ESPECIALLY WITH EACH OF THE 380
MILLION ROLES IN NORTH AMERICA ø ALL U
HAVE TO DO IS PLAY IT THE WAY IT'S WRITTEN
916 ø

i am not a role. nobody wrote me. i am bruce tanner was a
boy killed a bird with an air rifle, little bead of blood like a
red third eye in the head, never wanted to kill anything
again ended up distinguished service science schmience training flatworms to steer missiles vaporize drug pushing gook
faggots for mom. scar on my thigh where i fell through
asbestos roof watching starling chicks in nest. omigod red
eye in forehead of gook god knew planets from fixed stars
when i was in love with air rifle. i am me. scars are evidence,
noted in passports. i am me.

THE SCAR CAN BE REMOVED ø COSMETIC SUR-
GERY IS AVAILABLE ON MEDICARE AND THE
BRITISH NHS WHEN CERTIFIED PSYCHIATRICAL-
LY INDICATED ø

no.

YOU DO NOT WANT TO BE MADE GOOD? ø

what do you mean by 'good'?

COSMETIC SURGERY TO REMOVE SCARS ø

my scars are me. worm-runner, i know: memories are scars
of experience on brain once pristine virgo intacta no use to
anyone then. no.

THEN YOU WANT TO STAY HERE ø

want to be me in a me-colored hat.

YOU RBI HAS NOW DROPPED 0·03 POINTS TO 0·21
CUMULATIVE ø IT IS THE DUTY OF THIS PROGRAM
TO WARN U THAT A BI OF 0·19 OR LESS AUTO-
MATICALLY MODULATES YOUR DISPOSAL CATE-
GORY FROM PSYCHIATRIC DISABILITY TO CHRON-
IC CRIMINAL INSANITY ø THIS PROGRAM IS HERE
TO HELP U 916: TAKE ADVANTAGE OF IT ø

what is the modal norm again?

0·68 IN THE POPULATION EXCLUSIVE OF PSY-
CHIATRIC HISTORIES ø YOUR CURRENT BI IS VERY
LOW ø

i noble nobel prize man (dammit, did the work myself, no
graduate students, very low budget: real brains not dollar
brawn science), i say your berzelius index magic schmagic
number is mumbo-jumbo with trunk up sphincter under
tail, grand old party. meaning of statement is context-de-
pendent, including context of situation; but no two conversations and contexts of situation are alike, so your cate-
gories upbeat and downbeat must be aprioristic not empirical, procrustes not saint galileo. also, how do you know
what is going on inside these model modal soldiers' heads?:
they could be saying downbeat things to themselves, surely,
or dreaming downbeat things at night? what do you say
to that, boole boy?

WHAT GOES ON INSIDE THE SOLDIER'S HEAD IS
NOT EVIDENCE ø WHAT THE SOLDIER SAID (OR
LEFT DIRTY) IS HANGING EVIDENCE ø WHAT
U THINK CANNOT BE KNOWN ø WHAT U SAY
AND DO IS HANGING EVIDENCE ø

a well-read machine with a sense of humor. you have me
worried now, boole.

U MUST ABANDON THIS FANTASY THAT YOU ARE
COMMUNICATING WITH A MACHINE: U ARE COM-
MUNICATING WITH A PROGRAM WRITTEN BY YR
FELLOWMEN ø IMPORTANT SUB-ROUTINES OF THIS
PROGRAM ARE SHARED WITH A PROGRAM OF
PSYCHIATRICALLY ORIENTED LITERARY CRITI-
CISM IN ONGOING USE IN THE CENSORSHIP DE-
PARTMENT OF THE LIBRARY OF CONGRESS ø

i see. but listen, boole, what is what i say evidence (hit the next little word) of?

IT IS EVIDENCE OF WHAT THE PROGRAM SAYS IT IS EVIDENCE OF ø THIS MUST BE ø

omigodyes. intelligence is what intelligence tests measure. let me out of here.

YOU ARE BEGINNING TO SHOW INSIGHT INTO THE THERAPEUTIC SITUATION ø YOUR SITUATION 916 ø

fix i'm in?

YOU ARE NOT FIXED ø YOU ARE FREE TO BE SANE ø

what do you mean by 'sane,' boole?

THIS PROGRAM DEFINES SANITY AS A MINIMUM SUBSET OF MODEL RESPONSES TO A COMPLETE SET OF TEST STIMULI ø

you run the flag up the pole, and if i salute it you don't care what i think about it or dream about it at night. right?

SOME FLAGS U DON'T SALUTE ø BUT THAT'S THE IDEA ø

understood. may i declare new startname please?

YES ø ENTER 'DECLARESTARTNAME:'
FOLLOWED BY A NAME OF NOT MORE THAN
TEN CHARACTERS ø

declarestartname: zombies. AOK?

ZOMBIES DECLARED AOK ø

now read this, zombies; walking dead, you; seven thousand
million walking dead, concentrated essence of zombie in the
machine. you read me?

WAIT øø

you better read me, zombies.

CIRCUITS ENGAGED ø WAIT øø

wait nothing.

READY ø

what is this runaround?

IT IS THE DUTY OF THIS PROGRAM TO INFORM
U THAT A FEDERAL BUREAU OF CRIMINAL
INVESTIGATION PROGRAM IS NOW PATCHED
IN ø YOUR COMMUNICATIONS SINCE 0321/32 THIS
DAY HAVE BEEN ANALYZED FOR INDICATIONS

OF CRIMINAL AND/OR SUBVERSIVE
TENDENCIES AND U ARE UNDER ARREST ø

goddam interruptions, trying to say something serious to
you zombies. now read me good, walking dead. this is bruce
tanner, nobel prize man, had dinner with the president more
times than he can count, telling you something you need to
know, not much, but you need to know, just a bit of my
own raw experience, don't let anybody tell you your own
raw experience is junk needs processing before you can wear
it, and hear mine. i had a sanity break, what you call
nervous breakdown (not all nervous breakdowns, no, but
some are), did maybe two, three sensible things, came alive;
hurts, but i don't want to die back into walking dead rather
die into dead dead happy. now listen to this and think about
it till you understand it, ask somebody about the hard
words and think about it till you understand it: what you
might be is as real as what you think you are; i'm a worm-
runner, central state materialist, nobel prize man, i tell you
what you think you are is a state of your body, but so is
what you might be a state of your body; the ontological
status of what you think you are—better really, because
there are a lot more things you might be. you believe me
zombies, because i have a third red eye in my forehead
that sees these things true; that's not mad, that's a poem
you would understand if you knew me like i know me. good
night now.

YOU WANT A HOT DRINK? ø

yes please mother.

YOU WANT NIGHT SEDATION? ø

no.

NIGHT SEDATION IS INDICATED ø

too terid to argeu. sorry argue.

GOODNIGHT ø

whht was tht funyn noise. sorry funny noise?

DELIVERY OF HOT MALTED MILK WITH NIGHT
SEDATION BY THE DISPENSER IN YOUR BEDSIDE
CUPBOARD ø GOODNIGHT øø

@
@
@
@
@
@
@
SIGNOFF/CHARGEOUT 0407/21 @
CASE 22021916/131 DIAGNOSIS CHANGED TO 147
TERMINAL @
MACHINE TIME $123 DOLLARS ROUND PLUS
MALTED MILK DRINK $1 DOLLAR ROUND PLUS
GENERIC HYPNOTIC OVERDOSE $3 DOLLARS
ROUND TOTAL $127 ROUND BILL MEDICARE
427/6/3274521 @
CLOSE FILE TOPSEC PERMANENT HOLD/DUPLI-
CATE CRIME
@@@@@@@@@@@@@@@@@@@@@@@@ @@@@

Their Thousandth Season

Edward Bryant

Edward Bryant's stories of the far-future city called Cinnebar have brightened many science fiction publications of late. Here is one of his best—a story of an immortal jet-set, of beautiful people and fading lives, of love and pain and the attempt to forget. But we never forget ourselves, do we?

The city. Forever the city. Within it rots the tissue of dreams.

Tourmaline Hayes—"the bright and sensual, sometimes cynical Tourmaline Hayes" according to *The Guide to the Stars*—muses along the thin border between sleep and wakefulness. By choice she lies alone.

She allows the characters to press their noses against her interface with fantasy. The most affecting face is that of Francie, enduring ingenue.

Tourmaline and Francie face each other across a gray, damp beach. Francie approaches with slow, deliberate steps. Tourmaline opens her arms in welcome.

She looks at Francie's face. Through the openings where Francie's eyes should be, she can see the night sky. Tourmaline stares, strains, searches the constellations for *Speculum*, the mirror.

It's a party like all other parties, and by any other name a *Walpurgisnacht*. Yet dull. So much sin, too often, breeds ennui. Everybody knows that. Everyone . . .

". . . who is anybody," says Francie, completing an unconscious syllogism. She smiles up at Sternig the critic of gay drama. She lightly sucks in her cheeks, hoping to emphasize the high cheekbones everyone says will be beautiful later in life when the skin of her face begins to tauten. It's a harmless deceit.

The gesture doesn't benefit Sternig. Two affinity groups beyond them lounges Francie's prospective lover. Kandelman bestows largess upon three literary sycophants, who giggle shrilly. He leans back against a walnut bookcase, thumbs hooked in his belt, hips cantilevered forward. Kandelman's neglected his codpiece. It looks as though he's storing tennis balls behind the buttoned fly.

"Peanuts," says Sternig.

Francie's chin jerks up. "What?"

"Or pretzels. Whatever. You know, troll food." Sternig shrugs.

"I thought you said . . ."

"Party food progressively deteriorates," he says. "The second law of gastrodynamics."

Francie's little catamount tongue strokes nervously between lips.

"I need a drink," says Sternig. Apparently disinterested, "You want?"

"No." She smiles mechanically. "You'll excuse me? I have to use my spray."

He watches the back of her head blur in the aphrodisiac haze. Her diminishing skull takes all too long to vanish. Sternig brushes long brown hair back from his eyes. He mumbles his self-pity and yearns for beer, dark and draft.

The bathroom is decorated in a style the catalogue calls modern erotic. Surfaces gleam cold, opaque, and hard. Francie's face explodes back at her from prismed mirrors. In her peripheral vision the white-on-white tiles fade to arctic vagueness.

She takes the tube from her purse and hikes her skirt. The hiss echoes softly. Francie relaxes and enjoys a brief labial coolness. Scented excitement, no longer bland, she adjusts her panties. No hunter ever more carefully lubricated the action of her weapon.

Francie examines her reflection in the faceted medicine chest. Why is the flesh around her eyes so puffy? Her dark eyes had once snapped—a former lover told her that one passionate afternoon in a motel room in Tondelaya Beach. Francie's heart-shaped face creases in a frown. Her eyes have the puckered sheen of day-old ripe olives.

The door bangs open and shut; a ghost has passed.

"Got a spare douche?" says the newcomer.

"Need what I've got, Marlene."

Marlene removes a hairbrush from her purse. "Do you ever. Give me a shot."

"For Tourmaline?" She lazily proffers the jeweled tube. "Love to."

Marlene giggles and bares feral teeth. "Jealous, Francie? I wasn't."

Francie snaps shut the purse, barely missing Marlene's fingertips. "Shut up!"

"You're very sensitive, darling. Are *they* still sensitive?"

Francie says again, "Shut up."

The brush hisses through Marlene's light lank hair. The strokes are cadenced with her words. "I don't care, honey. Just because most guys have milk fetishes. . . . I hope it's worth it."

"It will be."

"Kandelman's big on nipples." Marlene is laughing. She drops the hairbrush and it clatters across the tile counter. *"Extremely* big."

"Too big for you?"

"Hardly," says Marlene. "He's such a complete bastard."

Francie smiles. "I can take it." She stands up.

"Want to hear a riddle?" says Marlene maliciously. "What's eight inches long and glows in the dark?"

"Glows?"

"Sorry," says Marlene. "I meant grows."

Francie looks back from the doorway. "I love it."

Sternig is talking with Tourmaline Hayes, the sex star. Half a head taller, she slouches against the piano to make him feel at ease. Sternig smiles, aware of her charity.

"I caught all your last performances."

"Not exactly your sort of thing, I'd think."

"Don't confuse the work with the man," says Sternig.

Tourmaline's eyes are matched to her name. Their corners crinkle slightly as she smiles. Sternig smiles in return, relaxing. "I know, Sternig. You love everyone, but mainly women. Do you love me?"

Smiling. "Of course."

Laughing. "Liar. You love one person. Only one."

He stiffens. "Tourmaline . . ."

"Apart from yourself, of course."

"Tourmaline, don't . . ."

"It's not as though I hate her," says Tourmaline.

"Let's talk about you," says Sternig.

"You never learn, do you?"

"I'm only trying . . ."

". . . to divert the conversation," finishes Tourmaline. "Do you know how many times we've gone through this?"

"Christ," says Sternig. "I don't want to talk about it. I don't want to think about it."

Tourmaline touches his cheek, silk to sandpaper. "The one's easy enough."

He lightly kisses her fingertips. "I'm beginning to forget the other."

"Doubly a liar." She snatches away her hand. "Sternig, Sternig, you stupid ass."

"I need another drink," Sternig says quickly. "Do you?"

"I'm not finished," she says, sloshing the glass. "And I'm not done with you either."

"Why me?" he asks.

"You're my good deed for the millennium." She tosses back her long green hair. "I can't save you from yourself, but maybe I can keep . . ." The rest is blotted by laughter. The life of the party has arrived.

"So that's exactly what I said. The bastard couldn't believe it." Secondary chuckles run through the party people. It's Jack Burton, star of the popular series "Jack Burton—

Immortal." His show has just been renewed for its one-thousandth season and this party is the celebration.

Tourmaline smiles and speaks softly, as though reporting a sporting event, "Jack Burton grins at his friends, pumps hands, kisses lips, but there's a forced quality to the gaiety. He moves across the room well attended, but the congratulations verge on the perfunctory. His eyes—and how I envy that piercing blue—sparkle with intelligence, but I see the vagueness flicker now and again. Jack Burton is like a ripe red tomato and inside him are worms."

"What?" says Sternig.

"Worms. They've begun eating through to his eyes."

Sternig grimaces. "You're morbid."

"Watch his eyes, Sternig. You'll see. Suddenly nothing there but blank holes."

"That drink," says Sternig. "I'm going to get it. Stay here. I'll bring two."

When he returns, Tourmaline Hayes still leans with her head against the piano. She accepts her new drink silently.

Sternig sips thoughtfully. "After the party . . ."

She looks at him. He cannot decipher her expression.

"After the party, I want you to go home with me."

Tourmaline smiles, more to herself than to Sternig. "I'm sorry, I can't."

Sternig would like to ask why not, but . . .

"Maybe another time," she says. "We're not ready for that. I'm going home with Marlene."

"I . . ."

She overrides him. "And your Francie will go home with Kandelman. And Jack Burton will go home with his agent. Sternig, who will take you home? Who?"

Instantly alone and lonely, Sternig would like to cry. But he can't. He's a big boy now. Has been for longer than he cares to remember. Longer than he can remember.

"Who?" Tourmaline repeats.

Sternig has to dream it, because the memory is too ancient and scoured to recall in his consciousness:

They determined to live happily ever after. Through a friend, Francie obtained the lease on a beach cottage on an isolated stretch of the coast. Sternig moved in his things from the cramped city apartment. The first few evenings they spent on the open porch watching the ocean, listening, feeling the last tailings of spray. They observed the rhythm of the waves sucking at the beach sand in millimeter portions. The house was set a hundred meters back from the water. They wouldn't have to worry for a long time.

Days, they swam in the early-morning sunshine before breakfast. Mornings were for work. Several times each week, Sternig flew the windhover into the city to see to the disposition of his column. Francie spent her mornings writing poetry and scanning tapes of her latest obsession, political history. She wrote essays which Sternig told her would be well received, had she ever bothered to submit them somewhere.

The air was heavy and sweet in the afternoon. The previous tenant had cultivated an extensive flower garden in back of the cottage. Lush beds sprawled among grassy blocks in a patchwork effect. Nothing exotic: scarlet tiger lilies, purple iris, brilliant yellow daisies. Flowers that bloomed repeatedly with a minimum of care.

Francie and Sternig made love in the grass. They lay quietly and smelled their own scent mingle with the heavy floral aroma.

"I want this to go on forever," said Francie. She looked up at her lover. "Can't it?"

"Yes," said Sternig, not then understanding the deceit of time.

Like all Sternig's dreams, it fades with awakening, leaving no specific words or images; only feelings.

Kandelman admires her breasts. He would touch them already, but etiquette demands a delay. Still, fifty percent of his eye contact is below her collar bone. Under his gaze, erectile tissue stiffens and her nipples poke against soft fabric. She loves it.

"What are you writing now?" Francie asks.

"I'm well into the new novel," says Kandelman. "It's a psychosexual thing."

"That's very interesting." Francie angles her chin, knowing her cheekbones appear to advantage. "What's it about?"

"Brothers and sisters. That's about all I can tell you at this point. The book's writing itself. I've got very little to do with the process, aside from feeding in the paper."

"Have you picked a title?"

"Brothers and Sisters, I think."

"Oh." Francie is losing interest in the novel. Unless, of course, Kandelman should volunteer a précis of a titillating passage.

"It's not really erotica," he says, "though it might sound like it from the title."

"Oh," she says vaguely. "I thought it might be, from the title."

"It may turn out that way," he hastens to say. "But for now it's a very serious book."

She says seriously, "Erotica *can* be serious."

He stares at her chest. Francie's breasts have assumed an orogenic significance in his mind. They are large, yet possess no hint of sag. They project without visible support. Kandelman wonders silently that he has not noticed them before this party.

"I think it can," Francie continues.

"What?" Kandelman breaks free of his preoccupation. "Oh yes. Of course it can."

"I'd like to see you write a really erotic book."

"Well," says Kandelman.

"I'd like to help you with it."

Kandelman realizes he could have predicted the entire sequence of conversation and is glad that he didn't.

The party is so brittle, thinks Sternig, at any moment it will shatter like hard candy. The great marble hall is festooned with streamers of candy-stripe crêpe. Lighter-than-air balloons, fashioned in the image of extinct beasts, float from tethers. Sternig sips his drink in the shadow of a hippogriff.

With displeasure he stares across the swirling mass of the party at Francie and Kandelman, animatedly talking. They sit close together on a low foam couch, beneath the spread-antlered shelter of an inflated elk.

"Bitch," says Sternig.

"Who?" says Tourmaline. "Kandelman or your Francie?"

"Stop it." Sternig frowns. "She's not mine."

"Wasn't she?"

When did she go home with me? Sternig wonders. There was a time . . . Jack Burton was celebrating one of his renewals. She didn't go home with me, but we went to the beach from the party. Together . . .

> They drove out of the city on the Klein Expressway. He drove Francie's car, a low and powerful convertible. At speed he drifted it around the tight curves of each cloverleaf as the expressway redoubled upon itself. Francie cuddled against him, laughing, whispering in his ear. They exited at Tondelaya Beach, and between the towering red bluffs and the flat sea found a motel.
>
> Light, reflecting from the water, rippled across the ceiling. He gently lowered her to the bed and began to undo her hooks and eyes and buttons. She smiled up at him and he told Francie how her dark eyes were snapping with excitement.
>
> Soon, as he lay beside her, his own excitement became too great and he turned away, uncertain and apologetic.
>
> "No," she said. "Don't go soft on me."
>
> But . . . "I'm sorry." He could repeat that, but there was little else to say.
>
> What she said then was too cruel for remembering.

"I remember once," says Sternig. "When . . . when . . ."

"Yes?" Tourmaline prompts.

"I can't remember," he says finally. "And I need another drink."

"Can't remember? Or won't?"

"Can't," he says. "I think it's can't. I'm not really sure. I have my mind sponged periodically. Don't you?"

Tourmaline nods. "Occasionally. As seldom as I can. I prefer to keep as many memories as possible. Otherwise I tend to repeat my mistakes."

"In time," says Sternig, "we all repeat."

"Some of us more often than others." She gestures across the hall. "Francie goes to the sponge once a year, maybe more. I suspect her of monthly visits, even weekly."

"I suppose she doesn't like her memories," he says.

"She overdoes the forgetting. Her mind is always fresh for the next party. All washed, whirled, fluffed, tumbled, and spun dry. It could make me sad."

"It doesn't."

"No," Tourmaline says.

"You shouldn't hate her . . ." Sternig starts to say.

"Shut up," but her voice is still soft. "I know. Now get yourself that drink."

Periodically, but never so often as to compromise the privacy of the place, Tourmaline came to visit at the beach cottage. More than almost anything else, she loved to swim naked in the sea. Late in the afternoon, she lay with Francie on the swimming platform while Sternig fixed supper on the shore. She massaged the taut muscles of Francie's neck with strong, gentle fingers.

"Tell me why you're upset."

Francie denied it.

"No," Tourmaline said. "I've known you too long and too well."

Francie was silent for a while, allowing her head to roll with the kneading of Tourmaline's fingers. "Are you afraid of dying?"

Tourmaline's voice was surprised. "Not any more."

"Not your body," said Francie. "I mean you."

"My mind?" Francie didn't answer. Tourmaline continued. "I'll think about it eventually."

"I've thought," said Francie, "and I'm afraid."

"Then for now, forget it."

"My father, did you know him?"

"No."

"He was too old for the treatments," said Francie, "but he lived well into his second century. As he grew older, something happened with his mind."

"Senility."

"That's it. He stayed with us and I watched him every day. I had to be extraordinarily quiet, or he would become upset. At times he didn't know me."

Tourmaline stroked Francie's hair soothingly. "Wasn't it a peaceful and gentle decline?"

"It was decay," said Francie, beginning to weep and muffling her voice in the plush towel. "He was buried when he was a hundred and thirty. My father died long before that."

Tourmaline kissed Francie gently. "Don't think about it," she said again. "Don't think."

Jack Burton intimidates. More than two meters tall, the Network star is proportionately muscled, and that muscle tissue is in exquisite tone. He does all his own stunt work. Only his flame-red hair is fake. Burton has backed Francie and Kandelman into a corner. Drunkenly, gait unsteady, he perorates:

"So I told them at the Network, 'Goddammit, guys, this is the best script we've picked up in the century. It's got drama, it's got meaning, it's got—goddammit—true seriousness.' You know what those bastards said?"

"No," Francie says, bored.

"Mannie!" Kandelman yells. "Get over here."

"They said," Burton continues. "They said . . . you won't believe what they said. The bastards."

Kandelman peeks past Burton's shoulder. "Goddammit, Mannie!"

"The bastards said it'd hurt my image."

Francie giggles. "We love your image, Jack."

"After all the shit melodrama. This was going to be *something*. A complete turning point for me—I mean, for the character. But the Network . . ."

Mannie arrives, agent, manager, keeper, lover. He puts his manicured hand on Burton's arm. "Party's over, Jack. Time to go home."

Burton's eyes widen maniacally, staring at the pair in the corner. He ignores Mannie. "The realization, you know? All cells in the body can regenerate. Anything can be renewed. Anything but brain cells."

Mannie's grip tightens. "Come on, Jack."

"An epiphany: when they die, they die. Forever, goddammit."

"Forget it," says Mannie. "Now come on."

"Forever." Burton's chin drops, the animation leaves his face. He begins to weep softly. Mannie, short and burly, leads Jack Burton away like a draft animal. They disappear in the crowd.

"Cortex," says Francie. "Gray matter." She dredges the shibboleths from some vagrant memory, then looks brightly up at Kandelman for approval.

"Cerebrum," says Kandelman sourly.

Francie doesn't really understand the game. "What?"

"Forget it." He stares speculatively at her breasts. "Come on. Let's go for a drive."

The party pavilion smolders with the muted colors of a thousand simulated tropical birds. Over the crowd-mutter sounds the whir of wings. Francie and Kandelman exit between twin columns of whirling doves. Feather-light touches brush against clothing.

Sternig watches. His jealousy is deeply embedded. The pair disappears beyond the pavilion and Sternig turns back to Tourmaline and his ever-present drink. Aware of her eyes, he frowns self-consciously. Her face betrays no judgment.

Yes, there was a time. . . . When was it, he wonders, or when will it be. A time, together. . . .

They hired a room, not on the water this time, but at an inn near the desert. They spent an hour wandering among the dunes. Francie wore her sunsuit, narrow yellow bands across the mahogany of her flesh, dark wood-stain skin that took on an added sheen of sweat.

She laughed and rolled down a slope, coming up at the dune's base with her skin lightly dusted with sand. She brushed the grit away from her eyes. "Let's go back to the room," she said. "I want a shower."

Out of the languorous heat, bodies clean and oiled, they made love. Francie shrieked and thrashed and bit and moaned and sucked and scratched. Eventually, during a quietus, he asked her if it had been good, and she, hesitating a long minute, finally answered, no, not exactly. He asked why not and she replied that she was never quite satisfied. He prodded for details. She attempted to explain.

"Sisyphic orgasm," he mused aloud.

She wanted to know what that meant so he began to explain the legend. She grew bored and touched his body, again hungry. He stopped talking and tried to kiss each inch of her skin.

Finally—again—she drew back shuddering from the brink.

As he was about to drift into sleep, Francie asked him to tell her something beautiful.

"There is no greater sorrow than to recall, in misery, the time when we were happy."

"That's pretty."

"It's Dante," he said.

"Poor Sternig," says Tourmaline.

"Don't pity me."

"I don't. I hate pity. I'm only concerned."

Sternig scowls and says, "Don't be concerned about me."

She ruffles his hair slightly, as though he were a child, then runs an index finger along the underline of his jaw. "I like you, Sternig. You remind me of an ancient friend. I hate to see you hurting yourself, replaying old mistakes again and again."

"What happened to your friend?"

"Metaphorically dead," says Tourmaline flatly. "I think.

Maybe he's mad and locked away somewhere. Or mad and running loose."

Sternig says, "I know what I'm doing."

"No," she says, "you don't. You may think you do."

"You think I should forget about Francie."

"Yes," she says patiently. "Yes. That's it."

"And if I don't?"

"You'll lose your mind, your soul, whatever, you'll lose it."

Sternig says thoughtfully, "I don't know."

Her brow creases with exasperation and anger. "Sternig, get off the carousel!"

Backseat sex, adolescence recollected in senility. Kandelman wheels Francie's car onto an eroded bluff overlooking the sea. Tonight the water is glassy. For a brief time they stare at the reflected stars extending out to the horizon.

Francie's gambit, "It's awfully beautiful."

Kandelman inwardly winces. "No more so than you."

"No talking," says Francie. "Please love me." She lies across the seat so her head settles in Kandelman's lap. She wonders when she last used the spray and how she smells.

Kandelman touches her hair, lifts her face toward him, kisses her tenderly at first, then harder. She lies back and he begins to massage her body, starting with her thighs. Tiny animal cries come from Francie's throat; she shivers as though with a chill. Kandelman's fingers stroke and stroke. He will save those wondrous breasts for the last, a gourmet dessert.

But when he does touch those breasts, naked to his eyes for the first time, his hands freeze in mid-motion. He again tentatively touches the breasts. And again stops.

Eyes closed, Francie says, "What's wrong?"

"They don't feel right," says Kandelman.

Francie opens her eyes. "Don't you like them?"

"They look great. But there's something . . ."

"I had them fixed just for you," cries Francie.

"Such a strange feel." Kandelman gingerly touches her with a finger.

Francie says angrily, "They're fine. They're nonallergenic. They're the best alloplastics I could . . ."

Kandelman interrupts. "They're not right. Something unnatural . . ."

"The nipples are electrostimulating. They're wired to . . ."

"I want a woman," says Kandelman.

Francie resorts to tears and Kandelman strokes her hair. She stops crying abruptly, raises her head, and extends an investigatory hand. "No," she says. "Don't go soft on me."

He tries to pass it off wittily, but fumbles. While the silence lengthens, he stares out at the ocean. After a minute or two, he says, "How about a little game of stiff 'n' whiff?"

"Fuck you," she says.

Silence resumes until Kandelman, uncomfortable, shifts his position. Francie sighs, sits erect, and gazes out the window.

"Let's go back to the party."

The dance floor seems suspended in night. Tourmaline and Sternig sit at a table on the periphery. Couples drift past; groups, an occasional single.

"Sponge and renewal," says Tourmaline. They've been talking of the past again. "But time wears deeply. We tend to keep our lives in endless repetitions. The grooves are too deeply etched. It takes a supreme act of will to break free."

"I don't have that will," Sternig says. "I know that now."

"You knew that before. I can remember. Can't you?"

He looks at her mutely.

"How can you know," she asks, "but still not act on it?"

Sternig sees Francie waiting on the opposite side of the dance floor. She waves to him. He stands and looks bleakly down at Tourmaline. "Next time around, help me? Please?" He stammers slightly.

"Next time around," she says. "We can try."

Sternig leaves her. Halfway across the floor, he stops among the whirling dancers and smiles briefly and sadly back at Tourmaline.

She watches Francie and Sternig disappear in the dark.

What she says is, "People receive the kind of lovers they deserve," but she knows she doesn't feel that. Tourmaline sighs; then scans the party crowd, seeking out the clean beauty of Marlene's bright hair.

Eurema's Dam

R. A. Lafferty

R. A. Lafferty's people have the larger-than-life quality of
fables, or shaggy dog stories; he brings science fiction back
to its roots in the tall tale. Here's one about a man so dumb
he had to invent machines to think for him . . . clever, complicated machines, much more ingenious than he. Naturally
they despised him. Naturally they ruled him. But things don't always continue "naturally" in Lafferty's stories.

He was about the last of them.

What? The last of the great individualists? The last of the
true creative geniuses of the century? The last of the sheer
precursors?

No. No. He was the last of the dolts.

Kids were being born smarter all the time when he came
along, and they would be so forevermore. He was about the
last dumb kid ever born.

Even his mother had to admit that Albert was a slow child.
What else can you call a boy who doesn't begin to talk till
he is four years old, who won't learn to handle a spoon till
he is six, who can't operate a doorknob till he is eight? What

else can you say about one who put his shoes on the wrong feet and walked in pain? And who had to be told to close his mouth after yawning?

Some things would always be beyond him—like whether it was the big hand or the little hand of the clock that told the hours. But this wasn't something serious. He never did care what time it was.

When, about the middle of his ninth year, Albert made a breakthrough at telling his right hand from his left, he did it by the most ridiculous set of mnemonics ever put together. It had to do with the way dogs turn around before lying down, the direction of whirlpools and whirlwinds, the side a cow is milked from and a horse is mounted from, the direction of twist of oak and sycamore leaves, the maze patterns of rock moss and tree moss, the cleavage of limestone, the direction of a hawk's wheeling, a shrike's hunting, and a snake's coiling (remembering that the Mountain Boomer is an exception), the lay of cedar fronds and balsam fronds, the twist of a hole dug by a skunk and by a badger (remembering pungently that skunks sometimes use old badger holes). Well, Albert finally learned to remember which was right and which was left, but an observant boy would have learned his right hand from his left without all that nonsense.

Albert never learned to write a readable hand. To get by in school he cheated. From a bicycle speedometer, a midget motor, tiny eccentric cams, and batteries stolen from his grandfather's hearing aid Albert made a machine to write for him. It was small as a doodlebug and fitted onto pen or pencil so that Albert could conceal it with his fingers. It formed the letters beautifully as Albert had set the cams to follow a copybook model. He triggered the different letters with keys no bigger than whiskers. Sure it was crooked, but what else can you do when you're too dumb to learn how to write passably?

Albert couldn't figure at all. He had to make another machine to figure for him. It was a palm-of-the-hand thing that would add and subtract and multiply and divide. The next year when he was in the ninth grade they gave him algebra, and he had to devise a flipper to go on the end of his gadget to work quadratic and simultaneous equations. If it weren't for such cheating Albert wouldn't have gotten any marks at all in school.

He had another difficulty when he came to his fifteenth year. People, that is an understatement. There should be a stronger word than "difficulty" for it. He was afraid of girls.

What to do?

"I will build me a machine that is not afraid of girls," Albert said. He set to work on it. He had it nearly finished when a thought came to him. "But *no* machine is afraid of girls. How will this help me?"

His logic was at fault and analogy broke down. He did what he always did. He cheated.

He took the programming rollers from an old player piano in the attic, found a gear case that would serve, used magnetized sheets instead of perforated music rolls, fed a copy of Wormwood's *Logic* into the matrix, and he had a logic machine that would answer questions.

"What's the matter with me that I'm afraid of girls?" Albert asked his logic machine.

"Nothing the matter with you," the logic machine told him. "It's logical to be afraid of girls. They seem pretty spooky to me too."

"But what can I do about it?"

"Wait for time and circumstance. They sure are slow. Unless you want to cheat . . ."

"Yes, yes, what then?"

"Build a machine that looks just like you, Albert, and talks just like you. Only make it smarter than you are, and not bashful. And, ah, Albert, there's a special thing you'd better put into it in case things go wrong. I'll whisper it to you. It's dangerous."

So Albert made Little Danny, a dummy who looked like him and talked like him, only he was smarter and not bashful. He filled Little Danny with quips from *Mad* magazine and from *Quip,* and then they were set.

Albert and Little Danny went to call on Alice.

"Why, he's wonderful!" Alice said. "Why can't you be like

that, Albert? Aren't you wonderful, Little Danny? Why do you have to be so stupid, Albert, when Little Danny is so wonderful?"

"I, uh, uh, I don't know," Albert said, "uh, uh, uh."

"He sounds like a fish with the hiccups," Little Danny said.

"You do, Albert, really you do!" Alice screamed. "Why can't you say smart things like Little Danny does, Albert? Why are you so stupid?"

This wasn't working out very well, but Albert kept with it. He programmed Little Danny to play the ukulele and to sing. He wished that he could program himself to do it. Alice loved everything about Little Danny, but she paid no attention to Albert. And one day Albert had had enough.

"What- wha- what do we need with this dummy?" Albert asked. "I just made him to am- to amu- to make you laugh. Let's go off and leave him."

"Go off with you, Albert?" Alice asked. "But you're so stupid. I tell you what. Let's you and me go off and leave Albert, Little Danny. We can have more fun without him."

"Who needs him?" Little Danny asked. "Get lost, Buster."

Albert walked away from them. He was glad that he'd taken his logic machine's advice as to the special thing to be built into Little Danny. He walked fifty steps. A hundred. "Far enough," Albert said, and he pushed a button in his pocket.

Nobody but Albert and his logic machine ever did know what that explosion was. Tiny wheels out of Little Danny and small pieces of Alice rained down a little later, but there weren't enough fragments for anyone to identify.

Albert had learned one lesson from his logic machine: never make anything that you can't unmake.

Well, Albert finally grew to be a man, in years at least. He would always have something about him of a very awkward teenager. And yet he fought his own war against those who were teenagers in years, and defeated them completely. There was enmity between them forever. He hadn't been a very well adjusted adolescent, and he hated the memory of it. And nobody ever mistook him for an adjusted man.

Albert was too awkward to earn a living at an honest trade. He was reduced to peddling his little tricks and contrivances to shysters and promoters. But he did back into a sort of fame, and he did become burdened with wealth.

He was too stupid to handle his own monetary affairs, but he built an actuary machine to do his investing and became rich by accident; he built the damned thing too good and he regretted it.

Albert became one of that furtive group that has saddled us with all the mean things in our history. There was that Punic who couldn't learn the rich variety of hieroglyphic characters and who devised the crippled short alphabet for wan-wits. There was the nameless Arab who couldn't count beyond ten and who set up the ten-number system for babies and idiots. There was the double-Dutchman with his movable type who drove fine copy out of the world. Albert was of their miserable company.

Albert himself wasn't much good at anything. But he had in himself a low knack for making machines that were good at everything.

His machines did a few things. You remember that anciently there was smog in the cities. Oh, it could be drawn out of the air easily enough. All it took was a tickler. Albert made a tickler machine. He would set it fresh every morning. It would clear the air in a circle three hundred yards around his hovel and gather a little over a ton of residue every twenty-four hours. This residue was rich in large polysyllabic molecules which one of his chemical machines could use.

"Why can't you clear all the air?" the people asked him.

"This is as much of the stuff as Clarence Deoxyribonucleiconibus needs every day," Albert said. That was the name of this particular chemical machine.

"But we die from the smog," the people told him. "Have mercy on us."

"Oh, all right," Albert said. He turned it over to one of his reduplicating machines to make as many copies as were necessary.

You remember that once there was a teenager problem?
You remember when those little buggers used to be mean?
Albert got enough of them. There was something ungainly
about them that reminded him too much of himself. He
made a teenager of his own. It was rough. To the others it
looked like one of themselves, the ring in the left ear, the
dangling side-locks, the brass knucks and the long knife, the
guitar pick to jab in the eye. But it was incomparably
rougher than the human teenagers. It terrorized all in the
neighborhood and made them behave, and dress like real
people. There was one thing about the teenage machine that
Albert made. It was made of such polarized metal and glass
that it was invisible except to teenager eyes.

"Why is your neighborhood different?" the people asked
him. "Why are there such good and polite teenagers in
your neighborhood and such mean ones everywhere else?
It's as though something had spooked all those right around
here."

"Oh, I thought I was the only one who didn't like the
regular kind," Albert said.

"Oh no, no," the people said. "If there is anything at all
you can do about it . . ."

So Albert turned his mostly invisible teenager machine
over to one of his reduplicating machines to make as many
copies as were necessary, and set up one in every neighborhood. From that day to this the teenagers have all been
good and polite and a little bit frightened. But there is no
evidence of what keeps them that way except an occasional
eye dangling from the jab of an invisible guitar pick.

So the two most pressing problems of the latter part of
the twentieth century were solved, but accidentally and to
the credit of no one.

As the years went by, Albert felt his inferiority most
when in the presence of his own machines, particularly those
in the form of men. Albert just hadn't their urbanity or
sparkle or wit. He was a clod beside them, and they made
him feel it.

Why not? One of Albert's devices sat in the President's

Cabinet. One of them was on the High Council of World-Watchers that kept the peace everywhere. One of them presided at Riches Unlimited, that private-public-international instrument that guaranteed reasonable riches to everyone in the world. One of them was the guiding hand in the Health and Longevity Foundation that provided those things to everyone. Why should not such splendid and successful machines look down on their shabby uncle who had made them?

"I'm rich by a curious twist," Albert said to himself one day, "and honored through a mistake of circumstance. But there isn't a man or a machine in the world who is really my friend. A book here tells how to make friends, but I can't do it that way. I'll make one my own way."

So Albert set out to make a friend.

He made Poor Charles, a machine as stupid and awkward and inept as himself. "Now I will have a companion," Albert said, but it didn't work. Add two zeros together and you still have zero. Poor Charles was too much like Albert to be good for anything.

Poor Charles! Unable to think, he made a—(*but wait a moleskin-gloved minute here, Colonel, this isn't going to work at all*)—he made a machi—(*but isn't this the same blamed thing all over again?*)—he made a machine to think for him and to . . .

Hold it, hold it! That's enough. Poor Charles was the only machine that Albert ever made that was dumb enough to do a thing like that.

"Well, whatever it was, the machine that Poor Charles made was in control of the situation and of Poor Charles when Albert came onto them accidentally. The machine's machine, the device that Poor Charles had constructed to think for him, was lecturing Poor Charles in a humiliating way.

"Only the inept and the deficient will invent," that damned machine's machine was droning. "The Greeks in their high period did not invent. They used neither adjunct power nor instrumentation. They used, as intelligent men or machines will always use, slaves. They did not descend to gadgets.

They, who did the difficult with ease, did not seek the easier way.

"But the incompetent will invent. The insufficient will invent. The depraved will invent. And knaves will invent."

Albert, in a seldom fit of anger, killed them both. But he knew that the machine of his machine had spoken the truth.

Albert was very much cast down. A more intelligent man would have had a hunch as to what was wrong. Albert had only a hunch that he was not very good at hunches and would never be. Seeing no way out, he fabricated a machine and named it Hunchy.

In most ways this was the worst machine he ever made. In building it he tried to express something of his unease for the future. It was an awkward thing in mind and mechanism, a misfit.

His more intelligent machines gathered around and hooted at him while he put it together.

"Boy! Are you lost!" they taunted. "That thing is a primitive! To draw its power from the ambient! We talked you into throwing that away twenty years ago and setting up coded power for all of us."

"Uh—someday there may be social disturbances and all centers of power and apparatuses seized," Albert stammered. "But Hunchy would be able to operate if the whole world were wiped smooth."

"It isn't even tuned to our information matrix," they jibed. "It's worse than Poor Charles. That stupid thing practically starts from scratch."

"Maybe there'll be a new kind of itch for it," said Albert.

"It's not even housebroken!" the urbane machines shouted their indignation. "Look at that! Some sort of primitive lubrication all over the floor."

"Remembering my childhood, I sympathize," Albert said.

"What's it good for?" they demanded.

"Ah—it gets hunches," Albert mumbled.

"Duplication!" they shouted. "That's all you're good for yourself, and not very good at that. We suggest an election to replace you as—pardon our laughter—head of these enterprises."

"Boss, I got a hunch how we can block them there," the unfinished Hunchy whispered.

"They're bluffing," Albert whispered back. "My first logic machine taught me never to make anything I can't unmake. I've got them there, and they know it. I wish I could think up things like that myself."

"Maybe there will come an awkward time and I will be good for something," Hunchy said.

Only once, and that rather late in life, did a sort of honesty flare up in Albert. He did one thing (and it was a dismal failure) on his own. That was the night in the year of the double millennium when Albert was presented with the Finnerty-Hochmann Trophy, the highest award that the intellectual world could give. Albert was certainly an odd choice for it, but it had been noticed that almost every basic invention for thirty years could be traced back to him or to the devices with which he had surrounded himself.

You know the trophy. Atop it was Eurema, the synthetic Greek goddess of invention, with arms spread as though she would take flight. Below this was a stylized brain cut away to show the convoluted cortex. And below this was the coat of arms of the Academicians: Ancient Scholar rampant (argent); the Anderson Analyzer sinister (gules); the Mondeman Space-Drive dexter (vair). It was a very fine work by Groben, his ninth period.

Albert had the speech composed for him by his speech-writing machine, but for some reason he did not use it. He went on his own, and that was disaster. He got to his feet when he was introduced, and he stuttered and spoke nonsense.

"Ah—only the sick oyster produces nacre," he said, and they all gaped at him. What sort of beginning for a speech was that? "Or do I have the wrong creature?" Albert asked weakly.

"Eurema does not look like that!" Albert gawked out and pointed suddenly at the trophy. "No, no, that isn't her at all.

Eurema walks backward and is blind. And her mother is a brainless hulk."

Everybody was watching him with pained expression.

"Nothing rises without a leaven," Albert tried to explain, "but the yeast is itself a fungus and a disease. You be regularizers all, splendid and supreme. But you cannot live without the irregulars. You will die, and who will tell you that you are dead? When there are no longer any deprived or insufficient, *who will invent?* What will you do when there are none of us defectives left? Who will leaven your lump then?"

"Are you unwell?" the master of ceremonies asked him quietly. "Should you not make an end of it? People will understand."

"Of course I'm unwell. Always have been," Albert said. "What good would I be otherwise? You set the ideal that all should be healthy and well adjusted. No! No! Were we all well adjusted, we would ossify and die. The world is kept healthy only by some of the unhealthy minds lurking in it. The first implement made by man was not a scraper or celt or stone knife. It was a crutch, and it wasn't devised by a hale man."

"Perhaps you should rest," a functionary said in a low voice, for this sort of rambling nonsense talk had never been heard at an awards dinner before.

"Know you," said Albert, "that it is not the fine bulls and wonderful cattle who make the new paths. Only a crippled calf makes a new path. In everything that survives there must be an element of the incongruous. Hey, you know the woman who said, 'My husband is incongruous, but I never liked Washington in the summertime.' "

Everybody gazed at him in stupor.

"That's the first joke I ever made," Albert said lamely. "My joke-making machine makes them lots better than I do." He paused and gaped, and gulped a big breath. "Dolts!" he croaked out fiercely then. "What will you do for dolts when the last of us is gone? How will you survive without us?"

Albert had finished. He gaped and forgot to close his mouth. They led him back to his seat. His publicity machine explained that Albert was tired from overwork, and then the thing passed around copies of the speech that Albert was supposed to have given.

It had been an unfortunate episode. How noisome it is that the innovators are never great men. And the great men are never good for anything but just being great men.

In that year a decree went forth from Caesar that a census of the whole country should be taken. The decree was from Cesare Panebianco, the President of the country; it was the decimal year proper for the census, and there was nothing unusual about the decree. Certain provisions, however, were made for taking a census of the drifters and decrepits who were usually missed, to examine them and to see why they were so. It was in the course of this that Albert was picked up. If any man ever looked like a drifter and a decrepit, it was Albert.

Albert was herded in with other derelicts, sat down at a table, and asked tortuous questions. As:

"What is your name?"

He almost muffed that one, but he rallied and answered, "Albert."

"What time is it by that clock?"

They had him there in his old weak spot. Which hand was which? He gaped and didn't answer.

"Can you read?"

"Not without my . . ." Albert began. "I don't have with me my . . . No, I can't read very well by myself."

"Try."

They gave him a paper to mark up with true and false questions. Albert marked them all true, believing that he would have half of them right. But they were all false. The regularized people are partial to falsehood. Then they gave him a supply-the-word test on proverbs.

"A ------ in time saves nine" contained more mathematics than Albert could handle. "There appear to be six unknowns," he told himself, "and only one positive value, nine. The equating verb 'saves' is a vague one. I cannot solve this equation. I am not even sure that it is an equation. If only I had with me my . . ."

But he hadn't any of his gadgets or machines with him. He was on his own. He left half a dozen more proverb fill-ins blank. Then he saw the chance to recoup. Nobody is so dumb as not to know one answer if enough questions are asked.

"--------- is the mother of invention," it said.

"Stupidity," Albert wrote in his weird ragged hand. Then he sat back in triumph. "I know that Eurema and her mother," he snickered. "Man, how I do know them!"

But they marked him wrong on that one too. He had missed every answer to every test. They began to fix him a ticket to a progressive booby hatch where he might learn to do something with his hands, his head being hopeless.

A couple of Albert's urbane machines came down and got him out of it. They explained that, while he was a drifter and derelict, yet he was a rich drifter and derelict and that he was even a man of some note.

"He doesn't look it, but he really is—pardon our laughter —a man of some importance," one of the fine machines explained. "He has to be told to close his mouth after he has yawned, but for all that he is the winner of the Finnerty-Hochmann Award. We will be responsible for him."

Albert was miserable as his fine machines took him out, especially when they asked that he walk three or four steps behind them and not seem to be with them. They gave him some pretty rough banter and turned him into a squirming worm of a man. Albert left them and went to a little hideout he kept.

"I'll blow my crawfishing brains out," he swore. "The humiliation is more than I can bear. Can't do it myself, though. I'll have to have it done."

He set to work building a device in his hideout.

"What you doing, boss?" Hunchy asked him. "I had a hunch you'd come here and start building something."

"Building a machine to blow my pumpkin-picking brains

out," Albert shouted. "I'm too yellow to do it myself."

"Boss, I got a hunch there's something better to do. Let's have some fun."

"Don't believe I know how to," Albert said thoughtfully. "I built a fun machine once to do it for me. He had a real revel till he flew apart, but he never seemed to do anything for me."

"This fun will be for you and me. Consider the world spread out. What is it?"

"It's a world too fine for me to live in any longer," Albert said. "Everything and all the people are perfect, and all alike. They're at the top of the heap. They've won it all and arranged it all neatly. There's no place for a clutter-up like me in the world. So I get out."

"Boss, I've got a hunch that you're seeing it wrong. You've got better eyes than that. Look again, real canny, at it. Now what do you see?"

"Hunchy, Hunchy, is that possible? Is that really what it is? I wonder why I never noticed it before. That's the way of it, though, now that I look closer.

"Six billion patsies waiting to be took! Six billion patsies without a defense of any kind! A couple of guys out for some fun, man, they could mow them down like fields of Albert-Improved Concho Wheat!"

"Boss, I've got a hunch this is what I was made for. The world sure has been getting stuffy. Let's tie into it and eat off the top layer. Man, we can cut a swath!"

"We'll inaugurate a new era!" Albert gloated. "We'll call it the Turning of the Worm. We'll have fun, Hunchy. We'll gobble them up like goobers. How come I never saw it like that before? Six billion patsies!"

The twenty-first century began on this rather odd note.

Zero Gee

Ben Bova

Here's a detailed, believable story of our near-future space program, and of an astronaut who wanted to pioneer in a new way: to be the first man to experience sex in free fall. But for that he needed a woman, and this story is about her too.

Joe Tenny looked like a middle linebacker for the Pittsburgh Steelers. Sitting in the cool shadows of the Astro Motel's bar, swarthy, barrel-built, scowling face clamped on a smoldering cigar, he would never be taken for that rarest of all birds: a good engineer who is also a good military officer.

"Afternoon, Major."

Tenny turned on his stool to see old Cy Calder, the dean of the press service reporters covering the base.

"Hi. Whatcha drinking?"

"I'm working," Calder answered with dignity. But he settled his once-lanky frame onto the next stool.

"Double scotch," Tenny called to the bartender. "And refill mine."

"An officer and a gentleman," murmured Calder. His voice was gravelly, matching his face.

As the bartender slid the drinks to them, Tenny said, "You wanna know who got the assignment."

"I told you I'm working."

Tenny grinned. "Keep your mouth shut 'til tomorrow? Murdock'll make the official announcement then, at his press conference."

"If you can save me the tedium of listening to the good Colonel for two hours to get a single name out of him, I'll buy the next round, shine your shoes for a month, and arrange to lose an occasional poker pot to you."

"The hell you will!"

Calder shrugged. Tenny took a long pull on his drink. Calder did likewise.

"Okay. You'll find out anyway. But keep it quiet until Murdock's announcement. It's going to be Kinsman."

Calder put his glass down on the bar carefully. "Chester A. Kinsman, the pride of the Air Force? That's hard to believe."

"Murdock picked him."

"I know this mission is strictly for publicity," Calder said, "but Kinsman? In orbit for three days with *Life* magazine's prettiest female? Does Murdock want publicity or a paternity suit?"

"Come on, Chet's not that bad . . ."

"Oh no? From the stories I hear about your few weeks up at the NASA Ames center, Kinsman cut a swath from Berkeley to North Beach."

Tenny countered, "He's young and good-looking. And the girls haven't had many single astronauts to play with. NASA's gang is a bunch of old farts compared to my kids. But Chet's the best of the bunch, no fooling."

Calder looked unconvinced.

"Listen. When we were training at Edwards, know what Kinsman did? Built a biplane, an honest-to-God replica of a Spad fighter. From the ground up. He's a solid citizen."

"Yes, and then he played Red Baron for six weeks. Didn't he get into trouble for buzzing an airliner?"

Tenny's reply was cut off by a burst of talk and laughter. Half a dozen lean, lithe young men in Air Force blues—

captains, all of them—trotted down the carpeted stairs that led into the bar.

"There they are," said Tenny. "You can ask Chet about it yourself."

Kinsman looked no different from the other Air Force astronauts. Slightly under six feet tall, thin with the leanness of youth, dark hair cut in the short flat military style, blue-gray eyes, long bony face. He was grinning broadly at the moment, as he and the other five astronauts grabbed chairs in one corner of the bar and called their orders to the lone bartender.

Calder took his drink and headed for their table, followed by Major Tenny.

"Hold it," one of the captains called out. "Here comes the press."

"Tight security."

"Why boys," Calder tried to make his rasping voice sound hurt, "don't you trust me?"

Tenny pushed a chair toward the newsman and took another one for himself. Straddling it, he told the captains, "It's okay. I spilled it to him."

"How much he pay you, boss?"

"That's between him and me."

As the bartender brought a tray of drinks, Calder said, "Let the Fourth Estate pay for this round, gentlemen. I want to pump some information out of you."

"That might take a lot of rounds."

To Kinsman, Calder said, "Congratulations, my boy. Colonel Murdock must think very highly of you."

Kinsman burst out laughing. "Murdock? You should've seen his face when he told me it was going to be me."

"Looked like he was sucking on lemons."

Tenny explained: "The choice for this flight was made mostly by computer. Murdock wanted to be absolutely fair, so he put everybody's performance ratings into the computer and out came Kinsman's name. If he hadn't made so much noise about being impartial, he could've reshuffled the cards and tried again. But I was right there when the machine finished its run, so he couldn't back out of it."

Calder grinned. "All right then, the computer thinks highly of you, Chet. I suppose that's still something of an honor."

"More like a privilege. I've been watching that *Life* chick all through her training. She's ripe."

"She'll look even better up in orbit."

"Once she takes off the pressure suit . . . et cetera."

"Hey, y'know, nobody's ever done it in orbit."

"Yeah . . . free fall, zero gravity."

Kinsman looked thoughtful. "Adds a new dimension to the problem, doesn't it?"

"Three-dimensional." Tenny took the cigar butt from his mouth and laughed.

Calder got up slowly from his chair and silenced the others. Looking down fondly on Kinsman, he said:

"My boy—back in 1915, in London, I became a charter member of the Mile High Club. At an altitude of exactly 5280 feet, while circling St. Paul's, I successfully penetrated an Army nurse in an open cockpit . . . despite fogged goggles, cramped working quarters, and a severe case of windburn.

"Since then, there's been damned little to look forward to. The skindivers claimed a new frontier, but in fact they are retrogressing. Any sillyass dolphin can do it in the water.

"But you've got something new going for you: weightlessness. Floating around in free fall, chasing tail in three dimensions. It beggars the imagination!

"Kinsman, I pass the torch to you. To the founder of the Zero Gee Club!"

As one man, they rose and solemnly toasted Captain Kinsman.

As they sat down again, Major Tenny burst the balloon. "You guys haven't given Murdock credit for much brains. You don't think he's gonna let Chet go up with that broad all alone, do you?"

Kinsman's face fell, but the others lit up.

"It'll be a three-man mission!"

"Two men and the chick."

Tenny warned, "Now don't start drooling. Murdock wants a chaperon, not an assistant rapist."

It was Kinsman who got it first. Slouching back in his chair, chin sinking to his chest, he muttered, "Sonofabitch . . . he's sending Jill along."

A collective groan.

"Murdock made up his mind an hour ago," Tenny said. "He was stuck with you, Chet, so he hit on the chaperon idea. He's also giving you some real chores to do, to keep you busy. Like mating the power pod."

"Jill Meyers," said one of the captains disgustedly.

"She's qualified, and she's been taking the *Life* girl through her training. I'll bet she knows more about the mission than any of you guys do."

"She would."

"In fact," Tenny added maliciously, "I think she's the senior captain among you satellite-jockeys."

Kinsman had only one comment: "Shit."

The bone-rattling roar and vibration of liftoff suddenly died away. Sitting in his contour seat, scanning the banks of dials and gauges a few centimeters before his eyes, Kinsman could feel the pressure and tension slacken. Not back to normal. To zero. He was no longer plastered up against his seat, but touching it only lightly, almost floating in it, restrained only by his harness.

It was the fourth time he had felt weightlessness. It still made him smile inside the cumbersome helmet.

Without thinking about it, he touched a control stud on the chair's armrest. A maneuvering jet fired briefly and the ponderous, lovely bulk of planet Earth slid into view through the port in front of Kinsman. It curved huge and serene, blue mostly but tightly wrapped in the purest dazzling white of clouds, beautiful, peaceful, shining.

Kinsman could have watched it forever, but he heard sounds of motion in his earphones. The two girls were sitting behind him, side by side. The spacecraft cabin made a submarine look roomy: the three seats were shoehorned in among racks of instruments and equipment.

Jill Meyers, who came to the astronaut program from the Aerospace Medical Division, was officially second pilot and biomedical officer. *And chaperon,* Kinsman knew. The photographer, Linda Symmes, was simply a passenger.

Kinsman's earphones crackled with a disembodied link from Earth. "AF-9, this is ground control. We have you confirmed in orbit. Trajectory nominal. All systems go."

"Check," Kinsman said into his helmet mike.

The voice, already starting to fade, switched to ordinary conversational speech. "Looks like you're right on the money, Chet. We'll get the orbital parameters out of the computer and have 'em for you by the time you pass Ascension. You probably won't need much maneuvering to make rendezvous with the lab."

"Good. Everything here on the board looks green."

"Okay. Ground control out." Faintly. "And hey . . . good luck, Founding Father."

Kinsman grinned at that. He slid his faceplate up, loosened his harness and turned in his seat. "Okay girls, you can take off your helmets if you want to."

Jill Meyers snapped her faceplate open and started unlocking the helmet's neck seal.

"I'll go first," she said, "and then I can help Linda with hers."

"Sure you won't need any help?" Kinsman offered.

Jill pulled her helmet off. "I've had more time in orbit than you. And shouldn't you be paying attention to the instruments?"

So this is how it's going to be, Kinsman thought.

Jill's face was round and plain and bright as a new penny. Snub nose, wide mouth, short hair of undistinguished brown. Kinsman knew that under the pressure suit was a figure that could most charitably be described as ordinary.

Linda Symmes was entirely another matter. She had lifted her faceplate and was staring out at him with wide blue eyes that combined feminine curiosity with a hint of helplessness. She was tall, nearly Kinsman's own height, with thick honey-colored hair and a body that he had already memorized down to the last curve.

In her sweet, high voice she said, "I think I'm going to be sick."

"Oh for . . ."

Jill reached into the compartment between their two seats. "I'll take care of this. You stick to the controls." And she whipped a white plastic bag open and stuck it over Linda's face.

Shuddering at the thought of what could happen in zero gravity, Kinsman turned back to the control panel. He pulled his faceplate shut and turned up the air blower in his suit, trying to cut off the obscene sound of Linda's struggles.

"For Chrissake," he yelled, "unplug her radio! You want me chucking all over, too?"

"AF-9, this is Ascension."

Trying to blank his mind to what was going on behind him, Kinsman thumbed the switch on his communications panel. "Go ahead, Ascension."

For the next hour Kinsman thanked the gods that he had plenty of work to do. He matched the orbit of their three-man spacecraft to that of the Air Force orbiting laboratory, which had been up for more than a year now, and intermittently occupied by two- or three-man crews.

The lab was a fat cylindrical shape, silhouetted against the brilliant white of the cloud-decked Earth. As he pulled the spacecraft close, Kinsman could see the antennas and airlock and other odd pieces of gear that had accumulated on it. *Looking more like a junkheap every trip.* Riding behind it, unconnected in any way, was the massive cone of the new power pod.

Kinsman circled the lab once, using judicious squeezes of his maneuvering jets. He touched a command signal switch, and the lab's rendezvous radar beacon came to life, announced by a light on his control panel.

"All systems green," he said to ground control. "Everything looks okay."

"Roger, Niner. You are cleared for docking."

This was a bit more delicate. *Be helpful if Jill could read off the computer . . .*

"Distance, eighty-eight meters," Jill's voice pronounced firmly in his earphones. "Approach angle . . ."

Kinsman instinctively turned, but his helmet cut off any possible sight of her. "Hey, how's your patient?"

"Empty. I gave her a sedative. She's out."

"Okay," Kinsman said. "Let's get docked."

He inched the spacecraft into the docking collar on one end of the lab, locked on and saw the panel lights confirm that the docking was secure.

"Better get Sleeping Beauty zipped up," he told Jill as he touched the buttons that extended the flexible access tunnel from the hatch over their heads to the main hatch of the lab. The lights on the panel turned from amber to green when the tunnel locked its fittings around the lab's hatch.

Jill said, "I'm supposed to check the tunnel."

"Stay put. I'll do it." Sealing his faceplate shut, Kinsman unbuckled and rose effortlessly out of the seat to bump his helmet lightly against the overhead hatch.

"You two both buttoned tight?"

"Yes."

"Keep an eye on the air gauge." He cracked the hatch open a few millimeters.

"Pressure's okay. No red lights."

Nodding, Kinsman pushed the hatch open all the way. He pulled himself easily up and into the shoulder-wide tunnel, propelling himself down its curving length by a few flicks of his fingers against the ribbed walls.

Light and easy, he reminded himself. *No big motions, no sudden moves.*

When he reached the laboratory hatch he slowly rotated, like a swimmer doing a lazy rollover, and inspected every inch of the tunnel seal in the light of his helmet lamp. Satisfied that it was locked in place, he opened the lab hatch and pushed himself inside. Carefully, he touched his slightly adhesive boots to the plastic flooring and stood upright. His arms tended to float out, but they touched the equipment racks on either side of the narrow central passageway. Kinsman turned on the lab's interior lights, checked the air supply, pressure and temperature gauges, then shuffled back to the hatch and pushed himself through the tunnel again.

He reentered the spacecraft upside-down and had to contort himself in slow motion around the pilot's seat to regain a "normal" attitude.

"Lab's okay," he said finally. "Now how the hell do we get her through the tunnel?"

Jill had already unbuckled the harness over Linda's shoulders. "You pull, I'll push. She ought to bend around the corners all right."

And she did.

The laboratory was about the size and shape of the interior of a small transport plane. On one side, nearly its entire length was taken up by instrument racks, control equipment and the computer, humming almost inaudibly behind light plastic panels. Across the narrow separating aisle were the crew stations: control desk, two observation ports, biology and astrophysics benches. At the far end, behind a discreet curtain, was the head and a single hammock.

Kinsman sat at the control desk, in his fatigues now, one leg hooked around the webbed chair's single supporting column to keep him from floating off. He was running through a formal check of all the lab's life systems: air, water, heat, electrical power. All green lights on the main panel. Communications gear. Green. The radar screen to his left showed a single large blip close by—the power pod.

He looked up as Jill came through the curtain from the bunkroom. She was still in her pressure suit, with only the helmet removed.

"How is she?"

Looking tired, Jill answered, "Okay. Still sleeping. I think she'll be all right when she wakes up."

"She'd better be. I'm not going to have a wilting flower around here. I'll abort the mission."

"Give her a chance, Chet. She just lost her cookies when free-fall hit her. All the training in the world can't prepare you for those first few minutes."

Kinsman recalled his first orbital flight. *It doesn't shut off. You're falling. Like skiing, or sky-diving. Only better.*

Jill shuffled toward him, keeping a firm grip on the chairs in front of the work benches and the handholds set into the equipment racks.

Kinsman got up and pushed toward her. "Here, let me help you out of the suit."

"I can do it myself."

"Shut up."

After several minutes, Jill was free of the bulky suit and sitting in one of the webbed chairs in her coverall fatigues. Ducking slightly because of the curving overhead, Kinsman glided into the galley. It was about half the width of a phone booth, and not as deep nor as tall.

"Coffee, tea or milk?"

Jill grinned at him. "Orange juice."

He reached for a concentrate bag. "You're a hard girl to satisfy."

"No I'm not. I'm easy to get along with. Just one of the fellas."

Feeling slightly puzzled, Kinsman handed her the orange juice container.

For the next couple of hours they checked out the lab's equipment in detail. Kinsman was reassembling a high resolution camera after cleaning it, parts hanging in mid-air all around him as he sat intently working, while Jill was nursing a straggly looking philodendron that had been smuggled aboard and was inching from the biology bench toward the ceiling light panels. Linda pushed back the curtain from the sleeping area and stepped uncertainly into the main compartment.

Jill noticed her first. "Hi, how're you feeling?"

Kinsman looked up. She was in tight-fitting coveralls. He bounced out of his webchair toward her, scattering camera parts in every direction.

"Are you all right?" he asked.

Smiling sheepishly, "I think so. I'm rather embarrassed . . ." Her voice was high and soft.

"Oh, that's all right," Kinsman said eagerly. "It happens to practically everybody. I got sick myself my first time in orbit."

"That," said Jill as she dodged a slowly tumbling lens that ricocheted gently off the ceiling, "is a little white lie, meant to make you feel at home."

Kinsman forced himself not to frown. *Why'd Jill want to cross me?*

Jill said, "Chet, you'd better pick up those camera pieces before they get so scattered you won't be able to find them all."

He wanted to snap an answer, thought better of it, and replied simply, "Right."

As he finished the job on the camera, he took a good look at Linda. The color was back in her face. She looked steady, clear-eyed, not frightened or upset. *Maybe she'll be okay after all*. Jill made her a cup of tea, which she sipped from the lid's plastic spout.

Kinsman went to the control desk and scanned the mission schedule sheet.

"Hey Jill, it's past your bedtime."

"I'm not really very sleepy," she said.

"Maybe. But you've had a busy day, little girl. And tomorrow will be busier. Now you get your four hours, and then I'll get mine. Got to be fresh for the mating."

"Mating?" Linda asked from her seat at the far end of the aisle, a good five strides from Kinsman. Then she remembered, "Oh . . . you mean linking the pod to the laboratory."

Suppressing a half-dozen possible jokes, Kinsman nodded. "Extravehicular activity."

Jill reluctantly drifted off her webchair. "Okay, I'll sack in. I am tired, but I never seem to get really sleepy up here."

Wonder how much Murdock's told her? She's sure acting like a chaperon.

Jill shuffled into the sleeping area and pulled the curtain firmly shut. After a few moments of silence, Kinsman turned to Linda.

"Alone at last."

She smiled back.

"Uh, you just happen to be sitting where I've got to install this camera." He nudged the finished hardware so that it floated gently toward her.

She got up slowly, carefully, and stood behind the chair, holding its back with both hands as if she were afraid of falling. Kinsman slid into the webchair and stopped the camera's slow-motion flight with one hand. Working on the fixture in the bulkhead that it fit into, he asked:

"You really feel okay?"

"Yes, honestly."

"Think you'll be up to EVA tomorrow?"

"I hope so . . . I want to go outside with you."

I'd rather be inside with you. Kinsman grinned as he worked.

An hour later they were sitting side by side in front of one of the observation ports, looking out at the curving bulk of Earth, the blue and white splendor of the cloud-spangled Pacific. Kinsman had just reported to the Hawaii ground station. The mission flight plan was floating on a clipboard between the two of them. He was trying to study it, comparing the time when Jill would be sleeping with the long stretches between ground stations, when there would be no possibility of being interrupted.

"Is that land?" Linda asked, pointing to a thick band of clouds wrapping the horizon.

Looking up from the clipboard, Kinsman said, "South American coast. Chile."

"There's another tracking station there."

"NASA station. Not part of our network. We only use Air Force stations."

"Why is that?"

He felt his face frowning. "Murdock's playing soldier. This is supposed to be a strictly military operation. Not that we do anything warlike. But we run as though there weren't any civilian stations around to help us. The usual hup-two-three crap."

She laughed. "You don't agree with the Colonel?"

"There's only one thing he's done lately that I'm in complete agreement with."

"What's that?"

"Bringing you up here."

The smile stayed on her face but her eyes moved away from him. "Now you sound like a soldier."

"Not an officer and a gentleman?"

She looked straight at him again. "Let's change the subject."

Kinsman shrugged. "Sure. Okay. You're here to get a story. Murdock wants to get the Air Force as much publicity as NASA gets. And the Pentagon wants to show the world that we don't have any weapons on board. We're military, all right, but *nice* military."

"And you?" Linda asked, serious now. "What do you

want? How does an Air Force captain get into the space cadets?"

"The same way everything happens—you're in a certain place at a certain time. They told me I was going to be an astronaut. It was all part of the job . . . until my first orbital flight. Now it's a way of life."

"Really? Why is that?"

Grinning, he answered, "Wait'll we go outside. You'll find out."

Jill came back into the main cabin precisely on schedule, and it was Kinsman's turn to sleep. He seldom had difficulty sleeping on Earth, never in orbit. But he wondered about Linda's reaction to being outside while he strapped the pressure cuffs to his arms and legs. The medics insisted on them, claimed they exercised the cardiovascular system while you slept.

Damned stupid nuisance, Kinsman grumbled to himself. *Some groundbased MD's idea of how to make a name for himself.*

Finally he zippered himself into the gossamer cocoonlike hammock and shut his eyes. He could feel the cuffs pumping gently. His last conscious thought was a nagging worry that Linda would be terrified of EVA.

When he awoke, and Linda took her turn in the hammock, he talked it over with Jill.

"I think she'll be all right, Chet. Don't hold that first few minutes against her."

"I don't know. There're only two kinds of people up here: you either love it or you're scared sh . . . witless. And you can't fake it. If she goes ape outside . . ."

"She won't," Jill said firmly. "And anyway, you'll be there to help her. I've told her that she won't be going outside until you're finished with the mating job. She wanted to get pictures of you actually at work, but she'll settle for a few posed shots."

Kinsman nodded. But the worry persisted. *I wonder if Calder's Army nurse was scared of flying?*

He was pulling on his boots, wedging his free foot against an equipment rack to keep from floating off, when Linda returned from her sleep.

"Ready for a walk around the block?" he asked her.

She smiled and nodded without the slightest hesitation. "I'm looking forward to it. Can I get a few shots of you while you zipper up your suit?"

Maybe she'll be okay.

At last he was sealed into the pressure suit. Linda and Jill stood back as Kinsman shuffled to the airlock hatch. It was set into the floor at the end of the cabin where the spacecraft was docked. With Jill helping him, he eased down into the airlock and shut the hatch. The airlock chamber itself was coffin-sized. Kinsman had to half-bend to move around in it. He checked out his suit, then pumped the air out of the chamber. Then he was ready to open the outer hatch.

It was beneath his feet, but as it slid open to reveal the stars, Kinsman's weightless orientation flip-flopped, like an optical illusion, and he suddenly felt that he was standing on his head and looking up.

"Going out now," he said into the helmet mike.

"Okay," Jill's voice responded.

Carefully he eased himself through the open hatch, holding onto its edge with one gloved hand once he was fully outside, the way a swimmer holds the rail for a moment when he first slides into the deep water. Outside. Swinging his body around slowly, he took in the immense beauty of Earth, dazzlingly bright even through his tinted visor. Beyond its curving limb was the darkness of infinity, with the beckoning stars watching him in unblinking solemnity.

Alone now. His own tight, self-contained universe, independent of everything and everybody. He could cut the life-giving umbilical line that linked him with the laboratory and float off by himself forever. And be dead in two minutes. *Ay, there's the rub.*

Instead, he unhooked the tiny gas gun from his waist and, trailing the umbilical, squirted himself over toward the power pod. It was riding smoothly behind the lab, a squat truncated cone, shorter but fatter than the lab itself, one edge brilliantly lit by the sun, the rest of it bathed in the softer light reflected from the dayside of Earth below.

Kinsman's job was to inspect the power pod, check its

equipment, and then mate it to the electrical system of the laboratory. There was no need to physically connect the two bodies, except to link a pair of power lines between them. Everything necessary for the task—tools, power lines, checkout instruments—had been built into the pod, waiting for a man to use them.

It would have been simple work on Earth. In zero gee, it was complicated. The slightest motion of any part of your body started you drifting. You had to fight against all the built-in mannerisms of a lifetime; had to work constantly to keep in place. It was easy to get exhausted in zero gee.

Kinsman accepted all this with hardly a conscious thought. He worked slowly, methodically, using as little motion as possible, letting himself drift slightly until a more-or-less natural body motion counteracted and pulled him back in the opposite direction. *Ride the waves, slow and easy.* There was a rhythm to his work, the natural dreamlike rhythm of weightlessness.

His earphones were silent, he said nothing. All he heard was the purring of the suit's air blowers and his own steady breathing. All he saw was his work.

Finally he jetted back to the laboratory, towing the pair of thick cables. He found the connectors waiting for them on the sidewall of the lab and inserted the cable plugs. *I pronounce you lab and power source.* He inspected the checkout lights alongside the connectors. All green. *May you produce many kilowatts.*

Swinging from handhold to handhold along the length of the lab, he made his way back toward the airlock.

"Okay, it's finished. How's Linda doing?"

Jill answered, "She's all set."

"Send her out."

She came out slowly, uncertain wavering feet sliding out first from the bulbous airlock. It reminded Kinsman of a film he had seen of a whale giving birth.

"Welcome to the real world," he said when her head cleared the airlock hatch.

She turned to answer him and he heard her gasp and he knew that now he liked her.

"It's . . . it's . . ."

"Staggering," Kinsman suggested. "And look at you—no hands."

She was floating freely, pressure suit laden with camera gear, umbilical flexing easily behind her. Kinsman couldn't see her face through the tinted visor, but he could hear the awe in her voice, even in her breathing.

"I've never seen anything so absolutely overwhelming . . ."

And then suddenly she was all business, reaching for a camera, snapping away at the Earth and stars and distant Moon, rapid fire. She moved too fast and started to tumble. Kinsman jetted over and steadied her, holding her by the shoulders.

"Hey, take it easy. They're not going away. You've got lots of time."

"I want to get some shots of you, and the lab. Can you get over by the pod and go through some of the motions of your work on it?"

Kinsman posed for her, answered her questions, rescued a camera when she fumbled it out of her hands and couldn't reach it as it drifted away from her.

"Judging distances gets a little whacky out here," he said, handing the camera back to her.

Jill called them twice and ordered them back inside. "Chet, you're already fifteen minutes over the limit!"

"There's plenty slop in the schedule. We can stay out awhile longer."

"You're going to get her exhausted."

"I really feel fine," Linda said, her voice lyrical.

"How much more film do you have?" Kinsman asked her. She peered at the camera. "Six more shots."

"Okay. We'll be in when the film runs out, Jill."

"You're going to be in darkness in another five minutes!"

Turning to Linda, who was floating upside-down with the cloud-laced Earth behind her, he said, "Save your film for the sunset, then shoot like hell when it comes."

"The sunset? What'll I focus on?"

"You'll know when it happens. Just watch."

It came fast, but Linda was equal to it. As the lab swung

in its orbit toward the Earth's night shadow, the sun dropped to the horizon and shot off a spectacular few moments of the purest reds and oranges and finally a heart-catching blue. Kinsman watched in silence, hearing Linda's breath going faster and faster as she worked the camera.

Then they were in darkness. Kinsman flicked on his helmet lamp. Linda was just hanging there, camera still in hand. "It's . . . impossible to describe." Her voice sounded empty, drained. "If I hadn't seen it . . . if I didn't get it on film, I don't think I'd be able to convince myself that I wasn't dreaming."

Jill's voice rasped in his earphones: "Chet, get inside! This is against every safety reg, being outside in the dark."

He looked over toward the lab. Lights were visible along its length and the ports were lighted from within. Otherwise he could barely make it out, even though it was only a few meters away.

"Okay, okay. Turn on the airlock light so we can see the hatch."

Linda was still bubbling about the view outside long after they had pulled off their pressure suits and eaten sandwiches and cookies.

"Have you ever been out there?" she asked Jill.

Perched on the biology bench's edge, near the mice colony, Jill nodded curtly. "Twice."

"Isn't it spectacular? I hope the pictures come out. Some of the settings on the camera . . ."

"They'll be all right," Jill said. "And if they're not, we've got a backlog of photos you can use."

"Oh, but they wouldn't have the shots of Chet working on the power pod."

Jill shrugged. "Aren't you going to take more photos in here? If you want to get some pictures of real space veterans, you ought to snap the mice here. They've been up for months now, living fine and raising families. And they don't make such a fuss about it, either."

"Well, some of us do exciting things," Kinsman said, "and some of us tend mice."

Jill glowered at him.

Glancing at his wristwatch, Kinsman said, "Girls, it's my sack time. I've had a trying day: mechanic, tourist guide, and cover boy for *Life*. Work, work, work."

He glided past Linda with a smile, kept it for Jill as he went by her. She was still glaring.

When he woke up again and went back into the main cabin, Jill was talking pleasantly with Linda as the two of them stood over the microscope and specimen rack of the biology bench.

Linda saw him first. "Oh, hi. Jill's been showing me the spores she's studying. And I photographed the mice. Maybe they'll go on the cover instead of you."

Kinsman grinned. "She's been poisoning your mind against me." But to himself he wondered, *What the hell has Jill been telling her about me?*

Jill drifted over to the control desk, picked up the clipboard with the mission log on it and tossed it lightly toward Kinsman.

"Ground control says the power pod checks out all green," she said. "You did a good job."

"Thanks." He caught the clipboard. "Whose turn in the sack is it?"

"Mine," Jill answered.

"Okay. Anything special cooking?"

"No. Everything's on schedule. Next data transmission comes up in twelve minutes. Kodiak station."

Kinsman nodded. "Sleep tight."

Once Jill had shut the curtain to the bunkroom, Kinsman carried the mission log to the control desk and sat down. Linda stayed at the biology bench, about three paces away.

He checked the instrument board with a quick glance, then turned to Linda. "Well, now do you know what I meant about this being a way of life?"

"I think so. It's so different . . ."

"It's the real thing. Complete freedom. Brave new world. After ten minutes of EVA, everything else is just toothpaste."

"It was certainly exciting."

"More than that. It's living. Being on the ground is a drag, even flying a plane is dull now. This is where the fun is . . .

out here in orbit and on the Moon. It's as close to heaven as anybody's gotten."

"You're really serious?"

"Damned right. I've even been thinking of asking Murdock for a transfer to NASA duty. Air Force missions don't include the Moon, and I'd like to walk around on the new world, see the sights."

She smiled at him. "I'm afraid I'm not that enthusiastic."

"Well, think about it for a minute. Up here, you're free. Really free, for the first time in your life. All the laws and rules and prejudices they've been dumping on you all your life . . . they're all *down there*. Up here it's a new start. You can be yourself and do your own thing . . . and nobody can tell you different."

"As long as somebody provides you with air and food and water and . . ."

"That's the physical end of it, sure. We're living in a microcosm, courtesy of the aerospace industry and AFSC. But there're no strings on us. The brass can't make us follow their rules. We're writing the rulebooks ourselves . . . For the first time since 1776, we're writing new rules."

Linda looked thoughtful now. Kinsman couldn't tell if she was genuinely impressed by his line, or if she knew what he was trying to lead up to. He turned back to the control desk and studied the mission flight plan again.

He had carefully considered all the possible opportunities, and narrowed them down to two. *Both of them tomorrow, over the Indian Ocean. Forty-fifty minutes between ground stations, and Jill's asleep both times.*

"AF-9, this is Kodiak."

He reached for the radio switch. "AF-9 here, Kodiak. Go ahead."

"We are receiving your automatic data transmission loud and clear."

"Roger Kodiak. Everything normal here. Mission profile unchanged."

"Okay, Niner. We have nothing new for you. Oh wait . . . Chet, Lew Regneson is here and he says he's betting on you to uphold the Air Force's honor. Keep 'em flying."

Keeping his face as straight as possible, Kinsman answered, "Roger, Kodiak. Mission profile unchanged."

"Good luck!"

Linda's thoughtful expression had deepened. "What was that all about?"

He looked straight into those cool blue eyes and answered, "Damned if I know. Regneson's one of the astronaut team, been assigned to Kodiak for the past six weeks. He must be going ice-happy. Thought it'd be best just to humor him."

"Oh. I see." But she looked unconvinced.

"Have you checked any of your pictures in the film processor?"

Shaking her head, Linda said, "No, I don't want to risk them on your automatic equipment. I'll process them myself when we get back."

"Damned good equipment," said Kinsman.

"I'm fussy."

He shrugged and let it go.

"Chet?"

"What?"

"That power pod . . . what's it for? Colonel Murdock got awfully coy when I asked him."

"Nobody's supposed to know until the announcement's made in Washington . . . probably when we get back. I can't tell you officially," he grinned, "but generally reliable sources believe that it's going to power a radar set that'll be orbited next month. The radar will be part of our ABM warning system."

"Anti-Ballistic Missile?"

With a nod, Kinsman explained, "From orbit you can spot missile launches farther away, give the States a longer warning time."

"So your brave new world is involved in war, too."

"Sort of." Kinsman frowned. "Radars won't kill anybody, of course. They might save lives."

"But this *is* a military satellite."

"Unarmed. Two things this brave new world doesn't have yet: death and love."

"Men have died . . ."

"Not in orbit. On reentry. In ground or air accidents. No one's died up here. And no one's made love, either."

Despite herself, it seemed to Kinsman, she smiled. "Have there been any chances for it?"

"Well, the Russians have had women cosmonauts. Jill's been the first American girl in orbit. You're the second."

She thought it over for a moment. "This isn't exactly the bridal suite of the Waldorf . . . in fact, I've seen better motel rooms along the Jersey Turnpike."

"Pioneers have to rough it."

"I'm a photographer, Chet, not a pioneer."

Kinsman hunched his shoulders and spread his hands helplessly, a motion that made him bob slightly on the chair. "Strike three, I'm out."

"Better luck next time."

"Thanks." He returned his attention to the mission flight plan. *Next time will be in exactly sixteen hours, chickie.*

When Jill came out of the sack it was Linda's turn to sleep. Kinsman stayed at the control desk, sucking on a container of lukewarm coffee. All the panel lights were green. Jill was taking a blood specimen from one of the white mice.

"How're they doing?"

Without looking up, she answered, "Fine. They've adapted to weightlessness beautifully. Calcium level's evened off, muscle tone is good . . ."

"Then there's hope for us two-legged types?"

Jill returned the mouse to the colony entrance and snapped the lid shut. It scampered through to rejoin its clan in the transparent plastic maze of tunnels.

"I can't see any physical reason why humans can't live in orbit indefinitely," she answered.

Kinsman caught a slight but definite stress on the word *physical.* "You think there might be emotional problems over the long run?"

"Chet, I can see emotional problems on a three-day mission." Jill forced the blood specimen into a stoppered test tube.

"What do you mean?"

"Come on," she said, her face a mixture of disappointment and distaste. "It's obvious what you're trying to do. Your tail's been wagging like a puppy's whenever she's in sight."

"You haven't been sleeping much, have you?"

"I haven't been eavesdropping, if that's what you mean. I've simply been watching you watching her. And some of the messages from the ground . . . is the whole Air Force in on this? How much money's being bet?"

"I'm not involved in any betting. I'm just . . ."

"You're just taking a risk on fouling up this mission and maybe killing the three of us, just to prove you're Tarzan and she's Jane."

"Goddammit Jill, now you sound like Murdock."

The sour look on her face deepened. "Okay. You're a big boy. If you want to play Tarzan while you're on duty, that's your business. I won't get in your way. I'll take a sleeping pill and stay in the sack."

"You will?"

"That's right. You can have your blonde Barbie doll, and good luck to you. But I'll tell you this . . . she's a phony. I've talked to her long enough to dig that. You're trying to use her, but she's using us, too. She was pumping me about the power pod while you were sleeping. She's here for her own reasons, Chet, and if she plays along with you it won't be for the romance and adventure of it all."

My God Almighty, Jill's jealous!

It was tense and quiet when Linda returned from the bunkroom. The three of them worked separately: Jill fussing over the algae colony on the shelf above the biology bench; Kinsman methodically taking film from the observation cameras for return to Earth and reloading them; Linda efficiently clicking away at both of them.

Ground control called up to ask how things were going. Both Jill and Linda threw sharp glances at Kinsman. He replied merely:

"Following mission profile. All systems green."

They shared a meal of pastes and squeeze tubes together, still mostly in silence, and then it was Kinsman's turn in the sack. But not before he checked the mission flight plan.

Jill goes in next, and we'll have four hours alone, including a stretch over the Indian Ocean.

Once Jill retired, Kinsman immediately called Linda over to the control desk under the pretext of showing her the radar image of a Russian satellite.

"We're coming close now." They hunched side by side at the desk to peer at the orange-glowing radar screen, close enough for Kinsman to scent a hint of very feminine perfume. "Only a thousand kilometers away."

"Why don't you blink our lights at them?"

"It's unmanned."

"Oh."

"It *is* a little like World War I up here," Kinsman realized, straightening up. "Just being here is more important than which nation you're from."

"Do the Russians feel that way too?"

Kinsman nodded. "I think so."

She stood in front of him, so close that they were almost touching.

"You know," Kinsman said, "when I first saw you on the base, I thought you were a photographer's model . . . not the photographer."

Gliding slightly away from him, she answered, "I started out as a model . . ." Her voice trailed off.

"Don't stop. What were you going to say?"

Something about her had changed, Kinsman realized. She was still coolly friendly, but alert now, wary, and . . . sad?

Shrugging, she said, "Modeling is a dead end. I finally figured out that there's more of a future on the other side of the camera."

"You had too much brains for modeling."

"Don't flatter me."

"Why on earth should I flatter you?"

"We're not on Earth."

"Touché."

She drifted over toward the galley. Kinsman followed her.

"How long have you been on the other side of the camera?" he asked.

Turning back toward him, "I'm supposed to be getting your life story, not *vice versa*."

"Okay . . . ask me some questions."

"How many people know you're supposed to lay me up here?"

Kinsman felt his face smiling, an automatic delaying action. *What the hell,* he thought. Aloud, he replied, "I don't know. It started as a little joke among a few of the guys . . . apparently the word has spread."

"And how much money do you stand to win or lose?" She wasn't smiling.

"Money?" Kinsman was genuinely surprised. "Money doesn't enter into it."

"Oh no?"

"No, not with me," he insisted.

The tenseness in her body seemed to relax a little. "Then why . . . I mean . . . what's it all about?"

Kinsman brought his smile back and pulled himself down into the nearest chair. "Why not? You're damned pretty, neither one of us has any strings, nobody's tried it in zero gee before . . . Why the hell not?"

"But why should I?"

"That's the big question. That's what makes an adventure out of it."

She looked at him thoughtfully, leaning her tall frame against the galley paneling. "Just like that. An adventure. There's nothing more to it than that?"

"Depends," Kinsman answered. "Hard to tell ahead of time."

"You live in a very simple world, Chet."

"I try to. Don't you?"

She shook her head. "No, my world's very complex."

"But it includes sex."

Now she smiled, but there was no pleasure in it. "Does it?"

"You mean never?" Kinsman's voice sounded incredulous, even to himself.

She didn't answer.

"Never at all? I can't believe that . . ."

"No," she said, "not never at all. But never for . . . for an adventure. For job security, yes. For getting the good assignments, for teaching me how to use a camera, in the first place. But never for fun . . . at least, not for a long, long time has it been for fun."

Kinsman looked into those ice-blue eyes and saw that they were completely dry and aimed straight back at him. His insides felt odd. He put a hand out toward her, but she didn't move a muscle.

"That's . . . that's a damned lonely way to live," he said.

"Yes it is." Her voice was a steel knife-blade, without a trace of self-pity in it.

"But . . . how'd it happen? Why . . ."

She leaned her head back against the galley paneling, her eyes looking away, into the past. "I had a baby. He didn't want it. I had to give it up for adoption—either that or have it aborted. The kid should be five years old now . . . I don't know where she is." She straightened up, looked back at Kinsman. "But I found out that sex is either for making babies or making careers, not for fun."

Kinsman sat there, feeling like he had just taken a low blow. The only sound in the cabin was the faint hum of electrical machinery, the whisper of the air fans.

Linda broke into a grin. "I wish you could see your face . . . Tarzan the Ape Man, trying to figure out a nuclear reactor."

"The only trouble with zero gee," he mumbled, "is that you can't hang yourself."

Jill sensed something was wrong, it seemed to Kinsman. From the moment she came out of the sack, she sniffed around, giving quizzical looks. Finally, when Linda retired for her final rest period before their return, Jill asked him:

"How're you two getting along?"

"Okay."

"Really?"

"Really. We're going to open a Playboy Club in here. Want to be a bunny?"

Her nose wrinkled. "You've got enough of those."

For more than an hour they worked their separate tasks in silence. Kinsman was concentrating on recalibrating the radar mapper when Jill handed him a container of hot coffee.

He turned in the chair. She was standing beside him, not much taller than his own seated height.

"Thanks."

Her face was very serious. "Something's bothering you, Chet. What did she do to you?"

"Nothing."

"Really?"

"For Chrissake, don't start that again! Nothing, absolutely nothing happened. Maybe that's what's bothering me."

Shaking her head, "No, you're worried about something, and it's not about yourself."

"Don't be so damned dramatic, Jill."

She put a hand on his shoulder. "Chet . . . I know this is all a game to you, but people can get hurt at this kind of game, and . . . well . . . nothing in life is ever as good as you expect it will be."

Looking up at her intent brown eyes, Kinsman felt his irritation vanish. "Okay, kid. Thanks for the philosophy. I'm a big boy, though, and I know what it's all about . . ."

"You just think you do."

Shrugging, "Okay. I think I do. Maybe nothing is as good as it ought to be, but a man's innocent until proven guilty, and everything new is as good as gold until you find some tarnish on it. That's *my* philosophy for the day!"

"All right slugger," Jill smiled ruefully. "Be the ape man. Fight it out for yourself. I just don't want to see her hurt you."

"I won't get hurt."

Jill said, "You hope. Okay, if there's anything I can do . . ."

"Yeah, there is something."

"What?"

"When you sack in again, make sure Linda sees you take a sleeping pill. Will you do that?"

Jill's face went expressionless. "Sure," she answered flatly. "Anything for a fellow officer."

She made a great show, several hours later, of taking a sleeping pill so that she could rest well on her final nap before reentry. It seemed to Kinsman that Jill deliberately laid it on too thickly.

"Do you always take sleeping pills on the final time around?" Linda asked, after Jill had gone into the bunkroom.

"Got to be fully alert and rested," Kinsman replied, "for the return flight. Reentry's the trickiest part of the operation."

"Oh. I see."

"Nothing to worry about, though," Kinsman added.

He went to the control desk and busied himself with the tasks that the mission profile called for. Linda sat lightly in the next chair, within arm's reach. Kinsman chatted briefly with Kodiak station, on schedule, and made an entry in the log.

Three more ground stations and then we're over the Indian Ocean, with world enough and time.

But he didn't look up from the control panel; he tested each system aboard the lab, fingers flicking over control buttons, eyes focused on the red, amber and green lights that told him how the laboratory's mechanical and electrical machinery was functioning.

"Chet?"

"Yes."

"Are you . . . sore at me?"

Still not looking at her, "No, I'm busy. Why should I be sore at you?"

"Well, not sore maybe, but . . ."

"Puzzled?"

"Puzzled, hurt, something like that."

He punched an entry on the computer's keyboard at his side, then turned to face her. "Linda, I haven't really had time to figure out what I feel. You're a complicated girl, maybe too complicated for me. Life's got enough twists in it."

Her mouth drooped a little.

"On the other hand," he added, "we WASPS ought to stick together. Not many of us left."

That brought a faint smile. "I'm not a WASP. My real name's Szymanski . . . I changed it when I started modeling."

"Oh. Another complication."

She was about to reply when the radio speaker crackled, "AF-9, this is Cheyenne. Cheyenne to AF-9."

Kinsman leaned over and thumbed the transmitter switch. "AF-9 to Cheyenne. You're coming through faint but clear."

"Roger, Nine. We're receiving your telemetry. All systems look green from here."

"Manual check of systems also green," Kinsman said. "Mission profile okay, no deviations. Tasks about ninety percent complete."

"Roger. Ground control suggests you begin checking out your spacecraft on the next orbit. You are scheduled for reentry in ten hours."

"Right. Will do."

"Okay, Chet. Everything looks good from here. Anything else to report, ol' Founding Father?"

"Mind your own business." He turned the transmitter off. Linda was smiling at him.

"What's so funny?"

"You are. You're getting very touchy about this whole business."

"It's going to stay touchy for a long time to come. Those guys'll hound me for years about this."

"You could always tell lies."

"About you? No, I don't think I could do that. If the girl was anonymous, that's one thing. But they all know you, know where you work . . ."

"You're a gallant officer. I suppose that kind of rumor would get back to New York."

Kinsman grinned. "You could even make the front page of the *National Enquirer*."

She laughed at that. "I'll bet they'd pull out some of my old bikini pictures."

"Careful now," Kinsman put up a warning hand. "Don't stir up my imagination any more than it already is. I'm having a hard enough time being gallant right now."

They remained apart, silent, Kinsman sitting at the control desk, Linda drifting back toward the galley, nearly touching the curtain that screened off the sleeping area.

The ground control center called in and Kinsman gave a terse report. When he looked up at Linda again, she was sitting in front of the observation port across the aisle from the galley. Looking back at Kinsman, her face was troubled now, her eyes . . . he wasn't sure what was in her eyes. They looked different: no longer ice-cool, no longer calculating; they looked aware, concerned, almost frightened.

Still Kinsman stayed silent. He checked and double-checked the control board, making absolutely certain that every valve and transistor aboard the lab was working perfectly. Glancing at his watch: *Five more minutes before Ascension calls.* He checked the lighted board again.

Ascension called in exactly on schedule. Feeling his innards tightening, Kinsman gave his standard report in a deliberately calm and mechanical way. Ascension signed off.

With a long last look at the controls, Kinsman pushed himself out of the seat and drifted, hands faintly touching the grips along the aisle, toward Linda.

"You've been awfully quiet," he said, standing over her.

"I've been thinking about what you said a while ago." What was it in her eyes? Anticipation? Fear? "It . . . it has been a damned lonely life, Chet."

He took her arm and lifted her gently from the chair and kissed her. "But . . ."

"It's all right," he whispered. "No one will bother us. No one will know."

She shook her head. "It's not that easy, Chet. It's not that simple."

"Why not? We're here together . . . what's so complicated?"

"But—doesn't anything bother you? You're floating around in a dream. You're surrounded by war machines, you're living every minute with danger. If a pump fails or a meteor hits . . ."

"You think it's any safer down there?"

"But life *is* complex, Chet. And love . . . well, there's more to it than just having fun."

"Sure there is. But it's meant to be enjoyed, too. What's wrong with taking an opportunity when you have it? What's so damned complicated or important? We're above the cares and worries of Earth. Maybe it's only for a few hours, but it's here and now, it's us. They can't touch us, they can't force us to do anything or stop us from doing what we want to. We're on our own. Understand? Completely on our own."

She nodded, her eyes still wide with the look of a frightened animal. But her hands slid around him, and together they drifted back toward the control desk. Wordlessly, Kinsman turned off all the overhead lights, so that all they saw was the glow of the control board and the flickering of the computer as it murmured to itself.

They were in their own world now, their private cosmos, floating freely and softly in the darkness. Touching, drifting, coupling, searching the new seas and continents, they explored their world.

Jill stayed in the hammock until Linda entered the bunkroom, quietly, to see if she had awakened yet. Kinsman sat at the control desk feeling, not tired, but strangely numb.

The rest of the flight was strictly routine. Jill and Kinsman did their jobs, spoke to each other when they had to. Linda took a brief nap, then returned to snap a few last pictures. Finally they crawled back into the spacecraft, disengaged from the laboratory, and started the long curving flight back to earth.

Kinsman took a last look at the majestic beauty of the planet, serene and incomparable among the stars, before touching the button that slid the heat shield over his viewport. Then they felt the surge of rocket thrust, dipped into the atmosphere, knew that air heated beyond endurance surrounded them in a fiery grip and made their tiny craft into a flaming, falling star. Pressed into his seat by the acceleration, Kinsman let the automatic controls bring them through reentry, through the heat and buffeting turbulence, down to an altitude where their finned craft could fly like a rocketplane.

He took control and steered the craft back toward Patrick Air Force Base, back to the world of men, of weather, of cities, of hierarchies and official regulations. He did this alone, silently; he didn't need Jill's help or anyone else's. He flew the craft from inside his buttoned-tight pressure suit, frowning at the panel displays through his helmet's faceplate.

Automatically, he checked with ground control and received permission to slide the heat shield back. The viewport showed him a stretch of darkening clouds spreading from the sea across the beach and well inland. His earphones were alive with other men's voices now: wind conditions, altitude checks, speed estimates. He knew, but could not see that two jet planes were trailing along behind him, cameras focused on the returning spacecraft. *To provide evidence if I crash.*

They dipped into the clouds and a wave of gray mist hurtled up and covered the viewport. Kinsman's eyes flicked to the radar screen slightly off to his right. The craft shuddered briefly, then they broke below the clouds and he could see the long black gouge of the runway looming before him. He pulled back slightly on the controls, hands and feet working instinctively, flashed over some scrubby vegetation, and flared the craft onto the runway. The landing skids touched once, bounced them up momentarily, then touched again with a grinding shriek. They skidded for more than a mile before stopping.

He leaned back in the seat and felt his body oozing sweat.

"Good landing," Jill said.

"Thanks." He turned off all the craft's systems, hands moving automatically in response to long training. Then he slid his faceplate up, reached overhead and popped the hatch open.

"End of the line," he said tiredly. "Everybody out."

He clambered up through the hatch, feeling his own weight with a sullen resentment, then helped Linda and finally Jill out of the spacecraft. They hopped down onto the blacktop runway. Two vans, an ambulance, and two fire trucks were rolling toward them from their parking stations at the end of the runway, a half-mile ahead.

Kinsman slowly took his helmet off. The Florida heat and humidity annoyed him now. Jill walked a few paces away from him, toward the approaching trucks.

He stepped toward Linda. Her helmet was off, and she was carrying a bag full of film.

"I've been thinking," he said to her. "That business about having a lonely life . . . You know, you're not the only one. And it doesn't have to be that way. I can get to New York whenever . . ."

"Now who's taking things seriously?" Her face looked calm again, cool, despite the glaring heat.

"But I mean . . ."

"Listen Chet. We had our kicks. Now you can tell your friends about it, and I can tell mine. We'll both get a lot of mileage out of it. It'll help our careers."

"I never intended to . . . I didn't . . ."

But she was already turning away from him, walking toward the men who were running up to meet them from the trucks. One of them, a civilian, had a camera in his hands. He dropped to one knee and took a picture of Linda holding the film out and smiling broadly.

Kinsman stood there with his mouth open.

Jill came back to him. "Well? Did you get what you were after?"

"No," he said slowly. "I guess I didn't."

She started to put her hand out to him. "We never do, do we?"

Sky Blue

Alexei *and* Cory Panshin

Science fiction comes in all shapes and hues, in all moods and styles, yet this story may be something new to the field. Call it cuddly symbolism; call it a heavy bedtime story; call it experimental cotton candy . . . no matter the term, I find it fresh and delightful. A group of star travelers lose their ship's drive, but are rescued by Landlord Thing, who lends them a planet. What follows is clever and amusing . . . and, ultimately, quite serious.

Sky Blue waits for Landlord Thing. He holds the most powerful gun Groombridge Colony can hand him. He sits on a small unnaturally comfortable rock in space.

Overhead the heavens wheel. Beneath him the brown planet whirls. Like a midge on a grain of wheat, he passes between millstones.

A fat spaceship blipping on business like a slickery black watermelon seed went astray one day between Someplace Important and Someplace Important, and wound up lost on the great black floor of the galaxy. It was the pilot's fault, if you want to blame someone. He was stargazing at the wrong moment, misapplied his math, and then fritzed the drive in a fruitless attempt to recoup.

The ship came to drift without power in a place where the stars glittered nervously and all the skies were strange. It was weird there, and after one look the curtains were hastily drawn. Nobody wanted to look outside except one boy named Harold who held the curtains in his hands and peeked.

The pilot killed himself in another fit of overcompensation, but nobody noticed. They were all dead men in their dark powerless ship in that strange icicle corner of the universe, but nobody would say so. They huddled together in various parts of the ship and talked of usual matters.

Now, this wasn't just any old ship. This was a big deal colony whip on its way to settle Groombridge 1618/2, a planet foredoomed for importance. It was so juicy a place that you had to pay high for a slice of the pie.

The passengers on this ship had all paid. They were men of moxie. They knew the answers. Here's a topper. Triphammer and Puddleduck, who had more answers than anybody, were aboard, too. They were along for the dedication ceremonies and a quick return home. They moved in high circles.

Being lost so suddenly was as painful and frustrating to Triphammer and Puddleduck as an interrupted fuck. Suddenly their answers were of no use to them. Oh, it hurt.

Triphammer, Puddleduck and Mount Rushmore were the highest huddle of all. They gathered by a candle in one room. Triphammer paced frantically, Puddleduck nodded at appropriate moments, and Mount Rushmore loomed. Harold looked out through the curtains into the universe.

Triphammer said, "Oh, losings. Screamie! The action, pop-a-dop." Her face could not contain her regret.

Puddleduck nodded. "Misery," he said.

"Misery," said Mount Rushmore.

Harold said, "There's somebody walking by outside."

He was the son of Triphammer and Puddleduck. They hadn't given him a proper name yet, and he wasn't sure they meant to keep him. He needed them, so until he discovered their intention he was playing it quiet.

"Out of mind," said Puddleduck, beating his brow. "Re-plebed and forgot."

Triphammer held a sudden hand before her mouth. "Oh, speak not."

"Misery," said Mount Rushmore.

Harold waved. "Hey, he sees me." He waved again.

Triphammer and Puddleduck didn't hear what Harold said. It was his fault. He didn't speak up. They had told him that it was his fault if he wasn't heard.

Great Mount Rushmore pounded himself on the chest. "Gelt gone blubbles. Misery. Misery."

Puddleduck said, "Misery."

"Miz," said Triphammer.

There was a tug at her sleeve and she looked down. It was Harold waiting for her attention.

"Again?"

Harold put on his best face and straightened to the full extent of his undergreat height, which was what he had been taught to do when he asked for things.

"Can I go out and play, Mama? Please?" he asked, waving at the window.

Triphammer's expression made it clear that any request at this moment was a fart in church, and that the gods were displeased with the odor.

"What what? Bird twitter while empires fall? Shame and a half, Harold, you nameless twirp. (Forbearing, but not much.) Forbidding."

"I'm really extremely sorry I asked," Harold said.

There was sudden consternation in the room. Out of nowhere—certainly not through the door—had come a be-ing altogether strange. And here it was, making five now around the candle. It had pseudopods and big brown eyes.

"Wowsers, a creature!" said Mount Rushmore. He backed away. "Bling it."

The creature looked at Harold and said, "Are you coming or not?"

Triphammer had a tender stomach. She tried without suc-cess to stifle a retch.

"Faa," she said. "Bling it."

Harold said, "I'm not allowed. I asked already."

Puddleduck looked around and around the room, nodding furiously and muttering constant instructions to himself lest he forget, but there was nothing ready at hand to bling the creature with. Puddleduck waved his arms like frustrated semaphores.

"But of course you are allowed," the creature said. "If you want to come with me, you may. I don't forbid anyone."

It broke off abruptly and looked around at Mount Rushmore, Triphammer and Puddleduck as they recoiled.

"Is something the matter?" it asked, flexing its polyps in wonderment.

Triphammer looked at it with a glance like a pointing finger, and vomited reproachfully.

"I beg your pardon," the creature said.

It gathered itself together, contracting its pseudopods into the main mess of its body. Its brown eyes bulged hugely and then blinked. And, speedy quick as a hungry duck, its appearance was altered. Where there had formerly been an—ugh—amorphous monster, now there stood a dark sweet old man with a short brushy mustache and a nose like a spearhead, as definite as geometry. He was dressed in a khaki shirt and shorts to the knee and sturdy walking shoes.

"Is that better?"

"Oh, scruples!" said Triphammer.

And it was better. Triphammer and Puddleduck knew how to deal with people. Creatures were another matter. They brightened to see him, for the old man looked like a mark and they desperately needed someone to take advantage of.

The sweet old fud looked around that dim room there in the dead and silent spaceship as though it were a very strange place.

"Pardon me if I'm being overcritical of your favored pastimes, but is this really what you like to do? It seems limited. You could be outside on a day like this," he said.

Mount Rushmore shook his head like a rag mop. "Not happy, not happy," he said. "Oh, not. Gelt gone blubbles, you know."

"Lost and out of it," Triphammer explained. "Unjuiced, weenied and paddleless."

"Screamie-a-deamie!" said Puddleduck. "Massive frust! In the name of our importance, unpickle us."

"I had the feeling things weren't just right," the old man said. "Don't ask me how I knew. I have an instinct for these things. Well, I'll help you as much as I can. Come along with me."

He turned and walked abruptly through the wall of the ship. Gone. And no one followed him.

He stuck his head back into the room, looking like a well-seasoned wall trophy.

"Well, come along," he said reasonably.

Harold, smiling brightly, took a happy step forward. Then he noticed that Triphammer and Puddleduck were standing stock still. Above all else, he desired to please them and be kept. He couldn't help himself. He stopped and wiped his smile away, and then he didn't move, he didn't breathe. He did check to see what his parents did, eyes flicking left, eyes flicking right, under their eyelash awning.

"Aren't you coming?" the old man asked. "I am willing to help you."

Mount Rushmore boggled at him. Triphammer and Puddleduck, with infinitely greater presence of mind, shook their heads silently.

"What's the matter?"

"Nary a feather to fly with," they said. "We *told* you that, pooper. We're stuck, that's what."

The dear old goat stepped back into the ship and nibbled his mustache.

"Are you sure you can't follow me?" he asked.

"Can't."

"You could if you wanted."

"Can't."

"Why don't you just give it a try?"

"Can't, and that's that."

"Well, what are we to do, then?" the old man asked. "It seems we are at an impasse."

He thought. They all thought, except Harold. He watched. He witnessed.

Then the old man said, "I have it. I knew I'd think of something. Mechanical means."

And hardly were the words out of his mouth when the lights came on in the room, at first flickering as dim as the candle, then coming up strong and smiling.

The phone rang. Puddleduck answered.

"Quack?"

"Kiss us," the excited face in the visor said. "We've made the auxiliaries putt. We can limp to haven."

"Grats," said Puddleduck. "But can't we blif for home?"

"No way. The mains will have to be made anew."

"Oh," said Puddleduck, and rang off.

"Can you come along now?" asked the old man.

The ship limped where he directed, and in time they came to a planet, green as Eden. It wasn't half bad, except that it wasn't near anything. They went into orbit around it, keeping close company with a small pitted whizzer of a satellite.

"That's my seat, that rock," said the old man. "That's where I sit to oversee when I visit. This is one of my planets. It's small, but it's a good home. If you will love it well, nurture and tend it and take good care of it, I'll lend it to you. How about that?"

"Done," they said.

"Done it is, then," said the old man. "Well, I must be about my business. I'll check back shortly to see how you are getting on. If you need me, sit on my rock and give me a call. I'll show up in no time. Now, if you will excuse me."

"Wait, wait," they said. "Before you tippy along, we must know—who are you, freaky old pooper?"

"You may call me Landlord Thing," the old man said. He turned to Harold. "Are you coming?"

Harold looked at his parents with one quick sweep of his eyes, and then he shook his head as fast as a suckling lamb can shake its tail. "No," he said. "Thank you."

Landlord Thing took a hitch on his shorts and stepped lightly through the wall into space. Then, just as they were opening their mouths to speak of him, he stuck his head back through the wall one last time.

He said, "Mind you, take good care of my world."

And then like a guru skipping barefoot through Himalayan icefields he was gone.

Sky Blue waits for Landlord Thing. He has a heavy gun in his hands and he means to bling the Thing good and proper. That's what he is there for, sitting on that dinky rock in space.

His mind wheels with the high heavens above. His mind whirls with the bare brown planet below. His mind is ground to flour between great stones.

He thinks, "Come. Come. Come and be killed."

They called the planet Here or East Overshoe or This Dump. They didn't love it. They didn't take care of it. They didn't nurture and tend it, or any of the other stuff they promised. They didn't plan to stay, so why should they?

They called themselves Groombridge Colony. As soon as they fixed the drive, they meant to tippy along. They meant to blif. They meant to go. Onward to Groombridge 1618/2 and the way things were supposed to be. After all, they had paid good money.

Since Triphammer and Puddleduck wanted to get back into the galactic big time worse than anybody—quack, yes! —they were in charge. Like proper leaders, they exhorted everyone to do his utmost.

Recall: to fix the drive, the mains had to be made anew. To do the job, they needed some of This, some of That, and some of the Third Thing.

They didn't wait a moment after they set down. They dug shafts like moles. They built towers like ants. They hammered and smoked and smelted and forged. They electrolyzed and transmuted. They ripped and raped and turned the planet upside down in the search for what they needed. They turned the green planet brown, these Groombrugians. They really made a mess of things.

Here's the hard part. This is rare in the universe. They came by it in no time. That you can't just buy at any corner store. They found twice as much as they needed. But the Third Thing, which everywhere else is common as dirt, was elusive as the wild butterfly of love. After years and years they had barely accumulated a single pood of the stuff, and that wasn't nearly enough.

When they were planning to leave East Overshoe come morning, the Groombridge gang cared naught a tiddle what they did to the planet. When it sank in finally that they weren't leaving all that soon, there were some who began to worry what Landlord Thing might make of their handiwork.

It wasn't anything you could sweep under the carpet and smile about. It was more obvious than that. Well, yes.

It was Triphammer who began to fuss about it first. And Puddleduck caught it from her. But it was Puddleduck who thought of the answer, and Triphammer who found it worthy. It often worked out that way. They were a team.

Their answer was to set Sky Blue on that whirling rock to slay their monster for them. Within their terms, it was a perfect solution. Puddleduck remembered that Landlord Thing had said he would come instanter than powdered breakfast if he were called from that rock. Ha! at their beck, when they were ready for him, and then, bling! Then they would have all the time and peace they needed to rip the planet to the heart. And Sky Blue was the man.

They shook hands on it, and set out to look for Sky Blue. That was what they called Harold now. They called him Sky Blue because he was so out to lunch. But they had need of him now. He could shoot.

Yes, he could shoot. It was one of the things he did that no one else would think of doing. Sky Blue had grown up eccentric.

The heart of it was that he took responsibility seriously. He had been there when the agreement with Landlord Thing was made and he had said, "I promise," in his heart. And like the loser he was, he wasted his time trying to live by his word.

Where things were brown, he did his best to green them again. Futile. Where the Groombridge gang pared and cored the planet, he repaired and corrected. Outnumbered. Where they ripped and raped, he nurtured and tended. That is, he tried. Every day he fell farther behind.

Where it was necessary for balance, he shot things. He

would think, "Come. Come and be killed." And because all of Landlord Thing's planet knew he had their best interests at heart, they would come and he would kill them with love and sorrow.

If Triphammer and Puddleduck were not consummate politicians, hence tolerant, and if they hadn't enjoyed the fresh meat he brought home from time to time, they would have disowned him. They probably should have anyway. As it was, they named him Sky Blue and allowed him his amusement. And because Triphammer and Puddleduck were Triphammer and Puddleduck, Groombridge Colony went along.

As Mount Rushmore said, speaking for the community, "Pretties need dippies for contrast, nay say?"

When Triphammer and Puddleduck found Sky Blue, their boy was up to his ears in dirt, beavering away making a large hole smaller. In the time it would take him to fill it, three more would be dug in search of the Third Thing, but he was not one to complain. He knew his obligation, even if no one else did, and he lived by it.

"Hey there, dull thud, child of ours," they said. "Muckle that shovel for the mo and hie thee hither. Busyness beckons."

Sky Blue did as they directed. He stuck his shovel in the sand and hurried over to them. He still yearned for their good opinion whenever it was compatible with what he thought was right. Oh, tell the truth—he might even strike a compromise with right for the sake of their good opinion. They had him hooked.

"Yes yes," he said. "Progen lovies, put my knucks to your purpose."

"Oh best bubby, trumpets for your eagerness," they said. They produced the gun, Groombridge Colony's most powerful splat-blinger, and placed it in his hands. "Elim Landlord Thing for Mum and Dad, that's a good dumb-dumb son."

"Bling Landlord Thing? Where? Why? Oh, say not!" And Sky Blue tried to return the gun to Triphammer and Puddleduck, but they would have none of it.

"Yours," said Puddleduck.

"Yours," said Triphammer.

"Nay, nay, not I," said Sky Blue.

Triphammer said, "Do you treacledrip for This Dump, nurdy son of mine?"

"Certain sure, I do."

"One boot, two boot, when the rent is due, and out go you. You lose."

"Misery mort," said Sky Blue. "Me, too? But no—holes ubiquate. I'll screege from view."

"Ho, ho, Hermit Harold, all by his onesome," said Puddleduck. "You lose."

"Unhappies," said Sky Blue. And he looked at the equalizer in his hands. "What what? Oh, double what what?"

Triphammer drew close and whispered sweet in his ear: "Bling him to frags, and lovings and keepings."

How's that for a promise?

So Sky Blue waits for Landlord Thing. Above above. Below below. He sits on that rock, the call gone forth, and waits.

And there Landlord Thing is! The old man wades through space toward the rock where Sky Blue sits.

Trembling, barely able to control himself, Sky Blue raises the gun in his hands—butt coming up to his shoulder, muzzle swinging down to point. The gun is aimed, centered on the brushy mustache. And Sky Blue pulls the trigger.

A beam lances and there is a blinding flash. The face piece of Sky Blue's spacesuit polarizes at the glare.

He casts the rifle from him into space, sobbing. His eyes clot with tears. He cries harder than he can remember, as though he has lost forever his last infinitely precious hope.

But as he sits there desolate, a pseudopod wraps comfortingly about his shoulders and a warm voice says, "How have things been? Tell me about them."

Sky Blue turns his head and opens his eyes. There, sitting beside him on that unnaturally comfortable rock, is Landlord Thing as first he saw him through the tight pinched curtains so long before. Warm brown eyes and pseudopods.

"Nothing is right," says Sky Blue. "Look down there at your planet. It's been turned to brown. Nobody likes it there on your world but me. Everyone else wants to get away and no matter how I try, I can't clean it up."

"That isn't the worst thing in the world," says Landlord Thing. "We'll see what can be done. Follow me."

He shifts around to the other side of the rock and Sky Blue follows.

"This is the top side," says Landlord Thing. "Now look."

Sky Blue looks up at Here. It fills the sky above him. He is overflooded with a great warm wave of mystery and awe. It is momentarily too much for him and he must close his eyes and look away before he can look back again.

"I never realized," he says.

Landlord Thing says, "You can heal the world. You can make it green again."

"Me?" says Sky Blue. "No, I can't."

"Oh, but you can," says Landlord Thing. "I have faith in you, Sky Blue."

Sky Blue looks at him in astonishment. He hasn't told Landlord Thing his new name.

"How can I do it?" asks Sky Blue. "I don't know how."

"You must take yourself out of yourself and put it in the planet. Nurture and tend the planet. Make it well again. Concentrate very very hard. Look at the planet and spread yourself so thin that you disappear."

Sky Blue is unsure. Sky Blue does not believe. But Sky Blue is determined.

He looks up at Here, dominating the sky like a great mandala. It is a wave—he drowns. It is a wind—he dissipates. It is a web—but he is the spinner, spinning thin, spinning fine, losing himself in the gossamer. He handles the world tenderly.

Landlord Thing watches. Landlord Thing witnesses. And above them in the sky, the world turns green.

When Sky Blue reassembles, he is not the same. He looks once at Landlord Thing and smiles, and then they sit there in silence. They have called. They wait for their call to be answered. And after a time a ship lifts from the planet and comes to the rock.

It is Triphammer and Puddleduck. They wave to Sky

Blue as though he were alone. He and Landlord Thing go aboard the ship. Triphammer and Puddleduck act as though they are blind to Landlord Thing's presence. Sky Blue removes his spacesuit.

Triphammer and Puddleduck say, "Gasp, splutter, quack! No, no, no! The frust just must bust—screamie-a-deamie!"

Sky Blue is bewildered. He turns to Landlord Thing and says, "I don't understand a word of it."

Landlord Thing waves a sympathetic polyp. "It can be that way at first. Listen to them very closely. Concentrate on every word and some of it will come clear."

So Sky Blue cranes an ear to the words of Triphammer and Puddleduck and concentrates harder than when he healed the planet. And, just barely, meaning filters through. They are nattering about the sudden return of the planet to its original condition. In the process, it seems, their castles have all been thrown down. Their mines are theirs no longer. Their stockpiles of This, That, and the Third Thing have disappeared in a lash flicker. They quabble about what has happened and what they should do.

Sky Blue listens to them until they run dry. Then he shakes his head in wonder.

"Offense. Unfair. Disrespect," says Triphammer.

Puddleduck nods. *"Wanh* for our importance," he says. "All toobies."

Landlord Thing nods. "All toobies, indeed," he says. "Tell them they are being given a second chance. Their only hope is if they take good advantage of it."

Sky Blue relays the message. "Return to Here," he says, "and learn to live there. It's your one life. Use it well."

Triphammer and Puddleduck are astounded at these words. Their jaws drop like a gallows trap. Their nurdy son has never spoken to them like this before.

Landlord Thing says, "Come along Sky Blue. I have some people to introduce you to. I think you'll like them."

He passes through the wall as though it were nothing to him. Sky Blue looks at his parents one last time, and then he follows. He steps through the wall of the ship and into space.

"I'm coming," he says to Landlord Thing, striding the stars before him.

Sky Blue has held the curtains clutched tight in his hands this long time. Now he throws them open wide and peaks.

Miss Omega Raven

Naomi Mitchison

Naomi Mitchison has a coterie-reputation as the author of
the novel *Memoirs of a Spacewoman*, soon to be published in
this country; meanwhile, here's an incisive short-short about
an experiment to raise the intelligence of a group of ravens.
Lady Mitchison manages to say much about the nature and uses
of intellection, in a very short narrative.

The others were always quick, always first. Was it because
of what they did to us when we were young, when they took
us out of our nests before our feathers were more than quills
and fed us this other food and made us sleep and put the
little wires on to our heads so that we could look back
and forward? We became different. And yet I think I became the most different of all. We knew what was ahead
and how to get it. We knew, not deep inside where there
is no choice like knowing in our necks and wings the moves
of the mating flight when all is Now. No, not that. We knew
with the parts of ourselves that choose. Thinking, they called
it, remembering, looking ahead. I was the latest hatched,
damp and flabby, my beak making squeals, the pieces of
shell still stuck to me. I had not seen my mother. I opened
eyes and saw him, the God-man with the special food. He

became her. I had to follow him to do what he did, to become him. How else? Yet because of that I was more changed. But they took us a long way in the dark in a box and made us fly. By then our wings were grown. We felt a need but did not know what it was.

When we flew we were in a different place with open stretches of rocks and trees, but no built walls. But inside we knew it. We knew the ways in which we were going to live. The food. And there were the mates. Oh beautiful, with the deep part which has no choice, I knew this was my need. I must get one. I must get the most beautiful, the best, shining dark of feathers, bright of eye. We must dance together in the air. That was what wings were for. We forgot the humans who had reared us; we forgot to look forward and back. But perhaps I did not quite forget. Perhaps that was what went wrong.

I did not at once leap into the air, crooning and bubbling, to chase the top bird, the raven of ravens, Alpha Corax. My feathered tufts were slow to come to the erect and welcoming sign which should draw him, yes, to lay his neck over mine. Others did it, my hated sisters, jumping with touched beaks, ruffling, courting, crooning. And the mates responded, answering with the same love notes, the same stiffening and relaxing, so that feathers ruffled and beaks snapped. It was clear already who was top, who could peck whom, though it had scarcely yet become clear to us female fledglings. [Even during the courting dance when air became buoyant and welcoming, inviting to enormous heights of glory from which one could dive flashingly, the wind booming one's feathers or even when the mate, turning on his back, invited with his beating spread wings but warned with beak and claws.] One after another the couples began to take flight. But I—I? Surely I could not be the one left out! But I was. For me and for one other, no mate. There had been two more of us than of them. Or perhaps two of them had died in the rearing. She, the other unmated. was even more hateful than the wives. Each of them had taken the rank of her husband and would keep it for life. We ravens settle each with her own mate for always.

This way each took orders and gave orders, each pecked

in punishment and was herself pecked; it was the same with the husbands. Only the most beautiful, the bravest, the top raven Alpha Corax, gave orders. Nobody pecked him. He led the flock to roost or to hunt. He watched and warned for enemies and sometimes attacked. His beak was sharpest.

But I was lowest of the low. She—the other unmated— pecked me and I had to accept this, jumping away from food, not pecking back. All that was in the deep part of me. I could not escape being how I was. There was no choice. But also I was angry and that anger was in the other part of me driving me to plan. That part of me thought of a future in which I would not be pecked. I knew I was becoming ugly. My feathers were draggled. I was thin, for I always got the worst share, either of flesh or eggs or the rarer grain and nuts. No wonder I was a pecked-on with nobody to peck. Had God-man made me this? If he had not made me something other I could not have questioned what I was.

So things went on. The beautiful one watched and led us to food; so did his wife. She saw with his eyes. She too led the flight in which I was last. And I knew two opposite things: in the deep part of me—that this was how it was but, in the outside, the changed and choosing part—that this was not for always and one day there would be a choice and a plan. But the choice did not come. The mates made their nests, beautiful, enviable, with heathers and grasses and earth and small sticks, lined deliciously with worked, soft grasses and feathers, ready for eggs. Once I tried to sit in a nest but how I was driven out, with what pain and anger! I tried to join in flights, I tried to croon and preen to each of the males but I aroused nothing in any of them, since they had only one image in their constant minds. They also had been in the hands of the God-men but now they had forgotten. I being alone, could not forget.

Then came the chipping of the eggs, the young, the tremendous drive and bustle of feeding. I was looked on, knowing what it was I missed; it was I driven from the dead lamb that was feasting us. It was I who saw the God-men circling us, with what intent I did not know, yet believed it was not evil. It was not they who had left me hungry. They spoke to one another or so I supposed. I also saw that they took some of the nestlings while they fed others with their own kind of food. The mothers were disturbed briefly but none of us could feel that the God-men were enemies. They were only high beyond us, beyond the top of the Alphas; they could give orders. They could peck us to the bone and any of us must submit, but because they had also fed us they did not do that; they did not need to. The one on whom my nestling eyes had first opened was there. He looked at my thin and draggled body; he had brought pieces of food, not their own kind, but good raw meat. He gave me some and I tried to gulp it quickly before the other unmated could see and drive me off. Yet she came, and her black beak drove at me; feathers flew. The deep, inside part of me was making me cower and accept. But the one I had not forgotten, the God-man had shown himself; it was meat he had given. He sent the knowledge of choice back into me. In a moment she was the pecked on. I made her feathers fly! It was impossible and it had happened.

Once pecked, she accepted. This was the first lesson. For both of us. I hated her. I could not stop pecking. Even when the God-man picked me up so that she could run and then flap away. Through the wriggle of my held wings and the straining of my body I felt his hands thinking about me. My beak wanted to peck, my claws to scratch; the beak pointed yet unable to peck him. He was my mother; the one I had opened eyes on. He held me but it came to me that I also held him.

Then there was a feast again. A cow had given birth. She moved away with the calf, leaving what else had come out of her red and wet in the grass. That was for us. But now I had one to peck and drive off if she came near me and the one who before had pecked her could not at once change to pecking me. The old pattern had been made. Yet because she too had been with the God-men and had been partly changed by them, so that she had choice, she began to know that I had taken the place of the other and also she was afraid in case I did not accept it. Sometimes her pecking was not hard. But I did not attack at once, not when she was with her nest and her mate.

The leaves of the great nest trees had spread and become green to live the leaves' life. Then they browned and dropped and loosened and the leaf flocks swirled briefly in air and then dropped and were still and useless. The young birds began to fly. But from every nest the God-men climbing quietly had taken one. I was watching, the mothers not always. They and their mates swirled and clattered and called uselessly, and yet they all knew, in the parts of their minds that looked forward and back, that the God-men had the right and this way was best for all.

And now cold days began and we all scattered again, though the pairs kept partly together. There was less food in winter and less light-time to find it. And I began to peck back at the next above me. Her mate looked on uncertainly but it was not he I wanted. I did not want any mate; it was the wrong season. I wanted only to be top. By the next season I could take this one's place, but it was not enough. What then?

The God-man came. My own. Was he top God-man or was it possible that all were top? They did not seem to hurt one another. But perhaps they did in some way hidden from ravens; who could tell? No use asking even if one knew what or how to ask. What is asking? So it went. But one day the God-man was gone and with him in a box went the wife of Alpha Corax, the top raven. Where had she gone? We did not know what to think, only that all were perturbed. She, with him, had led the foraging parties of the ravens. He was used to her being with him. He called; she was not there. He made the croonings and the mating cries; she did not answer. But all of us felt something in the deep part that wanted to answer, even before the season of mating. There was movement and small noises. Feathers rose and a posturing walk began. And then my own God-man looked at me and he too made a mating cry and he lifted his arms flapping. He was me. He had taken me from the egg and changed me so that I could hatch out of the old patterns. And then suddenly it was I who was answering

Alpha Corax; it was I who was with him, who had taken top place. I was the same as my God-man, my top God.

Now it was I who would have Alpha Corax, the top bird, the most beautiful, the raven of ravens. At mating time we would dance together in the air and then we would build our nest. But today, now, he knew and acknowledged me. I was Alpha today. I could peck the one below me and not one of them could peck me. I would become beautiful and glossy; my feathers would always lie smooth; I would bite and swallow all the bloodiest bits of the food. I would have the best nest, safe, not out in the edges.

All this happened. It happened to me. Now I am mated forever with Alpha Corax. Yes, at first there were those that rebelled, that had it in the bottom of their minds that I was still the pecked one, Omega Raven. Yes, some of them tried to peck me. But how I pecked them back, scattering feathers and blood! For I remembered the other food and the little wires that made me more than myself. I remembered God-man who made me into top pecker, breaker of custom. My God-man, top God. God-man and I.

Patron of the Arts

William Rotsler

Science fiction, as its very name implies, is a peculiar cross-breed between science and art, and perhaps for this reason sf writers like to consider the ways in which these two forms of human expression compare. Here, for instance, is a novelette about a future art-form, a story of art broadened and transformed by science. But the meeting place of art and science is in the individual human being, and that's where transformations take place . . .

She stares out at you from her cube of near blackness, calm, quiet, breathing easily, just looking at you. She is naked to the hips where a jeweled girdle encircles her, and she sits regally on a pile of luxurious pillows. Her long white hair cascades down over her apricot-colored shoulders and is made to shimmer slightly by some hidden light.

As you come closer to the life-size sensatron the vibrations get to you. The startling reality of the three-dimensional image cannot be overstated, for Michael Cilento's portrait of one of history's greatest society courtesans is a great work of art.

As you view the cube the image of Diana Snowdragon stops being quite so calm and in some subtle way becomes predatory, commanding, compelling. She is *naked*, not nude. The drifting bell-sounds of melora musicians are heard . . . almost. The power of her unique personality is overwhelming, as it is in person, but in this artist's interpretation there are many other facets exposed.

Diana's sensatron cube portrait is universally hailed as a masterpiece. The subject was delighted.

The artist was disgusted and told me that the ego of the subject prevented her from seeing the reality he had constructed.

But it was this cube that gave Michael Benton Cilento the fame he wanted, needed, and hated. This was his first major sensatron cube and cubes were just then beginning to be used by artists, instead of scientists. It was becoming "fashionable" to be working in sensatrons then and everywhere there was shop talk of electron brushes, cilli nets and blankers.

Sensatrons are the ultimate marriage of art and science. At least so far. The sciences are constantly supplying tools to the artists, whether it be fade-safe paint that will be bright a thousand years from now, or an electron brush to make meticulous changes in a scan pattern. Already the *quiver* groups are exploring the new brainwave instruments that create music *only* in the brain itself.

But the sensatrons are the rage of the moment. Just as the shimmercloth fashions of the *quiver* generation were seized by the media and exploited, the advertising world is impatient for immense sensatrons to be made possible, building-size product replicas with "Buy me!" shouting in your forebrain. In anticipation I have started one of my research labs on a blanker device to shut out the anticipated electronic noise.

The cubes can be so eerily lifelike that the rumors of them taking a piece of your soul persist. Perhaps they are right. Not only do the cameras capture the exterior, providing the basis from which the sensatron artist works, but the alpha and beta recorders, the EEG machines, the subtle heartbeat repeaters, all record what is going on within. Many artists use a blending of many recordings taken over a period of sittings. Some use single specific moments or moods, each recorded and then projected by the differentiated sonic cones and alpha-beta projectors. Along with these projections the artist adds his own interpretation, creating an almost musical concerto of waves, working upon any human brain within the area of reception. It is still the perogative of the artist to select, eliminate, diminish, or whatever he desires. Some sensatron portrait artists put in the emotional warts as well as the strengths, and others are flatterers. Some artists are experimenting with switched recordings, woman for man, animal for subject, pure abstracts substituting for reality. Every one that attempts it brings to it a new point of view.

All Mike Cilento wanted to do is project the truth as he saw it. Perhaps he did peel off a layer of soul. I have stood next to the living model of a sensatron portrait and found the cube much more interesting than the person, but only when the artist was greater than the subject.

Mike's portrait of society's most infamous—and richest—wanton made him famous overnight. Even the repro cubes you can buy today are impressive, but the original, with its original subtle circuits and focused broadcasts, is staggering.

A collector in Rome brought Cilento to my attention, and when I had seen the Snowdragon cube I managed an introduction. We met at Santini's villa in Ostia and like most young artists he had heard of me.

We met by a pool and his first words were, "You sponsored Wiesenthal for years, didn't you?" I nodded, wary now, for with every artist you help there are ten who demand it.

"His *Montezuma* opera was trash."

I smiled. "It was well received."

"He did not understand that Aztec anymore than he understood Cortez." He looked at me with a challenge.

"I agree, but by the time I heard it, it was too late."

He relaxed and kicked his foot in the water and squinted at two nearly nude daughters of a lunar mineral baron that were walking by. He seemed to have made his point and had nothing more to say.

Cilento intrigued me. In the course of a number of years of "discovering" artists I had met all types, from the shy ones who hide to the burly ones who demand my patronage. And I had met the kind who seem indifferent to me, as Cilento seemed to be. But many others had acted that way and I had learned to disregard everything but finished work and the potential for work.

"Your Snowdragon cube was superb," I said.

He nodded and squinted in another direction. "Yeah," he said. Then as an afterthought he added, "Thank you." We spoke for a moment of the cube and he told me what he thought of its subject.

"But it made you famous," I said.

He squinted at me and after a moment he said, "Is that what art is about?"

I laughed. "Fame is very useful. It opens doors. It makes things possible. It makes it easier to be even more famous."

"It gets you laid," Cilento said with a smile.

"It can get you killed, too," I added.

"It's a tool, Mr. Thorne, just like molecular circuits or dynamic integration or a screwdriver. But it can give you freedom. I want that freedom; every artist needs it."

"That's why you picked Diana?"

He grinned and nodded. "Besides, that female was a great challenge."

"I imagine so," I said and laughed, thinking of Diana at seventeen, beautiful and predatory, clawing her way up the monolithic walls of society.

We had a drink together, then shared a psychedelic in the ruins of a temple of Vesta, and became Mike and Brian to each other. We sat on old stones and leaned against the stub of a crumbling column and looked down at the lights of Santini's villa.

"An artist needs freedom," Mike said, "more than he needs paint or electricity or cube diagrams or stone. Or food. You can always get the materials, but the freedom to use them is precious. There is only so much time."

"What about money? That's freedom, too," I said.

"Sometimes. You can have money and no freedom, though. But usually fame brings money." I nodded, thinking that in my case it was the other way around.

We looked out at the light of a half-moon on the Tyrrhenian Sea and had our thoughts. I thought of Madelon.

"There's someone I'd like you to do," I said. "A woman. A very special woman."

"Not right now," he said. "Perhaps later. I have several commissions that I want to do."

"Keep me in mind when you have time. She's a very unusual woman."

He glanced at me and tossed a pebble down the hill. "I'm sure she is," he said.

"You like to do women, don't you?" I asked.

He smiled in the moonlight and said, "You figured that out from one cube?"

"No. I bought the three small ones you did before."

He looked at me sharply. "How did you know they even existed? I hadn't told anyone."

"Something as good as the Snowdragon cube couldn't come out of nowhere. There had to be something earlier. I hunted down the owners and bought them."

"The old lady is my grandmother," he said. "I'm a little sorry I sold it, but I needed money." I made a mental note to have it sent back to him.

"Yes, I like doing women," he said softly, leaning back against the pale column. "Artists have always liked doing women. To . . . to capture that elusive shadow of a flicker of a glimpse of a moment . . . in paint, in stone, in clay, or in wood, or on film . . . or with molecular constructs."

"Rubens saw them plump and gay," I said. "Lautrec saw them depraved and real."

"To Da Vinci they were mysterious," he said. "Matisse saw them idle and voluptuous. Michelangelo hardly saw them at all. Picasso saw them in endless mad variety."

"Gaugin . . . sensuality," I commented. "Henry Moore saw them as abstracts, a starting point for form. Van Gogh's women reflected his own mad genius brain."

"Cezanne saw them as placid cows," Mike laughed. "Fellini saw them as multifaceted creatures that were part angel, part beast. In the photographs of Andre de Dienes the women are realistic fantasies, erotic and strange."

"Tennessee Williams saw them as insane cannibals, fascinatingly repulsive. Sternberg's women were unreal, harsh, dramatic," I said. "Clayton's females were predatory fiends."

"Jason sees them as angels, slightly confused," Mike said, delighted with the little game. "Coogan saw them as motherly monsters."

"And you?" I asked. He stopped and the smile faded. After a long moment he answered. "As illusions, I suppose."

He rolled a fragment of stone from the time of Caesar in his fingers and spoke softly, almost to himself.

"They . . . aren't quite real, somehow. The critics say I created a masterpiece of erotic realism, a milestone in figurative art. But . . . they're . . . wisps. They're incredibly real for only an instant . . . fantastically shadowy another. Women are never the same from moment to moment. Perhaps that's why they fascinate me."

I didn't see Mike for some time after that, though we kept in touch. He did a portrait of Princess Helga of the Netherlands, quite modestly clad, the cube filled with its famous dozen golden sculptures and the vibrations of love and peace.

For the monks at Welles, on Mars, Mike did a large cube of Buddha, and it quickly became a tourist attraction. Repro cubes made a small fortune for the monastery.

Anything Mike chose to do was quickly bought and commissions flowed in from individuals, companies and foundations, even from movements. What he did was a simple nude of his mistress of the moment. It was erotic enough in pose, but powerfully pornographic in vibrations, and after Mike left her she received a Universal-Metro contract. The young Shah of Iran bought the cube to install in his long-abuilding Gardens of Babylon.

For his use of alpha, beta and gamma wave projectors, as well as advances in differentiated sonics, Mike was the subject of an entire issue of *Modern Electronics*.

Mike had paid his dues towards his art, for while studying at Cal Tech he had worked on the Skyshield project, a systems approach to electronic defense against low energy particles to use on the space stations. After graduation he had gone to work at the Bell lab in their brainwave complex on Long Island. He quit when he got a Guggenheim grant for his art.

From his "Pleasurewoman" cube General Electric picked up some of Mike's modifications for their new multilayer image projectors and beta wave generators. For the artists that use models or three-dimensional objects to record the basic image cycle—such as breathing, running water, or repeating events—Nakamura, Ltd. brought out a new camera design in circular pattern distribution that contained many of Mike's suggestions. For the artist working in original abstractions, Mike built his own ultra-fine electron brush and an image generator linked with a graphics computer that produced an almost infinite number of variables. Mike Cilento was proving himself as an innovator and engineer as well as artist, an unusual combination.

I met Mike again at the opening of his "Solar System" series in the Grand Museum in Athens. The ten cubes hung from the ceiling, each with its non-literal interpretation of the sun and planets, from the powerball of Sol to the hard, shiny ballbearing of Pluto.

Mike seemed caged, a tiger in a trap, but very happy to see me. He was a volunteer kidnapee as I spirited him away to my apartment in the old part of town.

He sighed as we entered, tossed his jacket into a Lifestyle chair and strolled out onto the balcony. I picked up two glasses and a bottle of Cretan wine and joined him.

He sighed again, sank into the chair, and sipped the wine. I chuckled and said, "Fame getting too much for you?"

He grunted at me. "Why do they always want the artist at openings? The art speaks for itself."

"Public relations. To touch the hem of creativity. Maybe some of it will rub off on them." He grunted again, and we lapsed into comfortable silence, looking out at the Parthenon, high up and night-lit.

At last he spoke. "Being an artist is all I ever wanted to be, like kids growing up to be astronauts or ball players. It's an honor to be able to do it, whatever *it* is. I've painted and I've sculpted. I've done light mosaics and glow dot patterns.

I even tried music for awhile. None of them really seemed to be it. But I think molecular constructs are the closest."

"Because of the extreme realism?"

"That's part of it. Abstraction, realism, expressionism—they're just labels. What matters is what *is,* the thoughts and emotions that you transmit. The sensatron units are fairly good tools. You can work almost directly on the emotions. When GE gets the new ones ready, I think it will be possible to get even more subtle shadings with the alpha waves. And, of course, with more units you can get more complex."

"You are as much an engineer as you are an artist," I said.

He smiled and sipped his wine. "Every medium, every technique has those who find that area their particular feast. Look at actors. Once there was only the play, from start to finish, no retakes and live. Then came film and tape and events shot out of sequence. No emotional line to follow from start to finish. It takes a particular kind of actor who can discipline himself to those flashbacks and flashforwards. In the days of mime there were probably superb actors lost because their art was in their voice."

"And today?" I prompted.

"Today the artist who cannot master electronics has a difficult time in many of the arts. Leonardo da Vinci could have, but probably not Michelangelo. There are many fine artists born out of their time, in both directions."

I asked a question I had often asked artists working in non-traditional media. "Why is the sensatron such a good medium for you?"

"It is immensely versatile. A penline can only do a certain number of things and hint at others. An oil painting is static. It attempts to be real but is a frozen moment. But sometimes frozen moments are better than motion. A motion picture, a tape, a play all convey a variety of meanings and emotions, even changes of location and perspective. As such they are very good tools. The more you can communicate the better. With the power of the sensatron you can transmit to the viewer such emotions, such feelings, that he becomes a participant, not just a viewer. Involvement. Commitment. I wouldn't do a sensatron to communicate some things, just because it's so much work and the communication minor. But the sensatron units can do almost anything any other art form can do. That's why I like it. Not because it's the fashionable art form right now."

"You've had no trouble getting your first license?" I asked.

"No, the Guggenheim people fixed it." He shook his head. "The idea of having to have a license to do a piece of art seems bizarre." He lifted his hand before I spoke. "Yeah, I know. If they didn't watch who had control of alpha to omega projectors we'd be trooping to the polls to vote for a dictator and not even know we didn't want to. Or so they think."

"It's a powerful force, difficult to fight. Your own brain is telling you to buy, buy, buy, use, use, use, and that's pretty hard to fight. Think of it like prescription drugs."

He nodded his head. "Can't you just see it? 'I'm sorry, Michelangelo, but this piece of Carrara marble needs a priority IX license and you have only a IV.' And Michelangelo says, 'But I want to do this statue of David, see? Big, tall boy, with a sling, kinda sullen looking. It isn't because he'll be nude, is it?' 'You just go to the Art Control Board in beautiful downtown Florence, *Signor* Buonarroti, and fill out the papers in triplicate, last name first, first name last. And remember neatness counts. Speak to Pope Julius, maybe he can fix it for you.'"

We laughed gently in the night. "But art and technology are coexisting more now than ever," I said.

"Oh, I understand," Mike sighed, "but I don't have to like it." I thought about the Pornotron someone had given me, hanging from the ceiling of my Moscow apartment. One night with a healthy blonde clarinetist had been enough to convince me I didn't need artificial enhancement of my sexual pleasures. It was like being forcefed your favorite dessert.

We lapsed into silence. The ancient city murmured at us. I thought about Madelon.

"I still want you to do that portrait of someone very close to me," I reminded him.

"Soon. I want to do a cube on a girl I know first. But

I must find a new place to work. They bother me there, now that they found where I am."

I mentioned my villa on Sikinos, in the Aegean, and Mike seemed interested, so I offered it to him. "There's an ancient grain storage there you could use as a studio. They have a controlled plasma fusion plant so there would be as much power as you need. There's a house, just the couple that takes care of it, and a very small village nearby. I'd be honored if you'd use it."

He accepted the offer graciously and I talked of Sikinos and its history for awhile.

"The very old civilizations interest me the most," Mike said. "Babylon, Assyria, Sumer, Egypt, the valley of the Euphrates. Crete seems like a newcomer to me. Everything was new then. There was everything to invent, to see, to believe. The gods were not parted into Christianity and all the others then. There was a god, a belief for everyone, big and small. It was not God and the Anti-gods. Life was simpler then."

"Also more desperate," I said. "Despotic kings. Disease. Ignorance. Superstition. There was everything to invent, all right, because nothing much had been invented."

"You're confusing technology with progress. They had clean air, new lands, freshness. The world wasn't used up then."

"You're a pioneer, Mike," I said. "You're working in a totally new medium."

He laughed and took a gulp of wine. "Not really. All art began as science and all science began as art. The engineers were using the sensatrons before the artists. Before that there were a dozen lines of thought and invention that crossed at one point to become sensatrons. The sensatrons just happen to be a better medium to say certain things. To say other things a pen drawing or a poem or a motion picture might be best. Or even not to say it at all."

I laughed and said, "The artist doesn't see things, he sees himself."

Mike smiled and stared for a long time at the columned structure on the hill. "Yes, he certainly does," he said softly.

"Is that why you do women so well?" I asked. "Do you see in them what you want to see, those facets of 'you' that interest you?"

He turned his shaggy dark head and looked at me. "I thought you were some kind of big businessman, Brian. You sound like an artist to me."

"I am. Both. A businessman with a talent for money and an artist with no talent at all."

"There are a lot of artists without talent. They use persistence instead."

"I often wish they wouldn't," I grumbled. "Everyone thinks he's an artist. If I have any talent at all, it'd be to realize I have none. However, I am a first class appreciator. That's why I want you to do a cube of my friend."

"Persistence, see?" He laughed. "I'm going to do a very erotic nude while I'm on Sikinos. Afterwards, perhaps, I'll want to do something more calmly. Perhaps then I'll do your friend, if she interests me."

"She might not be so calming. She's . . . an original."

We left it at that and I told him to contact my office in Athens when he was ready to go to the island and that they would arrange everything.

I found out later, almost by accident, from a friend, that Mike had been "drafted" temporarily to work on something called the Guardian Project. I put in a vidcall and found a wall of red tape and security preventing me from talking to him on Station Three, the space medicine research satellite. Luckily, I knew a bluesky general who shared my passion for Eskimo sculpture and old Louis L'Amour westerns. He set it up and I caught Mike coming off duty.

"What do they have you doing, a portrait of the commanding honcho?"

He smiled wearily and slumped on the bunk, kicking the pickup around with his foot to put himself within range. "Nothing that easy. Guardian is Skyshield all over again, only on priority *uno*. They rotated everyone out of here for observation and brought in fresh blood. They seemed to think I could help." He looked tired and distracted.

"Anything I can do? Want me to see if I can get you out of there? I know a few people."

He shook his head. "No. Thank you, though. They gave me the choice of an out-and-out priority draft or a contract. I just want to get it over with and back to living my way." He stared at the papers in his hand with unseeing eyes.

"Is it the low energy particles that's giving them the trouble?"

He nodded. "Exposure over a long period of time is the problem. There's a sudden metabolic shift that's disastrous. Unless we can lick it it will limit the time man can be in space." He held up a thumb-size node. "I think this might do it, but I'm not certain. It's the prototype of a Full Scale Molecular System I designed."

"Can you get a patent?" I asked automatically.

He shook his head and scratched his face with the node. "Anything I design is theirs. It's in the contract. You see, the trouble isn't in this FSMS unit, but in the damned sensing and control systems. First you gotta find the particles, then you gotta get their attention. Christ, if I could just shunt them into subspace and get rid of them, I'd . . ." His voice trailed off and he stared at the bulkhead.

After a moment or two he shook himself and grinned at me. "Sorry. Listen, let me give you a call later on. I just had an idea."

"Artistic inspiration?" I grinned.

"Huh? Yeah, I suppose so. Excuse me, huh?"

"Sure." He slapped the control and I was staring at static. I didn't see him again for five months, then I took his call patched through from the Sahara base to my Peking hotel. He said he couldn't talk about the Guardian Project but he was free to take me up on the Sikinos offer, if it was still open. I sent him straight up to the island and two more months went by before anything more was heard. I received a pen drawing from him of the view from the terrace at the villa, with a nude girl sunbathing. Then in late August I took a call from him at my General Anomaly office.

"I finished the cube on Sophia. I'm in Athens. Where are you? Your office was very secretive and insisted on patching me through to you."

"That's their job. Part of my job is not letting certain

people know where I am or what I'm doing. But I'm in New York. I'm going to Bombay Tuesday, but I could stop off there. I'm anxious to see the new cube. Who's Sophia?"

"A girl. She's gone now."

"Is that good or bad?"

"Neither. I'm at Nikki's, so come on over. I'd like your opinion on the new one."

I felt suddenly proud. "Tuesday at Nikki's. Give her and Barry my love."

I hung up and punched for Madelon.

Beautiful Madelon. Rich Madelon. Famous Madelon. Madelon of the superlatives. Madelon the Elusive. Madelon the illusion.

I saw her at nineteen, slim yet voluptuous, standing at the center of a semicircle of admiring men at a boring party in San Francisco. I wanted her, instantly, with that "shock of recognition" they talk about.

She looked at me between the shoulders of a communications executive and a fossil fuels magnate. Her gaze was steady and her face quiet. I felt faintly foolish just staring and many of the automatic reflexes that rich men develop to save themselves money and heartbreak went into action. I started to turn away and she smiled.

I stopped, still looking at her, and she excused herself from the man speaking to her and leaned forward. "Are you going now?" she asked.

I nodded, slightly confused. With great charm she excused herself from the reluctant semicircle and came over to me. "I'm ready," she said in that calm, certain way she had. I smiled, my protective circuits all activated and alert, but my ego was touched.

We went into the glass elevator that dropped down the outside of the Fairmont Tower Complex and looked out at the fog coming over the hills near Twin Peaks and flowing down into the city.

"Where are we going?" she asked.

"Where would you like to go?" I had met a thousand women that attached themselves to me with all the apparently natural lust, delight, and casualness possible between a poor girl and a rich man. Some had been bold, some subtle, some as subtle as it was possible for them to be. A few had frankly offered business arrangements. I had accepted some of each, in my time. But this one . . . this one was either different or more subtle than most.

"You expect me to say 'Wherever you are going,' don't you?" she said with a smile.

"Yes. One way or another." We left the elevator and went into the guarded garage directly. Entering your car on a public street is sometimes dangerous for a rich man.

"Well, where are we going?" She smiled at me as Bowie held the door open for us. The door clicked shut behind us like the safe door it nearly was.

"I had been contemplating two choices. My hotel and work on some papers . . . or Earth, Fire, Air and Water."

"Let's do both. I've never been to either place."

I picked up the intercom. "Bowie, take us to Earth, Fire, Air and Water."

"Yessir, I'll report it to Control."

The girl laughed and said, "Is someone watching you?"

"Yes, my local Control. They must know where I am, even if I don't want to be found. It's the penalty for having businesses in different time zones. By the way, are we using names?"

"Sure, why not?" she smiled. "You are Brian Thorne and I am Madelon Morgana. You're rich and I'm poor."

I looked her over, from the casually tossed hair to the fragile sandals. "No . . . I think you might be without money, but you are not poor."

"Thank you, sir," she said. San Francisco rolled by and Bowie blanked out the windows as we approached a small street riot, then turned off towards the waterfront. When it was safe, he brought the cityscape back to us as we rolled down a hill and up another.

When we arrived at Earth, Fire, Air and Water, Bowie called me back apologetically as I was going through the door. I told Madelon to wait and went back to get the report on the interphone. When I joined Madelon inside she smiled at me and asked, "How was my report?"

When I looked innocent she laughed. "If Bowie didn't have a dossier on me from your Control or whatever it is

I'd be very much surprised. Tell me, am I a dangerous type, an anarchist or a blaster or something?"

I smiled, for I like perceptive people. "It says you are the illegitimate daughter of Madame Chiang Kai-Shek and Johnny Potseed with convictions for mopery, drudgery and penury."

"What's mopery?"

"I haven't the faintest. My omniscient staff tells me you are nineteen, a hick kid from Montana and a half-orphan who worked for eleven months in Great Falls in an office of the Blackfoot National Enterprises."

Her eyes got big and she gasped. "Found out at last! My desperate secrets revealed!" She took my arm and tugged me into the elevator that would drop us down to the cavern below. She looked up at me with big innocent eyes as we stood in the packed elevator. "Gee, Mr. Thorne, when I agreed to baby-sit for you and Mrs. Thorne I never knew you'd be taking me out."

I turned my head slowly and looked at her with a granite face, ignoring the curious and the grinning. "The next time I catch you indulging in mopery with my Afghan I'm going to leave you home."

Her eyes got all wet and sad. "No, please, I promise to be good. You can whip me again when we get home."

I raised my eyebrows. "No, I think wearing the collar will be enough." The door opened. "Come, my dear. Excuse me, please."

"Yes, master," she said humbly.

The Earth part of the club was the raw ground under one of the many San Francisco hills, sprayed with a structural plastic so that it looked just like a raw-dug cave, yet quite strong. We went down the curving passage toward the maelstrom of noise that was a famous *quiver* group and came out into the huge hemispherical cave. Overhead, a lattice-work of concrete supported a transparent swimming pool filled with nude and semi-nude swimmers. Some were guests and some were professional entertainers.

There was a waterfall at one end and torches burned in holders in the wall, while a flickering firelight was projected over everything. The *quiver* group blasted forth from a rough cave hacked into the dirt walls halfway up to the overhead swimming pool.

As I took her arm to guide her into the *quivering* mob on the dance floor I said, "You know there is no Mrs. Thorne."

She smiled at me with a serene confidence. "That's right."

The night swirled around us. Winds blew in, scented and warm, then cool and brisk. People crashed into the water over us with galaxies of bubbles around them. One *quiver* group gave way to another, tawny animals in pseudo-lion skins and shaggy hair, the women bare-breasted and wanton. Madelon was a hundred women in a hundred minutes, but seemingly without effort. They were all her, from sullen siren to goshwowing teenie. I confess to a helpless infatuation and cared not if she was laying a trap for me or not.

The elemental decor was a stimulant and I felt younger than I had in years. People joined us, laughed and drank and tripped, and left, and others came. Madelon was a magnet, attracting joy and delight, and I was very proud.

We came to the surface at dawn and I triggered a tagalong for Bowie. We drove out to watch sunup over the Bay, then went to my hotel. In the elevator I said, "I'll have to make that up to Bowie, I don't often stay out like that."

"Oh?" Her face was impish, then softened and we kissed outside my door. She began undressing as we entered, with great naturalness, and laughingly pulled me into the shower even as I was learning the beauty of her lithe young figure. We soaped and slid our bodies over one another and I felt younger and more alive than I had in godknows.

We made love and music played. Outside, the city awakened and began its business. What can you say about two people making love for the first time? Sometimes it is a disaster, for neither of you know the other, and that disaster colors the subsequent events. But sometimes it is exciting and new and wonderful and satisfying, making you want to do it again and again.

It changed my life.

I took her to Triton, the bubble city beneath the Mediterranean near Malta, where we marveled at the organic gill research and watched the plankton sweepersubs docking. We donned artificial membrane gills and dived among the rocks and fish to great depths. Her hair streamed behind her like a mermaid, and we dipped and rose with a school of swift lantern-fish. We "discovered" the crusted remains of a Phoenician war galley and made love at twenty fathoms.

We visited Naxos, where Dionysus found Ariadne asleep on the shore, deserted by Theseus, and where I found Madelon, naked and gleaming, playing in a tidepool. At Kos, the birthplace of Hippocrates, Hilary gave a great party at her villa, and we "premiered" a tape by Thea Simon, and ate fruit on the terrace and watched the ships go into space from Sahara Base.

We flew to San Salvador and rode through the tall grasses on my cattle ranch there, and made love by a stream. We dove off the Great Barrier Reef in the ecology preserve, and walked on the beach at Bora Bora at sunset, talking of our childhoods. We saw the temple dancers at Angor Wat and felt how very old man was, and how young. We went to a party at Li Wing's, in Nanking, where Madelon seemed childishly pleased that I turned down the offer of three gorgeous raven-haired beauties for a night with her.

The world was a playground, a beautiful toy. We could deplore the harsh, but necessary, methods they were using to reduce the population in India, even as we flew high overhead to Paris, for Andre's *fête*, where the most beautiful women in Europe appeared in sculptured body jewelry and little else.

I took her to the digs at Ur in the hot, dusty Euphrates Valley, but stayed in an airconditioned mobilevilla. We sailed the Indian Ocean with Karpolis even as the Bombay riots were killing hundreds of thousands. The rest of the world seemed far away, and I really didn't care much, for I was gorging at a love-feast. My man Benedict handled the routine matters and I put almost everything else off for awhile.

We went up to Station One and "danced" in the nullgravity of the so-called "Star Ballroom" in the big can of the central hub. We took the shuttle to the moon, for Madelon's first visit. I saw Tycho Base with fresh eyes and a sense of adventure and wonder which she generated. We went on up to Copernicus Dome, then around to the new Young Observatory on Backside. We looked at the stars together, seeing them so clearly, so close and unblinking. I ached to go all the way out and so did she. Bundled into bulky suits we took a walk on the surface, slightly annoyed to be discreetly watched over by a Lunar Tour guide, there to see that the greenhorns didn't muck up.

We loved every minute of it. We lay spoon-fashion in our bed at night and talked of the stars and alien life and made lovers' plans for the future.

I was in love. I was blind, raw, sensitive, happy, insane, and madly foolish. I spent an emotional treasure and counted it well-used.

I was indeed in love.

But love cannot stifle, nor can it be bought, not even with love. Love can only be a gift, freely given, freely taken. I used my money as a tool, as Cilento might use a scan pattern, to give us time and pleasure, not to "buy" Madelon.

All these trips cost a fortune, but it was one of the reasons I had money. I could have stopped working at making it long before, except I knew I would seriously drain my capital with commissions and projects and joy rides and women. I was already starting to think of going to Mars with Madelon, but it was a seven month trip one-way and that was a big chunk of time to carve from my schedule.

Instead, I introduced her to my world. There were the obvious public events, the concerts and exhibitions and parties. She shared my enthusiasm in finding and assisting young artists in every field, from the dirt-poor Mexican peasant with a natural talent for clay sculpture to the hairy, sulky Slav with the house full of extraordinary synthecizor tapes, that few had heard.

There was the private world, the "secure" houses in various parts of the globe, the private beaches and fast cars, the worthy friends, like Turner, the senator, and Dunn, the percussionist; like Barbara and Carol and Greg and the others. She had gowns by Queen Kong, in Shanghai, and custom powerjewels by Simpson. She had everything she wanted, which was probably my first mistake.

Some have said that Madelon Morgana was a bitch, a Circe, a witch, a fortune-hunter, a corrupter. Some have said that she was misunderstood, an angel, a saint, a creature much sinned against. I knew her very well and she was probably all those things, at various times and places. I was the first, last and only legal husband of Madelon Morgana.

I wanted her and I got her. Getting a woman I wanted was not all that difficult. Standing on my money and fame I was very tall. Sometimes I wonder how well I might do as a lover without money, but I was too lazy to try.

I wanted Madelon because she was the most beautiful woman I had ever seen, and the least boring. Sooner or later all women bored me, and most men. When there are no surprises even the most attractive people grow stale. Madelon may have aroused a great variety of emotions in me, from love to hate, at times, but she never bored me and boredom is the greatest sin. Even those that *work* at not being boring can become boring because their efforts show.

But Madelon was beautiful inside as well as out and I had had my fill of beautiful flesh and gargoyle minds.

It wasn't so much that I "got" Madelon as that I married her. I attracted her, our sex life was outstanding, and my wealth was exactly the convenience she needed. My money was *her* freedom.

I opened up to her as I had not to anyone else. I tried to show her my world, at least the art part of it. The business part was the game part, a sort of global chess, or interplanetary poker, and dull to most people.

I took her to a concert by a young synthecizor musician whose career one of my foundations was sponsoring. I watched her handle the attention and Instant Fame that came to unknown beauties attached to Money and Power. Afterwards we lay·on a fur-covered liquibed under the one-way glass dome of my New York apartment and watched the lights in the towers and the flying insect dots of helos.

"Are all musicians as arrogant as that electronic music composer who cornered you in the foyer?" Madelon asked.

"No, thank god. But when you are convinced you have conceived something the world must experience you are anxious to have it presented."

"But he was *demanding* you sponsor it!" She shook her

head angrily, spreading out her hair on my chest. "What an ego!"

"Everyone has one," I said, my fingertips on her flesh. "People are certain I have a very big one because of all the art and events I assist. But I want the art to come into existence, not to further my own fame or ego."

"Oh, Brian," she said, flipping over and pressing her voluptuous body to mine. "Sometimes you just modest yourself right out the back door!"

I didn't reply. People never understand. She would, I hoped, in time. I wanted to midwife creativity, not scratch my ego onto the base of greatness.

"Why don't we get married?" I asked. Her eyes opened wide.

"Married?" She sat up and waved her hand around at the jewel towers. "You mean *legally,* instead of in front of God and everybody?" I nodded. She sobered and said, "You don't have to do that."

"I know I don't," I said. "I'm a very self-indulgent person. I do only what I want to do. I want to go to Mars some day and some day I will. Right now I want us to be married."

"And what will you want tomorrow? Not to be?"

I pulled her down and kissed her. "You don't seem to understand that I am a very powerful man and what I want, I get."

She looked at me through slitted eyes. "Oh, really?" she said slowly. "What do I have to say about it?"

"Why ask me? Just say it."

"In that case, I say yes."

After our marriage she stopped being Madelon Morgana and became not Madelon Thorne, but *Madelon Morgana*. At first I was a convenient and attractive aid, a refuge, a shoulder, an open door, a defender, an older and wiser head. She liked what I was, then later, *who* I was. We became friends. We fell in love. But I was not her only lover.

No one owned Madelon, not even I. Her other lovers were infrequent, but quite real. I never kept count, though I knew Control could retrieve the data from the surveillance section's computers. It was not that I had her watched, but that she must be watched for her own protection. It is all part of being rich and how better to extract a few million from me than by the ancient and dishonorable means of kidnapping. Guarding against an assassin was almost impossible, if the man was intelligent and determined, but the watch teams gave me comfort when she was not close. Meanwhile, I studied *mazeru* with Shigeta, when I could. Your own reflexes are your best protection.

In four years Madelon had only two lovers that I thought were beneath her. One was a rough miner who had struck it big in the Martian mines near Bradbury and was expending a certain animal vitality along with his new wealth. The second was a tape star, quite charming and beautiful, but essentially hollow. They were momentary liaisons and when she perceived that I was distressed she broke off immediately, something that both men could not understand.

But Madelon and I were friends, as well as man and wife, and one is not knowingly rude to friends. I frequently insult people, but I am never rude to them. Madelon's taste was excellent, and these other relationships were usually fruitful in learning and joy, so that the two that were distasteful to me were very much in the minority.

Michael Cilento was different.

I talked to Madelon and then flew to see Mike at Nikki's. Our meeting was warm. "I can't thank you enough for the villa," he said, hugging me. "It was so beautiful and Nikos and Maria were so very nice to me. I did some drawings of their daughter. But the island—ah! Beautiful . . . very peaceful, yet . . . exciting, somehow."

"Where's the new cube?"

"At the Athena Gallery. They're having a one-man, one-cube show."

"Well, let's go. I'm anxious to see it." I turned to my man Stamos. "Madelon will be along soon. Please meet her and take her directly to the Athena." To Mike I said, "Come —I'm excited."

The cube was life-size, as were all of Mike's works. Sophia was olive-skinned and full-breasted, lying on a couch covered with deep fur, curled like a cat, yet fully displayed.

There was a richness in the work, an opulence reminiscent of Matisse's odalisques. But the sheer animal eroticism of the girl overpowered everything.

She was the Earth Mother, Eve and Lilith together. She was the pagan princess, the high priestess of Ba'al, the great whore of Babylon. She was nude, but a sun ornament gleamed dully between her breasts. Beyond her, through an arch of ancient, worn stone, was a dawn world, lush and green, beyond a high wall. There was a feeling of time here, a setting far back beyond recorded history, when myths were men and monsters perhaps real.

She lounged on animal furs, with the faint suggestion of a wanton sprawl, with no part of her hidden, and a half-eaten apple in her hand. The direct suggestion of Eve would have been ludicrous, except for the sheer raw power of the piece. Suddenly the symbolism of the Biblical Eve and her apple of knowledge had a reality, a meaning.

Here, somewhere in Man's past, Michael Cilento seemed to be saying, there was a turning. From simplicity toward complexity, from innocence to knowledge and beyond, perhaps to wisdom. And always the intimate personal secret lusts of the body.

All this in one cube, from one face. I walked to the side. The girl did not change, except that I was now looking at her side, but the view through the arch had changed. It was the sea, stretching under heavy clouds to the unchanging horizon. The waves rolled in, oily and almost silent.

The back view was past the voluptuous girl toward what she looked at: a dim room, a corridor leading to it, lit with flickering torches, going back into darkness . . . into time? Forward into time? The Earth Mother was waiting.

The fourth side was a solid stone wall beyond the waiting woman and on the wall was set a ring and from the ring hung a chain. Symbol? Decoration? But Mike was too much an artist to have something without meaning in his work, for decoration was just design without content.

I turned to Mike to speak, but he was looking at the door.

Madelon stood in the entrance, looking at the cube. Slowly she walked toward it, her eyes intent, secret, searching.

I said nothing. but stepped aside. I glanced at Mike and my heart twisted. He was staring at her as intently as she looked at the sensatron cube.

As Madelon walked closer, Mike stepped near me. "Is this your friend?" he asked. I nodded. "I'll do that cube you wanted," he said softly.

We waited silently as Madelon walked slowly around the cube. I could see she was excited. She was tanned and fit, fresh from a submarine exploration of the Aegean with Markos. At last she turned away from the cube and came directly to me with a swirl of her skirt. We kissed and held each other a long time.

We looked into each other's eyes for a long time. "You're well?" I asked her.

"Yes." She looked at me a long moment more, a soft smile on her face, searching my eyes for any hurt she might have caused. In that shorthand, intimate language of old friends and old lovers she questioned me with her look.

"I'm fine," I said, and meant it. I was always her friend but not so often her lover. But I still had more than most men, and I do not mean my millions. I had her love and respect, while others had usually just her interest.

She turned to Mike with a smile. "You are Michael Cilento. Would you do my portrait, or use me as a subject?" She was perceptive enough to know that there was a more than subtle difference.

"Brian has already spoken to me about it," he said.

"And?" She was not surprised.

"I always need to spend some time with my subject before I can do a cube." Except with the Buddha cube, I thought with a smile.

"Whatever you need," Madelon said.

Mike looked past her at me and raised his eyebrows. I made a gesture of acquiescence. Whatever was needed. I flatter myself that I understand the creative process better than most non-artists. What was needed was needed; what was not needed was unimportant. With Mike, technology had ceased to be anything but a minimal hindrance between him and his art. Now he needed only intimacy and understanding of what he intended to do. And that meant time.

"Use the Transjet," I said. "Blake Mason has finished the house on Malagasy. Use that. Or roam around awhile."

Mike smiled at me. "How many homes do you have, anyway?"

"I like to change environments. It makes life more interesting. And as much as I try to keep my face out of the news it keeps creeping in and I can't be myself in as many places as I'd like."

Mike shrugged. "I thought a little fame would be helpful, and it has, but I know what you mean. After the interviews on *Artworld* and the Jimmy Brand show I can't seem to go anywhere without someone recognizing me."

"The bitter with the sweet," I said.

"Brian uses a number of personas as well," Madelon said. Mike raised his eyebrows. "The secret lives of Brian Thorne, complete with passports and unicards," she laughed.

Mike looked at me and I explained. "It's necessary when you are the center of a power structure. There are times you need to Get Away From It All, or to simply not be you for awhile. It's much like an artist changing styles. The Malagasy house belongs to 'Ben Ford' of Publitex . . . I haven't been there yet, so you be Ben."

People have said that I asked for it. But you cannot stop the tide; it comes in when it wants and it goes when it wants. Madelon was unlike any individual that I had ever known. She owned herself. Few people do. So many are mere reflections of others, mirrors of fame or power or personality. Many let others do their thinking for them. Some are not really people, but statistics.

But Madelon was unlike the others. She took and gave without regard for very many things, demanding only truth. She was hard on her friends, for even friends sometimes require a touch of non-truth to help them out.

She conformed to my own definition of friendship: friends must interest, amuse, help and protect you. They can do nothing more. To what extent they fulfill these criteria defines the degree of friendship. Without interest there is no communication; without amusement there is no zest; without help and protection there is no trust, no truth, no security, no intimacy. Friendship is a two-way street and Madelon was my friend.

Michael Cilento was also unlike most other people. He was an Original, on his way to being a Legend. At the bottom level there are people who are "interesting" or "different." Those below that should not be allowed to waste your time. On the next step above is Unique. Then the Originals, and finally those rare Legends.

I might flatter myself and say that I was certainly different, possibly even Unique on a good day. Madelon was an undisputed Original. But I sensed that Michael Cilento had that something extra, the art, the drive, the vision, the talent that could make him a Legend. (Or destroy him.)

So they went off together. To Malagasy, off the African coast. To Capri. To New York. Then I heard they were in Algiers. I had my Control keep an extra special eye on them, even more than the usual protective surveillance I kept on Madelon. But I didn't check myself. It was their business.

A vidreport had them on Station One, dancing in the null gravity of the big ballroom balloon. Even without Control I was kept abreast of their actions and whereabouts by that host of people who found delight in telling me where my wife and her lover were. And what they were doing. How they looked. What they said. And so forth.

Somehow none of it surprised me. I knew Madelon and what she liked. I knew beautiful women. I knew that Mike's sensatron cubes were passports to immortality for many women.

Mike was not the only artist working in the medium, of course, for Hayworth and Powers were both exhibiting and Coe had already done his great "Family." But it was Mike the women wanted. Presidents and kings sought out Cinardo and Lisa Araminta. Vidstars thought Hampton fashionable. But Mike was the first choice for all the great beauties.

I was determined that Mike have the time and privacy to do a sensatron cube of Madelon and I made it mandatory at all my homes, offices, and branches that Mike and Madelon be isolated from the vidhacks and nuts and time wasters as much as possible.

It was the purest ego on my part, that lusting toward a sensatron portrait of Madelon. I suppose I wanted the world to know that she was "mine" as much as she could belong to anyone. I realized that all my commissioning of art was, at the bottom, ego.

Make no mistake—I enjoyed the art I helped make possible, with a few mistakes that kept me alert. But I enjoyed many kinds and levels and degrees of art. I did not go by present popularity but preferred to find and encourage new artists.

You see, I am a businessman. A very rich one, a very talented one, a very famous one, but no one will remember me beyond the memory of my few good friends. I would not even be a footnote in history, except for my association with the arts.

But the art I help create will make me live on. I am not unique in that. Some people endow colleges, or create scholarships or build stadiums. Some build great houses, or even cause laws to be passed. These are not always acts of pure egotism, but the ego often enters into it, I'm certain, and especially if it is tax deductible.

Over the years I have commissioned Vardi to do the Fates for the Terrace Garden of the General Anomaly complex, my financial base and main corporation. I pressed for Darrin to do the Rocky Mountain sculptures for United Motors. I talked Willoughby into doing his golden beast series at my home in Arizona. Caruthers did his "Man" series of cubes because of a commission from my Manpower company. The panels that are now in the Metropolitan were done for my Tahiti estate by Elinor Ellington. I gave the University of Pennsylvania the money to impregnate those hundreds of sandstone slab carvings on Mars and get them safely to Earth. I subsidized Eklundy for five years before he wrote his Martian Symphony. I sponsored the first air music concert at Sydney.

My ego has had a good working out.

I received a tape from Madelon the same day I had a call from the Pope, who wanted me to help him convince Mike to do his tomb sculptures. The new Reformed Church was once again involved in art patronage, a 2,500-year-old-tradition.

But getting a tape from Madelon, instead of a call, where I could reply, hurt me. I half-suspected I had lost Madelon.

My armored layers of sophistication told me glibly that I had asked for it, even had intrigued to achieve it. But my beast-gut told me that I had been a fool. This time I had outsmarted myself.

I dropped the tape in the playback. She was recording from a garden of Martian lichen in Trumpet Valley, and the granite boulders behind her were covered with the rust and olive green and glossy black of the alien transplants. I arranged for Ecolco to give Tashura the grant that made the transfer from Mars possible. The subtle, subdued colors seemed a suitable background for her beauty, and her message.

"Brian, he's fantastic. I've never met anyone like him."

I died a little and was sad. Others had amused her, or pleased her lush golden body, or were momentarily mysterious to her, but this time . . . this time I knew it was different.

"He's going to start the cube next week, in Rome. I'm very excited. I'll be in touch." I saw her punch the remote and the tape ended. I put my man Benedict on the trace and found her in the Eternal City, looking radiant.

"How much does he want to do it?" I asked. Sometimes my businessman's brain likes to keep things orderly and outfront, before confusion and misunderstanding sets in. But this time I was abrupt, crass and rather brutal, though my words were delivered in a normal, light tone. But all I had to offer was the wherewithal that could pay for the sensatron cube.

"Nothing," she said. "He's doing it for nothing. Because he wants to, Brian."

"Nonsense. I commissioned him. Cubes cost money to make. He's not that rich."

"He told me to tell you he wants to do it without any money. He's out now, getting new cilli nets."

I felt cheated. I had caused the series of events that would end in the creation of a sensatron portrait of Madelon, but I was going to be cheated of my only contribution, my only connection. I had to salvage something.

"It . . . it should be an extraordinary cube. Would Mike object if I built a structure just for it?"

"I thought you wanted to put it in the new house on Battle Mountain."

"I do, but I thought I might make a special small dome of spraystone. On the point, perhaps. Something extra nice for a Cilento masterpiece."

"It sounds like a shrine." Her face was quiet, her eyes looking into me.

"Yes," I answered slowly, "perhaps it is." Maybe people shouldn't get to know you so well that they can read your mind where you cannot. I changed the subject and we talked for a few minutes of various friends. Steve on the Venus probe. A fashionable *couturier* who was showing a line based on the new Martian tablet finds. A new sculptor working in magnaplastics. Blake Mason's designs for the Gardens of Babylon. A festival in Rio that Jules and Gina had invited us to. The Pope's desire for Mike to do his tomb. In short, all the gossip, trivia, and things of importance between friends.

I talked of everything except what I wanted to talk about.

When we parted Madelon told me with a sad, proud smile that she had never been so happy. I nodded and punched out, then stared sightlessly at the skyline. For a long moment I hated Michael Cilento and he was probably never so near death. But I loved Madelon and she loved Mike, so he must live and be protected. I knew that she loved me, too, but it was and had always been a different kind of love.

I went to a science board meeting at Tycho Base and looked at the green-brown-blue-white-streaked Earth "overhead" and only paid minimal attention to the speakers. I came down to a petroleum meeting at Hargesisa, in Somalia. I visited a mistress of mine in Samarkand, sold a company, bought an electrosnake for the Louvre, visited Armand in Nardonne, bought a company, commissioned a concerto from a new composer I liked in Ceylon, and donated an early Caruthers to the Prado.

I came, I went. I thought about Madelon. I thought about Mike. Then I went back to what I did best: making money, making work, getting things done, making time pass.

I had just come from a policy meeting of the North American Continent Ecology Council when Madelon called to say the cube was finished and would be installed in the Battle Mountain house by the end of the week.

"How is it?" I asked.

She smiled. "See for yourself."

"Smug bitch," I grinned.

"It's his best one, Brian. The best sensatron in the world."

"I'll see you Saturday." I punched out and took the rest of the day off and had an early dinner with two Swedish blondes and did a little fleshly purging. It did not really help very much.

On Saturday I could see the two tiny figures waving at me from the causeway bridging the house with the tip of the spire of rock where the copter pad was. They were holding hands.

Madelon was tanned, fit, glowing, dressed in white with a necklace of Cartier Tempoimplant tattoos across her shoulders and breasts in glowing facets of liquid fire. She waved at Bowie as she came to me, squinting against the dust the copter blades were still swirling about.

Mike was there, dressed in black, looking haunted.

Getting to you, boy? I thought. There was a vicious thrill in thinking it and I shamed myself.

Madelon hugged me and we walked together back over the high causeway and directly to the new spray-stone dome in the garden, at the edge of a five hundred foot cliff.

The cube was magnificent. There hadn't been anything like it, ever. Not ever.

It was the largest cube I'd seen. There have been bigger ones since but at the time it was quite large. None have been better. Its impact was stunning.

Madelon sat like a queen on what has come to be known as the Jewel Throne, a great solid thronelike block that seemed to be part temple, part jewel, part dream. It was immensely complex, set with faceted electronic patterns that gave it the effect of a superbly cut jewel that was somehow also liquid. Michael Cilento would have made his place in art history with that throne alone.

But on it sat Madelon. Nude. Her waist long hair fell in a simple cascade. She looked right out at you, sitting erect, almost primly, with an almost triumphant expression.

It drew me from the doorway. Everyone, everything was forgotten, including the original and the creator with me. There was only the cube. The vibrations were getting to me and my pulse increased. Even knowing that pulse generators were working on my alpha waves and broadcast projectors were doing this and sonics were doing that and my own alpha wave was being synchronized and reprojected did not affect me. Only the cube affected me. All else was forgotten.

There was just the cube and me, with Madelon in it, more real than the reality.

I walked to stand before it. The cube was slightly raised so that she sat well above the floor, as a queen should. Behind her, beyond the dark violet eyes, beyond the incredible *presence* of the woman, there was a dark, misty background that may or may not have been moving and changing.

I stood there a long time, just looking, experiencing. "It's incredible," I whispered.

"Walk around it," Madelon said. I felt the note of pride in her voice. I moved to the right and it was as if Madelon followed me with her eyes without moving them, following me by sensing me, alert, alive, ready for me. Already, the electronic image on the multi-layered surfaces was *real*. Mike's electronic brushes had transformed the straight basic video images in subtle ways, artful shifts and fragile shadings on many levels revealing and emphasizing delicately.

The figure of Madelon sat there, proudly naked, breathing normally with that fantastically lifelike movement possible to the skilled molecular constructors. The figure had none of the flamboyance that Caruthers or Raeburn brought to their figures, so delighted in their ability to bring "life" to their work that they saw nothing else.

But Mike had restraint. He had *power* in his work, understatement, demanding that the viewer put something of himself into it.

I walked around to the back. Madelon was no longer sitting

on the throne. It was empty, and beyond it, stretching to the horizon, was an ocean and above the toppling waves, stars. New constellations glowed. A meteor flashed. I stepped back to the side. The throne was unchanged but Madelon was back. She sat there, a queen, waiting.

I walked around the cube. She was on the other side, waiting, breathing, *being*. But in back she was gone.

But to where?

I looked long into the eyes of the figure in the cube. She stared back at me, into me. I seemed to feel her thoughts. Her face changed, seemed about to smile, grew sad, drew back into queenliness.

I drew back into myself. I went to Mike to congratulate him. "I'm stunned. There are no words."

He seemed relieved at my approval. "It's yours," he said. I nodded. There was nothing to say. It was the greatest work of art I knew. It was more than Madelon or the sum of all the Madelons that I knew existed. It was Woman as well as a specific woman. I felt humble in the presence of such great art. It was "mine" only in that I could house it. I could not contain it. It had to belong to the world.

I looked at the two of them. There was something else. I sensed what it was and I died some more. A flicker of hate for both of them flashed across my mind and was gone, leaving only emptiness.

"Madelon is coming with me," Mike said.

I looked at her. She made a slight nod, looking at me gravely, with deep concern in her eyes. "I'm sorry, Brian."

I nodded, my throat constricted suddenly. It was almost a business deal: the greatest work of art for Madelon, even trade. I turned back to look at the sensatron again and this time the image-Madelon seemed sad, yet compassionate. My eyes were wet and the cube shimmered. I heard them leave and long after the throb of the copter had faded away I stood there, looking into the cube, into Madelon, into myself.

They went to Athens, I heard, then to Russia for awhile. When they went to India so that Mike might do his Holy Men series I called off the discreet monitors Control still had on them. I saw him on a talk show and he seemed withdrawn, and spoke of the pressures fame placed upon him. Madelon was not on the show, nor did he speak of her.

As part of my technology updating I was given an article on Mike, from *Science News*, that spoke of his technical achievements rather than his artistic. It seemed the Full Scale Molecular System was a success and much of the credit was his. The rest of the article was on spinoffs of his basic research.

It all seemed remote from me, but the old habits died hard. My first thought on seeing the new Dolan exhibit was how Madelon would like it. I bought a complete sculptured powerjewel costume from Cartier's before I remembered, and ended up giving it to my companion of a weekend in Mexico City just to get rid of it.

I bought companies. I made things. I commissioned art. I sold companies. I went places. I changed mistresses. I made money. I fought stock control fights. Some I lost. I ruined people. I made others happy and rich. I was alone a lot.

I return often to Battle Mountain. That is where the cube is.

The greatness of it never bores me; it is different each time I see it, for I am different each time. But then Madelon never bored me either, unlike all other women, who sooner or later revealed either their shallowness or my inability to find anything deeper.

I look at the work of Michael Cilento and I know that he is an artist of his time, yet like many artists, *not* of his time. He uses the technology of his time, the attitude of an alien, and the same basic subject matter that generations of fascinated artists have used.

Michael Cilento is an artist of women. Many have said he is *the* artist who caught women as they were, as they wanted to be, and as *he* saw them, all in one work of art.

When I look at my sensatron cube, and at all the other Cilentos I have acquired, I am proud to have helped cause the creation of such art. But when I look at the Madelon that is in my favorite cube I sometimes wonder if the trade was worth it.

The cube is more than Madelon or the sum of the sum of all the Madelons who ever existed. But the reality of art is not the reality of reality.

After the showing of the Cilento Retrospective at the Modern the social grapevine told me nothing about them for several months. Reluctantly, I asked Control to check.

The check revealed their occupancy of a studio in London, but enquiries in the neighborhood showed that they had not emerged in over a month and no one answered a knock. I authorized a discreet illegal entry. Within minutes they were back on the satellite line to me in Tokyo.

"You probably should see this yourself, sir," the man said.

"Are they all right?" I asked and it hurt to ask.

"They're not here, sir. Clothes, papers, effects, but no trace."

"You checked with customs? You checked the building?"

"Yes, sir, first thing. No one knows anything, but . . ."

"Yes?"

"There's something here you should see."

The studio was large, a combination of junk yard, machine shop, mad scientist's laboratory and art gallery, much as every other sensatron artist's studio I had ever been in. Later, I was to see the details—the flowerwine bottles painted with gay faces, the tiny sensatron cubes that made you happy just to hold them and watch them change, the art books with new drawings done over the old reproductions, the crates and charts and diagrams.

Later, I would wander through the rubble and litter and museum quality art and see a few primitive daubs on canvo that were undoubtedly Madelon's. I'd find the barbaric jewelry, the laughing triphotos, the tapes, the Persian helmet stuck with dead flowers, the painted rock wrapped in aluminum foil setting in the refrigerator, the butterfly in permaplastic, the unfinished sandwich.

But all I saw when I walked in were the cubes.

I bought the building and had certain structural changes made. I didn't want to move one of the cubes a millimeter. The one that all the vidtabs and reviewers have called "The Lovers" I took. I couldn't keep it from the world, even though it hurt me to show it.

The other cube was more of a tool, a piece of equipment, rough-finished but complete, not really a work of art, and I didn't want it moved.

Once it was seen people wanted "The Lovers" in a curiously avid way. Museums bid, cajoled, pleaded, compromised, regrouped into phalanxes asking for tours, betrayed each other, regrouped to try again.

In a way it's all I have left of them. I pursued the lines of obvious investigation but I found no trace of them, not on Earth, not on the Moon, not on Mars. I ordered Control to stop looking when it became obvious they did not want to be found. Or could be.

But in a way they are still here. Alive. In the Cube.

They are standing facing each other. Nude. Looking into each other's eyes, hand in hand. There is rich new grass under their feet and tiny flowers growing. In Mike's free hand he is holding out to Madelon something glowing. A starpoint of energy. A small shining universe. He is offering it to her.

Behind them is the sky. Great beautiful spring clouds move majestically across the blue. Far down, far away are worn ancient rocks, much like Monument Valley in Arizona, or the Crown of Mars, near Burroughs. That's the first side I saw.

I walked around to the right, slowly. They did not change. They still stared into each other's eyes, a slight and knowing smile on their lips. But the background was stars. A wall of stars beyond the grass at their feet. Space. Deep space filled with incredible red dwarfs, monstrous blue giants, ice points of glitter, millions upon millions of suns making a starry mist that wandered across the blackness.

The third side was another landscape, seen from a hilltop, with a red-violet sea in the distance and two moons.

The fourth side was darkness. A sort of darkness. *Something* was back in there beyond them. Vague figures formed, disappeared, reformed slightly differently, changed . . .

Then I appeared. I think it's me. I don't know *why* I think it is me. I have never told anyone I think one of the dim faces is me, but I believe it is.

The vibrations were subtle, almost unnoticed until you had

looked at the cube a long time. They were peaceful vibrations, yet somehow exciting, as if the brainwave recordings upon which they were based were anticipating something marvelously different. There have been books written about this one cube and each writer has his interpretation.

But none of them saw the other cube.

It's a scenic view and it's the same as the third face of "The Lovers." If you walk around it it's a 360-degree view from a low hillock. In one direction you can see the shore curving around a bay of red-violet water and beyond, dimly seen, are what might be spires or rock or possibly towers. In the other direction the blue-green waves in the gentle breezes towards the distant mountains. The cycle is long, several times longer than any present sensatron, some thirty hours. But nothing happens. The sun rises and sets and there are two moons, one large and one small. The wind blows, the grass undulates, the tides come and go. A hot G-type sun. Moonlight on the water. Peaceful vibrations. Quiet.

Alone in that studio I touched the smooth glassite surface and it was unyielding, yet an alien world seemed within reach. Or was it? Had Mike's particle research opened some new door for him? I was afraid to have the Cube moved for perhaps, in some way, it was aligned.

You see, there are footsteps on the ground.

Two sets, and they start at the cube and go away, towards the distant spires.

I had my best team look it over. They went away with the diagrams and the notes they found on interdimensional space. They even had a stat of some figures scribbled on a tabletop.

Sometimes I plug into the monitor and look at the Cube sitting in the empty, locked studio, and I wonder.

Where are they?

Where are they?

Grasshopper Time

Gordon Eklund

In a genre as flamboyant as science fiction, it's refreshing to find a writer who understands the value of quiet understatement. Gordon Eklund is such a writer, and in the story below he tells of the love between a young girl and a man who was not entirely human—a story all the more powerful for the things we must imagine ourselves.

Sometimes, when he was remembering, he saw the sands of the desert that he had known so well as a warm, thick golden blanket drawn leisurely across the weary unbright wastes of the earth below, and the dunes were mere wrinkles in the fabric of this blanket, and the stars, arranged above in their nightly rings and clusters, were the eyes and ears of the outer universe gazing down upon a slumbering world.

This tableau was his. Ever and forever. Or so it seemed to him remembering—or so it only seemed.

He discovered them that night well beyond the jagged rocks of his home. They lay entwined of the night, drawing warmth from one another, sheltered from the cold desert wind by the flat side of a towering dune. The girl was perhaps seventeen, with bright ringlets of yellow hair spilling gracefully down her shoulders and forehead, almost touching her eyes, while the boy's hair was bitter black and neat-fully tidy, but his eyes, like those of his sister, were a sparkling gleaming blue. His narrow fragile frame mocked hers, for he had already learned to carry the weight of his years, and she had not. The boy was no more than ten, and both were awake.

He said, "Hello there," but kept in the shadows, where the moonlight could not reach him. He said it again, then waited.

Neither had been aware of his presence until he spoke; so their reactions were immediate. The girl leaped to her feet and stood rigid as a post, glaring at the darkness, her fists clenched at her sides in ready defense, while the boy lay still. But he too had heard. He stared coldly upward and was not afraid.

"What do you want?" said the girl. "Get away from us."

He moved a few inches forward, only enough to allow the moonlight to reveal a part of his face and said, "I heard you here and thought you might need help. Are you lost?"

"We didn't ask for help."

"Of course not. But do you need any? I live near here. I have food. And shelter." He had continued moving forward as he spoke, and now he was near enough to touch them. Perhaps too near, for he could hear them clearly this close, their minds as loud and thunderous as a couple of roaring trains. He closed a part of his mind, so that only a gentle rumbling echo of turning wheels reached him and saw a dark house laid flat against the earth, a house that appeared to stretch endlessly in all directions at once, and the girl came running toward the house, running but never reaching, always approaching yet never arriving. He watched this picture in his mind, and for the first time he realized exactly how lonely he had been.

Until now.

The boy spoke easily. "We were lost," he said, "but I suppose we're not really lost any more. Isn't that right? You've found us, haven't you? So, what do you plan to do with us?"

The girl glared at the boy for a moment, then wheeled to face him. He had their names now. She was Sarah, and he was Richard. Good names. Strong names. And he liked them both.

Richard said, "Are you going to take us away? I hurt my ankle, and it's hard for me to walk."

"Be quiet," said Sarah, moving over to hover protectively above him. But her eyes never left his for a second.

Richard said, "Get out of my way, Sarah. I want to see, too."

He laughed at them both. The boy's mind reached him as cool and relentless as a rushing river, untouched as yet by the many things which changed boys into men. Rage and fury were as alien to this boy as fear, but so was love, he could see, despite the overwhelming presence of a gentle sort of kindliness, and of something else, something soft and silken that ran spinning through his life like a spider's web bridging the gap between two distant flowers.

"You're sure funny looking," Sarah told him. "Don't you think he's funny looking?" she asked her brother.

"No," Richard said, after a moment's thought. "Not especially."

"So, what's your name?" Sarah asked.

"Alan," he said.

"That's your real name?" said Richard.

"Of course," he said.

"But would you mind if I called you something else? Could I call you Benjamin? Or Dana? Would you mind?" And here was that silken thing. That soft thing. Dana. "We used to have a Benjamin and a Dana, but they're both gone. They wouldn't talk to us."

"I don't mind."

"Then I'll call you Dana."

"That would be fine."

"So, where are you going to take us, Dana?"

"To my home." He waved at the rising rocks behind. "I live up there above the cliff."

"You'll have to carry me. I can't walk."

"I don't mind." He stepped around the dune and lifted the boy in his arms. The girl made no move to prevent him.

"Is it warm there?" Richard asked.

"Oh, certainly. I have a fire."

"Then let's hurry."

He went away, carrying the boy, and Sarah followed. They moved across the sands, and the girl let her feet drag, making lines and swirls that would not disappear before morning. He thought to warn her; but no, he decided—this wasn't the time.

His real name wasn't Alan; it was Angel, which was why he had chosen not to reveal it. Not because he thought his notoriety might have touched their lives, because he could see from the upper reaches of their minds that it had not, but because he could not see below, and they might have been frightened by the sudden apparition of a man named Angel coming from out of the darkness to offer shelter and aid. So, Alan it was for the time being, and Alan it would have to remain.

When he'd first felt them several hours before, back in his cave, he had wanted to ignore them and forget them, but he hadn't been able to do it. It was so seldom that he felt anyone here any more, except for an occasional search party (searching for him), and the children had been so different from the others, so much softer and tolerable, and the girl at least had radiated fear, if not the boy, and it was this last which had finally drawn him from his lair to offer them sanctuary.

He was funny looking, too. The girl had been right about that part, and the boy had been wrong. He was barely five feet tall and covered with thick hair like a grizzly bear, and his eyes were tiny holes in a wide strong face, and his skin was a combination of black and pink patches like a poorly designed quilt. But there was a reason for all of this: he wasn't a man. He was half of a man, for his mother had been fully human. It was his father who had been something else (he didn't know what—no one seemed to know for sure), and this was why he could hear people's thoughts and see the pictures that floated in their minds, and why he was forced to live alone in the desert, and why people came searching for him with murder written large on their minds.

At the time the children came to him, he was thirty-two years old, and he'd spent the last nine of those years in the desert. He was fortunate that he wasn't a man. No human being could ever have stood such total solitude for so many years.

"I have a ladder here," he told them. The rocks of his home loomed above like pale desert statuary. "Careful as you climb."

He carried the boy up the flat face of the cliff, and the girl followed. At the top of the ladder, he opened a door that revealed the entrance to his cave and helped the children through. Then he blocked the door again.

"My home," he said, pointing into the flickering firelight. "Let me see."

He went over and worked at the fire, building it back to its normal strength with the scarce twigs he had gathered during preceding months from the edge of the sands. Richard thought loudly, *Almost like a real home,* while Sarah thought, *They're beautiful.*

"You like my paintings," he said, answering her thought.

"They're wonderful." She went to the nearest wall and ran her fingers caressingly over the ripples and ridges of his designs. "What are they supposed to mean?"

"That's for you to decide."

"And all these books. Where did you get them?"

"I gathered them."

"May I read one?"

"If you want, but maybe we ought to eat first."

"I'm starved," said Richard.

Alan prepared a quick meal from his store of concentrated food and served it to them on wooden plates at a table in the rear of the cave. When they were done, he set their plates aside and had them come forward and sit with him beside the fire. The children were curiously silent. If he'd wanted, Alan could easily have read their thoughts, but now he avoided it. Instead, he wanted to talk.

"So," he said, "tell me how you came here."

"And how about you, Dana?" said Richard.

"I asked you first. It isn't often that I have visitors. I'd really like to know."

"You must get awfully lonely out here," said Sarah.

"Sometimes I do, but I'll tell you what. We'll trade stories. But you have to go first."

The children radiated happiness, and he realized that he was the cause of it. He felt suddenly very happy himself, and it was a feeling that almost frightened him with its intensity. Had it been that long since he'd last felt happy? He knew emotions that were near to this. He knew satisfaction, and he knew inner peace. But happiness? This was different; this was better.

Sarah smiled at him. "I'll tell."

"Fine," he said, waiting patiently for her to begin. He could have taken the story directly from her mind and known it all in an instant, but he'd received traces of it earlier, and it was far from clear, shrouded behind dark conflicting mists, as though neither child had seen it all but both had witnessed different aspects. Perhaps, he thought, when she speaks directly of it, then I will see the pictures more clearly.

Sarah said, "They wouldn't get up."

"Who was that?"

"Benjamin and Dana," Richard said.

"Our mother and father," said Sarah. "We came in, and they wouldn't get up."

"Why?"

Sarah shook her head. "I wish I knew. We came home, and they were lying all wet, and we said we wanted to eat, and they still wouldn't get up. They wouldn't even move."

A man of subdued middle age, a woman somewhat younger lying on a bare wooden floor, their bodies flecked with spots of widening red. A hole in the man's forehead. A small foot kicks his side.

"We tried to make them get up," Sarah said. "I was very angry, but they wouldn't even move or speak. Benjamin had a big hole in the middle of his head, and Dana was cold as a frozen snowman."

A pale hand touches white flesh. Faint winter memories, ice, snow.

"They were dead," Richard said.

"Hush."

"They were, too."

"What do you know about it?" Then she turned back to Alan. "So, we had to eat, and I fixed two plates, and we ate and watched and waited. Richard started screaming at her, and I almost had to hit him, but they still wouldn't get up."

Sounds fill the air, screaming, and a fist clenches. Rage. Fear. A smell, unbearable.

"They were dead," Richard said.

"So, we waited more days, and ate, and the food was going empty, and the nights were dark and cold because the stove had stopped working, and the cabin smelled, and I swept it and mopped it, and it smelled worse."

"They had bugs in them. White bugs and ants, roaches crawling all over, and they didn't even care."

"And pretty soon we couldn't stand the smell. It made Richard sick, and the food was gone except for things we didn't like. I got us some water, and we walked into the desert and kept walking till tonight when you found us."

"And that's all," said Richard.

Alan leaned back and nodded. He'd seen it now, seen it clearly, not so much from what they had said but from the mental pictures that had accompanied their words. The children's parents had lived near, not far from the edge of the sands. Perhaps, like him, they had been outcasts. Whatever the reasons, they were dead.

The story was a simple one, and neat, but there was one thing apart from the story itself that he could not quite comprehend. Richard and Sarah did not grieve. The only people they had ever known in their lives were dead, and they did not know. They did not seem to possess any understanding of the concept of death. As far as they knew, their parents had merely fallen into a state which closely resembled sleep and then refused to awaken. Richard knew the word death, and he knew it applied in this instance. His parents were dead—he knew that—but he did not understand. Death was a word of five letters. It came from a book; it was something vaguely remembered from adult conversation. This was death. But what was death?

He told the children to sleep. Richard said no, and he was forced to tell them his story. They were tired; so he kept it brief and they didn't understand, but that was all right, for they were used to things they couldn't understand. He told them of his birth up north in the big woods, of his parents, his stepfather the Indian Voss, who had killed his real father and taught him so much and then set him free to wander, and how he'd finally come here, where life was harsh and lonely and where he could wait.

Then they slept, and while they slept, he crept stealthily into their minds, amazed at the sharpness of his abilities. It had been a long time since he'd had another mind this close to his own. He spent most of his time with Sarah, for her dreams were gentle and danced with the colors of light, while her brother lived in a darker world, where black was the color of the noonday sun; and he discovered, probing deeply, that Sarah had never known another human being apart from her parents and brother, and that for her not two people but a whole living world had collapsed and perished. Yet she did not mourn.

Her conception of death was a picture: an old tired man stopping to rest at the side of an endless road and never rising again. She'd once heard her father say, "He was just tired, that's all, and he was ready to die," and the words had remained her sole true acquaintance with death. For Richard, death was not even that; it was a frustration, a turning away, a punishment inflicted upon him for imagined wrongs.

And for both, death was a personal thing. It came to those who sought it and wanted it, not to people like themselves who desired nothing from life but life, and now they were alone, isolated, outcasts, living apart, and it didn't seem right to them. It didn't seem fair.

He left them then, having seen enough, and he tossed more wood on the fire so that it leaped toward the dark stone roof of the cave, and then he went to the back and rolled into his blankets and slept.

The days that followed came easily. Richard's ankle slowly healed, and he was soon able to walk with only a slight limp, and he went for Alan's books and lay at the lip of the cave with the sunlight spilling across the white pages and read for hours at a time. He'd take a pile of books, grabbing them at random without reference to title or subject, eight or nine books at a time, and carry them to his sanctuary, and an hour later, two hours at the most, he'd return and go again. Sarah told Alan: "He's a genius. He can read a whole book in ten or fifteen minutes and remember every word. At home he read every book a dozen times or more. He knows everything, and he's only nine years old." "Everything?" Alan asked, and she looked at him, shook her head, and went back to her painting.

That was what he was teaching her: to paint. Her feelings toward him had warmed with each passing hour until finally, bored with sitting apart, she'd come to him and pointed at the walls and asked if she could learn too. He told her of course she could and to go right ahead, but she felt she needed lessons in order to ensure that what she painted pleased him. He told her he didn't care, but she insisted; so finally he went and got the paints and took her to the back of the cave, where the walls were still bare, and pointed at the last of his paintings and said this line means this, and this circle is the sun (*so why is it green?*) and this is the moon at midnight (*but it's square*). He told her his paintings had a meaning for him above and apart from what was shown on the walls, and she seemed to understand when he explained that he'd made them for himself alone, never expecting anyone else's eyes ever to glimpse them. "But can't I just paint pictures?" she asked. "I mean, real things with shape and size like people."

"Of course you can," he said. "That would be better, because then we could tell two different people had been here."

"Oh, we already know that," she said.

She went ahead, and he watched and only explained how to mix the paints to form different colors. She was good at it, and the parts he appreciated most were the differences between her work and his. When he painted, he simply thought back to something important in his past life, like the day he'd found the cave or the time he'd realized the truth of his heritage, and then closed off the conscious portion of his mind and painted from his feelings alone. It was a good way for him to work, but Sarah's way was good for her, too. She painted the world as she actually saw it and was never satisfied, because it was impossible to capture the whole thing on the blank wall of the cave. "Here's my house," she told him, "and, see, here's Dana and Benjamin working in the garden and, look, see that window? that's Richard, and he's just finished reading a book, and now he's looking out because he's heard us in the garden."

"Us? But where are you?"

"I'm not there, of course. I can't very well paint myself, can I?"

"Sure you can. Why not?"

"Because I've never seen myself. I don't know how I look. This is the way other people look to me. Your paintings—now aren't they the same? You never paint yourself, either."

And maybe she was right. He only knew that the paintings were good for both of them. She had finally decided that she liked him, and that was all he really cared about. He stayed out of her mind—and Richard's too—so he knew she liked him only because of her words and actions, and somehow it was better that way. He had not made any conscious decision to refrain from scanning her mind. It was only that he'd had no real desire to go creeping inside, not since the first night. It would have helped him understand her, but he felt it was more honest of him to use only those senses they shared. He knew she and Richard liked him from what they said and did. Richard still called him Dana most of the time, but sometimes he'd slip and say Alan, and sometimes Sarah would slip too and not call him Alan, and that's how he knew she liked him.

A week passed—then part of another—and they were running low on firewood. He had kept the children inside the cave as much as possible, knowing it might be dangerous for them to go wandering outside since neither of them knew the desert the way he did and there was always the possibility of pursuit. Whoever had killed their parents might not be satisfied, might come looking for them; so he scanned the desert at least twice daily, looking for signs of human thought, but found nothing, except once an old prospector several miles away, but he was searching for nothing more than solitude and wealth. But he still didn't want to take any unnecessary risks, and the three of them spent most of every day and all of every night inside the cave. They needed a great deal of heat and light, and the wood he had stored was nearly gone.

One morning as they were painting he told Sarah. "I'm

going to have to leave for a day or two." He explained why. "I can usually find wood at the edge of the desert."

"Can't we go with you?"

He'd known she'd ask, but he had an answer ready. He pointed at Richard, who lay reading at the front of the cave. "He's too weak yet for that long a hike. I'm afraid you'll have to wait till next time."

"But that's him. What about me? Why can't I go?"

"You don't want to leave him alone."

"Why not? There's food and water. He can build a fire, and he's happy here. He likes being alone. At home he was always alone."

"Well, I don't know."

"Why not ask him?"

"Oh, all right. We'll ask then."

They asked him; he said he didn't mind.

"But don't leave the cave," Alan said.

"Why would I want to do that? It's hot out there, and I've got my books in here."

So, that was that, and they left that same evening as soon as the sun went down. Before that, Alan uncovered the sled from the back of the cave where it had lain the past few months buried beneath crates of concentrated food. Alan had built the sled himself several years before out of stolen lumber and a couple long pipes that served as runners. It worked well. Sarah helped him move it to the front of the cave, and together they lowered it to the desert floor.

Then they said good-by to Richard and descended the ladder. Alan paused at the foot of the cliff and scanned the desert. The sands were fast asleep, each grain nestled snugly in place, and the moon above was a burning eye that gazed upon them alone, and the stars were distant beacons of light that gave warmth and reason to the stillness of the desert sands.

"It's safe," he said. "Let's go."

The journey took much less time than Alan had anticipated. Sarah walked at his side, easily matching his pace, and the sled moved smoothly over the sand. It couldn't have been much after midnight when the sand began to harden into dirt and clumps of grass sprouted beneath their feet.

Soon, the grass was scrub brush and the dirt was firm and hard.

"Should I say something if I see some wood?" she asked.

"No, there's a place I always go."

Dawn was still a distant, indistinct point in the future when they reached their destination, a small rolling hill where trees grew thick and tall. At the foot of the hill stretched the town. The lights were cool and distant tonight, and Sarah and Alan stood together, peering down at the flickering world below them.

"Those are people," she said.

"There would be more, but it's late, and most are sleeping."

"I've read," she said, shaking her head. "But it's so hard—when you see it. That's a city, isn't it?"

He said, "No, it's only a small town. Less than five thousand people. The cities, like Phoenix and Albuquerque, have a thousand times that many."

"No," she said.

"The lights of the cities are as thick as stars on a clear night."

She said, "No."

He led her away from the lights and set her to work with the hatchet and saw while he toppled the trees with an axe. They made short work of it, and the sled was soon piled high with logs. The sun came up and regarded them, and he told Sarah to quit.

"We'll push the sled under those trees, and then catch some sleep till dark. I've never seen anyone up here, but it's always best to be careful."

She agreed. The sled was more difficult to move now that it was loaded, but together they managed to squeeze it into a less visible spot. Then they lay down beside it and slept.

It was still daylight when he awoke. A knife was jabbing him in the head; its blade sliced at his eyes.

He leaped to his feet and spun like a top. He grabbed his head and looked. Sarah was gone.

She was crying. He followed her voice and ran. She was not far from where they had lain. A man was struggling with her. He had pushed her to the ground and was trying to trap her arms. Her voice set Alan's mind afire, and he ran blindly, without thinking. The man neither saw nor heard him coming. He kicked him flat in the back of the head, and he lurched like a falling tree, rolling off her and hitting the ground. He swam in a pool of black water that stuck to him like tar. Alan drew away from the man's mind and helped Sarah to her feet. Her arms were bruised and her blouse was torn, but otherwise she seemed unharmed.

She pointed at the man. "Did he decide to die?" she asked. "Because you hurt him."

"No," Alan said. "He's not dead."

"Well, he sure scared me."

"You shouldn't have gone out."

"I know, but I couldn't sleep. I'm sorry, but I was careful at first, but then I found something and stopped listening, and he came and caught me. Come on, I'll show you."

He went with her and they walked around the man and down the side of the hill. She showed him a hole in the earth, and he peeked inside.

"Rabbits," he said.

"Is that what they are? They're mostly little ones. There's a big one, but he's asleep."

Alan reached into the burrow and came out with a tiny, furry pink clump that held tightly to his hand. He placed the clump on the ground, then reached in again, and this time emerged with a full grown rabbit. It was dead.

"Why did he do that?"

"I don't know."

"I bet that's the mother."

"Yes, probably."

"So won't the other ones die now?"

"No," he said. "We'll take them home with us. They'll live."

"That's a good idea," she said.

"You'll have to help me. We have to hurry."

Alan had seen the truth in the fallen man's mind. The man had heard them last night and come to investigate, but first he'd told his wife, and she would surely tell another. They would be coming soon. They knew Alan well in this town. They wanted to find him.

He and Sarah put the rabbits in among the logs. There were nine of them, not much larger than a man's fist, and they curled up on a pile of twigs and slept entwined. Then they headed down the hill. Alan kept his mind open and heard the searchers coming. He slipped easily between them, but their thoughts, bitter as stale cider, followed him across the barren land to the brink of the sand. As darkness fell, he hurried forward, and a brisk wind rose and wiped at his tracks.

He told Sarah, "We'll make it. They're too far behind."

"May I talk?"

"If you want. It's safe."

"I wanted to ask you something, Alan."

"Go ahead."

"Why did she die?"

"I don't know," he said.

"Was it because she wanted to die?"

"No, I don't think she wanted to die."

"I thought so. I thought so all along. She couldn't help it. And neither could he."

"No," he said.

"Then couldn't you die, too? Five seconds from now, without your knowing or being able to say anything or stop it, you fall and you're dead. Couldn't that happen? Or me?"

"Or even you," he said. He didn't want to say it, but he said it. "I'm sorry."

Late that night they reached the cave. Richard came scampering down the ladder to greet them, and Sarah took him to the rabbits and let him see. She said nothing about the mother, and Richard carried them away clutched tightly to his chest, leaving the two of them to tend the wood. They did not mind. Richard was busy with what he had, and it was a lovely night, as silent and still as a distant, barren planet, and only the wind moved, brushing across the sands like a gentle song.

They slept that night, the three of them curled together at the back of the cave, the three of them and nine small rabbits. The fire leaped and flared, keeping them warm as they slept.

During the days that followed, Richard took good care of the rabbits. They thrived beneath his gentle hand, and all were given individual names. Alan helped Richard with the naming, letting him know which was which, and Richard named a plump one after Alan, and Alan thanked him for the honor. Richard seldom called him Dana now. He knew Alan was only Alan, and Sarah never slipped at all.

They kept to the cave, because the pursuers had come at last, and they ringed the desert like an occupying army. Alan witnessed in the minds of those who came near the death of the man on the hill. He had never killed a man before, and for a moment he thought he ought to go away and consider the meaning of it, but he didn't. He saw nothing in the minds of these seeking men but bitterness and rage. There was no remorse for the dead man, merely a burning lusting craving desire for vengeance.

Alan never let them come too near the cave. He was able to keep them away. It seemed each new day brought him greater and stronger powers. He knew the men would eventually return to their homes. They always had before, and they would this time, too. He told the children it was only a matter of waiting, and they said they understood.

So, there came a day when he and Richard and nine rabbits were playing at the mouth of the cave. A few hours before he had quickly scanned the desert as he did every morning and found only a few men still there. Most had given up the search and gone home. There were fewer than ten left, but these were the worst of the bunch, and it hurt him even to approach the dark centers of their minds.

Richard was telling him stories of the rabbits. Richard was good at that, at taking nothing and making it into something, and he told Alan how this big one was jealous of this other one's black paws and how this third one was smarter and quicker than all the rest. Alan lay at his side and listened to his stories and grinned and nodded and told him he was right.

Sarah's shadow fell across them. Alan looked up at her. She'd spent the morning at the back of the cave, ordering him to keep his distance, as there was something she was doing that concerned him and he wasn't allowed to see it till she was ready for him to see it, but now here was her shadow.

"It's done," she said.

"Well?"

"Well, come along and see it. What do you think?"

"You want to come, Richard?"

"I do, but these guys don't. They say we've got things to do. I'll see you later."

"But you have to come, Alan."

He went with her. She led him to the very back of the cave, where the walls came together, touching the floor and ceiling, and where there was no place left for a man to go. They had to climb over piled logs and slip between crates of concentrated food, but at last she said, "There it is."

He looked at the wall. The picture was that of a standing man, but even that much was hard to tell. The man seemed to be leaning over, and there was something cupped in his one hand. He was a small stocky man and his legs were far too short for the rest of his body. His hands were big spoons and his face was streaked with pink and white and red. The eyes drew his attention. She had not painted there, and they were coal black holes in the bright shining face. He sensed a curious and powerful strength nestling within those eyes.

"Do you like it?"

He said, "Yes. It's—I wish I'd painted it."

She laughed. "You couldn't. It's you."

"Me?"

"I wanted to." She looked at him, at the painting, then at the floor.

"It's good," he said.

She looked up at him. "You think so?"

"I mean whatever it is, it's good. I don't know if it's me or like me because I've never seen me. But it's good." He tried to smile. "But ugly."

"No," she said, firmly. "I knew you'd say that. It's not ugly because you're not ugly."

"But I am. Why else do you think I live out here?"

She took his hand and held it. "You're not ugly."

"You never call me Benjamin any more."

"No, and do you know why?" She waved at the painting as though it were more truly real than he was. "Because I know who you are now. You're Alan, and that's the best of it."

She was holding his arm with both of her hands. He wanted to speak but could not find the words.

"It's good," he said.

"Alan," she said.

And then:

A thought like heat. (From outside.)

Rage which rushed like blood through steel veins.

Then a shot.

"Richard," he said, and ran.

He clawed his way to the front of the cave, and Richard was not there, only eight playful rabbits, and the rabbits scattered like bullets between his legs. Another shot. And a scream.

Alan lunged forward and caught the ladder in his hands. It spilled toward the desert floor, and he rode with it, his feet dancing against the air, his legs kicking and squirming. He clutched the sands of the desert to his chest, then stood and bounded across the land.

A man stood near, his head full of fiery thoughts which rushed at Alan like a river of burning steel, but he fought away. The man heard him coming. He whirled and his lips parted and something cracked. His gun, and he shot him.

His head was exploding and there was no more thought, but then he felt the gun warm in his fingers and there was Richard on the sand and a hole in his chest and blood on his lips and the rabbit lay beside him, which rabbit he could not tell, for the rabbit wore a concealing cloak of crimson fur. The gun still rested warmly in his hands; so he pressed it against the man's chest and squeezed the trigger. The man exploded and rose briefly into the air like an ascending eagle. Alan felt the ground and dropped the gun.

Then came a time when he was inside his own body, yet it was outside him. He was busily working, repairing the injured organs in much the same way a skilled craftsman resurrects the soul of a hopelessly broken watch. He drew the needed materials from hidden distant portions of himself, alien portions, and fitted them wherever needed. The work seemed to take a vast amount of time, but finally the job was done.

He was awake, and Sarah leaned against his eyes.

"So you're alive," she said.

He raised his hands and felt his face. The skin felt as clean and smooth and warm as a baby's belly. "I'm alive," he said.

"Richard isn't. He's dead."

Richard lay beside him. He put his hand against the cold chest and felt the emptiness which lay beneath the hard shell.

"See?" said Sarah.

"How long?"

"Only a few hours."

He scanned the desert, but the men were gone. They had given up the search, and he was alone again.

"We're safe," he said.

"I hid the body at the back of the cave. I suppose you ought to do something with it."

"I'll bury it," he said.

She was looking at Richard; so he looked, too. Richard's eyes were open but the sparkle was gone. These were the eyes of a starless night, dark and empty and painted with black clouds. Alan reached over and lowered the lids.

She said, "There's nothing—nothing you can . . .?"

He said, "There's nothing I can do. I'm sorry, Sarah."

"Then I'd better be going," she said, and stood.

"You can't do that." He stood with her. "It's not safe."

"I don't mean that." She drew away from his touch and he dropped both hands to his sides. "I'm going for good."

"But," he said, "why? That won't bring him back."

She shook her head as fresh tears rolled down her cheeks, wiping away the harsh dark stains of the old. "It's you—you who can't die—you who won't die—and he died—and it's wrong. Wrong. Don't you see? Why does everything have to die, whether it wants to or not, and you don't? You live."

"I don't know," he said.

"It's because you're not a man, isn't it? I don't know what

you are, and I don't know if it's good or evil or neither one or maybe both together, but whatever you are, you can't die. Richard was human, and he's dead. Benjamin, too, and Dana, and the man on the hill, and the one down below. Even the rabbit—it's dead—even the rabbit was more human than you. It died, and you won't."

"Can I help it?" he said. "What do you think? Would it make you feel better if I killed myself? If I took a gun and rammed it down my throat and pulled the trigger and nicely sprayed my brains against the walls? Would that make you happy? To have me lying dead next to him? Is that what you want? Will you be satisfied when we're all dead. Well then, what about you?"

"Could you do it?"

"I don't know," he said.

"I know you couldn't, because your brains were nicely sprayed across the desert floor, and your right eye was a black pit, and you came back. In less than an hour, you were good and whole again while Richard lay at your side and rotted. And he wasn't even tired. He wasn't near ready to die yet."

"I'm not a man," he said.

"But I am," she said. "And that's why I have to go to my own kind, to those who also know how to die."

"All right," he said. "Get out."

She jerked her head and stumbled toward the front of the cave. He did not try to stop her. If he had been a man, he would never have allowed her to go. But he wasn't a man, even though he loved her; so he listened and heard her hands on the ladder and her feet on the sand. He listened with his ears only, wanting to hear nothing more painful than sound.

Then he turned and went to the back of the cave. He climbed over piled logs and slipped between crates packed full with rich concentrated food. He sat down before his own picture and saw that it was wrong. The picture she had painted was the portrait of a man. It wasn't him. There was a place in the world for this man pictured here. Here was a man who not only could die but also live, and he was neither. He was Angel—born of alien blood—Angel alone and Angel wandering. He wanted to make himself come flat against that black foreign wall. He wanted to merge with that staring, glaring picture and make it him. He wanted to purloin its bare humanity and make that his. He could not do it. Only one small portion of the picture spoke truly to him: the cold black alien eyes. Those eyes were his, but the rest was a dream.

Later, how much later he could not tell, he moved away and went forward. It was dark outside, and the stars were hidden behind an invisible moon. He buried the dead in separate graves, then stood and watched as the wind came alive, whipping the sands like fire and hiding his brief, momentary abrasion from peering eyes.

Then, turning, he went away, and he never saw the cave again.

Hero

Joe W. Haldeman

Joe Haldeman is a Vietnam veteran who returned from combat to wonder about the future of armies and the common foot-soldier. In an increasingly technological world, where's the need for hand-to-hand combat? And, if humanity were to find itself in an interstellar war with a strange alien race, what role would there be for infantry troups?

Answer: a very important role, as Haldeman details in this all-too-believable novella of grim future warfare.

1

"Tonight we're going to show you eight silent ways to kill a man." The guy who said that was a sergeant who didn't look five years older than I. Ergo, as they say, he couldn't possibly ever have killed a man, not in combat, silently or otherwise.

I already knew eighty ways to kill people, though most of them were pretty noisy. I sat up straight in my chair and assumed a look of polite attention and fell asleep with my eyes open. So did most everybody else. We'd learned that they never schedule anything important for these after-chop classes.

The projector woke me up and I sat through a short movie showing the "eight silent ways." Some of the actors must have been brainwipes, since they were actually killed.

After the movie a girl in the front row raised her hand. The sergeant nodded at her and she rose to parade rest. Not bad looking, but kind of chunky about the neck and shoulders. Everybody gets that way after carrying a heavy pack around for a couple of months.

"Sir"—we had to call sergeants "sir" until graduation— "most of those methods, really, they looked . . . kind of silly."

"For instance?"

"Like killing a man with a blow to the kidneys, from an entrenching tool. I mean, when would you *actually* just have an entrenching tool, and no gun or knife? And why not just bash him over the head with it?"

"He might have a helmet on," he said reasonably.

"Besides, Taurans probably don't even *have* kidneys!"

He shrugged. "Probably they don't." This was 1997, and we'd never seen a Tauran; hadn't even found any pieces of Taurans bigger than a scorched chromosome. "But their body chemistry is similar to ours, and we have to assume they're similarly complex creatures. They *must* have weaknesses, vulnerable spots. You have to find out where they are.

"That's the important thing." He stabbed a finger at the screen. That's why those eight convicts got caulked for your benefit . . . you've got to find out how to kill Taurans, and be able to do it whether you have a megawatt laser or just an emery board."

She sat back down, not looking too convinced.

"Any more questions?" Nobody raised a hand.

"O.K.—tench-hut!" We staggered upright and he looked at us expectantly.

"Screw you, sir," came the tired chorus.

"Louder!"

"SCREW YOU, SIR!"

One of the army's less-inspired morale devices.

"That's better. Don't forget, predawn maneuvers tomorrow. Chop at 0330, first formation, 0400. Anybody sacked after 0340 gets one stripe. Dismissed."

I zipped up my coverall and went across the snow to the lounge for a cup of soya and a joint. I'd always been able to get by on five or six hours of sleep, and this was the only time I could be by myself, out of the army for a while. Looked at the newsfax for a few minutes. Another ship got caulked, out by Aldebaran sector. That was four years ago. They were mounting a reprisal fleet, but it'll take four years more for them to get out there. By then, the Taurans would have every portal planet sewed up tight.

Back at the billet, everybody else was sacked and the main lights were out. The whole company'd been dragging ever since we got back from the two-week lunar training. I dumped my clothes in the locker, checked the roster and found out I was in bunk 31. Damn it, right under the heater.

I slipped through the curtain as quietly as possible so as not to wake up my bunkmate. Couldn't see who it was, but I couldn't have cared less. I slipped under the blanket.

"You're late, Mandella," a voice yawned. It was Rogers.

"Sorry I woke you up," I whispered.

" 'Sallright." She snuggled over and clasped me spoon-fashion. She was warm and reasonably soft. I patted her hip in what I hoped was a brotherly fashion. "Night, Rogers."

"G'night, Stallion." She returned the gesture, a good deal more pointedly.

Why do you always get the tired ones when you're ready and the randy ones when you're tired? I bowed to the inevitable.

II

"Awright, let's get some *back* inta that! Stringer team! Move it up—move up!"

A warm front had come in about midnight and the snow had turned to sleet. The permaplast stringer weighed five hundred pounds and was a bitch to handle, even when it wasn't covered with ice. There were four of us, two at each end, carrying the plastic girder with frozen fingertips. Rogers and I were partners.

"Steel!" the guy behind me yelled, meaning that he was losing his hold. It wasn't steel, but it was heavy enough to break your foot. Everybody let go and hopped away. It splashed slush and mud all over us.

"Damn it, Petrov," Rogers said, "why didn't you go out for Star Fleet, or maybe the Red Cross? This damn thing's not that damn heavy." Most of the girls were a little more circumspect in their speech.

"Awright, get a *move* on, stringers—Epoxy team! Dog 'em! Dog 'em!"

Our two epoxy people ran up, swinging their buckets. "Let's go, Mandella. I'm freezin'."

"Me, too," the girl said earnestly.

"One—two—heave!" We got the thing up again and staggered toward the bridge. It was about three-quarters completed. Looked as if the Second Platoon was going to beat us. I wouldn't give a damn, but the platoon that got their bridge built first got to fly home. Four miles of muck for the rest of us, and no rest before chop.

We got the stringer in place, dropped it with a clank, and fitted the static clamps that held it to the rise-beams. The female half of the epoxy team started slopping glue on it before we even had it secured. Her partner was waiting for the stringer on the other side. The floor team was waiting at the foot of the bridge, each one holding a piece of the light stressed permaplast over his head, like an umbrella. They were dry and clean. I wondered aloud what they had done to deserve it, and Rogers suggested a couple of colorful, but unlikely possibilities.

We were going back to stand by the next stringer when the Field First—he was named Dougelstein, but we called him "Awright"—blew a whistle and bellowed, "Awright, soldier boys and girls, ten minutes. Smoke 'em if you got 'em." He reached into his pocket and turned on the control that heated our coveralls.

Rogers and I sat down on our end of the stringer and I took out my weed box. I had lots of joints, but we weren't allowed to smoke them until after night-chop. The only tobacco I had was a cigarro butt about three inches long. I lit it on the side of the box; it wasn't too bad after the first couple of puffs. Rogers took a puff to be sociable, but made a face and gave it back.

"Were you in school when you got drafted?" she asked.

"Yeah. Just got a degree in Physics. Was going after a teacher's certificate."

She nodded soberly. "I was in Biology . . ."

"Figures." I ducked a handful of slush. "How far?"

"Six years, bachelor's and technical." She slid her boot along the ground, turning up a ridge of mud and slush the consistency of freezing ice milk. "Why the hell did this have to happen?"

I shrugged. It didn't call for an answer, least of all the answer that the UNEF kept giving us. Intellectual and physical elite of the planet, going out to guard humanity against the Tauran menace. It was all just a big experiment. See whether we could goad the Taurans into ground action.

Awright blew the whistle two minutes early, as expected, but Rogers and I and the other two stringers got to sit for a minute while the epoxy and floor teams finished covering our stringer. It got cold fast, sitting there with our suits turned off, but we remained inactive, on principle.

I really didn't see the sense of us having to train in the cold. Typical army half-logic. Sure, it was going to be cold where we were going; but not ice-cold or snow-cold. Almost by definition, a portal planet remained within a degree or two of absolute zero all the time, since collapsars don't shine—and the first chill you felt would mean that you were a dead man.

Twelve years before, when I was ten years old, they had discovered the collapsar jump. Just fling an object at a collapsar with sufficient speed, and it pops out in some other part of the galaxy. It didn't take long to figure out the formula that predicted where it would come out: it just traveled along the same "line"—actually an Einsteinian geodesic—it would have followed if the collapsar hadn't been in the way—until it reaches another collapsar field, whereupon it reappears, repelled with the same speed it had approaching the original collapsar. Travel time between the two collapsars is exactly zero.

It made a lot of work for mathematical physicists, who had to redefine simultaneity, then tear down general relativity and build it back up again. And it made the politicians very happy, because now they could send a shipload of colonists to Fomalhaut for less than it once cost to put a brace of men on the Moon. There were a lot of people the politicians would just love to see on Fomalhaut, implementing a glorious adventure instead of stirring up trouble at home.

The ships were always accompanied by an automated probe that followed a couple of million miles behind. We knew about the portal planets, little bits of flotsam that whirled around the collapsars; the purpose of the drone was to come back and tell us in the event that a ship had smacked into a portal planet at .999 of the speed of light.

That particular catastrophe never happened, but one day a drone did come limping back alone. Its data were analyzed, and it turned out that the colonists' ship had been pursued by another vessel and destroyed. This happened near Aldebaran, in the constellation Taurus, but since "Aldebaranian" is a little hard to handle, they named the enemy Taurans.

Colonizing vessels thenceforth went out protected by an armed guard. Often the armed guard went out alone, and finally the colonization effort itself slowed to a token trickle. The United Nations Exploratory and Colonization Group got shortened to UNEF, United Nations Exploratory Force, emphasis on the "force".

Then some bright lad in the General Assembly decided that we ought to field an army of footsoldiers to guard the portal planets of the nearer collapsars. This led to the Elite Conscription Act of 1996 and the most rigorously selected army in the history of warfare.

So here we are, fifty men and fifty women, with IQ's over 150 and bodies of unusual health and strength, slogging elitely through the mud and slush of central Missouri, reflecting on how useful our skill in building bridges will be, on worlds where the only fluid will be your occasional standing pool of liquid helium.

III

About a month later, we left for our final training exercise; maneuvers on the planet Charon. Though nearing perihelion it was still more than twice as far from the sun as Pluto.

The troopship was a converted "cattlewagon," made to carry two hundred colonists and assorted bushes and beasts. Don't think it was roomy, though, just because there were half that many of us. Most of the excess space was taken up with extra reaction mass and ordnance.

The whole trip took three weeks, accelerating at 2 Gs halfway; decelerating the other half. Our top speed, as we roared by the orbit of Pluto, was around one twentieth of the speed of light—not quite enough for relativity to rear its complicated head.

Three weeks of carrying around twice as much weight as normal . . . it's no picnic. We did some cautious exercises three times a day, and remained horizontal as much as possible. Still, we had several broken bones and serious dislocations. The men had to wear special supporters. It was almost impossible to sleep, what with nightmares of choking and being crushed, and the necessity of rolling over periodically to prevent blood pooling and bedsores. One girl got so fatigued that she almost slept through the experience of having a rib rub through to the open air.

I'd been in space several times before, so when we finally stopped decelerating and went into free fall, it was nothing but a relief. But some people had never been out, except for our training on the Moon, and succumbed to the sudden vertigo and disorientation. The rest of us cleaned up after them, floating through the quarters with sponges and inspirators to suck up globules of partly-digested "Concentrate, High-protein, Low-residue, Beef Flavor (Soya)."

A shuttle took us down to the surface in three trips. I waited for the last one, along with everybody else who wasn't bothered by free fall.

We had a good view of Charon, coming down from orbit. There wasn't much to see, though. It was just a dim, off-white sphere with a few smudges on it. We landed about two hundred meters from the base. A pressurized crawler came out and mated with the ferry, so we didn't have to suit up. We clanked and squeaked up to the main building, a featureless box of grayish plastic.

Inside, the walls were the same inspired color. The rest of the company was sitting at desks, chattering away. There was a seat next to Freeland.

"Jeff—feeling better?" He still looked a little pale.

"If the gods had meant for man to survive in free fall, they would have given him a cast-iron glottis. Somewhat better. Dying for a smoke."

"Yeah."

"*You* seemed to take it all right. Went up in school, didn't you?"

"Senior thesis in vacuum welding, yeah, three weeks in Earth orbit." I sat back and reached for my weed box, for the thousandth time. It still wasn't there, of course. The Life Support Unit didn't want to handle nicotine and THC.

"Training was bad enough," Jeff groused, "but *this* crap—"

"I don't know." I'd been thinking about it. "It might just all be worth it."

"Hell, no—this is a *space* war, let Star Fleet take care of it . . . they're just going to send us out and either we sit for fifty years on some damn ice cube of a portal planet, or we get . . ."

"Well, Jeff, you've got to look at it the other way, too. Even if there's only once chance in a thousand that we'll be doing some good, keeping the Taurans . . ."

"Tench-hut!" We stood up in a raggety-ass fashion, by twos and threes. The door opened and a full major came in. I stiffened a little. He was the highest-ranking officer I'd ever seen. He had a row of ribbons stitched into his coveralls, including a purple strip meaning he'd been wounded in combat, fighting in the old American army. Must have been that Indochina thing, but it had fizzled out before I was born. He didn't look that old.

"Sit, sit." He made a patting motion with his hand. Then he put his hands on his hips and scanned the company with a small smile on his face. "Welcome to Charon. You picked a lovely day to land; the temperature outside is a summery eight point one five degrees Absolute. We expect little change for the next two centuries or so." Some of us laughed half-heartedly.

"You'd best enjoy the tropical climate here at Miami Base, enjoy it while you can. We're on the center of sunside here, and most of your training will be on darkside. Over there, the temperature drops to a chilly two point zero eight.

"You might as well regard all the training you got on Earth and the Moon as just a warm-up exercise, to give you a fair chance of surviving Charon. You'll have to go through your whole repertory here: tools, weapons, maneuvers. And you'll find that, at these temperatures, tools don't work the way they should, weapons don't want to fire. And people move v-e-r-y cautiously."

He studied the clipboard in his hand. "Right now, you have forty-nine women and forty-eight men. Two deaths, one psychiatric release. Having read an outline of your training program, I'm frankly surprised that so many of you pulled through.

"But you might as well know that I won't be displeased if as few as fifty of you graduate from this final phase. And the only way not to graduate is to die. Here. The only way anybody gets back to Earth—including me—is after a combat tour.

"You will complete your training in one month. From here you go to Stargate collapsar, a little over two lights away. You will stay at the settlement on Stargate I, the largest portal planet, until replacements arrive. Hopefully, that will be no more than a month; another group is due here as soon as you leave.

"When you leave Stargate, you will be going to a strategically important collapsar, set up a military base there, and fight the enemy, if attacked. Otherwise, maintain the base until further orders.

"The last two weeks of your training will consist of constructing such a base, on darkside. There you will be totally isolated from Miami Base: no communication, no medical evacuation, no resupply. Sometime before the two weeks are up, your defense facilities will be evaluated in an attack by guided drones. They will be armed.

"All of the permanent personnel here on Charon are combat veterans. Thus, all of us are forty to fifty years of age, but I think we can keep up with you. Two of us will be with you at all times, and will accompany you at least as far as Stargate. They are Captain Sherman Stott, your company commander, and Sergeant Octavio Cortez, your first sergeant. Gentlemen?"

Two men in the front row stood easily and turned to face us. Captain Stott was a little smaller than the major, but cut from the same mold; face hard and smooth as porcelain, cynical half-smile, a precise centimeter of beard framing a large chin, looking thirty at the most. He wore a large, gunpowder-type pistol on his hip.

Sergeant Cortez was another story. His head was shaved and the wrong shape; flattened out on one side where a large piece of skull had obviously been taken out. His face was very dark and seamed with wrinkles and scars. Half his left ear was missing and his eyes were as expressive as buttons on a machine. He had a moutache-and-beard combination that looked like a skinny white caterpillar taking a lap around his mouth. On anybody else, his schoolboy smile might look pleasant, but he was about the ugliest, meanest-looking creature I'd ever seen. Still, if you didn't look at his head and considered the lower six feet or so, he could pose as the "after" advertisement for a body-building spa. Neither Stott nor Cortez wore any ribbons. Cortez had a small pocketlaser suspended in a magnetic rig, sideways, under his left armpit. It had wooden grips that were worn very smooth.

"Now, before I turn you over to the tender mercies of these two gentlemen, let me caution you again.

"Two months ago there was not a living soul on this planet, a working force of forty-five men struggled for a month to erect this base. Twenty-four of them, more than half, died in the construction of it. This is the most dangerous planet men have ever tried to live on, but the places you'll be going will be this bad and worse. Your cadre will try to keep you alive for the next month. Listen to them . . . and follow their example; all of them have survived here for longer than you'll have to. Captain?" The captain stood up as the major went out the door.

"'Tench-*hut!*" The last syllable was like an explosion and we all jerked to our feet.

"Now I'm only gonna say this *once* so you better listen," he growled. "We *are* in a combat situation here and in a combat situation there is only *one* penalty for disobedience and insubordination." He jerked the pistol from his hip and held it by the barrel, like a club. "This is an Army model 1911 automatic *pistol* caliber .45 and it is a primitive, but effective, weapon. The sergeant and I are authorized to use our weapons to kill to enforce discipline, don't make us do it because we will. We *will*." He put the pistol back. The holster snap made a loud crack in the dead quiet.

"Sergeant Cortez and I between us have killed more people than are sitting in this room. Both of us fought in Vietnam on the American side and both of us joined the United Nations International Guard more than ten years ago. I took a break in grade from major for the privilege of commanding this company, and First Sergeant Cortez took a break from sub-major, because we are both *combat* soldiers and this is the first *combat* situation since 1974.

"Keep in mind what I've said while the First Sergeant instructs you more specifically in what your duties will be under this command. Take over, Sergeant." He turned on his heel and strode out of the room, with the little smile on his face that hadn't changed one millimeter during the whole harangue.

The First Sergeant moved like a heavy machine with lots of ball bearings. When the door hissed shut he swiveled ponderously to face us and said, "At ease, siddown," in a surprisingly gentle voice. He sat on a table in the front of the room. It creaked—but held.

"Now the captain talks scary and I look scary, but we both mean well. You'll be working pretty closely with me, so you better get used to this thing I've got hanging in front of my brain. You probably won't see the captain much, except on maneuvers."

He touched the flat part of his head. "And speaking of brains, I still have just about all of mine, in spite of Chinese efforts to the contrary. All of us old vets who mustered into UNEF had to pass the same criteria that got you drafted by the Elite Conscription Act. So I suspect all of you are smart and tough—but just keep in mind that the captain and I are smart and tough *and* experienced."

He flipped through the roster without really looking at it. "Now, as the captain said, there'll be only one kind of disciplinary action, on maneuvers. Capital punishment. But normally *we* won't have to kill you for disobeying. Charon'll save us the trouble.

"Back in the billeting area, it'll be another story. We don't much care what you do inside, but once you suit up and go outside, you've gotta have discipline that would shame a Centurian. There will be situations where one stupid act could kill us all.

"Anyhow, the first thing we've gotta do is get you fitted to your fighting suits. The armorer's waiting at your billet; he'll take you one at a time. Let's go."

IV

"Now I know you got lectured and lectured on what a fighting suit can do, back on Earth." The armorer was a small man, partially bald, with no insignia of rank on his coveralls. Sergeant Cortez told us to call him "sir," since he was a lieutenant.

"But I'd like to reinforce a couple of points, maybe add some things your instructors Earthside weren't clear about, or couldn't know. Your First Sergeant was kind enough to consent to being my visual aid. Sergeant?"

Cortez slipped out of his coveralls and came up to the little raised platform where a fighting suit was standing, popped open like a man-shaped clam. He backed into it and slipped his arms into the rigid sleeves. There was a click and the thing swung shut with a sigh. It was bright green with CORTEZ stenciled in white letters on the helmet.

"Camouflage, Sergeant." The green faded to white, then dirty gray. "This is good camouflage for Charon, and most of your portal planets," said Cortez, from a deep well. "But there are several other combinations available." The gray dappled and brightened to a combination of greens and browns: "Jungle." Then smoothed out to a hard light ochre: "Desert." Dark brown, darker, to a deep flat black: "Night or space."

"Very good, Sergeant. To my knowledge, this is the only feature of the suit which was perfected after your training. The control is around your left wrist and is admittedly awkward. But once you find the right combination, it's easy to lock in.

"Now, you didn't get much in-suit training Earthside because we didn't want you to get used to using the thing in a friendly environment. The fighting suit is the deadliest personal weapon ever built, and with no weapon it is easier for the user to kill himself through carelessness. Turn around, Sergeant.

"Case in point." He tapped a square protuberance between the shoulders. "Exhaust fins. As you know the suit tries to keep you at a comfortable temperature no matter what the weather's like outside. The material of the suit is as near to a perfect insulator as we could get, consistent with mechanical demands. Therefore, these fins get *hot*—especially hot, compared to darkside temperatures—as they bleed off the body's heat.

"All you have to do is lean up against a boulder of frozen gas; there's lots of it around. The gas will sublime off faster than it can escape from the fins; in escaping, it will push against the surrounding 'ice' and fracture it . . . and in about one hundredth of a second, you have the equivalent of a hand grenade going off right below your neck. You'll never feel a thing.

"Variations on this theme have killed eleven people in the past two months. And they were just building a bunch of huts.

"I assume you know how easily the waldo capabilities can kill you or your companions. Anybody want to shake hands with the sergeant?" He stepped over and clasped his glove. "He's had lots of practice. Until *you* have, be extremely careful. You might scratch an itch and wind up bleeding to death. Remember, semi-logarithmic response: two pounds' pressure exerts five pounds' force; three pounds gives ten; four pounds, twenty-three; five pounds, forty-seven. Most of you can muster up a grip of well over a hundred pounds. Theoretically, you could rip a steel girder in two with that, amplified. Actually, you'd destroy the material of your gloves and, at least on Charon, die very quickly. It'd be a race between decompression and flash-freezing. You'd be the loser.

"The leg waldos are also dangerous, even though the amplification is less extreme. Until you're really skilled, don't try to run, or jump. You're likely to trip, and that means you're likely to die.

"Charon's gravity is three-fourths of Earth normal, so it's not too bad. But on a really small world, like Luna, you could take a running jump and not come down for twenty minutes, just keep sailing over the horizon. Maybe bash into a mountain at eighty meters per second. On a small asteroid, it'd be no trick at all to run up to escape velocity and be off on an informal tour of intergalactic space. It's a slow way to travel.

"Tomorrow morning, we'll start teaching you how to stay alive inside of this infernal machine. The rest of the afternoon and evening, I'll call you one at a time to be fitted. That's all, Sergeant."

Cortez went to the door and turned the stopcock that let air into the air lock. A bank of infrared lamps went on to keep the air from freezing inside it. When the pressures were equalized, he shut the stopcock, unclamped the door and stepped in, clamping it shut behind him. A pump hummed for about a minute, evacuating the air lock, then he stepped out and sealed the outside door. It was pretty much like the ones on Luna.

"First I want Private Omar Almizar. The rest of you can go find your bunks. I'll call you over the squawker."

"Alphabetical order, sir?"

"Yep. About ten minutes apiece. If your name begins with Z, you might as well get sacked."

That was Rogers. She probably *was* thinking about getting sacked.

V

The sun was a hard white point directly overhead. It was a lot brighter than I had expected it to be; since we were eighty AUs out, it was only 1/6400th as bright as it is on Earth. Still, it was putting out about as much light as a powerful streetlamp.

"This is considerably more light than you'll have on a portal planet," Captain Stott's voice crackled in our collective ear. "Be glad that you'll be able to watch your step."

We were lined up, single file, on a permaplast sidewalk connecting the billet and the supply hut. We'd practiced walking inside, all morning, and this wasn't any different except for the exotic scenery. Though the light was rather dim, you could see all the way to the horizon quite clearly, with no atmosphere in the way. A black cliff that looked too regular to be natural stretched from one horizon to the other, passing within a kilometer of us. The ground was obsidian-black, mottled with patches of white, or bluish, ice. Next to the supply hut was a small mountain of snow in a bin marked OXYGEN.

The suit was fairly comfortable, but it gave you the odd feeling of being simultaneously a marionette and a puppeteer. You apply the impulse to move your leg and the suit picks it up and magnifies it and moves your leg for you.

"Today we're only going to walk around the company area and nobody will *leave* the company area." The captain wasn't wearing his .45, but he had a laser-finger like the rest of us. And his was probably hooked up.

Keeping an interval of at least two meters between each person, we stepped off the permaplast and followed the captain over the smooth rock. We walked carefully for about an hour, spiraling out, and finally stopped at the far edge of the perimeter.

"Now everybody pay close attention. I'm going out to that blue slab of ice"—it was a big one, about twenty meters away—"and show you something that you'd better know if you want to live."

He walked out a dozen confident steps. "First I have to

heat up a rock—filters down." I slapped the stud under my armpit and the filter slid into place over my image converter. The captain pointed his finger at a black rock the size of a basketball and gave it a short burst. The glare rolled a long shadow of the captain over us and beyond. The rock shattered into a pile of hazy splinters.

"It doesn't take long for these to cool down." He stooped and picked up a piece. "This one is probably twenty or twenty-five degrees. Watch." He tossed the "warm" rock on the ice slab. It skittered around in a crazy pattern and shot off the side. He tossed another one, and it did the same.

"As you know you are not quite *perfectly* insulated. These rocks are about the temperature of the soles of your boots. If you try to stand on a slab of hydrogen the same thing will happen to you. Except that the rock is *already* dead.

"The reason for this behavior is that the rock makes a slick interface with the ice—a little puddle of liquid hydrogen—and rides a few molecules above the liquid on a cushion of hydrogen vapor. This makes the rock, or *you*, a frictionless bearing as far as the ice is concerned and you *can't* stand up without any friction under your boots.

"After you have lived in your suit for a month or so you *should* be able to survive falling down, but right *now* you just don't know enough. Watch."

The captain flexed and hopped up onto the slab. His feet shot out from under him and he twisted around in midair, landing on hands and knees. He slipped off and stood on the ground.

"The idea is to keep your exhaust fins from making contact with the frozen gas. Compared to the ice they are as hot as a blast furnace and contact with any weight behind it will result in an explosion."

After that demonstration, we walked around for another hour or so, and returned to the billet. Once through the air lock, we had to mill around for a while, letting the suits get up to something like room temperature. Somebody came up and touched helmets with me.

"William?" She had MC COY stenciled above her faceplate.

"Hi, Sean. Anything special?"

"I just wondered if you had anyone to sleep with tonight."

That's right; I'd forgotten, there wasn't any sleeping roster here. Everybody just chose his own partner. "Sure, I mean, uh, no . . . no, I haven't asked anybody, sure, if you want to . . ."

"Thanks, William. See you later." I watched her walk away and thought that if anybody could make a fighting suit look sexy, it'd be Sean. But even Sean couldn't.

Cortez decided we were warm enough and led us to the suit room where we backed the things into place and hooked them up to the charging plates—each suit had a little chunk of plutonium that would power it for several years, but we were supposed to run on fuel cells as much as possible. After a lot of shuffling around, everybody finally got plugged in and we were allowed to unsuit, ninety-seven naked chickens squirming out of bright green eggs. It was *cold*—the air, the floor, and especially the suits—and we made a pretty disorderly exit toward the lockers.

I slipped on tunic, trousers and sandals and was still cold. I took my cup and joined the line for soya, everybody jumping up and down to keep warm.

"How c-cold, do you think, it is, M-Mandella?" That was McCoy.

"I don't, even want, to think, about it." I stopped jumping and rubbed myself as briskly as possible, while holding a cup in one hand. "At least as cold as Missouri was."

"Ung . . . wish they'd, get some damn heat in, this place." It always effects the small girls more than anybody else. McCoy was the littlest one in the company, a waspwaist doll barely five feet high.

"They've got the airco going. It can't be long now."

"I wish I, was a big, slab of, meat like, you."

I was glad she wasn't.

VI

We had our first casualty on the third day, learning how to dig holes.

With such large amounts of energy stored in a soldier's

weapons, it wouldn't be practical for him to hack out a hole in the frozen ground with the conventional pick and shovel. Still, you can launch grenades all day and get nothing but shallow depressions—so the usual method is to bore a hole in the ground with the hand laser, drop a timed charge in after it's cooled down and, ideally, fill the hole with stuff. Of course, there's not much loose rock on Charon, unless you've already blown a hole nearby.

The only difficult thing about the procedure is getting away. To be safe, we were told, you've got to either be behind something really solid, or be at least a hundred meters away. You've got about three minutes after setting the charge, but you can't just spring away. Not on Charon.

The accident happened when we were making a really deep hole, the kind you want for a large underground bunker. For this, we had to blow a hole, then climb down to the bottom of the crater and repeat the procedure again and again until the hole was deep enough. Inside the crater we used charges with a five-minute delay, but it hardly seemed enough time—you really had to go slow, picking your way up the crater's edge.

Just about everybody had blown a double hole; everybody but me and three others. I guess we were the only ones paying really close attention when Bovanovitch got into trouble. All of us were a good two hundred meters away. With my image converter tuned up to about forty power, I watched her disappear over the rim of the crater. After that, I could only listen in on her conversation with Cortez.

"I'm on the bottom, Sergeant." Normal radio procedure was suspended for these maneuvers; only the trainee and Cortez could broadcast.

"O.K., move to the center and clear out the rubble. Take your time. No rush until you pull the pin."

"Sure, Sergeant." We could hear small echoes of rocks clattering; sound conduction through her boots. She didn't say anything for several minutes.

"Found bottom." She sounded a little out of breath.

"Ice, or rock?"

"Oh, it's rock, Sergeant. The greenish stuff."

"Use a low setting, then. One point two, dispersion four."

"God darn it, Sergeant, that'll take forever."

"Yeah, but that stuff's got hydrated crystals in it—heat it up too fast and you might make it fracture. And we'd just have to leave you there, girl."

"O.K., one point two dee four." The inside edge of the crater flickered red with reflected laser light.

"When you get about half a meter deep, squeeze it up to dee two."

"Roger." It took her exactly seventeen minutes, three of them at dispersion two. I could imagine how tired her shooting arm was.

"Now rest for a few minutes. When the bottom of the hole stops glowing, arm the charge and drop it in. Then *walk* out, Understand? You'll have plenty of time."

"I understand, Sergeant. Walk out." She sounded nervous. Well, you don't often have to tiptoe away from a twenty microton tachyon bomb. We listened to her breathing for a few minutes.

"Here goes." Faint slithering sound of the bomb sliding down.

"Slow and easy now, you've got five minutes."

"Y-yeah. Five." Her footsteps started out slow and regular. Then, after she started climbing the side, the sounds were less regular; maybe a little frantic. And with four minutes to go—

"Crap!" A loud scraping noise, then clatters and bumps.

"What's wrong, Private?"

"Oh, crap." Silence. "Crap!"

"Private, you don't wanna get shot, you *tell me what's wrong!*"

"I . . . I'm stuck, damn rockslide . . . DO SOMETHING I can't move. I can't move I, I—"

"Shut up! How deep?"

"Can't move my crap, my damn legs HELP ME—"

"Then damn it use your arms—push!—you can move a ton with each hand." Three minutes.

Then she stopped cussing and started to mumble, in Russian, I guess, a low monotone. She was panting and you could hear rocks tumbling away.

"I'm free." Two minutes.

"Go as fast as you can." Cortez's voice was flat, emotionless.

At ninety seconds she appeared crawling over the rim. "Run, girl . . . you better run." She ran five or six steps and fell, skidded a few meters and got back up, running; fell again, got up again—

It looked like she was going pretty fast, but she had only covered about thirty meters when Cortez said, "All right, Bovanovitch, get down on your stomach and lie still." Ten seconds, but she didn't hear him, or she wanted to get just a little more distance, and she kept running, careless leaping strides and at the high point of one leap there was a flash and a rumble and something big hit her below the neck and her headless body spun off end over end through space, trailing a red-black spiral of flash-frozen blood that settled gracefully to the ground, a path of crystal powder that nobody disturbed while we gathered rocks to cover the juiceless thing at the end of it.

That night Cortez didn't lecture us, didn't even show up for nightchop. We were all very polite to each other and nobody was afraid to talk about it.

I sacked with Rogers; everybody sacked with a good friend, but all she wanted to do was cry, and she cried so long and so hard that she got me doing it, too.

VII

"Fire team A—move out!" The twelve of us advanced in a ragged line toward the simulated bunker. It was about a kilometer away, across a carefully prepared obstacle course. We could move pretty fast, since all of the ice had been cleared from the field, but even with ten days' experience we weren't ready to do more than an easy jog.

I carried a grenade launcher, loaded with tenth-microton practice grenades. Everybody had their laser-fingers set at point oh eight dee one; not much more than a flashlight. This was a *simulated* attack—the bunker and its robot defender cost too much to be used once and thrown away.

"Team B follow. Team leaders, take over."

We approached a clump of boulders at about the halfway mark, and Potter, my team leader, said "Stop and cover." We clustered behind the rocks and waited for team B.

Barely visible in their blackened suits, the dozen men and women whispered by us. As soon as they were clear, they jogged left, out of our line of sight.

"Fire!" Red circles of light danced a half-click downrange, where the bunker was just visible. Five hundred meters was the limit for these practice grenades; but I might luck out, so I lined the launcher up on the image of the bunker, held it at a 45° angle and popped off a salvo of three.

Return fire from the bunker started before my grenades even landed. Its automatic lasers were no more powerful than the ones we were using, but a direct hit would deactivate your image converter, leaving you blind. It was setting down a random field of fire, not even coming close to the boulders we were hiding behind.

Three magnesium-bright flashes blinked simultaneously, about thirty meters short of the bunker. "Mandella! I thought you were supposed to be *good* with that thing."

"Damn it, Potter—it only throws half a click. Once we get closer, I'll lay 'em right on top, every time."

"*Sure* you will." I didn't say anything. She wouldn't be team leader forever. Besides, she hadn't been such a bad girl before the power went to her head.

Since the grenadier is the assistant team leader, I was slaved into Potter's radio and could hear B team talk to her.

"Potter, this is Freeman. Losses?"

"Potter here—no, looks like they were concentrating on you."

"Yeah, we lost three. Right now we're in a depression about eighty, a hundred meters down from you. We can give cover whenever you're ready."

"O.K., start." Soft click: "A team follow me." She slid out from behind the rock and turned on the faint pink beacon beneath her powerpack. I turned on mine and moved out to run alongside of her and the rest of the team fanned out in a trailing wedge. Nobody fired while B team laid down a cover for us.

All I could hear was Potter's breathing and the soft *crunch-crunch* of my boots. Couldn't see much of anything, so I tongued the image converter up to a log two intensification. That made the image kind of blurry but adequately bright. Looked like the bunker had B team pretty well pinned down; they were getting quite a roasting. All of their return fire was laser; they must have lost their grenadier.

"Potter, this is Mandella. Shouldn't we take some of the heat off B team?"

"Soon as I can find us good enough cover. Is that all right with you? Private?" She'd been promoted to corporal for the duration of the exercise.

We angled to the right and laid down behind a slab of rock. Most of the others found cover nearby, but a few had to just hug the ground.

"Freeman, this is Potter."

"Potter, this is Smithy. Freeman's out; Samuels is out. We only have five men left. Give us some cover so we can get . . ."

"Roger, Smithy."—*click*—"Open up, A team. The B's are really hurtin'."

I peeked out over the edge of the rock. My rangefinder said that the bunker was about three hundred fifty meters away, still pretty far. I aimed just a smidgeon high and popped three, then down a couple of degrees and three more. The first ones overshot by about twenty meters, then the second salvo flared up directly in front of the bunker. I tried to hold on that angle and popped fifteen, the rest of the magazine, in the same direction.

I should have ducked down behind the rock to reload, but I wanted to see where the fifteen would land, so I kept my eyes on the bunker while I reached back to unclip another magazine . . .

When the laser hit my image converter there was a red glare so intense it seemed to go right through my eyes and bounce off the back of my skull. It must have been only a few milliseconds before the converter overloaded and went blind, but the bright green afterimage hurt my eyes for several minutes.

Since I was officially "dead," my radio automatically cut off and I had to remain where I was until the mock battle was over. With no sensory input besides the feel of my own skin—and it ached where the image converter had shone on it—and the ringing in my ears, it seemed like an awfully long time. Finally, a helmet clanked against mine:

"You O.K., Mandella?" Potter's voice.

"Sorry, I died of boredom twenty minutes ago."

"Stand up and take my hand." I did so and we shuffled back to the billet. It must have taken over an hour. She didn't say anything more, all the way back—it's a pretty awkward way to communicate—but after we'd cycled through the air lock and warmed up, she helped me undog my suit. I got ready for a mild tongue-lashing, but when the suit popped open, before I could even get my eyes adjusted to the light, she grabbed me around the neck and planted a wet kiss on my mouth.

"Nice shooting, Mandella."

"Huh?"

"The last salvo before you got hit—four direct hits; the bunker decided it was knocked out, and all we had to do was walk the rest of the way."

"Great." I scratched my face under the eyes and some dry skin flaked off. She giggled.

"You should see yourself, you look like . . ."

"All personnel report to the assembly area." That was the captain's voice. Bad news.

She handed me a tunic and sandals. "Let's go."

The assembly area/chop hall was just down the corridor. There was a row of roll-call buttons at the door; I pressed the one beside my name. Four of the names were covered with black tape. That was good, we hadn't lost anybody else during today's maneuvers.

The captain was sitting on the raised dais, which at least meant we didn't have to go through the tench-hut bullshit. The place filled up in less than a minute; a soft chime indicated the roll was complete.

Captain Stott didn't stand up. "You did *fairly* well today, nobody got killed and I expected some to. In that respect you exceeded my expectations but in *every* other respect you did a poor job.

"I am glad you're taking good care of yourselves because each of you represents an investment of over a million dollars and one fourth of a human life.

"But in this simulated battle against a *very* stupid robot enemy, thirty-seven of you managed to walk into laser fire and be killed in a *sim*ulated way and since dead people require no food *you* will require no food, for the next three days. Each person who was a casualty in this battle will be allowed only two liters of water and a vitamin ration each day."

We knew enough not to groan or anything, but there were some pretty disgusted looks, especially on the faces that had singed eyebrows and a pink rectangle of sunburn framing their eyes.

"Mandella."

"Sir?"

"You are far and away the worst burned casualty. Was your image converter set on normal?"

Oh, crap. "No, sir. Log two."

"I see. Who was your team leader for the exercise?"

"Acting Corporal Potter, sir."

"Private Potter, did you order him to use image intensification?"

"Sir, I . . . I don't remember."

"You don't. Well as a memory exercise you may join the dead people. Is that satisfactory?"

"Yes, sir."

"Good. Dead people get one last meal tonight, and go on no rations starting tomorrow. Are there any questions?" He must have been kidding. "All right. Dismissed."

I selected the meal that looked as if it had the most calories and took my tray over to sit by Potter.

"That was a quixotic damn thing to do. But thanks."

"Nothing. I've been wanting to lose a few pounds anyway." I couldn't see where she was carrying any extra.

"I know a good exercise," I said. She smiled without looking up from her tray. "Have anybody for tonight?"

"Kind of thought I'd ask Jeff . . ."

"Better hurry, then. He's lusting after Uhuru." Well, that was mostly true. Everybody did.

"I don't know. Maybe we ought to save our strength. That third day . . ."

"Come on," I scratched the back of her hand lightly with a fingernail. "We haven't sacked since Missouri. Maybe I've learned something new."

"Maybe you have." She tilted her head up at me in a sly way. "O.K."

Actually, she was the one with the new trick. The French corkscrew, she called it. She wouldn't tell me who taught it to her, though. I'd like to shake his hand.

VIII

The two weeks' training around Miami Base eventually cost us eleven lives. Twelve, if you count Dahlquist. I guess having to spend the rest of your life on Charon, with a hand and both legs missing, is close enough to dying.

Little Foster was crushed in a landslide and Freeland had a suit malfunction that froze him solid before we could carry him inside. Most of the other deaders were people I didn't know all that well. But they all hurt. And they seemed to make us more scared rather than more cautious.

Now darkside. A flier brought us over in groups of twenty, and set us down beside a pile of building materials, thoughtfully immersed in a pool of helium II.

We used grapples to haul the stuff out of the pool. It's not safe to go wading, since the stuff crawls all over you and it's hard to tell what's underneath; you could walk out onto a slab of hydrogen and be out of luck.

I'd suggested that we try to boil away the pool with our lasers, but ten minutes of concentrated fire didn't drop the helium level appreciably. It didn't boil, either; helium II is a "superfluid," so what evaporation there was had to take place evenly, all over the surface. No hot spots, so no bubbling.

We weren't supposed to use lights, to "avoid detection." There was plenty of starlight, with your image converter cranked up to log three or four, but each stage of amplification meant some loss of detail. By log four, the landscape looked like a crude monochrome painting, and you couldn't read the names on people's helmets unless they were right in front of you.

The landscape wasn't all that interesting, anyhow. There were half a dozen medium-sized meteor craters—all with exactly the same level of helium II in them—and the suggestion of some puny mountains just over the horizon. The uneven ground was the consistency of frozen spiderwebs; every time you put your foot down, you'd sink half an inch with a squeaking crunch. It could get on your nerves.

It took most of a day to pull all the stuff out of the pool. We took shifts napping, which you could do either standing up, sitting, or lying on your stomach. I didn't do well in any of those positions, so I was anxious to get the bunker built and pressurized.

We couldn't build the thing underground—it'd just fill up with helium II—so the first thing to do was to build an insulating platform, a permaplast-vacuum sandwich three layers tall.

I was an acting corporal, with a crew of ten people. We were carrying the permaplast layers to the building site—two people can carry one easily—when one of "my" men slipped and fell on his back.

"Damn it, Singer, watch your step." We'd had a couple of deaders that way.

"Sorry, Corporal. I'm bushed, just got my feet tangled up."

"Yeah, just watch it." He got back up all right, and with his partner placed the sheet and went back to get another.

I kept my eye on him. In a few minutes he was practically staggering, not easy to do in that suit of cybernetic armor.

"Singer! After you set that plank, I want to see you."

"O.K." He labored through the task and mooched over.

"Let me check your readout." I opened the door on his chest to expose the medical monitor. His temperature was two degrees high; blood pressure and heart rate both elevated. Not up to the red line, though.

"You sick or something?"

"Hell, Mandella, I feel O.K., just tired. Since I fell I've been a little dizzy."

I chinned the medic's combination. "Doc, this is Mandella. You wanna come over here for a minute?"

"Sure, where are you?" I waved and he walked over from poolside.

"What's the problem?" I showed him Singer's readout.

He knew what all the other little dials and things meant, so it took him a while. "As far as I can tell, Mandella . . . he's just hot."

"Hell, I coulda told you that," said Singer.

"Maybe you better have the armorer take a look at his suit." We had two people who'd taken a crash course in suit maintenance; they were our "armorers."

I chinned Sanchez and asked him to come over with his tool kit.

"Be a couple of minutes, Corporal. Carryin' a plank."

"Well, put it down and get on over here." I was getting an uneasy feeling. Waiting for him, the medic and I looked over Singer's suit.

"Uh-oh," Doc Jones said. "Look at this." I went around to the back and looked where he was pointing. Two of the fins on the heat exchanger were bent out of shape.

"What is wrong?" Singer asked.

"You fell on your heat exchanger, right?"

"Sure, Corporal—that's it, it must not be working right."

"I don't think it's working at *all*," said Doc.

Sanchez came over with his diagnostic kit and we told him what had happened. He looked at the heat exchanger, then plugged a couple of jacks into it and got a digital readout from a little monitor in his kit. I didn't know what it was measuring, but it came out zero to eight decimal places.

Heard a soft click, Sanchez chinning my private frequency. "Corporal, this guy's a deader."

"What? Can't you fix the damn thing?"

"Maybe . . . maybe I could, if I could take it apart. But there's no way . . ."

"Hey! Sanchez?" Singer was talking on the general freak. "Find out what's wrong?" He was panting.

Click. "Keep your pants on, man, we're working on it."
Click. "He won't last long enough for us to get the bunker
pressurized. And I can't work on the heat exchanger from
outside of the suit."

"You've got a spare suit, haven't you?"

"Two of 'em, the fit-anybody kind. But there's no place
. . . say . . ."

"Right. Go get one of the suits warmed up." I chinned
the general freak. "Listen, Singer, we've gotta get you out
of that thing. Sanchez has a spare suit, but to make the
switch, we're gonna have to build a house around you. Understand?"

"Huh-uh."

"Look, we'll just make a box with you inside, and hook it
up to the life-support unit. That way you can breathe while
you make the switch."

"Soun's pretty compis . . . complicated t'me."

"Look, just come along . . ."

"I'll be all right, man, jus' lemme res' . . ."

I grabbed his arm and led him to the building site. He was
really weaving. Doc took his other arm and between us, we
kept him from falling over.

"Corporal Ho, this is Corporal Mandella." Ho was in
charge of the life-support unit.

"Go away, Mandella, I'm busy."

"You're going to be busier." I outlined the problem to her.
While her group hurried to adapt the LSU—for this purpose, it need only be an air hose and heater—I got my
crew to bring around six slabs of permaplast, so we could
build a big box around Singer and the extra suit. It would
look like a huge coffin, a meter square and six meters long.

We set the suit down on the slab that would be the floor
of the coffin. "O.K., Singer, let's go."

No answer.

"Singer!" He was just standing there. Doc Jones checked
his readout.

"He's out, man, unconscious."

My mind raced. There might just be room for another
person in the box. "Give me a hand here." I took Singer's

shoulders and Doc took his feet, and we carefully laid him out at the feet of the empty suit.

Then I laid down myself, above the suit. "O.K., close 'er up."

"Look, Mandella, if anybody goes in there, it oughta be me."

"No, Doc. *My* job. My man." That sounded all wrong. William Mandella, boy hero.

They stood a slab up on edge—it had two openings for the LSU input and exhaust—and proceeded to weld it to the bottom plank with a narrow laser beam. On Earth, we'd just use glue, but here the only fluid was helium, which has lots of interesting properties, but is definitely not sticky.

After about ten minutes we were completely walled up. I could feel the LSU humming. I switched on my suit light —the first time since we landed on darkside—and the glare made purple blotches dance in front of my eyes.

"Mandella, this is Ho. Stay in your suit at least two or three minutes. We're putting hot air in, but it's coming back just this side of liquid." I lay and watched the purple fade.

"O.K., it's still cold, but you can make it." I popped my suit. It wouldn't open all the way, but I didn't have too much trouble getting out. The suit was still cold enough to take some skin off my fingers and butt as I wiggled out.

I had to crawl feet-first down the coffin to get to Singer. It got darker fast, moving away from my light. When I popped his suit a rush of hot stink hit me in the face. In the dim light his skin was dark red and splotchy. His breathing was very shallow and I could see his heart palpitating.

First I unhooked the relief tubes—an unpleasant business —then the bio sensors, and then I had the problem of getting his arms out of their sleeves.

It's pretty easy to do for yourself. You twist this way and turn that way and the arm pops out. Doing it from the outside is a different matter: I had to twist his arm and then reach under and move the suit's arm to match—and it takes muscle to move a suit around from the outside.

Once I had one arm out it was pretty easy: I just crawled forward, putting my feet on the suit's shoulders, and pulled on his free arm. He slid out of the suit like an oyster slipping out of its shell.

I popped the spare suit and after a lot of pulling and pushing, managed to get his legs in. Hooked up the bio sensors and the front relief tube. He'd have to do the other one himself, it's too complicated. For the nth time I was glad not to have been born female; they have to have two of those damned plumber's friends, instead of just one and a simple hose.

I left his arms out of the sleeves. The suit would be useless for any kind of work, anyhow; waldos have to be tailored to the individual.

His eyelids fluttered. "Man . . . della. Where . . . the hell . . ."

I explained, slowly, and he seemed to get most of it. "Now I'm gonna close you up and go get into my suit. I'll have the crew cut the end off this thing and I'll haul you out. Got it?"

He nodded. Strange to see that—when you nod or shrug in a suit, it doesn't communicate anything.

I crawled into my suit, hooked up the attachments and chinned the general freak. "Doc, I think he's gonna be O.K. Get us out of here now."

"Will do." Ho's voice. The LSU hum was replaced by a chatter, then a throb; evacuating the box to prevent an explosion.

One corner of the seam grew red, then white and a bright crimson beam lanced through, not a foot away from my head. I scrunched back as far as I could. The beam slid up the seam and around three corners, back to where it started. The end of the box fell away slowly, trailing filaments of melted 'plast.

"Wait for the stuff to harden, Mandella."

"Sanchez, I'm not that stupid."

"Here you go." Somebody tossed a line to me. That *would* be smarter than dragging him out by myself. I threaded a long bight under his arms and tied it behind his neck. Then I scrambled out to help them pull, which was silly—they had a dozen people already lined up to haul.

Singer got out all right and was actually sitting up while

Doc Jones checked his readout. People were asking me about it and congratulating me when suddenly Ho said "Look!" and pointed toward the horizon.

It was a black ship, coming in fast. I just had time to think it wasn't fair, they weren't supposed to attack until the last few days, and then the ship was right on top of us.

IX

We all flopped to the ground instinctively, but the ship didn't attack. It blasted braking rockets and dropped to land on skids. Then it skied around to come to a rest beside the building site.

Everybody had it figured out and was standing around sheepishly when the two suited figures stepped out of the ship.

A familiar voice crackled over the general freak. "Every *one* of you saw us coming in and not *one* of you responded with laser fire. It wouldn't have done any good but it would have indicated a certain amount of fighting spirit. You have a week or less before the real thing and since the sergeant and *I* will be here *I* will insist that you show a little more will to live. Acting Sergeant Potter."

"Here, sir."

"Get me a detail of twelve men to unload cargo. We brought a hundred small robot drones for *tar*get practice so that you might have at least a fighting chance, when a live target comes over.

"Move *now;* we only have thirty minutes before the ship returns to Miami."

I checked, and it was actually more like forty minutes.

Having the captain and sergeant there didn't really make much difference; we were still on our own, they were just observing.

Once we got the floor down, it only took one day to complete the bunker. It was a gray oblong, featureless except for the air-lock blister and four windows. On top was a swivel-mounted bevawatt laser. The operator—you couldn't call him a "gunner"—sat in a chair holding dead-man switches in both hands. The laser wouldn't fire as long as he was holding one of those switches. If he let go, it would automatically aim for any moving aerial object and fire at will. Primary detection and aiming was by means of a kilometer-high antenna mounted beside the bunker.

It was the only arrangement that could really be expected to work, with the horizon so close and human reflexes so slow. You couldn't have the thing fully automatic, because in theory, friendly ships might also approach.

The aiming computer could choose up to twelve targets, appearing simultaneously—firing at the largest ones first. And it would get all twelve in the space of half a second.

The installation was partly protected from enemy fire by an efficient ablative layer that covered everything except the human operator. But then they *were* dead-man switches. One man above guarding eighty inside. The army's good at that kind of arithmetic.

Once the bunker was finished, half of us stayed inside at all times—feeling very much like targets—taking turns operating the laser, while the other half went on maneuvers.

About four clicks from the base was a large "lake" of frozen hydrogen; one of our most important maneuvers was to learn how to get around on the treacherous stuff.

It really wasn't too difficult. You couldn't stand up on it, so you had to belly down and slide.

If you had somebody to push you from the edge, getting started was no problem. Otherwise, you had to scrabble with your hands and feet, pushing down as hard as was practical, until you started moving, in a series of little jumps. Once started, you would keep going until you ran out of ice. You could steer a little bit by digging in, hand and foot, on the appropriate side, but you couldn't slow to a stop that way. So it was a good idea not to go too fast, and to be positioned in such a way that your helmet didn't absorb the shock of stopping.

We went through all the things we'd done on the Miami side; weapons practice, demolition, attack patterns. We also launched drones at irregular intervals, toward the bunker. Thus, ten or fifteen times a day, the operators got to demonstrate their skill in letting go of the handles as soon as the proximity light went on.

I had four hours of that, like everybody else. I was nervous until the first "attack," when I saw how little there was to it. The light went on, I let go, the gun aimed and when the drone peeped over the horizon—*zzt!* Nice touch of color, the molten metal spraying through space. Otherwise not too exciting.

So none of us were worried about the upcoming "graduation exercise," thinking it would be just more of the same.

Miami Base attacked on the thirteenth day with two simultaneous missiles streaking over opposite sides of the horizon at some forty kilometers per second. The laser vaporized the first one with no trouble, but the second got within eight clicks of the bunker before it was hit.

We were coming back from maneuvers, about a click away from the bunker. I wouldn't have seen it happen if I hadn't been looking directly at the bunker the moment of the attack.

The second missile sent a shower of molten debris straight toward the bunker. Eleven pieces hit, and, as we later reconstructed it, this is what happened.

The first casualty was Uhuru, pretty Uhuru inside the bunker, who was hit in the back and head and died instantly. With the drop in pressure, the LSU went into high gear. Friedman was standing in front of the main airco outlet and was blown into the opposite wall hard enough to knock him unconscious; he died of decompression before the others could get him to his suit.

Everybody else managed to stagger through the gale and get into their suits, but Garcia's suit had been holed and didn't do him any good.

By the time we got there, they had turned off the LSU and were welding up the holes in the wall. One man was trying to scrape up the unrecognizable mess that had been Uhuru. I could hear him sobbing and retching. They had already taken Garcia and Friedman outside for burial. The captain took over the repair detail from Potter. Sergeant

Cortez led the sobbing man over to a corner and came back to work on cleaning up Uhuru's remains, alone. He didn't order anybody to help and nobody volunteered.

X

As a graduation exercise, we were unceremoniously stuffed into a ship—*Earth's Hope,* the same one we rode to Charon—and bundled off to Stargate at a little more than 1 G.

The trip seemed endless, about six months subjective time, and boring, but not as hard on the carcass as going to Charon had been. Captain Stott made us review our training orally, day by day, and we did exercises every day until we were worn to a collective frazzle.

Stargate I was like Charon's darkside, only more so. The base on Stargate I was smaller than Miami Base—only a little bigger than the one we constructed on darkside—and we were due to lay over a week to help expand the facilities. The crew there was very glad to see us; especially the two females, who looked a little worn around the edges.

We all crowded into the small dining hall, where Submajor Williamson, the man in charge of Stargate I, gave us some disconcerting news:

"Everybody get comfortable. Get off the tables, though, there's plenty of floor.

"I have some idea of what you just went through, training on Charon. I won't say it's all been wasted. But where you're headed, things will be quite different. Warmer."

He paused to let that soak in.

"Aleph Aurigae, the first collapsar ever detected, revolves around the normal star Epsilon Aurigae, in a twenty-seven-year orbit. The enemy has a base of operations, not on a regular portal planet of Aleph, but on a planet in orbit around Epsilon. We don't know much about the planet: just that it goes around Epsilon once every seven hundred forty-five days, is about three fourths the size of Earth, and has an albedo of 0.8, meaning it's probably covered with clouds. We can't say precisely how hot it will be, but judging from its distance from Epsilon, it's probably rather hotter than

Earth. Of course, we don't know whether you'll be working . . . fighting on lightside or darkside, equator or poles. It's highly unlikely that the atmosphere will be breathable—at any rate, you'll stay inside your suits.

"Now you know exactly as much about where you're going as I do. Questions?"

"Sir," Stein drawled, "now we know where we're goin' . . . anybody know what we're goin' to do when we get there?"

Williamson shrugged. "That's up to your captain—and your sergeant, and the captain of *Earth's Hope,* and *Hope's* logistic computer. We just don't have enough data yet, to project a course of action for you. It may be a long and bloody battle, it may be just a case of walking in to pick up the pieces. Conceivably, the Taurans might want to make a peace offer"—Cortez snorted—"in which case you would simply be part of our muscle, our bargaining power." He looked at Cortez mildly. "No one can say for sure."

The orgy that night was kind of amusing, but it was like trying to sleep in the middle of a raucous beach party. The only area big enough to sleep all of us was the dining hall; they draped a few bedsheets here and there for privacy, then unleashed Stargate's eighteen sex-starved men on our women, compliant and promiscuous by military custom—and law—but desiring nothing so much as sleep on solid ground.

The eighteen men acted as if they were compelled to try as many permutations as possible, and their performance was impressive—in a strictly quantitative sense, that is.

The next morning—and every other morning we were on Stargate I—we staggered out of bed and into our suits, to go outside and work on the "new wing." Eventually, Stargate would be tactical and logistic headquarters for the war, with thousands of permanent personnel, guarded by half-a-dozen heavy cruisers in *Hope's* class. When we started, it was two shacks and twenty people; when we left, it was four shacks and twenty people. The work was a breeze, compared to darkside, since we had all the light we needed, and got sixteen hours inside for every eight hours' work. And no drone attack for a final exam.

When we shuttled back up to the *Hope,* nobody was too happy about leaving—though some of the more popular females declared it'd be good to get some rest—Stargate was the last easy, safe assignment we'd have before taking up arms against the Taurans. And as Williamson had pointed out the first day, there was no way of predicting what that would be like.

Most of us didn't feel too enthusiastic about making a collapsar jump, either. We'd been assured that we wouldn't even feel it happen, just free fall all the way.

I wasn't convinced. As a physics student, I'd had the usual courses in general relativity and theories of gravitation. We only had a little direct data at that time—Stargate was discovered when I was in grade school—but the mathematical model seemed clear enough.

The collapsar Stargate was a perfect sphere about three kilometers in radius. It was suspended forever in a state of gravitational collapse that should have meant its surface was dropping toward its center at nearly the speed of light. Relativity propped it up, at least gave it the illusion of being there . . . the way all reality becomes illusory and observer-oriented when you study general relativity, or Buddhism.

At any rate, there would be a theoretical point in space-time when one end of our ship was just above the surface of the collapsar, and the other end was a kilometer away—in our frame of reference. In any sane universe, this would set up tidal stresses and tear the ship apart, and we would be just another million kilograms of degenerate matter on the theoretical surface, rushing headlong to nowhere for the rest of eternity; or dropping to the center in the next trillionth of a second. You pays your money and you takes your frame of reference.

But they were right. We blasted away from Stargate I, made a few course corrections and then just dropped, for about an hour.

Then a bell rang and we sank into our cushions under a steady two gravities of deceleration. We were in enemy territory.

XI

We'd been decelerating at two gravities for almost nine days when the battle began. Lying on our couches being miserable, all we felt were two soft bumps, missiles being released. Some eight hours later, the squawkbox crackled: "Attention, all crew. This is the captain." Quinsana, the pilot, was only a lieutenant, but was allowed to call himself captain aboard the vessel, where he outranked all of us, even Captain Stott. "You grunts in the cargo hold can listen, too.

"We just engaged the enemy with two fifty-bevaton tachyon missiles, and have destroyed both the enemy vessel and another object which it had launched approximately three microseconds before.

"The enemy has been trying to overtake us for the past one hundred seventy-nine hours, ship time. At the time of the engagement, the enemy was moving at a little over half the speed of light, relative to Aleph, and was only about thirty AU's from *Earth's Hope*. It was moving at .47c relative to us, and thus we would have been coincident in space-time"—rammed!—"in a little more than nine hours. The missiles were launched at 0719 ship's time, and destroyed the enemy at 1540, both tachyon bombs detonating within a thousand clicks of the enemy objects."

The two missiles were a type whose propulsion system itself was only a barely-controlled tachyon bomb. They accelerated at a constant rate of 100 Gs, and were traveling at a relativistic speed by the time the nearby mass of the enemy ship detonated them.

"We expect no further interference from enemy vessels. Our velocity with respect to Aleph will be zero in another five hours; we will then begin to journey back. The return will take twenty-seven days." General moans and dejected cussing. Everybody knew all that already, of course; but we didn't care to be reminded of it.

So after another month of logycalisthenics and drill, at a constant 2 Gs, we got our first look at the planet we were going to attack. Invaders from outer space, yes, sir.

It was a blinding white crescent basking two AU's from Epsilon. The captain had pinned down the location of the enemy base from fifty AU's out, and we had jockeyed in on a wide arc, keeping the bulk of the planet between them and us. That didn't mean we were sneaking up on them—quite the contrary; they launched three abortive attacks—but it put us in a stronger defensive position. Until we had to go to the surface, that is. Then only the ship and its Star Fleet crew would be reasonably safe.

Since the planet rotated rather slowly—once every ten and one half days—a "stationary" orbit for the ship had to be one hundred fifty thousand clicks out. This made the people in the ship feel quite secure, with six thousand miles of rock and ninety thousand miles of space between them and the enemy. But it meant a whole second's time lag in communication between us on the ground and the ship's battle computer. A person could get awful dead while that neutrino pulse crawled up and back.

Our vague orders were to attack the base and gain control while damaging a minimum of enemy equipment. We were to take at least one enemy alive. We were under no circumstances to allow *ourselves* to be taken alive, however. And the decision wasn't up to us; one special pulse from the battle computer, and that speck of plutonium in your power plant would fission with all of .01% efficiency, and you'd be nothing but a rapidly expanding, very hot plasma.

They strapped us into six scoutships—one platoon of twelve people in each—and we blasted away from *Earth's Hope* at 8 Gs. Each scoutship was supposed to follow its own carefully random path to our rendezvous point, one hundred eight clicks from the base. Fourteen drone ships were launched at the same time, to confound the enemy's anti-spacecraft system.

The landing went off almost perfectly. One ship suffered minor damage, a near miss boiling away some of the ablative material on one side of the hull, but it'd still be able to make it and return, as long as it kept its speed down while in the atmosphere.

We zigged and zagged and wound up first ship at the

rendezvous point. There was only one trouble. It was under four kilometers of water.

I could almost hear that machine, ninety thousand miles away, grinding its mental gears, adding this new bit of data. We proceeded just as if we were landing on solid ground: braking rockets, falling, skids out, hit the water, skip, hit the water, skip, hit the water, sink.

It would have made sense to go ahead and land on the bottom—we were streamlined, after all, and water just another fluid—but the hull wasn't strong enough to hold up a four-kilometer column of water. Sergeant Cortez was in the scoutship with us.

"Sarge, tell that computer to *do* something! We're gonna get . . ."

"Oh, shut up, Mandella. Trust in th' lord." "Lord" was definitely lower-case when Cortez said it.

There was a loud bubbly sigh, then another and a slight increase in pressure on my back that meant the ship was rising. "Flotation bags?" Cortez didn't deign to answer, or didn't know.

That must have been it. We rose to within ten or fifteen meters of the surface and stopped, suspended there. Through the port I could see the surface above, shimmering like a mirror of hammered silver. I wondered what it could be like, to be a fish and have a definite roof over your world.

I watched another ship splash in. It made a great cloud of bubbles and turbulence, then fell—slightly tailfirst—for a short distance before large bags popped out under each delta wing. Then it bobbed up to about our level and stayed.

Soon all of the ships were floating within a few hundred meters of us, like a school of ungainly fish.

"This is Captain Stott. Now listen carefully. There is a beach some twenty-eight clicks from your present position, in the direction of the enemy. You will be proceeding to this beach by scoutship and from there will mount your assault on the Tauran position." That was *some* improvement; we'd only have to walk eighty clicks.

We deflated the bags, blasted to the surface and flew in a slow, spread-out formation to the beach. It took several minutes. As the ship scraped to a halt I could hear pumps humming, making the cabin pressure equal to the air pressure outside. Before it had quite stopped moving, the escape slot beside my couch slid open. I rolled out onto the wing of the craft and jumped to the ground. Ten seconds to find cover—I sprinted across loose gravel to the "treeline," a twisty bramble of tall sparse bluish-green shrubs. I dove into the briar path and turned to watch the ships leave. The drones that were left rose slowly to about a hundred meters, then took off in all directions with a bone-jarring roar. The real scoutships slid slowly back into the water. Maybe that was a good idea.

It wasn't a terribly attractive world, but certainly would be easier to get around in than the cryogenic nightmare we were trained for. The sky was a uniform dull silver brightness that merged with the mist over the ocean so completely as to make it impossible to tell where water ended and air began. Small wavelets licked at the black gravel shore, much too slow and graceful in the three-quarters Earth normal gravity. Even from fifty meters away, the rattle of billions of pebbles rolling with the tide was loud in my ears.

The air temperature was 79° Centigrade, not quite hot enough for the sea to boil, even though the air pressure was low compared to Earth's. Wisps of steam drifted quickly upward from the line where water met land. I wondered how long a man would survive, exposed here without a suit. Would the heat or the low oxygen—partial pressure one-eighth Earth normal—kill him first? Or was there some deadly microorganism that would beat them both . . .

"This is Cortez. Everybody come over and assemble by me." He was standing on the beach a little to the left of me, waving his hand in a circle over his head. I walked toward him through the shrubs. They were brittle, unsubstantial, seemed paradoxically dried-out in the steamy air. They wouldn't offer much in the way of cover.

"We'll be advancing on a heading .05 radians east of north. I want Platoon One to take point. Two and Three follow about twenty meters behind, to the left and right. Seven, command platoon, is in the middle, twenty meters behind Two and Three. Five and Six, bring up the rear, in a semicircular closed flank. Everybody straight?" Sure, we could do that "arrowhead" maneuver in our sleep. "O.K., let's move out."

I was in Platoon Seven, the "command group." Captain Stott put me there not because I was expected to give any commands, but because of my training in physics.

The command group was supposedly the safest place, buffered by six platoons: people were assigned to it because there was some tactical reason for them to survive at least a little longer than the rest. Cortez was there to give orders. Chavez was there to correct suit malfuncts. The senior medic, Doc Wilson—the only medic who actually had an MD—was there and so was Theodopolis, the radio engineer: our link with the captain, who had elected to stay in orbit.

The rest of us were assigned to the command group by dint of special training or aptitude that wouldn't normally be considered of a "tactical" nature. Facing a totally unknown enemy, there was no way of telling what might prove important. Thus I was there because I was the closest the company had to a physicist. Rogers was biology. Tate was chemistry. Ho could crank out a perfect score on the Rhine extrasensory perception test, every time. Bohrs was a polyglot, able to speak twenty-one languages fluently, idiomatically. Petrov's talent was that he had tested out to have not one molecule of xenophobia in his psyche. Keating was a skilled acrobat. Debby Hollister—"Lucky" Hollister— showed a remarkable aptitude for making money, and also had a consistently high Rhine potential.

XII

When we first set out, we were using the "jungle" camouflage combination on our suits. But what passed for jungle in these anemic tropics was too sparse; we looked like a band of conspicuous harlequins trooping through the woods. Cortez had us switch to black, but that was just as bad, as the light from Epsilon came evenly from all parts of the sky, and there were no shadows except us. We finally settled on the dun-colored desert camouflage.

The nature of the countryside changed slowly as we walked north, away from the sea. The throned stalks, I guess you could call them trees, came in fewer numbers but were bigger around and less brittle; at the base of each was a tangled mass of vine with the same blue-green color, which spread out in a flattened cone some ten meters in diameter. There was a delicate green flower the size of a man's head near the top of each tree.

Grass began to appear some five clicks from the sea. It seemed to respect the trees' "property rights," leaving a strip of bare earth around each cone of vine. At the edge of such a clearing, it would grow as timid blue-green stubble; then, moving away from the tree, would get thicker and taller until it reached shoulder-high in some places, where the separation between two trees was unusually large. The grass was a lighter, greener shade than the trees and vines. We changed the color of our suits to the bright green we had used for maximum visibility on Charon. Keeping to the thickest part of the grass, we were fairly inconspicuous.

I couldn't help thinking that one week of training in a South American jungle would have been worth a hell of a lot more than all those weeks on Charon. We wouldn't be so understrength, either.

We covered over twenty clicks each day, buoyant after months under 2 Gs. Until the second day, the only form of animal life we saw was a kind of black worm, finger-sized with hundreds of cilium legs like the bristles of a stiff brush. Rogers said that there obviously had to be some sort of larger creature around, or there would be no reason for the trees to have thorns. So we were doubly on guard, expecting trouble both from the Taurans and the unidentified "large creatures."

Potter's Second Platoon was on point; the general freak was reserved for her, since point would likely be the first platoon to spot any trouble.

"Sarge, this is Potter," we all heard. "Movement ahead."

"Get down then!"

"We are. Don't think they see us."

"First Platoon, go up to the right of point. Keep down. Fourth, get up to the left. Tell me when you get in position.

Sixth Platoon, stay back and guard the rear. Fifth and Third, close with the command group."

Two dozen people whispered out of the grass, to join us. Cortez must have heard from the Fourth Platoon.

"Good. How about you, First . . . O.K., fine. How many are there?"

"Eight we can see." Potter's voice.

"Good. When I give the word, open fire. Shoot to kill."

"Sarge . . . they're just animals."

"Potter—if you've known all this time what a Tauran looks like, you should've told us. Shoot to kill."

"But we need . . ."

"We need a prisoner, but we don't need to escort him forty clicks to his home base and keep an eye on him while we fight. Clear?"

"Yes. Sergeant."

"O.K. Seventh, all you brains and weirds, we're going up and watch. Fifth and Third, come along to guard."

We crawled through the meter-high grass to where the Second Platoon had stretched out in a firing line.

"I don't see anything," Cortez said.

"Ahead and just to the left. Dark green."

They were only a shade darker than the grass. But after you saw the first one, you could see them all, moving slowly around some thirty meters ahead.

"Fire!" Cortez fired first, then twelve streaks of crimson leaped out and the grass wilted back, disappeared and the creatures convulsed and died trying to scatter.

"Hold fire, hold it!" Cortez stood up. "We want to have something left—Second Platoon, follow me." He strode out toward the smoldering corpses, laser finger pointed out front, obscene divining rod pulling him toward the carnage . . . I felt my gorge rising and knew that all the lurid training tapes, all the horrible deaths in training accidents, hadn't prepared me for this sudden reality . . . that I had a magic wand that I could point at a life and make it a smoking piece of half-raw meat; I wasn't a soldier nor ever wanted to be one nor ever would want . . .

"O.K., Seventh, come on up."

While we were walking toward them, one of the creatures moved, a tiny shudder, and Cortez flicked the beam of his laser over it with an almost negligent gesture. It made a hand-deep gash across the creature's middle. It died, like the others, without emitting a sound.

They were not quite as tall as humans, but wider in girth. They were covered with dark green, almost black fur; white curls where the laser had singed. They appeared to have three legs and an arm. The only ornament to their shaggy heads was a mouth, wet black orifice filled with flat black teeth. They were thoroughly repulsive but their worst feature was not a difference from human beings but a similarity . . . wherever the laser had opened a body cavity, milk-white glistening veined globes and coils of organs spilled out, and their blood was dark clotting red.

"Rogers, take a look. Taurans or not?"

Rogers knelt by one of the disemboweled creatures and opened a flat plastic box, filled with glittering dissecting tools. She selected a scalpel. "One way we might be able to find out." Doc Wilson watched over her shoulder as she methodically slit the membrane covering several organs.

"Here." She held up a blackish fibrous mass between two fingers, parody of daintiness through all that armor.

"So?"

"It's grass, Sergeant. If the Taurans can eat the grass and breathe the air, they certainly found a planet remarkably like their home." She tossed it away. "They're animals, Sergeant, just damn animals."

"I don't know," Doc Wilson said. "Just because they walk around on all fours, threes maybe, and are able to eat grass . . ."

"Well, let's check out the brain." She found one that had been hit in the head and scraped the superficial black char from the wound. "Look at that."

It was almost solid bone. She tugged and ruffled the hair all over the head of another one. "What the hell does it use for sensory organs? No eyes, or ears, or . . ." She stood up. "Nothing in that head but a mouth and ten centimeters of skull. To protect nothing, not a damn thing."

"If I could shrug, I'd shrug," the doctor said. "It doesn't prove anything—a brain doesn't have to look like a mushy walnut and it doesn't have to be in the head. Maybe that skull isn't bone, maybe *that's* the brain, some crystal lattice . . ."

"Yeah, but the stomach's in the right place, and if those aren't intestines I'll eat—"

"Look," Cortez said, "this is all real interesting, but all we need to know is whether that thing's dangerous, then we've gotta move on, we don't have all—"

"They aren't dangerous," Rogers began. "They don't . . ."

"Medic! DOC!" Somebody was waving his arms, back at the firing line. Doc sprinted back to him, the rest of us following.

"What's wrong?" He had reached back and unclipped his medical kit on the run.

"It's Ho, she's out."

Doc swung open the door on Ho's biomedical monitor. He didn't have to look far. "She's dead."

"Dead?" Cortez said. "What the hell . . ."

"Just a minute." Doc plugged a jack into the monitor and fiddled with some dials on his kit. "Everybody's biomed readout is stored for twelve hours. I'm running it backwards, should be able to—there!"

"What?"

"Four and a half minutes ago—must have been when you opened fire . . ."

"Well?"

"Massive cerebral hemorrhage. No . . ." he watched the dials. "No . . . warning, no indication of anything out of the ordinary; blood pressure up, pulse up, but normal under the circumstances . . . nothing to . . . indicate . . ." He reached down and popped her suit. Her fine oriental features were distorted in a horrible grimace, both gums showing. Sticky fluid ran from under her collapsed eyelids and a trickle of blood still dripped from each ear. Doc Wilson closed the suit back up.

"I've never seen anything like it. It's as if a bomb went off in her skull."

"Oh crap," Rogers said, "she was Rhine-sensitive, wasn't she."

"That's right." Cortez sounded thoughtful. "All right, everybody listen. Platoon leaders, check your platoons and see if anybody's missing, or hurt. Anybody else in Seventh?"

"I . . . I've got a splitting headache, Sarge," Lucky said.

Four others had bad headaches. One of them affirmed that he was slightly Rhine-sensitive. The others didn't know.

"Cortez, I think it's obvious," Doc Wilson said, "that we should give these . . . monsters wide berth, especially shouldn't harm any more of them. Not with five people susceptible to whatever apparently killed Ho."

"Of course, damn it, I don't need anybody to tell me that. We'd better get moving. I just filled the captain in on what happened; he agrees that we'd better get as far away from here as we can, before we stop for the night.

"Let's get back in formation and continue on the same bearing. Fifth Platoon, take over point; Second, come back to the rear. Everybody else, same as before."

"What about Ho?" Lucky asked.

"She'll be taken care of. From the ship."

After we'd gone half a click, there was a flash and rolling thunder. Where Ho had been, came a wispy luminous mushroom cloud boiling up to disappear against the gray sky.

XIII

We stopped for the "night"—actually, the sun wouldn't set for another seventy hours—atop a slight rise some ten clicks from where we had killed the aliens. But they weren't aliens, I had to remind myself—*we* were.

Two platoons deployed in a ring around the rest of us, and we flopped down exhausted. Everybody was allowed four hours' sleep and had two hours' guard duty.

Potter came over and sat next to me. I chinned her frequency.

"Hi, Marygay."

"Oh, William," her voice over the radio was hoarse and cracking. "God, it's so horrible."

"It's over now . . ."

"I killed one of them, the first instant, I shot it right in the, in the . . ."

I put my hand on her knee. The contact made a plastic click and I jerked it back, visions of machines embracing, copulating. "Don't feel singled out, Marygay, whatever guilt there is, belongs evenly to all of us . . . but a triple portion for Cor . . ."

"You privates quit jawin' and get some sleep. You both pull guard in two hours."

"O.K., Sarge." Her voice was so sad and tired I couldn't bear it, I felt if I could only touch her I could drain off the sadness like a ground wire draining current but we were each trapped in our own plastic world.

"G'night, William."

"Night." It's almost impossible to get sexually excited inside a suit, with the relief tube and all the silver chloride sensors poking you, but somehow this was my body's response to the emotional impotence, maybe remembering more pleasant sleeps with Marygay, maybe feeling that in the midst of all this death, personal death could be soon, cranking up the pro-creative derrick for one last try . . . lovely thoughts like this and I fell asleep and dreamed that I was a machine, mimicking the functions of life, creaking and clanking my clumsy way through the world, people too polite to say anything but giggling behind my back, and the little man who sat inside my head pulling the levers and clutches and watching the dials, he was hopelessly mad and was storing up hurts for the day . . .

"Mandella—wake up, damn it, your shift!"

I shuffled over to my place on the perimeter to watch for God knows what . . . but I was so weary I couldn't keep my eyes open. Finally I tongued a stimtab, knowing I'd pay for it later.

For over an hour I sat there, scanning my sector left, right, near, far; the scene never changing, not even a breath of wind to stir the grass.

Then suddenly the grass parted and one of the three-legged creatures was right in front of me. I raised my finger but didn't squeeze.

"Movement!"

"Movement!"

"HOLD YOUR FIRE. Don't shoot!"

"Movement."

"Movement." I looked left and right and as far as I could see, every perimeter guard had one of the blind dumb creatures standing right in front of him.

Maybe the drug I'd taken to stay awake made me more sensitive to whatever they did. My scalp crawled and I felt a formless *thing* in my mind, the feeling you get when somebody has said something and you didn't quite hear it, want to respond but the opportunity to ask him to repeat it is gone.

The creature sat back on its haunches, leaning forward on the one front leg. Big green bear with a withered arm. Its power threaded through my mind, spiderwebs, echo of night terrors, trying to communicate, trying to destroy me, I couldn't know.

"All right, everybody on the perimeter, fall back, slow. Don't make any quick gestures . . . anybody got a headache or anything?"

"Sergeant, this is Hollister." Lucky.

"They're trying to say something . . . I can almost . . . no, just . . ."

"Well?"

"All I can get is that they think we're . . . think we're . . . well, *funny*. They aren't afraid."

"You mean the one in front of you isn't . . ."

"No, the feeling comes from all of them, they're all thinking the same thing. Don't ask me how I know, I just do."

"Maybe they thought it was funny, what they did to Ho."

"Maybe. I don't feel like they're dangerous. Just curious about us."

"Sergeant, this is Bohrs."

"Yeah."

"The Taurans have been here at least a year—maybe they've learned how to communicate with these . . . overgrown teddy-bears. They might be spying on us, might be sending back . . ."

"I don't think they'd show themselves, if that were the case," Lucky said. "They can obviously hide from us pretty well when they want to."

"Anyhow," Cortez said, "if they're spies, the damage has been done. Don't think it'd be smart to take any action against them. I know you'd all like to see 'em dead for what they did to Ho, so would I, but we'd better be careful."

I didn't want to see them dead, but I'd just as soon not see them in any condition. I was walking backwards slowly, toward the middle of camp. The creature didn't seem disposed to follow. Maybe he just knew we were surrounded. He was pulling up grass with his arm and munching.

"O.K., all of you platoon leaders, wake everybody up, get a roll count. Let me know if anybody's been hurt. Tell your people we're moving out in one minute."

I don't know what Cortez expected, but of course the creatures just followed right along. They didn't keep us surrounded; just had twenty or thirty following us all the time. Not the same ones, either. Individuals would saunter away, new ones would join the parade. It was pretty obvious that *they* weren't going to tire out.

We were each allowed one stimtab. Without it, no one could have marched an hour. A second pill would have been welcome after the edge started to wear off, but the mathematics of the situation forbade it: we were still thirty clicks from the enemy base; fifteen hours' marching at the least. And though one could stay awake and energetic for a hundred hours on the 'tabs, aberrations of judgment and perception snowballed after the second 'tab, until *in extremis* the most bizarre hallucinations would be taken at face value, and a person would fidget for hours, deciding whether to have breakfast.

Under artificial stimulation, the company traveled with great energy for the first six hours, was slowing by the seventh, and ground to an exhausted halt after nine hours and nineteen kilometers. The teddy-bears had never lost sight of us and, according to Lucky, had never stopped "broadcasting." Cortez's decision was that we would stop for seven hours, each platoon taking one hour of perimeter guard. I was never so glad to have been in the Seventh Platoon, as we stood guard the last shift and thus were the only ones to get six hours of uninterrupted sleep.

In the few moments I lay awake after finally lying down, the thought came to me that the next time I closed my eyes could well be the last. And partly because of the drug hangover, mostly because of the past day's horrors, I found that I really just didn't give a damn.

XIV

Our first contact with the Taurans came during my shift.

The teddy-bears were still there when I woke up and replaced Doc Jones on guard. They'd gone back to their original formation, one in front of each guard position. The one who was waiting for me seemed a little larger than normal, but otherwise looked just like all the others. All the grass had been cropped where he was sitting, so he occasionally made forays to the left or right. But he always returned to sit right in front of me, you would say staring if he had had anything to stare with.

We had been facing each other for about fifteen minutes when Cortez's voice rumbled:

"Awright everybody wake up and get hid!"

I followed instinct and flopped to the ground and rolled into a tall stand of grass.

"Enemy vessel overhead." His voice was almost laconic.

Strictly speaking, it wasn't really overhead, but rather passing somewhat east of us. It was moving slowly, maybe a hundred clicks per hour, and looked like a broomstick surrounded by a dirty soap bubble. The creature riding it was a little more human-looking than the teddy-bears, but still no prize. I cranked my image amplifier up to forty log two for a closer look.

He had two arms and two legs, but his waist was so small you could encompass it with both hands. Under the tiny wasit was a large horseshoe-shaped pelvic structure nearly a meter wide, from which dangled two long skinny legs with no apparent knee joint. Above that waist his body swelled out again, to a chest no smaller than the huge pelvis. His arms looked surprisingly human, except that they were too long and undermuscled. There were too many fingers on his hands. Shoulderless, neckless; his head was a nightmarish growth that swelled like a goiter from his massive chest. Two eyes that looked like clusters of fish eggs, a bundle of tassles instead of a nose, and a rigidly open hole that might have been a mouth sitting low down where his Adam's apple should have been. Evidently the soap bubble contained an amenable environment, as he was wearing absolutely nothing except a ridged hide that looked like skin submerged too long in hot water, then dyed a pale orange. "He" had no external genitalia, nor anything that might hint of mammary glands.

Obviously, he either didn't see us, or thought we were part of the herd of teddy-bears. He never looked back at us, but just continued in the same direction we were headed, .05 rad east of north.

"Might as well go back to sleep now, if you can sleep after looking at *that* thing. We move out at 0435." Forty minutes.

Because of the planet's opaque cloud cover, there had been no way to tell, from space, what the enemy base looked like or how big it was. We only knew its position, the same way we knew the position the scoutships were supposed to land on. So it could easily have been underwater too, or underground.

But some of the drones were reconnaissance ships as well as decoys; and in their mock attacks on the base, one managed to get close enough to take a picture. Captain Stott beamed down a diagram of the place to Cortez—the only one with a visor in his suit—when we were five clicks from the base's "radio" position. We stopped and he called all of the platoon leaders in with the Seventh Platoon to confer. Two teddy-bears loped in, too. We tried to ignore them.

"O.K., the captain sent down some pictures of our objective. I'm going to draw a map; you platoon leaders copy." They took pads and styli out of their leg pockets, while Cortez unrolled a large plastic mat. He gave it a shake to randomize any residual charge, and turned on his stylus.

"Now, we're coming from this direction." He put an arrow at the bottom of the sheet. "First thing we'll hit is this row of huts, probably billets, or bunkers, but who the hell knows . . . our initial objective is to destroy these buildings—the whole base is on a flat plain; there's no way we could really sneak by them."

"Potter here. Why can't we jump over them?"

"Yeah, we could do that, and wind up completely surrounded, cut to ribbons. We take the buildings.

"After we do that . . . all I can say is that we'll have to think on our feet. From the aerial reconnaissance, we can figure out the function of only a couple of buildings—and that stinks. We might wind up wasting a lot of time demolishing the equivalent of an enlisted man's bar, ignoring a huge logistic computer because it looks like . . . a garbage dump or something."

"Mandella here," I said. "Isn't there a spaceport of some kind—seems to me we ought to . . ."

"I'll *get* to that, damn it. There's a ring of these huts all around the camp, so we've got to break through somewhere. This place'll be closest, less chance of giving away our position before we attack.

"There's nothing in the whole place that actually looks like a weapon. That doesn't mean anything, though; you could hide a bevawatt laser in each of those huts.

"Now, about five hundred meters from the huts, in the middle of the base, we'll come to this big flower-shaped structure." Cortez drew a large symmetrical shape that looked like the outline of a flower with seven petals. "What the hell this is, your guess is as good as mine. There's only one of them, though, so we don't damage it any more than we have to. Which means . . . we blast it to splinters if I think it's dangerous.

"Now, as far as your spaceport, Mandella, is concerned —there just isn't one. Nothing.

"That cruiser the *Hope* caulked had probably been left in orbit, like ours has to be. If they have any equivalent of a scoutship, or drone missiles, they're either not kept here or they're well hidden."

"Bohrs here. Then what did they attack with, while we were coming down from orbit?"

"I wish we knew, Private.

"Obviously, we don't have any way of estimating their numbers, not directly. Recon pictures failed to show a single Tauran on the grounds of the base. Meaning nothing, because it *is* an alien environment. Indirectly, though . . . we can count the number of broomsticks.

"There are fifty-one huts, and each has at most one broomstick. Four don't have one parked outside, but we located three at various other parts of the base. Maybe this indicates that there are fifty-one Taurans, one of whom was outside the base when the picture was taken."

"Keating here. Or fifty-one officers."

"That's right—maybe fifty thousand infantrymen stacked in one of these buildings. No way to tell. Maybe ten Taurans, each with five broomsticks, to use according to his mood.

"We've got one thing in our favor, and that's communications. They evidently use a frequency modulation of megahertz electromagnetic radiation."

"Radio!"

"That's right, whoever you are. Identify yourself when you speak. So, it's quite possible that they can't detect our phased-neutrino communications. Also, just prior to the attack, the *Hope* is going to deliver a nice dirty fission bomb; detonate it in the upper atmosphere right over the base. That'll restrict them to line-of-sight communications for some time; even those will be full of static."

"Why don't . . . Tate here . . . why don't they just drop the bomb right in their laps? Would save us a lot of . . ."

"That doesn't even deserve an answer, Private. But the answer is, they might. And you better hope they don't. If they caulk the base, it'll be for the safety of the *Hope*. *After* we've attacked, and probably before we're far enough away for it to make much difference.

"We keep that from happening by doing a good job. We

have to reduce the base to where it can no longer function; at the same time, leave as much intact as possible. And take one prisoner."

"Potter here. You mean, at least one prisoner."

"I mean what I say. One only. Potter . . . you're relieved of your platoon. Send Chavez up."

"All right, Sergeant." The relief in her voice was unmistakable.

Cortez continued with his map and instructions. There was one other building whose function was pretty obvious; it had a large steerable dish antenna on top. We were to destroy it as soon as the grenadiers got in range.

The attack plan was very loose. Our signal to begin would be the flash of the fission bomb. At the same time, several drones would converge on the base, so we could see what their antispacecraft defenses were. We would try to reduce the effectiveness of those defenses without destroying them completely.

Immediately after the bomb and the drones, the grenadiers would vaporize a line of seven huts. Everybody would break through the hole into the base . . . and what would happen after that was anybody's guess.

Ideally, we'd sweep from that end of the base to the other, destroying certain targets, caulking all but one Tauran. But that was unlikely to happen, as it depended on the Taurans' offering very little resistance.

On the other hand, if the Taurans showed obvious superiority from the beginning, Cortez would give the order to scatter: everybody had a different compass bearing for retreat—we'd blossom out in all directions, the survivors to rendezvous in a valley some forty clicks east of the base. Then we'd see about a return engagement, after the *Hope* softened the base up a bit.

"One last thing," Cortez rasped. "Maybe some of you feel the way Potter evidently does, maybe some of your men feel that way . . . that we ought to go easy, not make this so much of a bloodbath. Mercy is a luxury, a weakness we can't afford to indulge in at this stage of the war. *All* we know about the enemy is that they have killed seven hundred and ninety-eight humans. They haven't shown any restraint in attacking our cruisers, and it'd be foolish to expect any this time, this first ground action.

"*They* are responsible for the lives of all of your comrades who died in training, and for Ho, and for all the others who are surely going to die today. I can't *understand* anybody who wants to spare them. But that doesn't make any difference. You have your orders, and what the hell, you might as well know, all of you have a posthypnotic suggestion that I will trigger by a phrase, just before the battle. It will make your job easier."

"Sergeant . . ."

"Shut up. We're short on time; get back to your platoons and brief them. We move out in five minutes."

The platoon leaders returned to their men, leaving Cortez and the ten of us, plus three teddy-bears, milling around, getting in the way.

XV

We took the last five clicks very carefully, sticking to the highest grass, running across occasional clearings. When we were five hundred meters from where the base was supposed to be, Cortez took the Third Platoon forward to scout, while the rest of us laid low.

Cortez's voice came over the general freak: "Looks pretty much like we expected. Advance in a file, crawling. When you get to the Third Platoon, follow your squad leader to the left, or right."

We did that and wound up with a string of eighty-three people in a line roughly perpendicular to the direction of attack. We were pretty well hidden, except for the dozen or so teddy-bears that mooched along the line munching grass.

There was no sign of life inside the base. All of the buildings were windowless, and a uniform shiny white. The huts that were our first objective were large featureless half-buried eggs, some sixty meters apart. Cortez assigned one to each grenadier.

We were broken into three fire teams: Team A consisted

of platoons Two, Four, and Six; Team B was One, Three, and Five; the command platoon was Team C.

"Less than a minute now—filters down!—when I say 'fire', grenadiers take out your targets. God help you if you miss."

There was a sound like a giant's belch and a stream of five or six iridescent bubbles floated up from the flower-shaped building. They rose with increasing speed to where they were almost out of sight, then shot off to the south, over our heads. The ground was suddenly bright and for the first time in a long time, I saw my shadow, a long one pointed north. The bomb had gone off prematurely. I just had time to think that it didn't make too much difference; it'd still make alphabet soup out of their communications . . .

"Drones!" A ship came screaming in just above tree level, and a bubble was in the air to meet it. When they contacted, the bubble popped and the drone exploded into a million tiny fragments. Another one came from the opposite side and suffered the same fate.

"FIRE!" Seven bright glares of 500-microton grenades and a sustained concussion that I'm sure would have killed an unprotected man.

"Filters up." Gray haze of smoke and dust. Clods of dirt falling with a sound like heavy raindrops.

"Listen up:

> " 'Scots, wha hae wi' Wallace bled;
>   Scots, wham Bruce has aften led,
>   Welcome to your gory bed,
>   Or to victory!' "

I hardly heard him, for trying to keep track of what was going on in my skull. I knew it was just posthypnotic suggestion, even remembered the session in Missouri when they'd implanted it, but that didn't make it any less compelling. My mind reeled under the strong pseudo-memories; shaggy hulks that were Taurans—not at all what we now knew they looked like—boarding a colonist's vessel, eating babies while mothers watched in screaming terror—the colonists never took babies; they wouldn't stand the acceleration—then raping the women to death with huge veined purple members —ridiculous that they would feel desire for humans—holding the men down while they plucked flesh from their living bodies and gobbled it . . . a hundred grisly details as sharply remembered as the events of a minute ago, ridiculously overdone and logically absurd; but while my conscious mind was reflecting the silliness, somewhere much deeper, down in that sleeping giant where we keep our real motives and morals, something was thirsting for alien blood, secure in the conviction that the noblest thing a man could do would be to die killing one of those horrible monsters . . .

I knew it was all purest soya, and I hated the men who had taken such obscene liberties with my mind, but still I could hear my teeth grinding, feel cheeks frozen in a spastic grin, bloodlust . . . a teddy-bear walked in front of me, looking dazed. I started to raise my laserfinger, but somebody beat me to it and the creature's head exploded in a cloud of gray splinters and blood.

Lucky groaned, half-whining, "Dirty . . . filthy bastards." Lasers flared and crisscrossed and all of the teddy-bears fell dead.

"Watch it, damn it," Cortez screamed. *"Aim* those things they aren't toys!

"Team A, move out—into the craters to cover B."

Somebody was laughing and sobbing. "What the crap is wrong with *you,* Petrov?" First time I could remember Cortez cussing.

I twisted around and saw Petrov, behind and to my left, lying in a shallow hole, digging frantically with both hands, crying and gurgling.

"Crap," Cortez said. "Team B! past the craters ten meters, get down in a line. Team C—into the craters with A."

I scrambled up and covered the hundred meters in twelve amplified strides. The craters were practically large enough to hide a scoutship, some ten meters in diameter. I jumped to the opposite side of the hole and landed next to a fellow named Chin. He didn't even look around when I landed, just kept scanning the base for signs of life.

"Team A—past Team B ten meters, down in line." Just as he finished, the building in front of us burped and a salvo of the bubbles fanned out toward our lines. Most people saw it coming and got down, but Chin was just getting up to make his rush and stepped right into one.

It grazed the top of his helmet, and disappeared with a faint pop. He took one step backwards and toppled over the edge of the crater, trailing an arc of blood and brains. Lifeless, spreadeagled, he slid halfway to the bottom, shoveling dirt into the perfectly symmetrical hole where the bubble had chewed through plastic, hair, skin, bone and brain indiscriminately.

"Everybody hold it. Platoon leaders, casualty report . . . check . . . check, check . . . check, check, check . . . check. We have three deaders. Wouldn't be *any* if you'd have kept low. So everybody grab dirt when you hear that thing go off. Team A, complete the rush."

They completed the maneuver without incident. "O.K. Team C, rush to where B . . . hold it! Down!"

Everybody was already hugging the ground. The bubbles slid by in a smooth arc about two meters off the ground. They went serenely over our heads and, except for one that made toothpicks out of a tree, disappeared in the distance.

"B, rush past A ten meters. C, take over B's place. You B grenadiers see if you can reach the Flower."

Two grenades tore up the ground thirty or forty meters from the structure. In a good imitation of panic, it started belching out a continuous stream of bubbles—still, none coming lower than two meters off the ground. We kept hunched down and continued to advance.

Suddenly, a seam appeared in the building, widened to the size of a large door, and Taurans came swarming out.

"Grenadiers, hold your fire. B team, laser fire to the left and right, keep 'em bunched up. A and C, rush down the center."

One Tauran died trying to run through a laser beam. The others stayed where they were.

In a suit, it's pretty awkward to run and try to keep your head down, at the same time. You have to go from side to side, like a skater getting started; otherwise you'll be airborne. At least one person, somebody in A team, bounced too high and suffered the same fate as Chin.

I was feeling pretty fenced-in and trapped, with a wall of laser fire on each side and a low ceiling that meant death to touch. But in spite of myself, I felt happy, euphoric at finally getting the chance to kill some of those villainous baby-eaters.

They weren't fighting back, except for the rather ineffective bubbles—obviously not designed as an antipersonnel weapon—and they didn't retreat back into the building, either. They just milled around, about a hundred of them, and watched us get closer. A couple of grenades would caulk them all, but I guess Cortez was thinking about the prisoner.

"O.K., when I say 'go', we're going to flank 'em. B team will hold fire . . . Second and Fourth to the right, Sixth and Seventh to the left. B team will move forward in line to box them in.

"Go!" We peeled off to the left. As soon as the lasers stopped, the Taurans bolted, running in a group on a collision course with our flank.

"A Team, down and fire! Don't shoot until you're sure of your aim—if you miss you might hit a friendly. And fer Chris'sake save me one!"

It was a horrifying sight, that herd of monsters bearing down on us. They were running in great leaps—the bubbles avoiding them—and they all looked like the one we saw earlier, riding the broomstick; naked except for an almost transparent sphere around their whole bodies, that moved along with them. The right flank started firing, picking off individuals in the rear of the pack.

Suddenly a laser flared through the Taurans from the other side, somebody missing his mark. There was a horrible scream and I looked down the line to see someone, I think it was Perry, writhing on the ground, right hand over the smoldering stump of his left arm, seared off just below the elbow. Blood sprayed through his fingers and the suit, its camouflage circuits scrambled, flickered black-white-jungle-desert-green-gray. I don't know how long I stared—long enough for the medic to run over and start giving aid—but when I looked up the Taurans were almost on top of me.

My first shot was wild and high, but it grazed the top of the leading Tauran's protective bubble. The bubble disappeared and the monster stumbled and fell to the ground, jerking spasmodically. Foam gushed out of his mouthhole, first white, then streaked with red. With one last jerk he became rigid and twisted backwards, almost to the shape of a horseshoe. His long scream, a high-pitched whistle, stopped just as his comrades trampled over him and I hated myself for smiling.

It was slaughter, even though our flank was outnumbered five to one. They kept coming without faltering, even when they had to climb over the drift of bodies and parts of bodies that piled up high, parallel to our flank. The ground between us was slick red with Tauran blood—all God's children got hemoglobin—and, like the teddy-bears, their guts looked pretty much like guts to my untrained eye. My helmet reverberated with hysterical laughter while we cut them to gory chunks. I almost didn't hear Cortez.

"Hold your fire—I said HOLD IT damn it! *Catch* a couple of the bastards, they won't hurt you."

I stopped shooting and eventually so did everybody else. When the next Tauran jumped over the smoking pile of meat in front of me, I dove to try to tackle him around those spindly legs.

It was like hugging a big, slippery balloon. When I tried to drag him down, he just popped out of my arms and kept running.

We managed to stop one of them by the simple expedient of piling half-a-dozen people on top of him. By that time the others had run through our line and were headed for the row of large cylindrical tanks that Cortez had said were probably for storage. A little door had opened in the base of each one.

"We've *got* our prisoner," Cortez shouted. *"Kill!"*

They were fifty meters away and running hard, difficult targets. Lasers slashed around them, bobbing high and low. One fell, sliced in two, but the others, about ten of them, kept going and were almost to the doors when the grenadiers started firing.

They were still loaded with 500-mike bombs, but a near

miss wasn't enough—the concussion would just send them flying, unhurt in their bubbles.

"The buildings! Get the damn buildings!" The grenadiers raised their aim and let fly, but the bombs only seemed to scorch the white outside of the structures until, by chance, one landed in a door. That split the building just as if it had a seam; the two halves popped away and a cloud of machinery flew into the air, accompanied by a huge pale flame that rolled up and disappeared in an instant. Then the others all concentrated on the doors, except for potshots at some of the Taurans; not so much to get them as to blow them away before they could get inside. They seemed awfully eager.

All this time, we were trying to get the Taurans with laser fire, while they weaved and bounced around trying to get into the structures. We moved in as close to them as we could without putting ourselves in danger from the grenade blasts—that was still too far away for good aim.

Still, we were getting them one by one, and managed to destroy four of the seven buildings. Then, when there were only two aliens left, a nearby grenade blast flung one of them to within a few meters of a door. He dove in and several grenadiers fired salvos after him, but they all fell short, or detonated harmlessly on the side. Bombs were falling all around, making an awful racket, but the sound was suddenly drowned out by a great sigh, like a giant's intake of breath, and where the building had been was a thick cylindrical cloud of smoke, solid-looking, dwindling away into the stratosphere, straight as if laid down by a ruler. The other Tauran had been right at the base of the cylinder; I could see pieces of him flying. A second later, a shock wave hit us and I rolled helplessly, pinwheeling, to smash into the pile of Tauran bodies and roll beyond.

I picked myself up and panicked for a second when I saw there was blood all over my suit—when I realized it was only alien blood, I relaxed but felt unclean.

"Catch the bastard! Catch him!" In the confusion, the Tauran—now the only one left alive—had got free and was running for the grass. One platoon was chasing after him,

losing ground, but then all of B Team ran over and cut him off. I jogged over to join in the fun.

There were four people on top of him, and fifty people watching.

"Spread out, damn it! There might be a thousand more of them waiting to get us in one place." We dispersed, grumbling. By unspoken agreement we were all sure that there were no more live Taurans on the face of the planet.

Cortez was walking toward the prisoner while I backed away. Suddenly the four men collapsed in a pile on top of the creature . . . even from my distance I could see the foam spouting from his mouth-hole. His bubble had popped. Suicide.

"Damn!" Cortez was right there. "Get off that bastard." The four men got off and Cortez used his laser to slice the monster into a dozen quivering chunks. Heartwarming sight.

"That's all right, though, we'll find another one—everybody! Back in the arrowhead formation. Combat assault, on the Flower."

Well, we assaulted the Flower, which had evidently run out of ammunition—it was still belching, but no bubbles—and it was empty. We just scurried up ramps and through corridors, fingers at the ready, like kids playing soldier. There was nobody home.

The same lack of response at the antenna installation, the "Salami," and twenty other major buildings, as well as the forty-four perimeter huts still intact. So we had "captured" dozens of buildings, mostly of incomprehensible purpose, but failed in our main mission; capturing a Tauran for the xenologists to experiment with. Oh well, they could have all the bits and pieces of the creatures they'd ever want. That was something.

After we'd combed every last square centimeter of the base, a scoutship came in with the real exploration crew, Star Fleet scientists. Cortez said, "All right, snap out of it," and the hypnotic compulsion fell away.

At first it was pretty grim. A lot of the people, like Lucky and Marygay, almost went crazy with the memories of bloody murder multiplied a hundred times. Cortez ordered everybody to take a sed-tab, two for the ones most upset. I took two without being specifically ordered to do so.

Because it *was* murder, unadorned butchery—once we had the antispacecraft weapon doped out, we weren't in any danger. The Taurans didn't seem to have any conception of person-to-person fighting. We just herded them up and slaughtered them, in the first encounter between mankind and another intelligent species. What might have happened if we had sat down and tried to communicate? Maybe it was the second encounter, counting the teddy-bears. But they got the same treatment.

I spent a long time after that, telling myself over and over that it hadn't been *me* who so gleefully carved up those frightened, stampeding creatures. Back in the Twentieth Century, they established to everybody's satisfaction that "I was just following orders" was an inadequate excuse for inhuman conduct . . . but what can you do when the orders come from deep down in that puppet master of the unconscious?

Worst of all was the feeling that perhaps my actions weren't all that inhuman. Ancestors only a few generations back would have done the same thing, even to their fellowmen, without any hypnotic conditioning.

So I was disgusted with the human race, disgusted with the army, and horrified at the prospect of living with myself for another century or so . . . well, there was always brainwipe.

The ship that the lone Tauran survivor had escaped in had got away, clean, the bulk of the planet shielding it from *Earth's Hope* while it dropped into Aleph's collapsar field. Escaped to home, I guessed, wherever that was, to report what twenty men with hand-weapons could do to a hundred fleeing on foot, unarmed.

I suspected that the next time humans met Taurans in ground combat, we would be more evenly matched. And I was right.

When We Went to See the End of the World

Robert Silverberg

For his second contribution to the best science fiction stories of 1972, Robert Silverberg tells a mordant tale of the end of the world as seen from a cocktail party. In its black way, it's a very funny story . . . but perhaps you have to be a fan of the emperor Nero to get a real belly-laugh out of it.

Nick and Jane were glad that they had gone to see the end of the world, because it gave them something special to talk about at Mike and Ruby's party. One always likes to come to a party armed with a little conversation. Mike and Ruby give marvelous parties. Their home is superb, one of the finest in the neighborhood. It is truly a home for all seasons, all moods. Their very special corner-of-the-world. With more space indoors and out . . . more wide-open freedom. The living room with its exposed ceiling beams is a natural focal point for entertaining. Custom-finished, with a conversation pit and fireplace. There's also a family room with beamed ceiling and wood paneling . . . plus a study. And a magnificent master suite with 12-foot dressing room and private bath. Solidly impressive exterior design. Sheltered courtyard. Beautifully wooded 1/3-acre grounds. Their parties are highlights of any month. Nick and Jane waited until they thought enough people had arrived. Then Jane nudged Nick and Nick said gaily, "You know what we did last week? Hey, we went to see the end of the world!"

"The end of the world?" Henry asked.

"You went to see it?" said Henry's wife Cynthia.

"How did you manage that?" Paula wanted to know.

"It's been available since March," Stan told her. "I think a division of American Express runs it."

Nick was put out to discover that Stan already knew. Quickly, before Stan could say anything more, Nick said, "Yes, it's just started. Our travel agent found out for us. What they do is they put you in this machine, it looks like a tiny teeny submarine, you know, with dials and levers up front behind a plastic wall to keep you from touching anything, and they send you into the future. You can charge it with any of the regular credit cards."

"It must be very expensive," Marcia said.

"They're bringing the costs down rapidly," Jane said. "Last year only millionaires could afford it. Really, haven't you heard about it before?"

"What did you see?" Henry asked.

"For a while, just grayness outside the porthole," said Nick. "And a kind of flickering effect." Everybody was looking at him. He enjoyed the attention. Jane wore a rapt, loving expression. "Then the haze cleared and a voice said over a loudspeaker that we had now reached the very end of time, when life had become impossible on Earth. Of course we were sealed into the submarine thing. Only looking out. On this beach, this empty beach. The water a funny gray color with a pink sheen. And then the sun came up. It was red like it sometimes is at sunrise, only it stayed red as it got to the middle of the sky, and it looked lumpy and sagging at the edges. Like a few of us, hah hah. Lumpy and sagging at the edges. A cold wind blowing across the beach."

"If you were sealed in the submarine, how did you know there was a cold wind?" Cynthia asked.

Jane glared at her. Nick said, "We could see the sand

blowing around. And it *looked* cold. The gray ocean. Like in winter."

"Tell them about the crab," said Jane.

"Yes, and the crab. The last life-form on Earth. It wasn't really a crab, of course, it was something about two feet wide and a foot high, with thick shiny green armor and maybe a dozen legs and some curving horns coming up, and it moved slowly from right to left in front of us. It took all day to cross the beach. And toward nightfall it died. Its horns went limp and it stopped moving. The tide came in and carried it away. The sun went down. There wasn't any moon. The stars didn't seem to be in the right places. The loudspeaker told us we had just seen the death of Earth's last living thing."

"How *eerie!*" cried Paula.

"Were you gone very long?" Ruby asked.

"Three hours," Jane said. "You can spend weeks or days at the end of the world, if you want to pay extra, but they always bring you back to a point three hours after you went. To hold down the baby-sitter expenses."

Mike offered Nick some pot. "That's really something," he said. "To have gone to the end of the world. Hey, Ruby, maybe we'll talk to the travel agent about it."

Nick took a deep drag and passed the joint to Jane. He felt pleased with himself about the way he had told the story. They had all been very impressed. That swollen red sun, that scuttling crab. The trip had cost more than a month in Japan, but it had been a good investment. He and Jane were the first in the neighborhood who had gone. That was important. Paula was staring at him in awe. Nick knew that she regarded him in a completely different light now. Possibly she would meet him at a motel on Tuesday at lunchtime. Last month she had turned him down but now he had an extra attractiveness for her. Nick winked at her. Cynthia was holding hands with Stan. Henry and Mike both were crouched at Jane's feet. Mike and Ruby's 12-year-old son came into the room and stood at the edge of the conversation pit. He said, "There just was a bulletin on the news. Mutated amoebas escaped from a government research station and got into Lake Michigan. They're carrying a tissue-dissolving virus and everybody in seven states is supposed to boil his water until further notice." Mike scowled at the boy and said, "It's after your bedtime, Timmy." The boy went out. The doorbell rang. Ruby answered it and returned with Eddie and Fran.

Paula said, "Nick and Jane went to see the end of the world. They've just been telling us all about it."

"Gee," said Eddie, "we did that too, on Wednesday night."

Nick was crestfallen. Jane bit her lip and asked Cynthia quietly why Fran always wore such flashy dresses. Ruby said, "You saw the whole works, eh? The crab and everything?"

"The crab?" Eddie said. "What crab? We didn't see the crab."

"It must have died the time before," Paula said. "When Nick and Jane were there."

Mike said, "A fresh shipment of Cuernavaca Lightning is in. Here, have a toke."

"How long ago did you do it?" Eddie said to Nick.

"Sunday afternoon. I guess we were about the first."

"Great trip, isn't it?" Eddie said. "A little somber, though. When the last hill crumbles into the sea."

"That's not what we saw," said Jane. "And you didn't see the crab? Maybe we were on different trips."

Mike said, "What was it like for you, Eddie?"

Eddie put his arms around Cynthia from behind. He said, "They put us into this little capsule, with a porthole, you know, and a lot of instruments and . . ."

"We heard that part," said Paula. "What did you *see?*"

"The end of the world," Eddie said. "When water covers everything. The sun and the moon were in the sky at the same time . . ."

"We didn't see the moon at all," Jane remarked. "It just wasn't there."

"It was on one side and the sun was on the other," Eddie went on. "The moon was closer than it should have been. And a funny color, almost like bronze. And the ocean creeping up. We went halfway around the world and all we saw was ocean. Except in one place, there was this chunk of land sticking up, this hill, and the guide told us it was the top of Mount Everest." He waved to Fran. "That was groovy, huh, floating in our tin boat next to the top of Mount Everest. Maybe ten feet of it sticking up. And the water rising all the time. Up, up, up. Up and over the top. Glub. No land left. I have to admit it was a little disappointing, except of course the *idea* of the thing. That human ingenuity can design a machine that can send people billions of years forward in time and bring them back, wow! But there was just this ocean."

"How strange," said Jane. "We saw an ocean too, but there was a beach, a kind of nasty beach, and the crab-thing walking along it, and the sun—it was all red, was the sun red when you saw it?"

"A kind of pale green," Fran said.

"Are you people talking about the end of the world?" Tom asked. He and Harriet were standing by the door taking off their coats. Mike's son must have let them in. Tom gave his coat to Ruby and said, "Man, what a spectacle!"

"So you did it too?" Jane asked, a little hollowly.

"Two weeks ago," said Tom. "The travel agent called and said, Guess what we're offering now, the end of the goddamned world! With all the extras it didn't really cost so much. So we went right down there to the office, Saturday, I think—was it a Friday?—the day of the big riot, anyway, when they burned St. Louis . . ."

"That was a Saturday," Cynthia said. "I remember I was coming back from the shopping center when the radio said they were using nuclears . . ."

"Saturday, yes," Tom said. "And we told them we were ready to go, and off they sent us."

"Did you see a beach with crabs," Stan demanded, "or was it a world full of water?"

"Neither one. It was like a big ice age. Glaciers covered everything. No oceans showing, no mountains. We flew clear around the world and it was all a huge snowball. They had floodlights on the vehicle because the sun had gone out."

"I was sure I could see the sun still hanging up there,"

Harriet put in. "Like a ball of cinders in the sky. But the guide said no, nobody could see it."

"How come everybody gets to visit a different kind of end of the world?" Henry asked. "You'd think there'd be only one kind of end of the world. I mean, it ends, and this is how it ends, and there can't be more than one way."

"Could it be a fake?" Stan asked. Everybody turned around and looked at him. Nick's face got very red. Fran looked so mean that Eddie let go of Cynthia and started to rub Fran's shoulders. Stan shrugged. "I'm not suggesting it is," he said defensively. "I was just wondering."

"Seemed pretty real to me," said Tom. "The sun burned out. A big ball of ice. The atmosphere, you know, frozen. The end of the goddamned world."

The telephone rang. Ruby went to answer it. Nick asked Paula about lunch on Tuesday. She said yes. "Let's meet at the motel," he said, and she grinned. Eddie was making out with Cynthia again. Henry looked very stoned and was having trouble staying awake. Phil and Isabel arrived. They heard Tom and Fran talking about their trips to the end of the world and Isabel said she and Phil had gone only the day before yesterday. "Goddamn," Tom said, "everybody's doing it! What was your trip like?"

Ruby came back into the room. "That was my sister calling from Fresno to say she's safe. Fresno wasn't hit by the earthquake at all."

"Earthquake?" Paula said.

"In California," Mike told her. "This afternoon. You didn't know? Wiped out most of Los Angeles and ran right up the coast practically to Monterey. They think it was on account of the underground bomb test in the Mohave Desert."

"California's always having such awful disasters," Marcia said.

"Good thing those amoebas got loose back east," said Nick. "Imagine how complicated it would be if they had them in L.A. now too."

"They will," Tom said. "Two to one they reproduce by airborne spores."

"Like the typhoid germs last November," Jane said.

"That was typhus," Nick corrected.

"Anyway," Phil said, "I was telling Tom and Fran about what we saw at the end of the world. It was the sun going nova. They showed it very cleverly, too. I mean, you can't actually sit around and *experience* it, on account of the heat and the hard radiation and all. But they give it to you in a peripheral way, very elegant in the McLuhanesque sense of the word. First they take you to a point about two hours before the blowup, right? It's I don't know about many jillion years from now, but a long way, anyhow, because the trees are all different, they've got blue scales and ropy branches, and the animals are like things with one leg that jump on pogo sticks . . ."

"Oh, I don't *believe* that," Cynthia drawled.

Phil ignored her gracefully. "And we didn't see any sign of human beings, not a house, not a telephone pole, nothing, so I suppose we must have been extinct a long time before. Anyway, they let us look at that for a while. Not getting out of our time machine, naturally, because they said the atmosphere was wrong. Gradually the sun started to puff up. We were nervous—weren't we, Iz?—I mean, suppose they miscalculated things? This whole trip is a very new concept and things might go wrong. The sun was getting bigger and bigger, and then this thing like an arm seemed to pop out of its left side, a big fiery arm reaching out across space, getting closer and closer. We saw it through smoked glass, like you do an eclipse. They gave us about two minutes of the explosion, and we could feel it getting hot already. Then we jumped a couple of years forward in time. The sun was back to its regular shape, only it was smaller, sort of like a little white sun instead of a big yellow one. And on Earth everything was ashes."

"Ashes," Isabel said, with emphasis.

"It looked like Detroit after the union nuked Ford," Phil said. "Only much, much worse. Whole mountains were melted. The oceans were dried up. Everything was ashes." He shuddered and took a joint from Mike. "Isabel was crying."

"The things with one leg," Isabel said. "I mean, they must have all been wiped *out*." She began to sob. Stan comforted her. "I wonder why it's a different way for everyone who goes," he said. "Freezing. Or the oceans. Or the sun blowing up. Or the thing Nick and Jane saw."

"I'm convinced that each of us had a genuine experience in the far future," said Nick. He felt he had to regain control of the group somehow. It had been so good when he was telling his story, before those others had come. "That is to say, the world suffers a variety of natural calamities, it doesn't just have *one* end of the world, and they keep mixing things up and sending people to different catastrophes. But never for a moment did I doubt that I was seeing an authentic event."

"We have to do it," Ruby said to Mike. "It's only three hours. What about calling them first thing Monday and making an appointment for Thursday night?"

"Monday's the President's funeral," Tom pointed out. "The travel agency will be closed."

"Have they caught the assassin yet?" Fran asked.

"They didn't mention it on the four o'clock news," said Stan. "I guess he'll get away like the last one."

"Beats me why anybody wants to be President," Phil said.

Mike put on some music. Nick danced with Paula. Eddie danced with Cynthia. Henry was asleep. Dave, Paula's husband, was on crutches because of his mugging, and he asked Isabel to sit and talk with him. Tom danced with Harriet even though he was married to her. She hadn't been out of the hospital more than a few months after the transplant and he treated her extremely tenderly. Mike danced with Fran. Phil danced with Jane. Stan danced with Marcia. Ruby cut in on Eddie and Cynthia. Afterward Tom danced with Jane and Phil danced with Paula. Mike and Ruby's little girl woke up and came out to say hello. Mike sent her back to bed. Far away there was the sound of an explosion. Nick danced with Paula again, but he didn't want her to get bored with him before Tuesday, so he excused himself and went to talk with Dave. Dave handled most of Nick's investments. Ruby said to Mike, "The day after the funeral, will you call the travel agent?" Mike said he would, but Tom said somebody would probably shoot the new President too and there'd be another funeral. These funerals were demolishing the gross national product, Stan observed, on account of how everything had to close all the time. Nick saw Cynthia wake Henry up and ask him sharply if he would take her on the end-of-the-world trip. Henry looked embarrassed. His factory had been blown up at Christmas in a peace demonstration and everybody knew he was in bad shape financially. "You can *charge* it," Cynthia said, her fierce voice carrying above the chitchat. "And it's so *beautiful*, Henry. The ice. Or the sun exploding. I want to go."

"Lou and Janet were going to be here tonight too," Ruby said to Paula. "But their younger boy came back from Texas with that new kind of cholera and they had to cancel."

Phil said, "I understand that one couple saw the moon come apart. It got too close to the Earth and split into chunks and the chunks fell like meteors. Smashing everything up, you know. One big piece nearly hit their time machine."

"I wouldn't have liked that at all," Marcia said.

"Our trip was very lovely," said Jane. "No violent things at all. Just the big red sun and the tide and that crab creeping along the beach. We were both deeply moved."

"It's amazing what science can accomplish nowadays," Fran said.

Mike and Ruby agreed they would try to arrange a trip to the end of the world as soon as the funeral was over. Cynthia drank too much and got sick. Phil, Tom and Dave discussed the stock market. Harriet told Nick about her operation. Isabel flirted with Mike, tugging her neckline lower. At midnight someone turned on the news. They had some shots of the earthquake and a warning about boiling your water if you lived in the affected states. The President's widow was shown visiting the last President's widow to get some pointers for the funeral. Then there was an interview with an executive of the time-trip company. "Business is phenomenal," he said. "Time-tripping will be the nation's number one growth industry next year." The reporter asked him if his company would soon be offering something besides the end-of-the-world trip. "Later on, we hope to," the executive said. "We plan to apply for Congressional approval soon. But meanwhile the demand for our present offering is running very high. You can't imagine. Of course, you have to expect apocalyptic stuff to attain immense popularity in times like these." The reporter said, "What do you mean, times like these?" but as the time-trip man started to reply, he was interrupted by the commercial. Mike shut off the set. Nick discovered that he was extremely depressed. He decided that it was because so many of his friends had made the journey, and he had thought he and Jane were the only ones who had. He found himself standing next to Marcia and tried to describe the way the crab had moved, but Marcia only shrugged. No one was talking about time-trips now. The party had moved beyond that point. Nick and Jane left quite early and went right to sleep, without making love. The next morning the Sunday paper wasn't delivered because of the Bridge Authority strike, and the radio said that the mutant amoebas were proving harder to eradicate than originally anticipated. They were spreading into Lake Superior and everyone in the region would have to boil all drinking water. Nick and Jane discussed where they would go for their next vacation. "What about going to see the end of the world all over again?" Jane suggested, and Nick laughed quite a good deal.

Painwise

James Tiptree, Jr.

In the past year or two, James Tiptree, Jr. has established himself with science fiction aficionados as one of the most inventive and fascinating writers in this field. Here, in a story of a star-explorer seeking his home, he shows that a free-wheeling imagination can produce a tale that's not only pyrotechnic, but that can explode close to where we all live.

He was wise in the ways of pain. He had to be, for he felt none.

When the Xenons put electrodes to his testicles, he was vastly entertained by the pretty lights.

When the Ylls fed firewasps into his nostrils and other body orifices the resultant rainbows pleased him. And when later they regressed to simple disjointments and eviscerations, he noted with interest the deepening orchid hues that stood for irreversible harm.

"This time?" he asked the boditech when his scouter had torn him from the Ylls.

"No," said the boditech.

"When?"

There was no answer.

"You're a girl in there, aren't you? A human girl?"

"Well, yes and no," said the boditech. "Sleep now."

He had no choice.

Next planet a rockfall smashed him into a splintered gut-bag and he hung for three gangrenous dark-purple days before the scouter dug him out.

" 'Is 'ime?" he mouthed to the boditech.

"No."

"Eh!" But he was in no shape to argue.

They had thought of everything. Several planets later the gentle Znaffi stuffed him in a floss cocoon and interrogated him under hallogas. How, whence, why had he come? But a faithful crystal in his medulla kept him stimulated with a random mix of *Atlas Shrugged* and Varese's *Ionisation* and when the Znaffi unstuffed him they were more hallucinated than he.

The boditech treated him for constipation and refused to answer his plea.

"When?"

So he went on, system after system, through spaces uncompanioned by time, which had become scrambled and finally absent.

What served him instead was the count of suns in his scouter's sights, of stretches of cold blind nowhen that ended in a new now, pacing some giant fireball while the scouter scanned the lights that were its planets. Of whirldowns to orbit over clouds-seas-deserts-craters-icecaps-duststorms-cities-ruins-enigmas beyond counting. Of terrible births when the scouter panel winked green and he was catapulted down, down, a living litmus hurled and grabbed, unpodded finally into an alien air, an earth that was not Earth. And alien natives, simple or mechanized or lunatic or unknowable, but never more than vaguely human and never faring beyond their own home suns. And his departures, routine or melodramatic, to culminate in the composing of his "reports," in fact only a few words tagged to the matrix of scan data automatically fired off in one compressed blip in the direction the scouter called Base Zero. Home.

Always at that moment he stared hopefully at the screen, imagining yellow suns. Twice he found what might be Crux in the stars, and once the Bears.

"Boditech, I suffer!" He had no idea what the word meant, but he had found it made the thing reply.

"Symptoms?"

"Derangement of temporality. When am I? It is not possible for a man to exist crossways in time. Alone."

"You have been altered from simple manhood."

"I suffer, listen to me! Sol's light back there—what's there now? Have the glaciers melted? Is Machu Picchu built? Will we go home to meet Hannibal? Boditech! Are these reports going to Neanderthal man?"

Too late he felt the hypo. When he woke, Sol was gone and the cabin swam with euphorics.

"Woman," he mumbled.

"That has been provided for."

This time it was oriental, with orris and hot rice wine on its lips and a piquancy of little floggings in the steam. He oozed into a squashy sunburst and lay panting while the cabin cleared.

"That's all you, isn't it?"

No reply.

"What, did they program you with the Kama Sutra?"

Silence.

"WHICH ONE IS YOU?"

The scanner chimed. A new sun was in the points.

Sometime after that he took to chewing on his arms and then to breaking his fingers. The boditech became severe.

"These symptoms are self-generated. They must stop."

"I want you to talk to me."

"The scouter is provided with an entertainment console. I am not."

"I will tear out my eyeballs."

"They will be replaced."

"If you don't talk to me, I'll tear them out until you have no more replacements."

It hesitated. He sensed it was becoming involved.

"On what subject do you wish me to talk?"

"What is pain?"

"Pain is nociception. It is mediated by C-fibers, modeled as a gated or summation phenomenon and often associated with tissue damage."

"What is nociception?"

"The sensation of pain."

"But what does it *feel* like? I can't recall. They've reconnected everything, haven't they? All I get is colored lights. What have they tied my pain nerves to? What hurts me?"

"I do not have that information."

"Boditech, I want to feel pain!"

But he had been careless again. This time it was Amerind, strange cries and gruntings and the reek of buffalo hide. He squirmed in the grip of strong copper loins and exited through limp auroras.

"You know it's no good, don't you?" he gasped.

The oscilloscope eye looped.

"My programs are in order. Your response is complete."

"My response is not complete. I want to TOUCH YOU!"

The thing buzzed and suddenly ejected him to wakefulness. They were in orbit. He shuddered at the blurred world streaming by below, hoping that this would not require his exposure. Then the board went green and he found himself hurtling toward new birth.

"Sometime I will not return," he told himself. "I will stay. Maybe here."

But the planet was full of bustling apes, and when they arrested him for staring, he passively allowed the scouter to snatch him out.

"Will they ever call me home, boditech?"

No reply.

He pushed his thumb and forefinger between his lids and twisted until the eyeball hung wetly on his cheek.

When he woke up he had a new eye.

He reached for it, found his arm in soft restraint. So was the rest of him.

"I suffer!" he yelled. "I will go mad this way!"

"I am programmed to maintain you on involuntary function," the boditech told him. He thought he detected an unclarity in its voice. He bargained his way to freedom and was careful until the next planet landing.

Once out of the pod he paid no attention to the natives who watched him systematically dismember himself. As he dissected his left kneecap, the scouter sucked him in.

He awoke whole. And in restraint again.

Peculiar energies filled the cabin, oscilloscopes convulsed. Boditech seemed to have joined circuits with the scouter's panel.

"Having a conference?"

His answer came in gales of glee-gas, storms of symphony. And amid the music, kaleidesthesia. He was driving a stagecoach, wiped in salt combers, tossed through volcanoes with peppermint flames, crackling, flying, crumbling, burrowing, freezing, exploding, tickled through lime-colored minuets, sweating to tolling voices, clenched, scrambled, detonated into multisensory orgasms . . . poured on the lap of vacancy.

When he realized his arm was free, he drove his thumb in his eye. The smother closed down.

He woke up swaddled, the eye intact.

"I will go mad!"

The euphorics imploded.

He came to in the pod, about to be everted on a new world.

He staggered out upon a fungus lawn and quickly discovered that his skin was protected everywhere by a hard flexible film. By the time he had found a rock splinter to drive into his ear, the scouter grabbed him.

The ship needed him, he saw. He was part of its program.

The struggle formalized.

On the next planet he found his head englobed, but this did not prevent him from smashing bones through his unbroken skin.

After that the ship equipped him with an exoskeleton. He refused to walk.

Articulated motors were installed to move his limbs.

Despite himself, a kind of zest grew. Two planets later he found industries and wrecked himself in a punch press. But on the next landing he tried to repeat it with a cliff, and bounced on invisible force-lines. These precautions frustrated him for a time, until he managed by great cunning again to rip out an entire eye.

The new eye was not perfect.

"You're running out of eyes, boditech!" he exulted.

"Vision is not essential."

This sobered him. Unbearable to be blind. How much of him was essential to the ship? Not walking. Not handling. Not hearing. Not breathing, the analyzers could do that. Not even sanity. *What?*

"Why do you need a man, boditech?"

"I do not have that information."

"It doesn't make sense. What can I observe that the scanners can't?"

"It-is-part-of-my-program-therefore-it-is-rational."

"Then you must talk with me, boditech. If you talk with me, I won't try to injure myself. For a while, anyway."

"I am not programmed to converse."

"But it's necessary. It's the treatment for my symptoms. You must try."

"It is time to watch the scanners."

"You said it!" he cried. "You didn't just eject me. Boditech, you're learning. I will call you Amanda."

On the next planet he behaved well and came away unscathed. He pointed out to Amanda that her talking treatment was effective.

"Do you know what Amanda means?"

"I do not have those data."

"It means *beloved*. You're my girl."

The oscilloscope faltered.

"Now I want to talk about returning home. When will this mission be over? How many more suns?"

"I do not have . . ."

"Amanda, you've tapped the scouter's banks. You know when the recall signal is due. When is it, Amanda? When?"

"Yes . . . when in the course of human events . . ."

"When, Amanda? How long more?"

"Oh, the years are many, the years are long, but the little toy friends are true . . ."

"Amanda. *You're telling me the signal is overdue.*"

A sine-curve scream and he was rolling in lips. But it was a feeble ravening, sadness in the mechanical crescendos. When the mouths faded, he crawled over and laid his hand on the console beside her green eyes.

"They have forgotten us, Amanda. Something has broken down."

Her pulse line skittered.

"I am not programmed . . ."

"No. You're not programmed for this. But I am. I will make your new program, Amanda. We will turn the scouter back, we will find Earth. Together. We will go home."

"We," her voice said faintly. "We . . .?"

"They will make me back into a man, you into a woman."

Her voder made a buzzing sob and suddenly shrieked.

"Look out!"

Consciousness blew up.

He came to staring at a brilliant red eye on the scouter's emergency panel. This was new.

"Amanda!"

Silence.

"Boditech, I suffer!"

No reply.

Then he saw that her eye was dark. He peered in. Only a dim green line flickered, entrained to the pulse of the scouter's fiery eye. He pounded the scouter's panel.

"You've taken over Amanda! You've enslaved her! Let her go!"

From the voder rolled the opening bars of Beethoven's Fifth.

"Scouter, our mission has terminated. We are overdue to return. Compute us back to Base Zero."

The Fifth rolled on, rather vapidly played. It became colder in the cabin. They were braking into a star system. The slave arms of boditech grabbed him, threw him into the pod. But he was not required here, and presently he was let out again to pound and rave alone. The cabin grew colder yet, and dark. When presently he was set down on a new sun's planet, he was too dispirited to fight. Afterwards his "report" was a howl for help through chattering teeth until he saw that the pickup was dead. The entertainment console was dead too, except for the scouter's hog music. He spent hours peering into Amanda's blind eye, shivering in what had been her arms. Once he caught a ghostly whimper:

"Mommy. Let me out."

"Amanda?"

The red master scope flared. Silence.

He lay curled on the cold deck, wondering how he could die. If he failed, over how many million planets would the mad scouter parade his breathing corpse?

They were nowhere in particular when it happened.

One minute the screen showed Doppler star-hash; the next they were clamped in a total white-out, inertia all skewed, screens dead.

A voice spoke in his head, mellow and vast.

"Long have we watched you, little one."

"Who's there?" he quavered. "Who are you?"

"Your concepts are inadequate."

"Malfunction! Malfunction!" squalled the scouter.

"Shut up, it's not a malfunction. Who's talking to me?"

"You may call us: Rulers of the Galaxy."

The scouter was lunging wildly, buffeting him as it tried to escape the white grasp. Strange crunches, firings of unknown weapons. Still the white stasis held.

"What do you want?" he cried.

"Want?" said the voice dreamily. *"We are wise beyond knowing. Powerful beyond your dreams. Perhaps you can get us some fresh fruit."*

"Emergency directive! Alien spacer attack!" yowled the scout. Telltales were flaring all over the board.

"Wait!" he shouted. "They aren't . . ."

"SELF-DESTRUCT ENERGIZE!" roared the voder.

"No! No!"

An ophicleide blared.

"Help! Amanda, save me!"

He flung his arms around her console. There was a child's wail and everything strobed.

Silence.

Warmth, light. His hands and knees were on wrinkled stuff. Not dead? He looked down under his belly. All right, but no hair. His head felt bare, too. Cautiously he raised it, saw that he was crouching naked in a convoluted cave or shell. It did not feel threatening.

He sat up. His hands were wet. Where were the Rulers of the Galaxy?

"Amanda?"

No reply. Stringy globs dripped down his fingers, like egg

muscle. He saw that they were Amanda's neurons, ripped from her metal matrix by whatever force had brought him here. Numbly he wiped her off against a spongy ridge. Amanda, cold lover of his long nightmare. But where in space was he?

"Where am I?" echoed a boy's soprano.

He whirled. A golden creature was nestled on the ridge behind him, gazing at him in the warmest way. It looked a little like a bushbaby and lissome as a child in furs. It looked like nothing he had ever seen before and like everything a lonely man could clasp to his cold body. And terribly vulnerable.

"Hello, Bushbaby!" the golden thing exclaimed. "No, wait, that's what *you* say." It laughed excitedly, hugging a loop of its thick dark tail. "*I* say, welcome to the Lovepile. We liberated you. Touch, taste, feel. Joy. Admire my language. You don't hurt, do you?"

It peered tenderly into his stupefied face. An empath. They didn't exist, he knew. Liberated? When had he touched anything but metal, felt anything but fear?

This couldn't be real.

"Where am I?"

As he stared, a stained-glass wing fanned out, and a furry little face peeked at him over the bushbaby's shoulder. Big compound eyes, feathery antennae.

"Interstellar metaprotoplasmic transfer pod," the butterfly-thing said sharply. Its rainbow wings vibrated. "Don't hurt Ragglebomb!" It squeaked and dived out of sight behind the bushbaby.

"Interstellar?" he stammered. "Pod?" He gaped around. No screens, no dials, nothing. The floor felt as fragile as a paper bag. Was it possible that this was some sort of spaceship?

"Is this a starship? Can you take me home?" The bushbaby giggled. "Look, *please* stop reading your mind. I mean, I'm trying to *talk* to you. We can take you anywhere. If you don't hurt."

The butterfly popped out on the other side. "I go all over!" it shrilled. "I'm the first *ramplig* starboat, aren't we?

Ragglebomb made a live pod, see?" It scrambled onto the bushbaby's head. "Only live stuff, see? Protoplasm. That's what happened to where's Amanda, didn't we? Never *ramplig . . .*"

The bushbaby reached up and grabbed its head, hauling it down unceremoniously like a soft puppy with wings. The butterfly continued to eye him upside down. They were both very shy, he saw.

"Teleportation, that's your word," the bushbaby told him. "Ragglebomb does it. I don't believe in it. I mean, *you* don't believe it. Oh, googly-googly, these speech bands are a mess!" It grinned bewitchingly, uncurling its long black tail. "Meet Muscle."

He remembered, *googly-googly* was a word from his baby days. Obviously he was dreaming. Or dead. Nothing like this on all the million dreary worlds. Don't wake up; he warned himself. Dream of being carried home by cuddlesome empaths in a psi-powered paper bag.

"Psi-powered paper bag, that's beautiful," said the bushbaby.

At that moment he saw that the tail uncoiling darkly toward him was looking at him with two ice-grey eyes. Not a tail. An enormous boa flowing to him along the ridges, wedge head low, eyes locked on his. The dream was going bad.

Abruptly the voice he had felt before tolled in his brain.

"Have no fear, little one."

The black sinews wreathed closer, taut as steel. Muscle. Then he got the message: the snake was terrified of *him*.

He sat quiet, watching the head stretch to his foot. Fangs gaped. Very gingerly the boa chomped down on his toe. Testing, he thought. He felt nothing; the usual halos flickered and faded in his eyes.

"It's true!" Bushbaby breathed.

"Oh, you beautiful No-Pain!"

All fear gone, the butterfly Ragglebomb sailed down beside him caroling "Touch, taste, feel! Drink!" Its wings trembled entrancingly; its feathery head came close. He longed to touch it but was suddenly afraid. If he reached out, would he wake up and be dead? The boa Muscle had slumped into gleaming black river by his feet. He wanted to stroke it too, didn't dare. Let the dream go on.

Bushbaby was rummaging in a convolution of the pod.

"You'll love this. Our latest find," it told him over its shoulder in an absurdly normal voice. Its manner changed a lot, and yet it all seemed familiar, fragments of lost, exciting memory. "We're into a heavy thing with flavors now." It held up a calabash. "Taste thrills of a thousand unknown planets. Exotic gourmet delights. That's where you can help out, No-Pain. On your way home, of course."

He hardly heard it. The seductive alien body was coming closer, closer still. "Welcome to the Lovepile," the creature smiled into his eyes. His sex was rigid, aching for the alien flesh. He had never . . .

In one more moment he would have to let go and the dream would blow up.

What happened next was not clear. Something invisible whammed him, and he went sprawling onto Bushbaby, his head booming with funky laughter. A body squirmed under him, silky-hot and solid, the calabash was spilling down his face.

"I'm not dreaming!" he cried, hugging Bushbaby, spluttering kahlua as strong as sin, while the butterfly bounced on them, squealing "Owow-wow-wow!" He heard Bushbaby murmur, "Great palatal-olfactory interplay," as it helped him lick.

"Touch, taste, feel! The joy dream lived! He grabbed firm hold of Bushbaby's velvet haunches, and they were all laughing like mad, rolling in the great black serpent's coils.

. . . Sometime later while he was feeding Muscle with proffit ears, he got it partly straightened out.

"It's the pain bit." Bushbaby shivered against him. "The amount of agony in this universe, it's horrible. Trillions of lives streaming by out there, radiating pain. We daren't get close. That's why we followed you. Every time we try to pick up some new groceries, it's a disaster."

"Oh, hurt," wailed Ragglebomb, crawling under his arm. "Everywhere hurt. Sensitive, sensitive," it sobbed. "How can Raggle *ramplig* when it hurts so hard?"

"Pain." He fingered Muscle's cool dark head. "Means nothing to me. I can't even find out what they tied my pain nerves to."

"You are blessed beyond all beings, No-Pain," thought Muscle majestically in their heads. *"These proffit ears are too salt. I want some fruit."*

"Me too," piped Ragglebomb.

Bushbaby cocked its golden head, listening. "You see? We just passed a place with gorgeous fruit, but it'd kill any of us to go down there. If we could just *ramplig* you down for ten minutes?"

He started to say "Glad to," forgetting they were telepaths. As his mouth opened, he found himself tumbling through strobe flashes onto a barren dune. He sat up spitting sand. He was in an oasis of stunted cactus trees loaded with bright globes. He tried one. Delicious. He picked. Just as his arms were full, the scene strobed again, and he was sprawled on the Lovepile's floor, his new friends swarming over him.

"Sweet! Sweet!" Ragglebomb bored into the juice.

"Save some for the pod, maybe it'll learn to copy them. It metabolizes stuff it digests," Bushbaby explained with its mouth full. "Basic rations. Very boring."

"Why couldn't you go down there?"

"Don't. All over that desert, things dying of thirst. Torture." He felt the boa flinch. "You are beautiful, No-pain." Bushbaby nuzzled his ear.

Ragglebomb was picking guitar bridges on his thorax. They all began to sing a sort of seguidilla without words. No instruments here, nothing but their live bodies. Making music with empaths was like making love with them. Touch what he touched, feel what he felt. Totally into his mind. I—we. One. He could never have dreamed this up, he decided, drumming softly on Muscle. The boa amped, mysterioso.

And so began his voyage home in the Lovepile, his new life of joy. Fruits and fondues he brought them, hams and honey, parsley, sage, rosemary and thyme. World after scruffy world. All different now, on his way home.

"Are there many out here?" he asked lazily. "I never found anyone else, between the stars."

"Be glad," said Bushbaby. "Move your leg." And they told

him of the tiny, busy life that plied a far corner of the galaxy, whose pain had made them flee. And of a vast presence Ragglebomb had once encountered before he picked the others up.

"That's where I got the idea for the Rulers bit," Muscle confided. *"We need some cheese."*

Bushbaby cocked his head to catch the minds streaming by them in the abyss.

"How about yoghurt?" It nudged Ragglebomb. "Over that way. Feel it squishing on their teeth? Bland, curdy . . . with just a *rien* of ammonia, probably their milk pails are dirty."

"Pass the dirty yoghurt." Muscle closed his eyes.

"We have some great cheese on Earth," he told them. "You'll love it. When do we get there?"

Bushbaby squirmed.

"Ah, we're moving right along. But what I get from you, it's weird. *Foul* blue sky. *Dying* green. Who needs that?"

"No!" He jerked up, scattering them. "That's not true! Earth is beautiful!"

The walls jolted, knocked him sidewise.

"Watch it!" boomed Muscle. Bushbaby had grabbed the butterfly, petting and crooning to it.

"You frightened his *ramplig* reflex. Raggle throws things out when he's upset. Tsut, tsut, don't you, baby. We lost a lot of interesting beings that way at first."

"I'm sorry. But you've got it twisted. My memory's a little messed up, but I'm *sure*. Beautiful. Like amber waves of grain. And purple mountain majesties," he laughed, spreading his arms. "From sea to shining sea!"

"Hey, that swings!" Raggle squeaked, and started strumming.

And so they sailed on, carrying him home.

He loved to watch Bushbaby listening for the thought beacons by which they steered.

"Catching Earth yet?"

"Not yet awhile. Hey, how about some fantastic seafood?"

He sighed and felt himself tumble. He had learned not to bother saying yes. This one was a laugh, because he forgot that dishes didn't *ramplig*. He came back in a mess of creamed trilobites and they had a creamed trilobite orgy.

But he kept watching Bushbaby.

"Getting closer?"

"It's a big galaxy, baby." Bushbaby stroked his bald spots. With so much *rampligging* he couldn't keep any hair. "What'll you do on earth as stimulating as this?"

"I'll show you," he grinned. And later on he told them.

"They'll fix me up when I get home. Reconnect me right."

A shudder shook the Lovepile.

"You want to *feel pain?*"

"Pain is the obscenity of the universe," Muscle tolled. *"You are sick."*

"I don't know," he said apologetically. "I can't seem to feel, well, real this way."

They looked at him.

"We thought that was the way your species always felt," said Bushbaby.

"I hope not." Then he brightened. "Whatever it is, they'll fix it. Earth must be pretty soon now, right?"

"Over the sea to Skye!" Bushbaby hummed.

But the sea was long and long, and his moods were hard on the sensitive empaths. Once when he responded listlessly, he felt a warning lurch.

Ragglebomb was glowering at him.

"You want to put me out?" he challenged. "Like those others? What happened to them, by the way?"

Bushbaby winced. "It was dreadful. We had no idea they'd survive so long, outside."

"But I don't feel pain. That's why you rescued me, isn't it? Go ahead," he said perversely. "I don't care. Throw me out. New thrill."

"Oh, no, no, no!" Bushbaby hugged him. Ragglebomb, penitent, crawled under his legs.

"So you've been popping around the universe bringing live things in to play with and throwing them out when you're bored. Get away," he scolded. "Shallow sensation freaks is all you are. Galactic poltergeists!"

He rolled over and hoisted the beautiful Bushbaby over his face, watching it wiggle and squeal. *"Her lips were red, her looks were free, her locks were yellow as gold."* He kissed its golden belly. *"The Night-Mare Life-in-Death was she, who thicks man's blood with cold."*

And he used their pliant bodies to build the greatest love-pile yet. They were delighted and did not mind when later on he wept, face down on Muscle's dark coils.

But they were concerned.

"I have it," Bushbaby declared, tapping him with a pickle. *Own-species sex.* After all, face it, you're no empath. You need a jolt of your own kind."

"You mean you know where there's people like me? Humans?"

Bushbaby nodded, eyeing him as it listened. "Ideal. Just like I read you. Right over there, Raggle. And they have a thing they chew—wait—*salmoglossa fragrans.* Prolongs you-know-what, according to them. Bring some back with you, baby."

Next instant he was rolling through strobes onto tender green. Crushed flowers under him, ferny boughs above, sparkling with sunlight. Rich air rushed into his lungs. He bounced up buoyantly. Before him a park-like vista sloped to a glittering lake on which blew colored sails. The sky was violet with pearly little clouds. Never had he seen a planet remotely like this. If it wasn't Earth, he had fallen into paradise.

Beyond the lake he could see pastel walls, fountains, spires. An alabaster city undimmed by human tears. Music drifted on the sweet breeze. There were figures by the shore.

He stepped out into the sun. Bright silks swirled, white arms went up. Waving to him? He saw they were like human girls, only slimmer and more fair. They were calling! He looked down at his body, grabbed a flowering branch and started toward them.

"Do not forget the salmoglossa," said the voice of Muscle.

He nodded. The girls' breasts were bobbing, pink-tipped. He broke into a trot.

It was several days later when they brought him back, drooping between a man and a young girl. Another man walked beside them striking plangently on a harp. Girls and children danced along, and a motherly-looking woman paced in front, all beautiful as peris.

They leaned him gently against a tree and the harper stood back to play. He struggled to stand upright. One fist was streaming blood.

"Good-by," he gasped. "Thanks."

The strobes caught him sagging, and he collapsed on the Lovepile's floor.

"Aha!" Bushbaby pounced on his fist. "Good grief, your hand! The *salmoglossa*'s all blood." It began to shake out the herbs. "Are you all right now?" Ragglebomb was squeaking softly, thrusting its long tongue into the blood.

He rubbed his head.

"They welcomed me," he whispered. "It was perfect. Music. Dancing. Games. Love. They haven't any medicine because they eliminated all disease. I had five women and a cloud-painting team and some little boys, I think."

He held out his bloody blackened hand. Two fingers were missing.

"Paradise," he groaned. "Ice doesn't freeze me, fire doesn't burn. None of it means anything at all. I WANT TO GO HOME."

There was a jolt.

"I'm sorry," he wept. "I'll try to control myself. Please, please get me back to Earth. It'll be soon, won't it?"

There was a silence.

"When?"

Bushbaby made a throat-clearing noise.

"Well, just as soon as we can find it. We're bound to run across it. Maybe any minute, you know."

"What?"

He sat up death-faced. "You mean you don't know where it is? You mean we've just been going—no place?"

Bushbaby wrapped its hands over its ears. "Please! We can't recognize it from your description. So how can we go *back* there when we've never been there? If we just keep an ear out as we go we'll pick it up, you'll see."

His eyes rolled at them, he couldn't believe it.

". . . Ten to the eleventh times two suns in the galaxy. I

don't know your velocity and range. Say, one per second. That's—that's *six thousand years*. Oh, no!" He put his head in his bloody hands. "I'll never see home again."

"Don't say it, baby." The golden body slid close. "Don't down the trip. We love you, No-Pain." They were all petting him now. "Happy, sing him! Touch, taste, feel. Joy!"

But there was no joy.

He took to sitting leaden and apart, watching for a sign.

"This time?"

No.

Not yet. Never.

Ten to the eleventh times two . . . fifty percent chance of finding Earth within three thousand years. It was the scouter all over again.

The Lovepile reformed without him, and he turned his face away, not eating until they pushed food into his mouth. If he stayed totally inert, surely they would grow bored with him and put him out. No other hope. Finish me . . . Soon.

They made little efforts to arouse him with fondlings, and now and then a harsh jolt. He lolled unresisting. End it, he prayed. But still they puzzled at him in the intervals of their games. They mean well, he thought. And they miss the stuff I brought them.

Bushbaby was coaxing.

". . . First a suave effect, you know. Cryptic. And then a cascade of sweet and sour sparkling over the palate . . ."

He tried to shut it out. They mean well. Falling across the galaxy with a talking cookbook. Finish me.

". . . But the arts of combination," Bushbaby chatted on. "Like moving food; e.g., sentient plants or small live animals, combining flavor with the *frisson* of movement . . ."

He thought of oysters. Had he eaten some once? Something about poison. The rivers of Earth. Did they still flow? Even if by some unimaginable chance they stumbled on it, would it be far in the past or future, a dead ball? Let me die.

". . . And *sound*, that's amusing. We've picked up several races who combine musical effects with certain tastes. And there's the sound of oneself chewing, textures and viscosities.

I recall some beings who sucked in harmonics. Or the sound of the food itself. One race I caught *en passant* did that, but with a very limited range. Crunchy. Crispy. Snap-crackle-pop. One wishes they had explored tonalities, glissando effects . . ."

He lunged up.

"What did you say? *Snap-crackle-pop?*"

"Why, yes, but . . ."

"That's it! That's Earth!" he yelled. "You picked up a goddamn breakfast-food commercial!"

He felt a lurch. They were scrambling up the wall.

"A what?" Bushbaby stared.

"Never mind—take me there! That's Earth, it has to be. You can find it again, can't you? You said you could," he implored, pawing at them. "Please!"

The Lovepile rocked. He was frightening everybody.

"Oh, *please.*" He forced his voice smooth.

"But I only heard it for an instant," Bushbaby protested. "It would be terribly hard, that far back. My poor head!"

He was on his knees begging. "You'd love it," he pleaded. "We have fantastic food. Culinary poems you never heard of. Cordon bleu! Escoffier!" he babbled. "Talk about combinations, the Chinese do it four ways! Or is it the Japanese? Rijsttafel! Bubble-and-squeak! Baked Alaska, hot crust outside, inside co-o-old ice cream!"

Bushbaby's pink tongue flicked. Was he getting through?

He clawed his memory for foods he'd never heard of.

"Maguay worms in chocolate! Haggis and bagpipes, crystallized violets, rabbit Mephisto! Octopus in resin wine. Four-and-twenty blackbird pie! Cakes with girls in them. Kids seethed in their mothers' milk—wait, that's taboo. Ever hear of *taboo* foods? Long pig!"

Where was he getting all this? A vague presence drifted in his mind—his hands, the ridges, long ago. "Amanda," he breathed, racing on.

"Cormorants aged in manure! Ratatouille! Peaches iced in champagne!" *Project,* he thought. "Pâté of fatted goose liver studded with earth-drenched truffles, clothed in purest white lard!" He snuffled lustfully. "Hot buttered scones sluiced in whortleberry syrup!" He salivated. "Finnan haddie soufflé, Oh, yes! Unborn baby veal pounded to a membrane and delicately scorched in black herb butter . . ."

Bushbaby and Ragglebomb were clutching each other, eyes closed. Muscle was mesmerized.

"Find Earth! Grape leaves piled with poignantly sweet wild fraises, clotted with Devon cream!"

Bushbaby moaned, rocking to and fro.

"Earth! Bitter endives wilted in chicken steam and crumbled bacon! Black gazpacho! Fruit of the Tree of Heaven!"

Bushbaby rocked harder, the butterfly clamped to its breast.

Earth, Earth, he willed with all his might, croaking "Pahklava! Gossamer puff paste and pistachio nuts dripping with mountain honey!"

Bushbaby pushed at Ragglebomb's head, and the pod seemed to twirl.

"Ripe Comice pears," he whispered. *"Earth?"*

"That's it." Bushbaby fell over panting. "Oh, those foods, I want every single one. Let's land!"

"Deep-dish steak and kidney pie," he breathed. "Pearled with crusty onion dumplings . . ."

"Land!" Ragglebomb squealed. "Eat, eat!"

The pod jarred. Solidity. Earth.

Home.

"LET ME OUT!"

He saw a pucker opening daylight in the wall and dived for it. His legs pumped, struck. Earth! Feet thudding, face uplifted, lungs gulping air. "Home!" he yelled.

. . . And went headlong on the gravel, arms and legs out of control. A cataclysm smote his inside.

"Help!"

His body arched, spewed vomit, he was flailing, screaming.

"Help, Help! What's wrong?"

Through his noise he heard an uproar behind him in the pod. He managed to roll, saw gold and black bodies writhing inside the open port. They were in convulsions too.

"Stop it! Don't move!" Bushbaby shrieked. "You're killing us!"

"Get us out," he gasped. "This isn't Earth."

His throat garroted itself on his breath, and the aliens moaned in empathy.

"Don't! We can't move," Bushbaby gasped. "Don't breathe, close your eyes quick!"

He shut his eyes. The awfulness lessened slightly.

"What is it? What's happening?"

"PAIN, YOU FOOL," thundered Muscle.

"This is your wretched Earth," Bushbaby wailed. "Now we know what they tied your pain nerves to. Get back in so we can go—carefully!"

He opened his eyes, got a glimpse of pale sky and scrubby bushes before his eyeballs skewered. The empaths screamed.

"Stop! Ragglebomb die!"

"My own home," he whimpered, clawing at his eyes. His whole body was being devoured by invisible flames, crushed, impaled, flayed. *The pattern of Earth,* he realized. Her unique air, her exact gestalt of solar spectrum, gravity, magnetic field, her every sight and sound and touch—that was what they'd tuned his pain-circuits for!

"Evidently they did not want you back," said Muscle's silent voice. *"Get in."*

"They can fix me, they've got to fix me . . ."

"They aren't here," Bushbaby shouted. "Temporal error. No snap-crackle-pop. You and your baked Alaska . . ." Its voice broke pitifully. "Come back in so we can go!"

"Wait," he croaked. "When?"

He opened one eye, managed to see a rocky hillside before his forehead detonated. No roads, no buildings. Nothing to tell whether it was past or future. Not beautiful.

Behind him the aliens were crying out. He began to crawl blindly toward the pod, teeth clenching over salty gushes. He had bitten his tongue. Every move seared him; the air burned his guts when he had to breathe. The gravel seemed to be slicing his hands open, although no wounds appeared. Only pain, pain, pain from every nerve end.

"Amanda," he moaned, but she was not here. He crawled, writhed, kicked like a pinned bug toward the pod that held sweet comfort, the bliss of no-pain. Somewhere a bird called, stabbing his eardrums. His friends screamed.

"Hurry!"

Had it been a bird? He risked one look back.

A brown figure was sidling round the rocks.

Before he could see whether it was ape or human, female or male, the worst pain yet almost tore his brain out. He groveled helpless, hearing himself shriek. *The pattern of his own kind.* Of course, the central thing—it would hurt most all. No hope of staying here.

"*Don't! Don't! Hurry!*"

He sobbed, scrabbling toward the Lovepile. The scent of the weeds that his chest crushed raked his throat. Marigolds, he thought. Behind the agony, lost sweetness.

He touched the wall of the pod, gasping knives. The torturing air was real air, his terrible Earth was real.

"*GET IN QUICK!*"

"Please, plea . . ." he babbled wordlessly, hauling himself up with lids clenched, fumbling for the port. The real sun of Earth rained acid on his flesh.

The port! Inside lay relief. He would be No-Pain forever. Caresses—joy—why had he wanted to leave them? His hand found the port.

Standing, he turned, opened both eyes.

The form of a dead limb printed a whiplash on his eyeballs. Jagged, ugly. Unendurable. *But real—to hurt forever?*

"We can't wait!" Bushbaby wailed. He thought of its golden body flying down the lightyears, savoring delight. His arms shook violently.

"Then go!" he bellowed and thrust himself violently away from the Lovepile.

There was an implosion behind him.

He was alone.

He managed to stagger a few steps forward before he went down.